Praise
for
End of Sto

CW0081181G

"With John Bowers' debut novel *End of Story*, we have perhaps the first important gay novel of the new century, linking *Maurice*, E.M. Forester's great posthumous tale on the same subject, with the tragedy of 9/11 through an ingenious and erudite weaving of characters and stories from wildly disparate times, all clothed in a moving and convincing investigation of the very nature of love itself. Sometimes raucous, sometimes funny, always sexy, *End of Story* is the novel John Bowers was born to write."
  —Richard Wiley, winner of the PEN/Faulkner Award for *Soldiers in Hiding*

"I don't know of any other fictional work that makes the gigantic effort of covering so much social change, so much history of intimacy, and so much literary freedom with sex as emotional expression—gay history almost as a metaphor of the civilization Bowers means to encapsulate."
  —Robert Cornfield, New York

"A novel rich in atmosphere and raunchy in the bedroom, brimming with both cultural and sociopolitical commentary. While *End of Story* contains traces of E.M. Forster's *Maurice* and Michael Cunningham's *The Hours*, its Rococo prose ultimately reveals an intelligent, passionate author whose first goal is to entertain. This refreshingly forthright novel will delight the literatus, the love-struck, and the lewd—often at the same time."
  —Miles Newbold Clark, editor, No Record Press

"Of course you could compare John Bowers' ambitious *End of Story*, with its broad historical and literary span, to Michael Cunningham's *The Hours*. But I also think of Neil Bartlett's *Who Is that Man?*. As Bartlett imagines Oscar Wilde ghosting London now, so does Bowers imagine that spirits of gay figures from the past—first and foremost E. M. Forster—come to inspire subsequent lives. Intricately interlacing gay stories from the entire stretch of the twentieth century and beyond, *End of Story* is a love song to twentieth-century gay culture, from its highest expressions to its lowest and sweatiest."
  —Carolyn Dinshaw, founding editor of
  GLQ: A Journal of Lesbian and Gay Studies

"As a Cuban American, I love the chronicling of the life and romance of the Cuban character Eddy Mallafré. Along with his other interests, including the sexy sequel to Forster's *Maurice*, Bowers has also written a novel that reflects the Latino face of America today. Here we meet the Puerto Rican firefighter on 9/11, the Chicano academic in Los Angeles, the AIDS researcher from Barcelona, and the whole cast of Hispanic natives of northern New Mexico—even characters who wander into the story from the classic *Milagro Bean Field War*."

—Ed Chisholm, San Diego

"As a Princeton undergraduate alum from the same 1970s era as Morgan Cabell, the main character of *End of Story*, I am amazed how well John Bowers captures the spirit of Old Nassau, one of the novel's many interwoven themes. As in a Bach fugue, the voices compete and blend and lead to one "Aha!" moment after another. The author sublimely uses his multiple plot as a vehicle for philosophy, emotions, history, religion (reverent or otherwise) while moving the reader from joy to sadness, relief to uneasiness, and back again. Congratulations, Mr. Bowers!"

—Brad Thompson, MD

"At its core all great novels are love stories. Whatever happened to E. M. Forster's Maurice and his obsession? Bowers' imaginative and inventive twist to their story and its contemporary counterpoint is a joy to read! What a film this would make!"

—G. Sterling Zinsmeyer, executive producer of *Latter Days* and *Adam & Steve*

"John Bowers' *End of Story* is part historical anthology, part morality play, and part fuck poem. Archetypal characters, who happen to be gay, crisscross time and geography, offering perspectives on recognized cultural landmarks such as Studio 54, AIDS and 9/11. They tell the too familiar story of love, lust and loss that are the emotional tattoos shared by gay boomers. *End of Story* is must reading for the rainbow elite."

—Philip Hitchcock, artist and *OUT* magazine's
100 most influential gays in America

"Hilarious, heartbreaking, and thought-provoking in equal measure, John Bowers' *End of Story* is a *Tales of the City* for the new millennium. And like the best of Maupin's work, Bowers seamlessly follows his cast through glittering epochs of gay history, beginning with the last time it was fun to be gay in the wonderland of the parks and baths and Studio 54, backward to the difficulties of early 20th-century society and propriety, and crash-landing in the recent-now, where sexual freedom and political activism have given way to a post-gay millennial hangover. The story moves easily through time, crafting an epic, interconnected generational tale that presents the gay experience and issues of partnering and family intertwined with history like nothing I've read before. The juxtaposition of real world events with the characters' inner turmoil (culminating in the fall of the World Trade Center) and those of fantasy (Tolkien's *Two Towers*) creates a world that is neither real nor false, neither true nor a lie—and in that quality Bowers is able to capture the purest essence of what it means to be gay: to be everything and nothing, in the world and of the world at the same time. The unabashedly happy ending amidst the ruins is not just the characters' fates, but speaks to all possibilities for gay men and women."

—R. D. T. Byrd, author of *Fag Magic* and *Forever People*

"I read a lot of fiction on the lookout for film material. When I got an advance copy of *End of Story*, I thought that I would read a chapter at bedtime—but got drawn in, could not put it down, and stayed up all night until I finished the whole novel. A great writer creates a whole world, and John Bowers has created three complete worlds spanning a hundred years from the beginning of the 20th century to the beginning of the 21st century, from England and Italy to New York and New Mexico, from the outbreak of the First World War to the 9/11 attacks on the World Trade Center, and beyond. I was reminded of Michael Cunningham's *The Hours*, only the storylines connect and overlap in much more interesting ways. I love the "Ah Ha!" moments. And I love the happy endings. Before he made *Brokeback Mountain*, Ang Lee filmed *The Wedding Banquet* where nobody dies, nobody ends up broken-hearted, and even the parents are happy. Smart and funny, sad and sexy, beautiful and wise—no wonder I stayed up all night until I finished *End of Story!*"

—Joel Castleberg, executive producer of *Mr. Jealousy* and *Sleep with Me*

END
of
STORY

A Novel

John M. Bowers

SUNSTONE
PRESS

SANTA FE

Sunstone books may be purchased for educational, business, or sales promotional use. For information please write: Special Markets Department, Sunstone Press, P.O. Box 2321, Santa Fe, New Mexico 87504-2321.

Book and Cover design ▸ Vicki Ahl
Body typeface ▸ Adobe Jenson Pro
Printed on acid free paper

Library of Congress Cataloging-in-Publication Data

Bowers, John M., 1949-
    End of story : a novel / by John M. Bowers.
       p. cm.
    ISBN 978-0-86534-773-1 (pbk. : alk. paper)
    I. Title.
    PS3602.O8965E53 2010
    813'.6--dc22

                                    2010028121

Published in

WWW.SUNSTONEPRESS.COM
SUNSTONE PRESS / POST OFFICE BOX 2321 / SANTA FE, NM 87504-2321 /USA
(505) 988-4418 / ORDERS ONLY (800) 243-5644 / FAX (505) 988-1025

CONTENTS

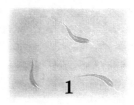

1

Facing the Sunshine

King's Old Boys—Cambridge, 1960

"Let us have one more gaudy night," Forster said to himself.

It was the end of the spring term in Cambridge, and King's College welcomed back its old boys from past generations for a reunion weekend. The wines were plentiful for luncheon on the Back Lawn. Gilmartin, the college steward, met the elderly novelist as he shuffled down the gravel pathway and offered a tray crowded with glasses. "The champagne comes highly recommended, sir."

"I don't normally indulge at midday."

"You seem uncommonly cheerful today, sir."

"Quite right!" The old man took the champagne and made a little toast. "Happy days!"

With glass in hand, Forster sought the seclusion of a bench against the wall toward the river. Beneath a trellis of the white-flowering vines he could enjoy the sunshine, sip his wine, and survey the men who had found their ways back to Cambridge. His one overwhelming desire was to be left alone with his thoughts.

He was celebrating. After so many years of waiting and worrying, the final revision of his novel *Maurice* had been completed that very morning. He had drafted the homosexual novel in 1913 but never published it, because the laws against obscenity and libel made it impossible. Again he said to himself, "Let us have one more gaudy night."

Forster sat very still beneath the blossoming vines. A grey man in a grey suit against a grey wall, he imagined himself invisible as he observed the old boys. Grouped in their little tribes that spanned decades, they gathered on the lawn to enjoy their wine and have the inevitable conversation of "Whatever happened to . . .? " and "No, how long ago?" The college cat emerged from the myrtle and rubbed against the writer's trousers twice before curling up at his feet.

Some of the old boys looked very old indeed, Forster thought, while others seemed like boys too young for freshmen. He had always imagined Cambridge as a place belonging to the very young and the very old. Yet he marveled at the tricks his eyes conspired with memory to play upon him. Over there stood a fine strapping lad who must surely be Evans, the very image of the beefy boy, even sporting the boat club tie. But this young graduate with his blond hair combed back in loose waves was hardly thirty. Evans had followed a year behind him and, if still alive, must be some bent and doddering travesty of fair-haired youth.

Only with effort could Forster recognize himself among these figures of hobbling antiquity. So he gazed with the eye of memory, the magical lens through which his novel's cad Clive Durham would always see his undergraduate friend Maurice Hall.

Out of some eternal Cambridge his friend began beckoning to him, clothed in the sun, and shaking out the scents and sounds of May term.

This sentence fell on the last page of the manuscript locked in the drawer of his writing table. There were no cross outs because the sentence was perfect after years of tinkering. Now the writer-in-residence could enjoy his champagne and savor the thought that Maurice and his friend Alec Scudder, as characters in his novel, would never become aged and ugly like these old boys gathering on the college lawn. They would remain boys eternal.

George Emerson was another. The young man standing alone nearest the river, so like Evans with backside glorious in white flannels, looked the way he imagined silent, dour George when he wrote *A Room with a View*. This fair-haired athlete looked like an American, though, big-boned and brawny, with a natural grace unmarred by English self-consciousness. At least the melancholy George, brooding over his world sorrow, would never know what it was to suffer old age like Evans a year behind him at King's, and eventually this monumental youth with his blond locks tousled about his forehead, his shoulders broad like an oarsman's.

George Emerson never grew a day older than the afternoon when he opened his heart to Lucy Honeychurch. "Choose a place where you won't do very much harm, and stand in it for all you are worth, facing the sunshine." These handsome young people lived in their own eternal present, a place where they buried their enchanted crocks of gold forever, safe from a changing world. George succeeded in marrying Lucy and—as the old saying goes—they lived happily ever after till the end of their days. They remained forever young and in love and filled with wonderful, wonderful promise. George and Lucy became more real to his readers than the author himself, now a dry old rag of a man who had dwindled into fame.

One day readers would look at *Maurice* much the same, as a palimpsest with layers written on top of layers, and secret stories hidden underneath. Who were his real-life models for Maurice and his friend Alec? What did the gentleman and the gamekeeper do in bed? And where did they escape after leaving the boathouse on Clive's country estate? Where could two such men live happily ever after till the end of *their* days?

Besotted after his first sex with another man, Maurice with his university education had fallen into fantasy. "We must live without relations and money." Alec the village lad, always more levelheaded, brought him back to reality. "Don't be daft. Your job in the City what gives you money and position? You can't chuck your job!"

True, men must work to build something lasting. He himself had spent an entire year drafting *Maurice*. Nobody could imagine the loneliness of such an effort. In 1913 the name of Oscar Wilde still could not be uttered without fear of giving offence. Such a waste of his good time, Forster thought, being a homosexual in England. But his novel was not written for an Edwardian public. Nor was it written for the friends who furtively read and returned the manuscript. It was written after visiting Edward Carpenter and his homosexual circle at his country estate—and meeting the astonishing couple Martin St. John Howell and his friend Alan Somebody—when he felt compelled to write something absolutely new for future readers.

Then came the regrets. Virginia Woolf wouldn't have understood, discovering once again only the lack of cohesion she found in all his books. She may have believed all our minds are threaded together, but he always felt she was poised to snap at him, so he never showed her the manuscript. His novels were never beautiful enough for her, never sad enough compared to her best works like *To the Lighthouse*—the book where nobody ever reached the bally lighthouse!—and far too dependent upon coincidences. Yet he no longer felt intimidated when he realized that his emotions were not hers. When the flesh educates the spirit, as Alec did for Maurice, the results ought to become staggeringly ordinary. Perhaps he built with bricks that needed to be lighted up, irradiated with something beyond themselves, but at the end of the day they remained plain bricks. That was their special beauty, to be exactly and abundantly what they were.

The Provost's wife was trying to catch his eye. The only woman at the party, she was wearing the indigo frock she reserved for festive occasions. Her white glove gripped the arm of a distinguished-looking government man who probably wanted to be introduced. Was Forster obliged to show his sociable side? He wondered if the

Provost's wife would be so keen for arranging these handshakes if she really knew. The hand that wrote such clever novels had done other things.

Forster took from his pocket a small book of Cavafy's poetry, its margins cluttered with his spidery handwriting. From long experience in basement restaurants and railway compartments, he knew nobody would bother him with his nose buried in a book, his eyes retreating farther behind his spectacles. He had done a little to spread Cavafy's fame, about the best thing he ever did, and now he opened the well-worn pages and pretended to read this poet who always stood at a slight angle to the universe. They met in Alexandria when he was struggling to revise *Maurice*—was it really as far back as 1916?—and for the first time in his life he parted with respectability with a soldier on the beach. Now all these long years later he didn't know why he suddenly became obsessed with finishing the novel. He had arranged a typist who could be trusted for publication after he died. Long ago he had rejected the original ending with the two men parting at Southampton. No, Alec would *not* sail away to South America while Maurice resigned himself to live as before, alone, his tear-streaked face toward England in a brave blur of exalted emotion. Resignation had been the tragic flaw of the modern age.

Now he had also cancelled the Arcadian epilogue in which Maurice's sister Kitty discovered her brother and his friend, many years later, working as woodcutters in the forest. After making these last changes, Forster felt the same sense of relief that Alec expressed in his last words in the boathouse: "And that's finished."

Never mind the review in the *Daily Telegraph*, his old friend Strachey already passed the harshest verdict. He believed that sex between the two men was unnatural not because it was diseased, but because there was so little of it. These healthy young men surely had erections. Could Alec continue Maurice's erotic education when the author himself could not imagine where those lessons led? And what about Maurice and Alec buggering? His young friend Isherwood grimaced at quaint words like *sharing* to describe two men having sex. But how could E. M. Forster have written otherwise? How could he say they fucked each other? He never wrote that George fucked Lucy. *Fuck* was not a word he liked seeing in print. For all its quiet cruelties and domestic horrors, the age of repression when he composed *Maurice* had also been an age of innocence and good taste.

Strachey and Isherwood were not alone. All of Forster's friends had appointed themselves experts on his books, when all he ever wanted from his critics was their praise. D. H. Lawrence said the unpublished manuscript was the cramp that kept him from writing other novels. *Lady Chatterley's Lover* was one book Forster truly envied because it included honest details of the sexual act, everything so utterly real about the coming together of two bodies in passion and love, all of the frank intimacies missing from his own novel *Maurice*. Yet the story of Lady

Chatterley and her gamekeeper Mellors ended no more satisfactorily, each lover saddled with a spouse who refused to grant a divorce, with no sense of where the couple could go and how they could live. Maybe Italy where the English always went to discover their passions.

On his first visit to Italy, Forster was taken to Herculaneum and recalled as a schoolboy reading Pliny's letter about the eruption of Mount Vesuvius. An American professor guided him through the Villa of the Papyri where excavations continued, showing him a great pile of charcoal lumps that had once been scrolls of poetry and philosophy. These books had been burnt to cinders when the volcano blasted through. A miniature of the great library at Alexandria had been reduced to nothingness in a few terrible moments. Was here the complete poetry of Sappho? Aristotle's lost treatise on comedy? What mattered the timing of *Maurice*'s publication, already consigned to a shadowland for half a century, when compared to all the lost classics heaped together in the ruined villa?

The Provost was walking in his direction, bringing Sir Somebody who wanted to be introduced and shake hands. Roused from napping at his feet, the college cat slipped back into the periwinkle.

Forster considered rising. He always liked the Provost. The man was literary. He wrote the biography of Virginia Woolf's father.

The Provost spoke with a genial smile, "Stay, stay."

Forster lied. "A bit wobbly in the legs today."

"You know Sir Adrian Fortescue, of course, the economist."

"Like my old friend Keynes, another King's man."

Sir Adrian extended his hand. "Of course you must have known Keynes. He was here at King's for ever so long."

"The Provost tells a wonderful story about Keynes, found pacing the chapel one afternoon. He had invested college funds in wheat futures, you see, and was afraid of being caught short. That would have meant several metric tons of wheat delivered to the front gate. Space would have been needed to store it."

Fortescue asked, "Did it really happen? How did things turn out? It's a wonderful story."

The Provost said, "The college wasn't caught short, I'm glad to report."

Forster added, "And wonderful stories don't really need to happen, just need to be wonderfully told."

"On the topic of stories, my wife and I enjoy your novels tremendously."

"I am surprised your work allows time for reading any novels."

"Oh, yes, all six of the very best, every year without fail."

Forster had published only five novels, and the winner of the Nobel Prize in Economics knew nothing about the unpublished manuscript of *Maurice*. Sir Adrian meant something else entirely. He was clearly referring to the six novels of Jane Austen. An awkward moment followed, relieved only when their little company was joined by Sutherland, the college's don in English literature.

The Provost said, "We are having a pleasant talk about novels."

Sutherland replied, "Forster is always pleasant when I'm around. I'm the official biographer. One swipe of my pen, and anything nasty might happen."

"Worse," Forster said. "You can make my life seem boring, which it is."

"Goebbels put you on the list for extermination when the Nazis conquered England. Call that boring?"

"Sir Adrian prefers Miss Austen's novels."

"Why shouldn't an economist? Our corporate alliances compare neatly with the marriage alliances in Austen's novels. And the happy endings, always happy endings. You can take your art, you can take your music, but give me a good story about young couples who get married and settle down. Austen grants us a wholly satisfying sense how these couples will live, even where they will live. I can see the Darcys happily settled at Pemberly, the Brandons at Delaford, and the Knightleys at Hartfield. Happy couples, happy homes, happy endings. Stories need to be life-affirming. That's the one principle we insist upon, my wife and I."

"I should be very glad if my works induced people to enjoy a bit more fully this marvelous world." Forster changed the subject. "When I lectured in America, readers constantly thanked me for creating Captain Horatio Hornblower."

Sutherland said, "Americans not knowing the difference between E. M. Forster and C. S. Forester—it's vintage. The episode belongs in your biography,"

"Are you putting this episode in? Enjoying this gaudy reunion, meeting Sir Adrian, and chatting about Jane Austen, my own favorite author?"

"Probably not, unless you choke on a cucumber sandwich. There is always a witness to history."

"Rubbish! A well-written biography is merely another form of storytelling—and then . . . and then . . . —but not a real life. Every time an episode goes missing because it doesn't fit, your biography becomes more like a novel, and myself no different from a character in it, what Lawrence called *the leavings of a life* spoiled by the novelist's touch, no coincidences and nothing improbable." Forster tapped his biographer's arm. "If the public thought I created Captain Hornblower *and* Lucy Honeychurch, posterity would remember me as a far more interesting writer."

"There *are* things that will make you far more interesting later on. The reading public always likes the unexpected." Sutherland knew all about *Maurice*. He knew its publication would provide a surprising coda to Forster's life.

The Provost said, "You novelists have a great advantage over us biographers.

Your stories are exactly what you make of them, no loose ends, no missing bits. Fiction writers foster the wonderful illusion of a more manageable human race."

Forster said, "Really? Nothing between the lines of a novel? No tantalizing foretaste of a sequel? Are not our characters, like ourselves, people whose secret lives remain invisible and their futures await a proper telling?"

Forster sank back on his bench, carefully, as if protecting brittle bones. He made a great show of feeling tired.

From the pavilion, the college steward brought forward his wines. Gilmartin lowered the tray so that Forester had an easier reach. "May I suggest another coupe of champers, sir? The claret is a bit corky."

The Provost led the way to the sandwiches, and the gentlemen moved along the gravel path with a parting compliment from Sir Adrian about *A Room with a View*. "Your one novel where none of the main characters dies!" Emerging from the myrtle verge, the college cat curled up again at Forster's feet.

Now where is our young Evans? Ah, Forster thought, there beside the river in front of a stand of willows, glorious backdrop to his summer whites and golden curls, jacket off and draped over his arm, better to show off the physique of a Nordic Apollo.

As a homosexual and a writer, Forster never penetrated much beyond the physical beauty of such men. Strachey noticed how the reader never truly grasped Alec's feelings in *Maurice*. What did the gamekeeper want when he climbed the ladder into Maurice's bedroom? The author himself couldn't say. Very clearly Maurice was the sort of man who thought himself into a muddle, but Alec felt directly and acted. Not every character is burdened with an inner life. Full of surprises, the gamekeeper might have turned out very different over time. Much as he believed lovers should act as if things lasted, experience taught that no human relationship is constant. Alec was strong, he was resourceful, and he had a wrestler's grit and agility for handling whatever the years threw his way. He had a spirit of adventure, even the soul of an artist, if only given the future denied him by the novel's abrupt ending.

But how could he and Maurice have remained anywhere in England? Maurice's medical nerve specialist said quite rightly when trying to cure the young man's homosexuality, "England has always been disinclined to accept human nature." Could Maurice and Alec live together anywhere in 1914 *and* live happily ever after?

Half a lifetime ago, Isherwood began asking for a continuation of the story. "There should be a sequel," he wrote from Berlin where he went looking for pretty boys before the Nazis. "Alec and Maurice have all their troubles before them. I should love to know what they're doing now." It became a game that the two writers never tired of playing. So many possibilities sprang to mind for Maurice Hall and Alec Scudder after they disappeared from England, so soon after first bedding each other.

The year was 1913, and the Great War was approaching with a speed that staggered everyone. Maurice had already joined the Territorials, then a peacetime militia. Could the two young men have been soldiers together, Maurice as an officer and Alec as his batman?

How to manage getting assigned to the same battalion? Clive Durham M.P. could arrange matters. Maurice with his wounded pride was determined never again to cross tracks with his former lover, but Alec enjoyed taking risks, like his plan for emigrating to Argentina and making a new life abroad. He remained the swaggering village buck with more than a country boy's instinct for criminality. Hadn't he written "*I know about you and Mr. Durham*" as threat of blackmail to Maurice? To Clive, the homosexual world would remain forever a cesspool, and one breath from it at election time could ruin him.

If Maurice and Alec become soldiers together in the Great War, what about their lives in the trenches? Alec might take sick. Influenza and trench fever killed more troopers than poison gas. Though gravely ill, the batman receives scant attention from the company doctor, a gentleman. So Maurice cares for Alec. He nurses him. He empties the patient's slop. Alec complains. "It's nasty. You mustn't have to do with my filth."

Talk goes round the mess of an officer caring for his servant. The brigadier insults Maurice in front of his men, saying sarcastically, "We'll have you wheeling the baby next!"

No, that won't do. They're back in the same damned problem over class.

Maurice has an old Cambridge friend in his battalion, by name Ramsey, who attended the same tutorials on Thucydides. Under the machineguns, their conversations relive the disastrous military expedition to Sicily, while Alec washes the cooking pans and looks sour. Andrew is a poet celebrating the band of brothers in the muck of the trenches. Brimming with short lyrics, his notebook has been passed around and his verses pronounced braver, more beautiful than Rupert Brooke's.

Then one sunny day after a night of intense shelling, in a dugout among the ruins of a farm house, Maurice and Andrew are sitting with a group of men and doing something as ordinary as sharing a meal, cheese perhaps, smoking, passing around a bottle of wine, tipping it back, complaining. Suddenly they hear the noise like a railway engine and an explosion that shakes the earth. There is a flash and a roar that goes red and a rush of wind. Maurice cannot breathe at first. One man is screaming next to him. The soldier's leg is gone, the stump twitching beside Maurice on the bare ground. An artillery shell has landed on the house. Andrew Ramsey is killed in an instant, his notebook blown up with him, gone.

Wounded slightly in the arm, Maurice mourns his friend's death while Alec feels jealous and wants to chuck the whole business of soldiering. The loss renders Maurice disillusioned, too, so he and Alec make their escape together, rowing across the alpine lake for safe haven in Switzerland.

No sooner in neutral territory than Alec becomes seriously ill, and Maurice takes him to hospital. He suffers one wave of fever after another. Maurice stays in the room, holding his friend's hand until the end. The country lad lies unconscious the whole time, and it does not take very long for him to die. Maurice thanks the doctor and turns off the light and closes the door. He feels that he is saying goodbye to a statue.

Maurice puts his friend's clothes in a paper sack, the old corduroys and woolen pullover, and he leaves the hospital and walks back in the rain to the boathouse where he had left the rowboat. After betraying his country rather than abandoning his friend, he has only this paper sack with Alec's scent clinging to the old clothes inside.

Call that a happy ending? Why are nearly all novels feeble at their conclusions? Perhaps if the two men leave Europe behind absolutely.

At the beginning of the fighting in 1914, Maurice joins the flying corps. He had loved speeding his motorbike through the fens outside Cambridge, so becomes an aviator who brings back pictures of enemy positions. Perhaps Alec operates the camera as he learns the science of photography.

Or perhaps Alec becomes Maurice's mechanic, always checking the petrol lines before takeoff. Nothing could appear more natural than that close relationship between an aviator and his mechanic. The country lad was good with his hands and understood tools. "They must have owned wonderful machinery to make a thing like that," Alec said when admiring the winged Assyrian bull at the British Museum, just before they were interrupted by the arrival of Mr. Ducie, Maurice's old school teacher, who prided himself on never forgetting a former pupil. But such an absurd coincidence, when the schoolmaster pops up and recognizes his old student, at such a critical moment in the action!

Next they join Lawrence of Arabia as part of his guerilla campaign against the Turks. The faraway desert was the right place for these two men. Disguised as Bedouin tribesmen, they lose almost completely their identities as Englishmen. They fight side by side and they sleep side by side, openly and without shame, people of the desert. Maurice pilots his two-seater over a landscape of creamy hills and scarlet valleys. He loves the arid region for the same reason that Lawrence did, because it is clean.

Then one day Maurice is flying alone and his aeroplane is struck by gunfire from the ground. Petrol leaks and soaks his seat. There is a spark from an electrical line. Flames are borne aloft by the rush of wind and engulf the cockpit, the pilot. Maurice crash-lands among the dry hills, horribly burned. His face is disfigured, almost beyond recognition, when the tribesmen bring him to a field hospital. Alec takes care of him and dresses his wounds and stays at his side. Sly and quick-handed, he pilfers ampoules of morphine in broad daylight.

They are evacuated back to Italy where Alec keeps them moving from one field hospital to the next, until they outrun the paperwork and Maurice falls between the cracks of the military bureaucracy, exactly what Alec wants for the injured officer known to the Italians as simply *the English patient*.

When the allies advance on retreating enemy troops, Alec arranges their passage northward to Lake Como, with stolen papers identifying Maurice as a French lieutenant educated at Cambridge, hence his perfect English, for when they are stopped at checkpoints. A sympathetic American ambulance driver, who claims he is writing a novel about the Caporetto retreat, transports them to the isolated village of Bellagio. Maurice and Alec remain in a hilltop villa, just the two of them among olive groves and azalea terraces, after the Prince and his household had fled across the lake to Switzerland.

Alec makes do with what little medicine he can scrounge, mostly codeine drops for sleep. Maurice's legs are so badly destroyed that bone shows through. His chest is scorched to dark purple. Bandages cover his body like a winding cloth. His head remains exposed, hairless and charred black. Alec pours calamine lotion on patches of burnt flesh, blowing on wounds too raw for ointment, as flakes of skin keep shedding off. Exposed for sponge baths, his penis has become grey and lifeless. Maurice complains, "Don't nanny me. Please, don't nanny me!"

Alec, still bossing things, chews an apple and passes the fruit from his mouth into Maurice's. He carts books from the library and keeps a fire ablaze through freezing alpine nights, all the while studying his friend's lengthening silences.

Maurice spends his days reading Thucydides in a battered student edition from 1890, one last keepsake of a Cambridge education. Between the pages, he inserts his own letters and diary entries, maps, leaves cut from other books, favorite poems by Whitman and Rumi copied in his own neat handwriting, all folded into the textbook, more a commonplace book now. There is so much new writing that Alec can smell the ink.

"Pliny must have walked down ancient paths like these," Maurice mutters in the middle of the night when his mind wanders, moving between dreams and waking delusions, his memories becoming more vivid as the codeine takes hold. "And Stendhal, too, because bits from *La Chartreuse de Parme* took place in this part of Italy."

When sunlight seeps through the curtains, Maurice looks down and contemplates what had been a boxer's body, agile and aggressive, offered to Alec for sexual pleasure, then in love and companionship, now hideously disfigured. "You have wedded yourself to a corpse," he hisses through charred lips. "A man with no face. A heap of charcoal. Nobody can love a ghost."

"Everyone loves a diamond. And what's a diamond but charcoal what's been under pressure for a goodish while?" Alec jokes to rescue him from morbid thoughts. "You've too much pluck to go under now."

At night the villa floats among cypress trees. The Prince must have been a fan of American adventure stories as a boy, because his library has *Last of the Mohicans* and *Huckleberry Finn* that Alec reads aloud by firelight. Maurice sucks on morphine tablets, his eyes fixed straight ahead, unfocused, in his poppy haze. The paraffin lamp casts light upward where painted figures of griffins and bagpipes come alive and dance across the ceiling.

There was less pain in the first weeks when nerve endings were burned off. Now that there is healing, there is pain, constant searing pain, and Maurice's eyes beg for an end to it. Warming his hands with a mug of horlicks foraged from a supply boat, Alec resolves upon a final loving act.

Alec's fingernail taps the glass syringe. He searches for a usable vein in an arm that lies like a flow of black lava upon the sheet. Both men drift away with the mildew smell of the old mattress, half imagining themselves back at the boathouse in Wiltshire, motionless while watching for squirrels to come down from the treetops to drink beside the lake.

The hearth blazes with the last books from the library. Alec crawls beneath the blanket. Maurice closes his eyes and slips into darkness, tugging at Alec's spirit as he goes. Breathing out and breathing in, breathing out and breathing in. Breathing out. The last exhalation parts his lips like a silk ribbon.

Alec's only keepsake is the volume of Thucydides filled with Maurice's letters, jottings, maps of their travels together, and postcards used as bookmarks. These were the pages where his hands had rested and his eyes scanned and scanned again the sentences. Glued inside the back cover are faded yellow petals from an evening primrose, one last relic of their long-lost English countryside.

Powerful but not exactly a happy ending, Forster thought, and too much like *The Charioteer* which Mary Renault sent him "with best wishes." Perhaps no happy outcome awaited any man who witnessed the horrors of the Great War. But why must the sodomite always die? He himself killed off the Italian fisher lad in "The Story of a Panic," and the African chieftain stabbed his missionary lover before throwing himself from the parapet in "The Life to Come." Why must there always be a murder, maybe two, or a youth dangling from a noose? Why must writers always kill the queer?

He admired Tolstoy's courage for showing his main characters growing old. With only the rearrangement of a few fundamentals, rather better luck all around, Maurice and Alec might have achieved something permanent. Surely these two men could prosper somewhere without their love lapsing into social habit or dwindling into mere marriage. There must be some wilderness where they could chop wood, drink from mountain streams, and live in a mud-brick house built with their own hands. And live free! Perhaps his real-life models Martin and Alan, wherever they disappeared after the weekend at Carpenter's, found the happy ending that the novelist could not properly imagine.

Ah, there is our young Evans again!

Lost among his musings as champagne sported with his brain, Forster suddenly realized that the golden-haired Evans was staring at him across the wide lawn. What did the monumental youth see? A famous author or a pitiful old man? It didn't signify, Forster thought, so long as the young man wanted to introduce himself and have a nice handshake. Where *was* the Provost's wife when he really needed her?

So big and athletic-looking, he must be an American.

2

Deep Breath Before the Plunge

Martin and Alan—Italy, 1914

One more time Martin St. John Howell recalled his first Latin sentence parsed as a schoolboy. *Sicilia est insula magna in Europa.* Their tour of Italy had started in the northern mountains and brought them in stages to Sicily, which was indeed a "large island in Europe."

He and his friend Alan Sutton had arrived at Syracuse in the heat of August, when even the English tourists retreated beneath the awnings of their hotels where they could settle back with lemonade and newspapers from home. After several mornings spent thumbing travel magazines, Martin's one overwhelming desire was to find some peaceful place on the map, remote from the dangers of a hostile world, where he and Alan could live together and not be bothered.

In the old limestone quarries that the Italians call the Latomia dei Cappuccini, with only his straw boater as protection from the sun, Martin sat with his student edition of the *Peloponnesian Wars* in his lap. He leaned his head against a column abandoned when it cracked during quarrying more than two thousand years before. In the hum of ancient silence, he wept. Martin had thought seldom about disease and death, but when he did it was with strong disapproval. Now he wept because he thought how here, on this spot outside ancient Syracuse, seven thousand Athenian warriors had died in squalid misery after being taken prisoners.

Their comrades had fought and died, the lucky ones, shoulder by shoulder with their fellows. Before mechanized battle dealing out death at a distance, a warrior felt the deep breath before the plunge. He saw his enemy's face and looked into his eyes as they jabbed with spears. The giving and receiving of blows, even death under another man's sword, had been filled with passion and intimacy, almost like the rapture of lovemaking in another man's embrace. After the battle, the Athenian survivors found themselves bloody but alive, living against the odds, while others lay dead around them on the ground. These warriors turned to each other in exhaustion. They wept openly. They embraced. Each man helped his friend unstrap his breastplate, wincing when they discovered wounds underneath they had not felt before. They attended one another, washing gashes and applying oil, with the tenderness of men bonded in the flesh.

The first time he felt the energy of Alan's body—Martin recalled—did not happen when the gamekeeper stole into his upstairs bedroom and embraced him. There had already been odd glances in the fields while shooting, and again in the apricot orchard when smoking after dinner. But the first time came when Alan helped him shift the pianoforte in the parlor at Pendersley, his university friend Colin Dunbar's country home in its wide green vale above Egdon Heath.

As rain pelted the manor house, the roof leaked and water dripped on the Broadwood grand's lid. After a shy little maid had brought a basin, all of the others had cleared out, servants as well as weekend guests. Martin lingered until the two men were alone together. Alan had a grim look, gruff and unsmiling, in reality self-conscious about the gap in his front teeth that he thought made him look common. Martin had taken off his dinner jacket and stood beside Alan, shoulder to shoulder, as they put their weight into the heavy instrument. Martin felt his strength join Alan's as the piano inched forward, each strong push and deep masculine grunt shifting it away from the water leaking through the ceiling.

The same secret attraction drew them together on the day after their first lovemaking, when they donned their cricket whites and sported in full English sunshine. Alan, the best batsman, captained the manor's team against the village in the annual match. Hitting and running, they passed each other between the wickets, exchanging glances, but careful not to attract Colin's notice. Martin heard the Dorset gamekeeper's hard breathing and knew that Alan, his brown eyes flashing in the sunlight, was listening for his own. They played for the sake of their physical friendship, partners in crime.

The Athenian warriors who survived the battle of Syracuse—Martin gazed into the shimmering heat—were not so lucky. With their ships destroyed, the prisoners were confined to this limestone quarry with its shallow caves. Here they died of hunger, disease, and parching thirst under the same savage sun that beat down upon his shoulders, denied even the rapture of death upon an enemy's spear. Perhaps Sophocles was right that it was best *not* to be born.

Martin had never experienced authentic feelings such as these, not before Alan came into his life and saved him from the slide downward into the greyness of the undeveloped heart. Before, his mindless routines seemed as much a prison as this ancient quarry, and his future seemed far worse, condemned to the sunless world of London's sodomites, trolling for rent boys in dockside pubs and relieving his insane urges among the cast-iron urinals of the public gents.

Before, as a Cambridge undergraduate plodding through Thucydides, Martin had been satisfied to get the translation right for his next tutorial. He memorized dates and places on a map, but never knew what stood behind names like Alcibiades, and never understood what a general's mistakes cost young men so far away from their homes and parents. Before, Martin had been a sleepwalker through life. But when Alan stole into his bed, for the first time Martin knew what a man's body felt like, what it smelled like, and what heat it gave off in sexual passion, including his own. His heart lost its sluggishness and his mind awoke.

Here at Syracuse, long-dead warriors had stripped themselves for battle and oiled their bodies, readying themselves to die under this same unrelenting sun. Somewhere in the dust coating his walking boot was the blood of some fair Athenian youth. Removing his boater, Martin pressed his ear to the column and quieted his breath, listening. He was straining to hear what the stone would surrender of the events that took place in the caves no longer visible beneath the narrow streets and tiled houses, when men clung desperately to life and to each other. He strained to hear what the limestone said. And as Martin pressed his ear harder to the stone and heard his own heartbeat echoed back, tears streamed from his eyes. "I feel that I lived here before, died here, too. And now it is all starting over again. Dear God, no—not us, not now."

"Jeminey! Are you wezzle-brained?" Alan was looking down where Martin sat with his head again the column. "Thought you'd given me the slip, eh? On your feet, double quick. You'll feel right enough when you've had your tea."

Martin donned his boater, remembering how Alexander the Great made a special trip with his lover Hephaestion and found the famous philosopher lying in the sun. The young general who was poised to conquer the world asked the old man if he wanted anything. The philosopher replied that he wanted only for Alexander to step from between him and the sunlight. Martin smiled weakly as he realized how his mind always reached for these ludicrous comparisons, something always needing to be *like* something else. His mind was permanently deranged by a first-rate English education. So he let Alan call him wezzle-brained and boss him. The working-class youngster would remain the practical one.

Rising on legs wobbly from long sitting, Martin reached out and mussed Alan's hair. "Whatever you say, Master Sutton."

On their first night together at Pendersley when Martin, in an agony of loneliness and shame, stood at that window and cried "Come here! Come here!" to the empty night, Alan had seized his chance. Through the mist that covered the lawn, he spotted the ladder leaning against his window where workmen were repairing roof tiles. The moon cast a shadow from the wych elm as he climbed up.

Alan pulled himself through the window and crept into the bedroom where he knew Martin slept alone. Almost without a sound from his heavy boots, he crossed the carpet and knelt beside the bed. Martin sat bolt upright and froze in panic, but made no retreat from the gamekeeper's advances. Alan's hand began stroking his pyjamas. "Sir, was you calling out for me to come here?"

Martin sank back and surrendered to the sensation of the hand moving strongly upon his chest. "Don't be afeard, sir," Alan said, running his hand farther under the bedclothes. "I've come here as you called. I've come."

Alan was nimble as he pulled back the blanket and unbuttoned Martin's shirt. The gamekeeper brought with him the scent of hedgerows soaked with rain. Martin sank back as he felt the night air flowing over him. Alan leaned further over the bed and pulled closer, kissing Martin's chest in the middle where a tuft of hair grew. Accustomed only to Colin's chaste pecks in their college rooms, Martin had never felt the full heat of a man's mouth upon his body before, certainly not a tongue playing hungrily as Alan moved against the grain of his chest hair.

Alan showed no shyness as he stripped himself, shaking off his boots and leaving his corduroys in a heap beside the bed. He slid under the covers and stretched his body next to Martin's, hardly touching as he settled beneath the blanket. Both men were almost the same height, Alan shorter by an inch or two, but matching shoulders and thighs as they faced each other under the covers. When Alan wiggled his toes, he felt Martin's feet stone cold from standing barefoot at the open window.

Martin was grabbed by his backside and pulled closer and felt the gamekeeper's flesh hardening where it pressed against his own. The bedroom darkened as clouds moved across the moon. Edging down, Alan started kissing his chest until his tongue found Martin's nipple, hard and button-like. He sniggered and gave a playful bite.

Sinking deeper under the sheets, Alan continued kissing his partner's belly and licking until his tongue burrowed into his navel. Lightly haired, Martin had a ridge of soft curls leading downward. Alan took the short hairs between his teeth and bit hard enough to make Martin wince. He gave a little blow, almost a whistle, and Martin took pleasure in his breath cooling his wet skin.

When Alan moved farther down, two completely ridiculous thoughts popped into Martin's mind. He remembered how Mr. Davis had called it the *membrum virile* in Latin, because the schoolmaster could not bring himself to use the common English name. Then Martin remembered later in the sixth form, when the older boys talked filth, he did not know the difference between the words *cock* and *cunt*. But these thoughts vanished as he sank back into the sensation of Alan's hot mouth moving up and down.

The gamekeeper gripped Martin by the elbows and pressed him against the mattress before sliding his palms along his flanks. He took hold of either side of Martin's hips and moved his haunches up and down, driving him deeper. Next he took him deep in the back of his throat, pausing until he gagged and came up gasping for air.

Alan crouched with his lean torso tented beneath the blanket. His knees forced Martin's legs wider apart as his free hand stroked it up and down with the motion of his mouth. Martin tried to prolong the sensation until he could not contain his crisis for one more moment. His whole body convulsed. Alan sank down to receive it deep in his throat and kept it there until the throbbing subsided. Martin wanted to shout "Thank you! Thank you! Thank you!" But some deep-down understanding made him realize Alan needed no words of gratitude, just as he needed no tip for helping with the day's shooting in the fields.

Wiping his mouth with the back of his hand as he emerged from beneath the blanket, Alan looked into Martin's eyes but did not say a word. With a low grunt, he curled up in the crook of his shoulder. Martin pulled the bedclothes high to muffle their words. "I like your body."

"Well we're quits, then, beens I like yours too," Alan replied. "An' happy birthday, sir. The other gentleman, he let slip you was twenty-one eesterday. I hope I gave full satisfaction just now, sir, better than the day's shooting."

"Ah, my birthday. You don't miss a trick, you sly boy. So that's why you wouldn't accept the money. I'm always slow at seeing. But please you mustn't call me *sir*. Martin. I'm Martin."

Alan lay motionless at his side. The gamekeeper had stayed awake for two whole nights beneath the window. He had lingered in the shadows of the laurel avenue keeping his yearnings to himself until this night. Alan was tired. He slept hard.

Martin slept scarcely at all, holding the young man's body close throughout the night, thrilled that the sexual frontier had been crossed after all the years of frustration. When his arm went numb, he endured the discomfort as long as he could because afraid of waking Alan. He heard owls. Finally he shifted to a more comfortable position.

Martin's mind was racing. He dozed a few times during the night, dreaming strange dreams, but nothing he could remember clearly when he awoke. Something about Alan as the faceless friend who haunted his sleeping fantasies for years, terrifying but also welcome, almost a premonition of the way the gamekeeper crept into his bed and whispered, "Don't be afraid, sir. I've come here as you called."

Martin felt headachy when he wakened near dawn, but happy to find Alan still at his side in heavy slumber. To pass time in the growing light, Martin studied the coarse hair and freckles on the gamekeeper's forearm.

Both men regretted their second night together, in the London hotel after their argument in the rain, when every feeling was tinged with fear, disappointment, and sadness. Alan had completed plans with his parents, his brother Bob, and his employer Mr. Dunbar to emigrate to the Argentine. The ticket was purchased. His kit was bought and needed just one last sorting through. Already he had a phrase book and was learning Spanish.

"Friday's the packing," Alan said as they lay close together in the musty-smelling room. "Saturday the *Normandie* sails from Southampton, so it's goodbye to Old England. Big responsibility, isn't it, going away. I mean, you got to work out all the details."

Martin found the courage to implore him, "Why don't you stay on in England? We'll never have this chance again, a find in a million, and you know it. Remain with me. We love each other."

"You reckerize, don't you, that's no excuse to get fuddled and act stupid-like." Alan turned surly as he had at the museum in front of the Elgin Marbles, when they argued about why Martin had not come to the estate's boathouse as he had implored in his letter, pausing only when a lady approached with her two boys and schoolmaster-looking husband.

Martin persisted. "Tell your brother you've changed your mind. I'll repay him for the ticket. Tell your parents that you are taking a position with Mr. Howell instead."

Alan tried sounding business-like. "Still, facts is facts, isn't it. My ticket is bought. Bob and his wife is expecting me. There's a definite job for me in Buenos Aires, and that's flat. You sort of trapping me with talk of loving each other. It's destiny we found each other. One chance in a million, it'll never happen again for the rest of my life. Ha! Bettermost we never met, you come to think of it."

Suddenly Alan's brave front collapsed and he burst into tears. "You're the only good thing happened to me at bloody Pendersley," he sniffled, pressing his face into Martin's shoulder. "The first time I saw you, I said to myself, wouldn't I like to have that one! You and your snooty ways, you almost missed having me. Near as nothing I never clomb that ladder."

Anger fueled their passion for what they believed was their last lovemaking. When Alan disappeared beneath the covers, though, Martin did not think that he could manage another explosion.

Throwing aside the covers, Alan drew back and spit. He cleared his throat and spit again. Martin was baffled. After sliding back and forth along his backside, Alan reached around and took Martin in his hand until he found the place. He stifled a little hiss of pain between clenched teeth as he sank farther on his haunches, eyes closed, until all the tension in his face relaxed into a broad smile.

Martin gasped. "What are you doing?"

"How's it feel?"

"It feels, well, strange and wonderful. But isn't it filthy?"

"Does it give you pleasure is what I'm asking."

"It gives me pleasure, yes, very great pleasure."

"Zame with me," Alan said, his eyes shut against the coming light.

Rising on his elbows, Martin drew near to kiss the gamekeeper as he rocked back and forth astride his flanks. Alan turned aside. He would grant the gentleman anything that his body had to offer, but not a kiss on the mouth.

Grief-stricken at their looming separation, Martin gladly lost himself in the pleasure of Alan riding his hips. The gamekeeper arched and unarched his body as his backside opened to receive him deeper. When Martin reached his crisis and shot hard, Alan fell backward and pressed his palms into the mattress on either side of Martin's ankles.

Adrift in the sexual afterglow, Martin was surprised when his partner suddenly righted himself, leaped from the bed, and made for the washstand, coming back with a towel dripping from the basin. "Look how nasty, you a gentleman and all," he joked as he wiped Martin clean with the wet end of the towel, then blotted him dry with the other.

Alan returned to the basin, splashed water in his face, and pulled on his clothes. He made a great show of being a man in a hurry, heading toward the door with a brusque goodbye. "Well, I'm off," Alan said with his hand on the doorknob. "I feel terrible rotten, one thing and another, but facts is facts." Then he was gone.

Carelessly dressed, Martin dragged himself into the London street to face the drizzly morning, wondering how he could endure never again seeing Alan. This sadness threatened to overwhelm him so he could not carry on. Perhaps they would not share another night of lovemaking, but he needed to see the gamekeeper just once more.

Martin looked up the schedule for the *Normandie*'s departure and rang his mother to send the car. The driver brought a note from his sister Kitty. She was the sly one, only a year younger, headstrong and clever, never bashful about speaking her mind.

Colin Dunbar keeps ringing the house. You bolted from Pendersley in such a state that everyone was alarmed. Such a great friend you have in Colin. Are you unwell? A crisis at the office? Desperately in love? I do so hope the latter—and high time it is! Please send word.

Chuckling to himself as he crumpled the paper into his pocket, Martin gave instructions to the front seat. One quick stop allowed him to purchase a farewell gift. It was a cricket set with bat, balls, wickets, pads and gloves, everything that Alan would need to introduce the English sport in the foreign land, each time remembering the special match they played together on a summer afternoon, two strong men against the world.

Nothing went according to expectations. Coming up from their village of East Egdon, Mr. and Mrs. Sutton had gone aboard to see off their son. They formed an uncomfortable little company struggling for conversation as they awaited Alan—who never appeared. Mrs. Sutton nattered on, "It's not like Alan. When Alan says a thing, Alan means it. It's just not like Alan."

"Maybe 'e stopped to smell the roses. You was always going on to him about smelling them bloody roses!" Mr. Sutton said angrily to his wife. "He'll come to grief, mark my words. The noggerhead will make a bad end in Queer Street."

Finally they needed to go ashore as the ship cast off on schedule, but without the Dorset gamekeeper. Mr. Sutton kept haranguing his wife as they stood on the quay. "You always bossing him, and Alan always digging in his heels, I shan't be surprised he missed the boat on purpose, just to spite *you!*"

Martin hardly knew what to feel. Certainly he was miffed for putting himself through the embarrassing episode with the parents, but mostly he felt thrilled that his friend was not at that moment heading across the Atlantic. Alan Sutton was in England. There was hope. He crushed his cigarette on the pavement and climbed into the back seat, smiling broadly. The afternoon had turned glorious with white clouds sailing over the waters and woods. Turning his face toward England in a brave blur of exalted emotion, Martin knew exactly where to go.

"The boathouse is a place I always fancied," Alan had told him as they lay together in the London hotel. "Looking over the pond, very quiet, now and then a fish jumps, and the cushions the way I stack them, I get real still and wait. Just as it gets dark, the squirrels what's been up in the welshnut trees all day, so timid, they come down to drink. I lie patient-like and watch for them. Just like I watched and waited for you, you bastard, not coming like I told you in my letter!"

Without a moment's hesitation Martin set out for the boathouse at Pendersley in its upland vale above the heath. Entering the estate through a gap in the hedgerow, he found Alan asleep inside the changing room on piled-up bedding, just visible in the fading light. He seemed groggy when he awoke. "So you got the wire."

"What wire?"

"The wire I sent to your office, telling you to come here without fail."

With a laugh at all the day's muddles, Martin threw off his overcoat and joined his friend on the cushions. As darkness descended and frogs began croaking, the hearth cast a red glow where they lay snug indoors. Alan yawned. "Excuse me beens I'm knackered, one thing and another."

"You sacrificed your career for my sake without any guarantee. I don't know if you're heroic or daft, only it's what you did, enough to make any man tired."

"Daft?" Alan scrubbed at Martin's cheek with the back of his hand. "That hurt, old gramfer, didn't it or oughter."

"As I suspected, you *are* a bit of a swine."

Then he drew Martin close. "It's the last hurt I'll give you, intending to. Now on, you have someone looking after you. Don't be afeard, now you're with me. Don't be afeard."

"I only meant that I'm daft, too. You've to learn I'm often in a muddle. But we shall find a way to live together and not be bothered. Promise!"

"Now we shan't be parted no more." He embraced Martin and kissed him on the neck. "That's settled and done with."

When Martin returned from the manor house after confronting Colin with the announcement he was in love with his gamekeeper, and had shared with him everything he had including his body—and Colin replied with disgust, "What a grotesque announcement!"—he found Alan still lying inside the boathouse. The young man had fed the fire. Rested and frisky, he stripped Martin of his business suit and wrestled with him in the firelight. Martin, a boxer at school, yielded to Alan's greater muscle power and grit, his hands strong and nimble.

"I'll lern you to fidget!" he said as he forced Martin over onto his belly. Searching beneath the cushion where he had hidden a tube of cream—"Hullo!"— Alan planted himself between Martin's legs and forced him spread-eagle, applying the cream to his partner before taking another dollop for himself. "Relax," he whispered as he moved forward, carefully thrusting where the cream lubricated. Martin did as he was ordered, accepting it because he wanted it. Alan was gentle as he slid inside. "You alright?"

"Never better."

"Just you wait!" Going slowly at first, Alan soon quickened his rhythm, grabbing Martin by the shoulders as he began thrusting harder.

"Dear God!" Martin was soon groaning as Alan pummeled his backside, the lad's large hands shackling his wrists to the cushion. "Oh oh oh oh oh *oh*!"

When Alan exploded, he stopped lunging and relaxed on top, his breathing hot on the back of his friend's neck. Sore, Martin surrendered to the weight of Alan's body as he felt, far up inside him, the throbbing slow and the bigness diminish. Alan slid off and caught Martin by the shoulder, turning him over. "Thanks, mate!"

Stroking his hair, Martin smiled as he caught the gamekeeper's sense of mischief. "When I met your parents on the ship, your old man said that your mother always told you to stop and smell the roses. Eh? Crawl down. I've got a long-stemmed beauty just for you."

"Gawd!"

"Come here!" Martin forced Alan's head down along his belly to where the cushions smelled of mildew and men's sweat. Alan started in, swirling him round and round until the swelling began. Then Martin felt a new sensation. Alan slipped his finger inside, moving in and out as he continued with his mouth. Startled, Martin began losing his hardness until Alan took him deeper in his throat and the stiffness returned.

When at last the sexual crisis came, the spasm hit Martin with a violence that he had never experienced before. The rapture left him panting and close to tears. Alan looked up from between his legs and grinned his gat-toothed smile, wiggling his finger inside until Martin begged him to stop. "Christ Almighty! Where did you learn these things?"

Alan gave a coarse laugh. "I'm not telling, so you're gonna die wondering." Removing his finger, he wiped it on the cushion and rested his head on Martin's belly, heaving in the aftermath of so much rough pleasure.

Afterwards Martin slept fitfully, drifting in and out of physical contentment. When he emerged from his dreamy half-slumber, he reached behind Alan's head, weaving his fingers in the lad's hair and pulling him close. Martin moved forward to kiss him on the lips. Alan pulled back, but Martin's hand held firm and would not let him escape. Suddenly all the struggle went out of Alan and he allowed himself to be drawn forward. Martin kissed him full on the mouth. No longer fighting, Alan drew forward and welcomed the kiss. He had eaten an apple while waiting and his spittle tasted sweet. Next Martin felt something unexpected when the gamekeeper pried open his mouth and thrust his tongue inside. With eyes closed, Martin widened his jaws to receive him.

More and more superstitious as the years passed, Alan came to believe the boathouse was an enchanted place—like the elf mound that his grandmother told about—preserving the memory of their whole life's happiness, like a magical crock of gold.

In the hotel room when Martin declared that he would chuck his job, Alan had said, "Don't be a berk. We've got to have money, that's plain. A man's nowhere free to live as he likes without hard cash."

So leaving the boathouse early the next morning, they returned to the same London hotel, not simply to spend another night of outlaw passion, but to begin arranging their new life together. After only one day's absence, Martin was back in his office, studying the stock exchange's movements and advising clients on their investments, while Alan stayed behind to read the racing sheets. Martin could not help teasing before leaving, "Just don't drop a parcel. Last time, I understand your nag fell so far behind it came in first in the *next* race."

"Bugger off!"

By day's end, Alan had wired his parents saying he had decided not to emigrate and was instead entering the employ of Mr. M. St. John Howell, Esq., of London. A letter followed with a cheque repaying the cost of the ticket and kit to be forwarded to his brother Bob in Buenos Aires. For his part, Martin went home to Richmond and announced to his mother and sisters that he planned on taking a flat in town. "It's more convenient for work. With talk of war, things are becoming hectic on the Exchange. I always enjoyed my weekends in town with Colin before he married Miss Adela Smith."

"But how will you manage, you noodle?" asked his sister Kitty, fixing him with a suspicious look, usually expert at winkling secrets out of him. "You've never concerned yourself with running a household. It sounds like absolute tosh."

Martin knew the question of servants would arise. "I've engaged a good man. He comes well recommended, previously in the employ of the Dunbars at Pendersley."

This was explanation enough to satisfy his mother, and certainly his sister Eva who was simply stopping at home for a fortnight while her husband Albert inspected factories in the north. But Kitty continued to query his plans. "Where in London do you intend setting up?"

"Bloomsbury seems promising. Several college chums have taken flats on Gordon Square. Besides, I have a soft spot for the British Museum and fancy popping in, whenever, to have a look at the Elgin Marbles."

Martin's immediate plan called for finding a well-appointed flat, large enough for a gentleman and his valet, on some quiet tree-lined street in Bloomsbury. For the time being they would lodge in the hotel, having engaged two adjoining rooms for the sake of appearances, but alternating back and forth in their lovemaking. "Maids need to see both beds been slept in," Alan remarked as he pulled back the covers and jumped between the sheets. "It'll throw dust in their eyes, that."

Martin slid under the covers beside him and snuggled close. "Are you going to mind awfully acting as my servant?"

"What's my wages to be?"

"Everything I own."

"Ha! Pull the other one!"

"We'll need to make you over completely, you understand. You'll need to learn how to behave in front of people when we are together, even when you go about on your own. Class never takes a holiday in England."

"An' when the front door closes and we're alone?"

"We are friends, full stop."

"Who washes up?"

Martin chuckled at Alan's unfailing practicality. "I hate when servants don't know to hold their tongues."

Alan raised his hand as if to strike. Martin caught him by the wrist and guided Alan's palm to his lips. "Not so rough as before. I almost miss the roughness."

Martin enjoyed making over Alan, taking satisfaction in every improvement that made his friend more fetching. The first order of business was a trip to his barber, Stanley, who had long practice at cutting his own hair just right, not to draw attention to his ears. Every school bully had pulled Martin's ears, teasing him brutally, so naturally he considered them ugly and spent the rest of his life doing his best to conceal them. The barber did much to transform Alan Sutton, even cleaned his fingernails. During the cricket match after their first night together, Colin's sister remarked that a haircut would go far at making the gamekeeper into someone attractive. And she was correct.

Next came new clothes. "Worcester's man James reports this haberdasher comes highly recommended," Martin remarked while the tailor's well-favoured assistant carefully measured Alan's inseam.

"Who're they when they're at home?"

"A school chum and his valet, damned brainy fellow. The butler James, I mean. Worcester is a wastrel as loopy as they come, a twit with not much brain power, who couldn't find a Cambridge college to take him, so ended up at Oxford instead, the home of lost causes. Which pretty much describe old Worcester to a tee, full of pure banana oil."

Alan echoed back. "A wastrel and a twit with not much brain power, loopy as they come. Ended up at Oxford, home of lost causes, full of pure banana oil."

With a keen ear for language, Alan proved a cunning mimic skilled at picking up any new accent. After only a week in London, he had already lost much of his provincial speech by imitating Martin's. No professor of elocution was needed to drill him in "the rain in Spain stays mainly in the plain." Colin's mother often remarked he was too smart for his station. His Dorset dialect came back whenever it suited his fancy, as when they tussled in bed—*I'll lern you to fidget, old gramfer, you see I'll lern you to fidget!*—and Martin did not complain.

Alan could now pass almost anywhere in society with a proper haircut and a gentleman's wardrobe. For their first real outing, Martin took him to a performance of *H.M.S. Pinafore* and hoped that he would like Gilbert and Sullivan. Alan laughed in all of the right places and left the theater humming the tunes. Martin was delighted and put his arm around his friend's shoulder as they strolled down the pavement, stopping only to buys a couple of boutonnieres from a flower girl with an appalling cockney accent, and then continued through Covent Garden singing together the musical finale.

> *And in spite of all temptations*
> *To belong to other nations,*
> *He remains an Englishman –*
> *He remaaaains an Eeeeenglishman.*

But if Alan Sutton was an Englishman, he was no gentleman and could never hope to become one in Edwardian society. He would always need to pose as Martin's servant.

They never took their flat on Gordon Square when Martin realized he could not abide a lifelong fraud. Next day, he came back to the hotel and announced that he had booked them passage abroad. The pretense that he and Alan were anything but friends, not some shameful parody of Tristram Worcester and his valet James, had already become intolerable for him.

His nerve specialist Dr. Lancelot Jones, who had failed to cure his sexual deviance through hypnosis, recommended removal to a country where the Code Napoléon made homosexuality no longer a crime. Martin decided upon Italy instead of France. Soon London's cobblestones would be slippery with fallen chestnut leaves. The sunny south beckoned. He was not chucking his job, he assured Alan, simply taking the long holiday that was his due as one of the hardworking partners in the firm of Howard and Howell, Stock Brokers.

Before he left the office for the last time, a letter arrived from Kitty.

> *Mother has been treated to an unexpected visit from a Mr. and Mrs. Sutton from some village near the Dunbar estate. I was spending the day at the Domestic Institute, preparing myself for the spinster's life in the event Prince Charming does not come courting with a bundle, but apparently the scene was ghastly. They practically accused you of kidnapping their son and selling him into white slavery. You didn't, did you? I almost hope you have. It would immediately install you in the annals of the few truly interesting characters in the St. John Howell family, eclipsing even father's youthful folly in Monte Carlo. Do write and tell all. You know that I shall be silent as the grave with Mother and Eva. I wish I had your courage. Maybe someday. For now I send you my very special love. You understand—my very special love!*

Leaving London on the night train, Martin and Alan continued by rail directly to Italy. Heading north from Milan, they transferred to a small steamer for a cruise around Lake Como until arriving at their immediate destination Bellagio, which had looked so inviting in the travel brochures. They lodged at a lakeside villa famous for its writers and composers, where Liszt composed his fiendishly difficult *Paganini Études*. Their suite had a mountain view framed out the window by cypresses. "These magic casements open upon perilous seas in fairyland forlorn," Martin announced as he threw open the shutters. "Something tremendous is happening, Alan. Do you feel it?"

Without a word of reply, Alan locked the bedroom door and shoved Martin onto the bed. They whispered each other's names as their clothes came off. All the while medieval knights watched motionless from the golden needlework of tapestries opposite their canopied four-poster.

Martin had arrived in Milan with a letter of introduction to the British consul from Colin Dunbar, M.P. The political life suited Colin. He thought of the welfare of his constituents and said so eloquently in speeches that he took great trouble writing. He was well liked by his party's leadership. He climbed the ladder. Adela proved to be the perfect wife for a politician, supportive of his ambitions, patient with his many absences, and brilliant at arranging parties. She knew exactly who belonged at particular social gatherings, who not. Almost always when entertaining at their Westminster home, Mrs. Dunbar said she would buy the flowers herself. Alan had bullied Martin before they left London, "Write your old chum. What's the good you having connections, you don't use them?"

The consul had then provided Martin with another introduction to the nobleman whose villa overlooked the lakeside village of Bellagio. Prince del Dongo gave them free run of his grounds, even inviting Martin and his companion to stay during their visit, but the Prince's hospitality would have left them no privacy and was therefore politely declined.

Far from England's pastures and hedgerows, Martin and Alan shouldered their picnic hampers and climbed through olive groves and azalea terraces on a gusty late-summer day. Up gravel paths twisting among pines, they trudged until reaching the wooded summit. There they found what Martin knew they would find—because his guidebook never failed him—the ruins of a castle built centuries ago to defend against lake pirates. Alan spread their blanket beneath the grey walls while Martin uncorked the wine. The bold promontory afforded two completely different views where the lake's arms, the one toward Como so voluptuously beautiful and the other toward Lecco, rocky and austere.

Forever restless, Alan never outgrew his love of the outdoors, leaving Martin in his reverie to explore the groves beyond the stone ruins. He returned with a fragment of red tile found beneath the laurels. "What's this?"

"The guidebook says that the ancient Roman writer Pliny built a villa on the top of this little mountain. Tiles from his villa can still be found, the book says, and you found one."

"Good job he did. No pirates sneaking up on him here."

Martin stretched out on the blanket and gazed toward the sunshine filtered through pine needles. "Pliny must have walked down ancient paths like these" he mused out loud, puffing on his pipe. "And Stendhal, too, because bits from *La Chartreuse de Parme* took place in this part of Italy. This landscape reminded the young countess how fleeting life is—and how we should enjoy whatever happiness offers itself to us."

"There's others walk here now." Alan motioned in the direction of the pines. One of the villa's gardeners, young and winsome with black curly hair, stood watching from the evergreens. He smiled and touched the brim of his cap when he saw they had spotted him. Alan remarked, "He's not ancient, neither, if you take my meaning."

"Stendhal was right. Beauty is nothing but the promise of happiness."

"Fancy a treat? Cook didn't pack a pudden."

"The Italian language provides phrases for every variation of pleasure, like *terzo comodo*, when a third man becomes convenient for the other two."

Taking the lead, Alan shouted "Hullo!" and beckoned the gardener to join them. Making a great show of shyness, the young man approached their blanket tentatively and greeted them in his own language. Alan produced his cigarette case, opening it for him to help himself. Alan took one first as encouragement. Finally accepting the offer, the Italian produced a box of matches and lit Alan's cigarette before lighting his own.

Reclining on his elbows, Martin watched the scene cautiously before offering some wine. The young man resisted with "no, no, no" before he was persuaded to have a glass, then another. Soon Martin was uncorking a second bottle, and they were tearing into loaves of bread and eating cheese and laughing.

An hour later when the gardener made an effort to rise and return to work, he fell back down on the blanket, too drunk to walk, or so he let on. Alan made the first move. His advances met no resistance. While Martin unbuttoned the young man's shirt, Alan undid his trousers and slipped his hand inside. It was the first time they tasted the ferocious passion of the Latin race, venturing outside their friendship to share a frolic with a third man. His name was Giorgio.

Back in Milan as autumn descended, his name was Ermenio. In Turin, he was a tram conductor who called himself Cesario. In Bergamo, he was Mario the glassblower. In Parma for Christmas, they found a bored and curious seminarian named Fabrizio. They never caught the name of their waiter in Genoa. Dante was the bellboy at their hotel in Siena. Giustino was the Lucca student who wanted desperately to improve his English. On a bright winter day in Naples, they secured the services of an off-duty bersagliero named Dominico as their guide to Herculaneum, where they sported in the ruins of one of the more remote villas still under excavation by the Americans.

Their Venetian gondolier was a beautiful husband and father, tall and well shaped, named Daniele. Venice was all commotion because the Archduke had been shot, and the Austrians were demanding to send troops into Serbia to arrest those who plotted the assassination. So Daniele moored his gondola and did his best to divert the English visitors at their hotel, once a notorious palazzo, where legend held that Lord Byron debauched a duchess, her daughter, and her precocious young son during a single afternoon.

Later the English travelers went off the beaten track to Monteriano. There a young artist named Gino, the local dentist's son, invited them to view the frescoes of Santa Deodata where they misconducted themselves in the sacristy. By the time they reached Florence in high summer, Martin was fatigued from travel and decided they needed to rest. They stayed at the same pensione where his sister Eva had come on honeymoon with his university chum Albert. The newlyweds had written ahead for a room with a view of the Arno, and they made good report of its cleanness upon their return to Bayswater.

Martin and Alan found themselves in possession of the same splendid room with a view. Its painted ceiling was a riot of griffins and bagpipes. Before unpacking, the two men reclined in the window seat and drank some local wine, intertwining their legs while enjoying their view of the river. They nuzzled each other's crotches with stocking feet. "Can't keep it in your pants?" Alan joked when he felt the hardness swelling inside Martin's trousers.

Soon they were tumbling into bed as Martin teased his friend, "Time to stop and smell the roses?"

After a late lunch, they visited the church of Santa Croce and bought postcards, and when they returned for dinner a letter had arrived from Kitty. Martin skimmed it in the smoking room.

Mother behaves as if you were away at school, not run off to Italy with Colin Dunbar's man on such a daring escapade. . . I almost wish that she would fling the cat about and make a loud fuss, instead of silently playing the Tragic Muse. . . Her favorite expression is "gone wrong"—"I don't know how such a sweet boy could have gone so wrong." To my mind, you remain so much the superior personage than I ever expected, utterly redeemed from the cut-to-pattern wretchedness of the City.

Finally reaching Rome, they enjoyed their hotel near the Spanish Steps and made a great friend of the facchino, whose name was Giovanni. Alan was eager to visit the Vatican, filling his pockets with grapes and apples at breakfast. "I understand there's sacred monkeys back of the Pope's palace. I'm hoping we have a chance to see them, maybe feed them. Catholics are a queer lot." But the square-jawed Swiss Guardsman knew nothing about sacred monkeys, so Alan sat beneath the colonnade, looking dejected, and shared his grapes with Martin.

Inside the Sistine Chapel, Martin read from the guidebook while Alan stood dumbstruck looking up at the ceiling frescos. "They made glorious things in those days. It took a lot of paint to make those men look alive. That's what I call art!"

Rome was where Martin bought Alan a deluxe camera for taking portraits as well as pictures of old churches. "You have a very talented eye," Martin assured him. "When we went shooting at Pendersley, you saw the rabbits the rest of us missed. You notice things and you're quick, like batting at cricket. Those talents can make you a brilliant photographer, professional if you work hard."

Their progress led southward to Sicily, where they had an invitation from another one of Martin's old Cambridge chums—Algernon Rotheley—a man who had suffered misfortune on a grand public scale.

Lord Rotheley had been the most conspicuous undergraduate at King's College in his year. Tall, dark-haired, and elegant in dress and manner, the Marquis of Ellesmere's son proved himself a brilliant debater at the Union, though in private conversation he always emphasized one word in every sentence and was positively *addicted* to superlatives. Nabbed with a marine behind a pub in Soho during the summer after taking his degree, Rotheley was tried and convicted of gross indecency. His position in society was forfeited by his ignominy—so the judge pronounced from the bench—and he was sentenced to six months of hard labor in Reading Gaol. Some friends feared that the public humiliation would drive him to suicide or the bottle. The English despise the beaten.

But Rotheley was made of sterner stuff. As he rode in the black wagon from the Old Bailey, he had made a firm resolution how he would face his imprisonment. First, he would refuse to view himself as a criminal. He had done nothing wrong because nobody had been harmed. Nor would he play the martyr. He would make a daily study of indifference. He would cultivate a sense of dignity incapable of recognizing scorn from others. If there was pain, he would find meaning in it. Nobody could take away his freedom to choose his attitude toward these dire reversals. The thought of suicide never entered his mind.

Rotheley had read about desert saints who made virtues of confinement and privation. No lifer, he knew the exact term of his suffering. The six months in prison became in his mind nothing more than a stay at a health spa. Long hours on the treadmill reduced his waistline while strengthening his limbs. Each night when he lay exhausted on his bunk, he ran his hand along his thighs and admired muscles that grew firmer every week. Nietzsche was right, he thought. Whatever did not kill him *did* make him stronger.

By the end of his ordeal, Rotheley felt almost thankful to prison for awakening his spirit. Its ugliness intensified his apprehension of beauty wherever he found it. Its solitude sharpened his appetite for love. He was grateful for the newfound ability to feel gratitude itself, appreciating even the smallest comforts. For a man whose whole existence was bent upon being conspicuous, he enjoyed becoming a nonentity. To meet death well was a great accomplishment, when it came, but better still to inhabit this world here and now with the fullest sense of being alive.

Lord Rotheley, strong as he never was as an undergraduate who disdained rowing and footer, walked from the prison a totally free man, so lean and serene he could have posed for the portrait of a saint. He gladly abandoned London to wander the world as a blithe exile. Without a homeland now, he felt himself everywhere at home, taking pleasure because he knew more pleasure waited around the next corner. He was in Paris for the beginning of the opera season, and in Venice for the raucous carnival of Redentore with its regatta and fireworks. He tanned his newly muscular legs on the beaches of Pampelonne, his favorite on the Côte d'Azur, and then tried his luck at the gaming tables of Marienbad.

Martin even heard a rumor during their weekend at Edward Carpenter's country estate—when he and Alan enjoyed a long sit-down with the novelist E. M. Forster—that the intrepid Rotheley had traveled as far as Japan. There he had assembled a large collection of shunga scrolls, which he brought back for sale in Paris with profit enough to purchase one of Rodin's bronze nude athletes, an artwork of undying beauty.

Back in Europe now, Lord Rotheley had drifted south to Sicily and taken up residence in the household of Baron von Gloeden, the photographer. The Englishman was artistic by temperament and made himself useful by attending the Baron's picture-taking sessions with local youths. For a small fee, these adolescents showed no hesitation in taking off every stitch to pose for the camera. Some youths were muscular, some had good-looking faces, and some possessed a rough arrogance and disdainful beauty that awakened Rotheley's sharpest yearnings too long stifled in prison.

Rotheley's invitation found them at the pensione in Florence with no immediate prospects after their midsummer stay in Rome. And why not enjoy a few country boys in the groves of Arcady? First Martin wanted to visit Syracuse where he could finish reading Thucydides, and then they could travel north to the German's seaside villa. Alan shared his enthusiasm. "The Baron can teach me about the camera, professional-like!"

But Martin and his friend never joined Lord Rotheley and the country lads disrobing for picture-taking. After a summer marked by exceptional tranquility throughout Europe, their holiday ended in Syracuse on a very hot day in August 1914. With massive disruptions in the rail service, Kitty's letter had taken two weeks to reach their hotel.

Dearest Martin, just a brief note in fear it will not get through. Things are nightmarish here. Nothing but patriotic rant about saving wives and daughters from the Huns. The men have lost their minds completely. You will not believe it, but we were enjoying a lovely family weekend when news arrived that Britain's ultimatum had been rejected by the Kaiser. Without a word Albert jumped up from the dinner table, rushed out the front door, and ran the streets looking for a recruiting officer. Never a thought of Eva! With everyone suspected as a traitor who does not pitch in, I have joined my friend Miss Tansy from the Domestic Institute in an ambulance company, and now we spend our evenings wrapping each other in bandages for practices. Please, wherever you are, do not return home to this madness.

Martin had been following the political scene throughout their Italian journeys, and anxiety over the momentum of military preparations fueled his passion for the great monuments of European civilization that might not survive the coming juggernaut. This urgency had also fueled his escapades with Giorgio, Ermenio, Daniele, and Giustino.

"Now it is all starting over again," Martin had muttered as he folded Kitty's letter into his Thucydides and leaned his head against the limestone column, surveying the ancient quarry in the shimmering heat. His student edition of *The Peloponnesian Wars* rested in his lap while tears streams down his cheeks. The book lay open to a paragraph marked in blue ink.

So Alcibiades and the other accused left Sicily in their own ship and sailed as though on their way back to Athens. But when they reached Thurii, they parted company with their companions and left their ship and went into hiding, since they were afraid to go back and stand trial with all the prejudice against them. And in the end, they were nowhere to be found.

When Alan discovered him in the quarry, called him wezzle-brained for sitting in the noonday sun, and lured him for some tea at the nearest taverna—"I feel nearly done in, too, the heat and all!"—Martin looked embarrassed that he had been caught weeping.

"Let me tell you the reality behind the patriotic bravado of the *Daily Telegraph*," Martin began gravely after the waiter settled the cups and cakes. "This coming war will not end with a quick victory by any nation. It will become a great war unleashing death across Europe. Armies will stand against armies in stalemate, and corpses will be stacked like cordwood. Look around us. This is one of the world's great battlefields and one of history's great killing fields. Because the Athenian expeditionary force was defeated here, Spartan victory on the mainland brought to an end the golden age that gave us the likes of Sophocles and Plato, the builders of the Parthenon and the inventors of democracy. And now? Tourists gather at the edge of the quarries, the clever ones wondering how the outcome might have been different if Alcibiades had remained in command."

Furrowing his brow, Alan tried grasping what Martin was going on about.

"What of this great war now starting?" Martin continued. "In a hundred years, sightseers will visit the battlefields of France and think how tragic, how unnecessary, what a horrific waste of human life. Digging anywhere in those green fields where hand-dug trenches once ran, men will find bits of barbed wire, shards of artillery shells, and rusted buttons and badges still filling the air with smell of rust on wet mornings. French farmers plowing their fields, a hundred years from today, will turn up the bones of the nameless dead soldiers who fell there, full of youth and beauty." His face turned grim with determination. "And one of them will *not* be me, Alan Sutton, and one of them will not be *you*!"

Alan sat tensely with his hands shoved in his trouser pockets, fiddling with the hotel key. "When I was making to emigrate to the Argentine, do you remember what you said? *England for me*. Right there in the apricot grove, me rubbing my breeks against your leg as we walked, you thinking I was waiting for one of the maids, all the time I was taking a chill waiting for you. *England for me*, you said."

"I also remember my quack hypnotist said that England has always been disinclined to accept human nature. Why die for a country whose laws condemn us as criminals? We're only bystanders. If faced with the choice between betraying my country or my friendship with you, I hope I have the guts to stand my ground, like a good Athenian warrior, for the sake of the comrade at my side. Not for king and country but for you, Alan Sutton."

"Where then? Here in Sicily, we've reached the end."

Martin stared at the cloudless sky. "We must search for big spaces, not some prison like this place became for the young Athenians, and England became for the two of us. We need some place where nothing modern and horrible can reach us, a place that has already existed forever, full of woods some of them, and arched with a clear blue sky like this one. We won't have a nationality. Wherever you and I can live together will become our Land of Hope and Glory. Two strong men *can* defy the world."

"I've trusted you this far, and it's plain we're meant to go together. Only I like a dry place best, not waterlogged like England. Is there somewhere we can go that's warm and dry like here?"

Martin had been making a study of tourist brochures and guidebooks for world travelers. He smiled bravely and nodded, "Rather!"

Time was pressing. Soon the telegraph would summon them home for mobilization. Martin had joined the Territorials after leaving university. By the next year, the militia would be fighting in the trenches at Belgium, where poison gas hung heavy over no man's land and their advance was halted by German machineguns. Next the Territorials would join the armies assembled for slaughter on a monumental scale at the Battle of the Somme, while conscription awaited Alan. Italy had declared its neutrality for the time being. If they acted quickly, they could bid their farewell to arms and chart their retreat ahead of the coming storm.

The next morning, a hired motorcar took them westward to Sicily's main port for international shipping. Turning their backs on the ancient parapets of Europe, Martin booked them passage on a steamer leaving Palermo and carrying other emigrants seeking new lives in far-off lands.

"So that's settled and done with," Alan said stonily as they stood on the ship's fantail after clearing the wide bay, their arms around each other's shoulders. Nearby, a very pretty Italian girl stood all by herself, looking forlorn, as a flock of gulls wheeled and cried above the ship's wake. Only these three passengers remained in the gathering darkness to watch the high summit of Monte Pellegrino recede into the sea mists.

Martin muttered, "*Sicilia est insula magna in Europa.*" His Latin schoolbook had correctly predicted their jumping-off point into the unknown. Just like a soldier in the front line of battle, he felt the deep breath before the plunge.

3

To the Boathouse

Morgan and Eddy—New York, 1977

"Just one more?"

Central Park on a summer afternoon looked like an update of Seurat's famous landscape. Joggers ran on pathways by the lake, schoolboys raced each other on bicycles, and teenagers threw Frisbees back and forth while their dogs in red bandanas chased after, barking. Brides posed for their wedding photos beside the Bethesda Angel fountain, and from the luxury apartments along Fifth Avenue, nannies pushed strollers, still exchanging stories about the citywide blackout the month before. At the boathouse restaurant waiters hurried back and forth while diners, sipping Chablis, watched tourists lining up for rides in gondolas. A curtain of green muffled the traffic noise and the roar of jetliners climbing to cruising altitude. But Central Park after dark told a different story.

It had been the hottest, muggiest day of August. Now long after midnight, Morgan's one overwhelming desire was to reach the boathouse. He came to these woods looking for one more sexual adventure before heading home. He always found what he needed sitting on a park bench, leaning along the pedestrian bridge, or lurking just off the pathway where the shadows deepened and men crouched in the bushes. Morgan felt completely free as soon as he reached the boulder beside the lake, his favorite place to sit and wait. He struck a bargain with himself and said aloud, "Just one more."

In almost moments he found himself in the bushes with a young man down on his knees, handsome with mustache and hungry eyes. They always had to be young. Morgan never gave a second look at any man ten minutes older than himself.

With his hands gripping Morgan's bare thighs, this guy looked like the Olympic swimmer who had won all the gold medals. Morgan Carr Cabell had been the freestyle champion at Princeton. His teammates elected him captain, but he carried a grudge because the vote was not unanimous. Coach said so. Morgan liked getting great head from a man who looked like the Olympic swimmer.

Morgan reached up and his hands grasped a low branch of the tree overhead and he stretched to full height, all six three of him, no longer caring if his khakis fell down around his ankles as he sank into all the sensations of the summer night. The breeze moved over his bare skin and through his hair, silky and sun-bleached from daily jogging. He closed his eyes and sank deeper into the physical encounter.

Morgan thought he heard a noise and glanced over his shoulder checking for cops, though he knew they never came into the park after midnight. Still, he felt an outlaw's fear of arrest that made his escapades more exciting. He imagined himself like Lord Byron in the dark byways of Venice seeking his erotic thrills in palazzos, in doorways, and in gondolas—with gondoliers. The night's long hunt for one more muscular body to plunder, and then the fierce grappling of two men or three, sometimes more, made his heart quicken and his senses come fully alive.

Morgan's eyes settled on what had momentarily distracted him—a young man not cruising and not pursuing, just standing alone under the lamppost beside the pathway. Other men started circling him. They paused and tried to catch his eye, but he stood with his hands in the pockets of his slacks, his tie loosened and collar open, the only motionless figure in the slow-moving shadowland of instant sexual release. He was staring in Morgan's direction.

Suddenly Morgan was embarrassed with his khakis down around his ankles and could feel his face flushing hot. Freezing, he stared out of the darkness into the eyes of this strangely beautiful man while still getting vigorous sex from the man who looked like the gold medal swimmer.

This was the same man from the disco, all bone structure and musculature, first spotted on the far side of the bar at Studio 54, good-looking in the way that men were good-looking in New York with great cheekbones and sculpted hair, thick and wavy like a mane. His face was the face of a twenty-something Nureyev with intense dark eyes, only he was leaner, tauter than the Russian dancer, his skin paler and his lionlike hair auburn, almost red.

This man with his movie star good looks had been wearing an Armani suit when he stepped up to the bar where cocaine was served as readily as cocktails, while Morgan was wearing the preppy uniform of alligator shirt, khaki slacks, and topsiders. This story will never have a happy ending, Morgan had thought as his eyes followed the man in his designer suit through the crowd. He's not all that good-looking anyway. His nose is too big, like the actor who put the gerbil up his butt. And he's too dressed up, probably a star-fucker, definitely Euro Trash. But, he could not help adding, the guy has the most amazing eyes.

Morgan had followed him to the dance floor and watched from a safe distance. He loved the hard-driving beat and catchy tunes like *Macho Man* and *If You Could Read My Mind* and his all-time favorite *I Will Survive*, truly the national anthem of the broken-hearted. But Morgan never danced because he felt awkward and afraid he might have to take off his shirt on the dance floor. So he stood on the sidelines, nursed his vodka tonic, and watched the other men dancing as they stripped off shirts revealing lean torsos glistening with sweat.

The man with the killer cheekbones was astonishing when he started dancing, easing into the crowd, in total control of his body, his movements confident and strong, the angular features of his face very masculine. He began dancing with a woman and then drifted by himself into the middle of the crowd, his eyes closed in his own private world. And this Armani man never took his shirt off, just loosened his tie and shoved up the sleeves of his jacket. He was what a trashy novelist would call painfully handsome, Morgan thought, as he kept running through his mind what his friend Claire always said, "Any man that good-looking can't be that straight."

Claire was his classmate from law school at University of Virginia, and she became the bar buddy who accompanied him to gay hot spots so he would not drink alone. She was the only woman permanently in his life besides his mother and the bitch goddess Success, who fired his sexual pursuits just as she drove his professional ambitions as an attorney. Even when they started bar-hopping back in Charlottesville, she scanned the crowd and helped Morgan spot his next one-night boyfriend. Morgan would ask cautiously, "Are you sure?" She would give him a knowing look, "He can be had."

Now both of them had ended up in New York where Claire was often the only woman in the bar, ordering one Harvey Wallbanger after another, her favorite. She loved the rowdy fun and make-believe of these homosexual haunts. "Now that I've found this place," she announced to everyone within earshot at Harry's Back East, "I'm going to be here every night for the rest of my life!" But she got huffy about being called a fag hag, proclaiming loudly one night at Ty's, "You know what I am? I'm a gay man trapped in a straight woman's body!" She also had strong opinions about Morgan's sex life and told him brutally whenever he mentioned finding a boyfriend and settling down some day, "You're not the marrying kind."

Her pronouncement had come back to Morgan as he stood in the crowd at Studio 54 watching *him*. He could not stop gazing at him and wanting this one man. He felt a great emotional abyss opening up somewhere deep inside as his eyes followed *him*.

Now long after midnight near the boathouse in Central Park, this stranger with the rust-red hair had shown up and was walking slowly into the shadows where Morgan lurked with his khakis down around his ankles. He stopped right next to Morgan and stood shoulder to shoulder, glancing down where the black hair of Morgan's sex partner could just barely be seen moving up and down, up and down. Then he fixed his eyes on Morgan's.

Morgan could hear his breathing. He felt bits of bark clinging to his sweaty palms as he released the branch and dropped his arms to his sides. As lamplight filtered through leaves overhead, a line of poetry popped into his mind—*Your eyes have shot their arrows into my heart*—but he said nothing, afraid that any talking would ruin the moment. He recalled a line from Dante while forgetting the Olympic lookalike down on his knees.

Already three months in Manhattan where he was working for a Wall Street law firm while cramming for the bar exam, Morgan should have been exhausted by the weekend. Instead he felt the need for release. "My horniness can be detected by NASA satellites," he told Claire as he turned on his barstool to survey the crowd.

"You," replied Claire as she put down her drink, empty, "would fuck a snake if someone would hold its head up. It's a well-known true fact."

It was the perfect time and place to be a man in his mid-twenties, gay and single in New York, eight years after the Stonewall Uprising when homosexuals fought back against the police. Everything had exploded wide open for latecomers like Morgan, and everything was happening in the bars, in the discos, in the parks, at the baths, among the truck in the meatpacking district, and down at the piers on West Street.

Actually Morgan never went to the piers because he heard grim tales how the wooden floors were rotten, planks gave way, and men fell through dark holes into the river below, knocked unconscious when struck by crossbeams on the way down. Their drowned bodies were found floating nude, bruised and bloated, with their cutoff jeans still down around their ankles. So he made a point of never roving as far as West Street, just as he never ventured south of the World Trade Center after sundown, way too dangerous for a man who wore Brooks Brothers.

Instead, he became an uptown guy subletting a one-bedroom apartment just off Central Park West, rent controlled so that he could afford the neighborhood. He was not supposed to bring home any overnight guests and he never needed to.

Morgan could not remember the last time he had sex with his shoes off. Night or day, he could enjoy himself in a backroom or a video arcade. He went to a restaurant and got sex from his waiter in the restroom. He went window-shopping, caught the eye of a clerk, and was beckoned inside to join him in the storeroom. He found himself on a crowded subway car with a crew-cut intern from St. Vincent's Hospital pressed against his body, rubbing up and down and getting each other hard, so that Morgan exited two stops early and followed the young doctor back to his apartment for a quickie.

Morgan went to a museum and ended up in a stall in the men's room, his body pressed against the cool marble wall, in a passionate embrace with an art student with curly hair and a tattered jean jacket. They had made eye contact in the American collection, circled the gallery, and finally converged in front of Georgia O'Keeffe's *Black Hollyhock Blue Larkspur* before the young man led the way to the restroom. For all his fancy Ivy League education and his professional ambitions as an attorney, Morgan had to admit that the one thing he wanted more than anything else in the whole wide world was his next blowjob.

This Saturday night when he encountered the Armani man had unfolded like every other Saturday night since he moved to the city. Morgan started on Christopher Street, going from bar to bar. He defended his promiscuity as making up for lost time, since he experienced his first gay sex only during his sophomore year at Princeton and did not become really active until his second year of law school at Virginia. And why not? His sporting life was just a sideshow. On some level he knew he was only playing hooky when he submerged into the sexual underworld of Manhattan, a tourist and not a true inhabitant of these gay bars and discos. Not yet twenty-five, he clung to the myth of immortal youth and endlessly unfolding possibilities. Morgan was willing to try almost everything because he knew he was risking nothing.

Earlier that night after three bars and three vodka tonics, he found himself drawn to a familiar backroom where sex was automatic and there was no conversation. Morgan hated small talk. Maybe too much *yak yak yak* ruined the experience, or maybe he just couldn't be bothered. The last evening he endured the ordeal of making chitchat, a Columbia undergraduate took an hour telling him about the deep interpersonal values of his est seminars. True, the sex was magnificent later. The student was an insatiable bottom who would not let Morgan stop slamming him doggie style, relentlessly pile driving so hard he worried about ripping his rubber. Morgan was fastidious about cleanliness to a degree almost unknown among his fellow butt-fuckers. His father had shocked him thoroughly with his unexpected birds-and-bees lecture while driving together to his Princeton admission interview. "Prophylactics prevent disease and unwanted pregnancy, also the need to worry about coping with either problem!" The advice about condoms actually sank in. But the hour of barroom conversation with the psychology major from Columbia was one hour of life, Morgan knew, he would never get back. He would rather screw a stranger than talk to him.

What Morgan really liked was the darkness of the bar's backroom.

Sometimes he followed a cute guy back, sometimes the cute guy followed him, no mystery, no crapshoot. There the young man stopped in front of him, got close enough to feel his body heat, sensed no resistance, fumbled with his belt buckle, went down, groped the bulge in his khakis and gave a squeeze. Morgan savored every second of it. The sex act was condensed to a few urgent movements as Morgan found himself unzipping, whipping out, and feeling himself consumed by the warm wet mouth down in the darkness.

Morgan was not picky about technique as long as the man on his knees didn't stop till the job was done. Afterwards he always leaned down and said, "Thanks, buddy!" Not only because he was a super polite Southerner who had been taught good manners as the surest means for getting what he wanted in life. But because Morgan wanted the other guy to know that the sexual encounter was *done*, and he was tucking in, zipping up, and moving on. His motto was simple. It's better to leave than get left.

That is exactly how his Saturday night began on Christopher Street before he headed uptown and spotted the Armani man.

Sometimes during a long evening spent prowling for sex, Morgan liked to stop at a piano bar called Five Oaks, walking around and around because he always got lost in the West Village. In this dimly lit haunt of older gay men and some straight couples, the legendary Marie Blake performed all the old songs. On this particular night, she was pounding out a Cole Porter favorite as he made his way down the stairs.

> Good authors too who once knew better words
> Now only use four-letter words
> Writing prose — Anything goes!

Morgan was introduced to this cabaret when he first came to New York for his interview with the law firm. After the business dinner, one of the senior partners, another transplanted Virginian like himself, offered to drop Morgan off at his hotel. Instead, they ended up having a nightcap at Five Oaks.

Even before his brandy arrived, Mr. Satterfield was explaining how he first met Marie when he was a young naval officer during World War II. The night before they shipped out, he and some other junior officers were "painting the town red" and ended up drinking in a joint where she was "tickling the ivories." Ensign Satterfield had passed out under the table and was abandoned by the drinking buddies, but Marie had overheard the junior officers mentioning the name of their ship and knew he needed to get back before dawn. So Marie loaded him into a taxi when the bar closed and delivered him to his battleship in the Brooklyn Naval Yard. Ever since that night, wherever she was performing in New York, no matter how louche the clientele, this senior partner of a prestigious Wall Street law firm sought her out, often emptying the contents of his wallet into her tip jar when leaving, with just enough left for a taxicab home to Sutton Place.

From his own first night at Five Oaks, Morgan too returned to hear Marie play whenever he wanted to nurse a drink and slide back into his own memories. Marie's voice with its raw sense of life's pains and losses spelled escape from the sunlit world of boring, boring, boring.

Some men drink to forget, but Morgan drank to remember. Over and over he thought back to his one great love when he was a Princeton undergraduate, his squash partner and best friend, Ethan Rees. Everyone called him the Golden Boy, and that was exactly how Morgan remembered Ethan. After a third drink in the course of an evening, Morgan could not help recalling the whole story. How they had been drawn to each other when they first met in their freshman English class writing term papers on *The Great Gatsby*. How they never ran out of things to talk about on the squash court, over meals at their eating club, and late at night over whiskey in the dorms, Morgan exhausted from swimming and Ethan bruised from lacrosse practice. And finally how they ended up, one winter night, drinking bourbon while listening to *Parsifal* in Morgan's room. They were lying side by side on a Turkish carpet, a gift from his grandmother when he went off to college, propped up on their elbows, close enough for Morgan to settle his gaze on Ethan's hair, amazed how the individual strands were really many different colors, not just blond and red but also white and auburn brown, a wonderful blend.

Morgan had found the courage to confess his darkest secret that he thought he was probably a homosexual, and instead of bolting for the door, Ethan said simply, "Gay? So why aren't you an English major?" Then Ethan shared his own deepest secret that he wanted to write a novel and already had the title picked out, *A Cry of Seagulls*. The story was about two buddies whose sailboat gets caught in a hurricane. The storm's violence rips a hole in the fabric of time, and they encounter Blackbeard's pirate ship in the eye of the tempest. Then all hell breaks loose. Listening about the novel, Morgan felt relieved that Ethan showed no panic over his gayness as he continued staring at his friend's multicolored hair.

Still recounting the plot of his novel, Ethan nudged closer on the antique carpet. Then he put his hand on Morgan's shoulder, grinning as he raised his eyes, "Want to give it a try?" And they did, trying everything, first on the carpet as their clothes came off, then in the dark bedroom as they stood facing each other with erections swatting back and forth, and finally in the narrow dorm bed. Their passionate grappling was more like wrestling as their arms and legs got tangled in the sheets. Drunk and sexually drained, Morgan fell asleep with his body pressed against the cold wall. He awoke in the gray light of a winter morning, alone.

Two days later, Ethan left a note taped to his door asking for a squash game. Nothing more was ever said. Ethan acted as if the whole thing never happened, and Morgan went along with the pretense. They played their fast-paced squash matches just as before. When the courts were booked solid, they retreated to the weight room in the Dillon Gym where they loaded the barbells and spotted each other for bench presses. In the usual jock way, they encouraged and shamed each other into one more lift. "Don't be a fucking sissy," Morgan mocked him as he straddled Ethan's head and rested his fingers lightly underneath the barbell, continuing to urge him, "Get it up, get it up!"

And all the while Morgan's heart was breaking as he yearned for the Golden Boy and longed for a friendship that was complete and would last a lifetime. Ethan became the emotional sinkhole that fell away beneath him and threatened to engulf Morgan's every waking thought. Steeped in failure, Morgan knew that his life might have been easier if they never saw each other again. Then he could have transformed Ethan into the villain of his tragic life history, the culprit who condemned him to the degrading future of the old queer professors who walked their dogs at night near the train station, hoping to find sex in the bushes with other old queer professors.

Instead he and Ethan remained friends, always good friends. They resumed their lives as before. They played squash and listened to records and drank Jack Daniels.

On the first snowfall of winter, Ethan pounded on Morgan's door at midnight and pulled him from bed where he was reading *Birth of Tragedy* to join one of Princeton's newest traditions, the Nude Olympics. Sophomores were stripping naked, streaking the campus, and converging in the darkness of one of the university's hallowed courtyards. In those early years when women were still new arrivals on the campus, this night of all-male revelry remained the great leveler when all distinctions disappeared between rugby jocks and astrophysics geeks.

Naked together in the mobbed quadrangle, Ethan passed a flask back and forth as protection against the freezing temperatures. Morgan took a swig and imagined the taste of Ethan's lips lingering on rim. As the frolic reached its climax, the two men howled with laughter and pressed their naked bodies together for warmth. They joined the conga line of white-limbed males snaking through the snowy quadrangle. Ethan stood behind, wrapping his arms around Morgan's chest and hugging so tightly that Morgan could feel his friend's heart pounding against his back.

On other nights, quiet indoors when they were alone together, their conversations became edgy and competitive. As the spring semester came to a close, each encounter seemed like intellectual arm wrestling. Their banter became a sad substitute for any physical grappling.

All the while Morgan spent sleepless nights writhing in emotional agony in his single bed. He felt so devastated that even his esophagus ached in sorrow as he curled up beside his imaginary lover. Always when he masturbated, he tried to catch the scent of Ethan's hair lingering somewhere deep inside his pillow, thinking over and over until he said aloud, "I'll spend a lifetime learning how to miss you."

Summer vacation before the junior year would have been the perfect time for them to go their separate ways. They could have drifted apart and never gotten together again when the fall semester started. But Ethan would not let Morgan sink into the gloomy solitude of his books, records, and swimming practices. Even in their senior year while writing the honors thesis, Ethan cadged a study carrel on the same floor of the Firestone Library where they could hole up together, with black construction paper taped over the windows, because it was unfashionable to be seen working hard at Princeton. His research project in microbiology and virology was so technical he could never simplify it enough for a philosophy major to grasp, while Morgan completed his vast comparative study of Friedrich Nietzsche and William James.

Ethan did not actually need a carrel, Morgan realized later, nor did he need to hide in the library to write up his lab results. He made this commitment mainly to prevent Morgan from sinking into the bottomless despair that befell so many Princeton undergraduates as they struggled to complete their senior projects. Ethan's steady gestures of friendship made Morgan feel only more frustrated. He desperately yearned for a masculine friendship which was loving *and* sexual, the way he hoped theirs would become after their one night together.

That never-repeated conjunction of hungry bodies happened more than five years before Morgan arrived in Manhattan, but he still revisited that one awesome night in his barroom reveries. He would always remember the Golden Boy best because he made him suffer the most. His mind did not conjure up some imaginary sex scene but the real thing, the night when they actually made love and Ethan whimpered when he achieved orgasm. He had pressed his face into Morgan's bare thigh and lingered, with tears and slobber, as the two men lay sixty-nine in the tangle of sheets.

Whenever recalling the sexual wrestling that began with Ethan's "Want to give it a try?" Morgan swore he would never fall in love again. The sleepless nights of tossing and turning in his dorm bed, as he rehearsed conversations he would never actually have with Ethan, brought him too much pain. With so many years still stretching into the future, his life already felt like one long aftermath.

So Morgan took comfort in the anonymity of gay bars, just as he did in the safe solitude of Marie Blake's piano lounge. These became his byways of exile.

Something about the black woman herself felt consoling, too. Morgan belonged to the last generation of Southern boys raised by colored women who looked just like the piano player, with names like Belle and Willie Bea, all brown eyes and red lips and no smiles. These older Negro women shaped his life in so many small ways that he could not count them all.

Belle read from the children's adventure story called *David and the Phoenix* as Morgan lay on the sofa with his head resting in her ample lap. These reading sessions kindled his passion for books and his earliest belief that if he only climbed the right mountain, he would discover the Phoenix's secret for endless boyhood. Willie Bea's husband worked in a baloney factory and told her exactly what went in—"Everything but the oink!"—so she would not eat baloney and would not even touch it to make sandwiches for Morgan and his younger brother T. J. For the rest of his life, Morgan avoided cold cuts and ate peanut butter instead, and did not realize exactly why.

So Morgan enjoyed a sense of comfort and security as he sat back all alone at the table nearest Marie's keyboard, nursing a couple of vodka tonics, sometimes wondering with regret why his mother insisted his kid brother take piano lessons while he got the swimming coach, but always savoring the songs of love and heartbreak as he thought over and over again about Ethan.

> Give me a kiss to build a dream on,
> And my imagination will thrive upon that kiss. . .

Just like Mr. Satterfield from the law firm, Morgan tipped heavily before leaving, even when money was tight, and always got a big hug from Marie. She left him with the same parting advice every night, "You be good now, boy, and act like you got some sense!" She seemed like a figure of timeless maternal care and judgment, the last in a centuries-old line of colored women who taught children to say *yes ma'am* and *no ma'am*. Morgan had found one place in Manhattan where he felt entirely at ease with Marie's remonstrance and her look of motherly disapproval. It was the security of a man who knew that he was a little safer in the world if he found a quiet place to curl up with a book, and did not eat baloney.

Five Oaks was also the place where his rampaging urges briefly subsided under the world-weary gaze of the woman at the keyboard. Morgan used her piano lounge to recharge his sexual batteries and savor the romantic lyrics of *a kiss to build a dream on* before launching himself back into the night.

Morgan had an uncanny knack for making taxicabs appear out of nowhere, and almost immediately he was heading uptown where he would meet the Armani man.

Morgan knew to charge the red velvet rope when arriving at Studio 54. Even as his taxi halted out front, he made a dash for the door and the infamous rope opened for him. Never did he need to stand in line with the "gray people," as the owner called the losers who came nightly from New Jersey hoping for a taste of the glitz and glamour. Steve Rubell had spotted Morgan the first night as a big athletic-looking man, classy in an Ivy League way. Steve hated sissies. Morgan had a VIP card but never needed to use it for instant access to this hallucinatory realm of drugs, dancing, and sexual escape.

One night when Morgan sprang from a limo and made his dash to the door with some Princeton classmates, he nearly tripped over Cher whose entourage was barred from entering. Morgan remembered thinking as he looked back over his shoulder, "Cher! Who'll remember *her* in twenty years?" Tonight Morgan felt the music before he actually heard the hard-pounding *Hot Stuff*. The speakers thundered so powerfully that the soles of his feet caught the beat through the floor. The theater was engulfed in artificial smoke and the heat was staggering as he melted into the hot bodies on his way to the bar.

Lasers lashed the darkness. Decibel levels were off the scale. Shirtless blond waiters blowing silver whistles moved through the crowd with champagne buckets, every one gorgeous enough to be a male model or porn star. Morgan considered this place the genuine Crisco Disco where reality slipped through his fingers, desperately wanting to get lost in the tangle of bare limbs and the labyrinth of sexual possibilities.

And all the beautiful people were dancing. There were girls in silky nothings, musclemen in studded collars, wolf-eyed youths with shaved heads, dykes with slicked-back hair, whores in red vinyl jumpsuits, aging vestals with lace to their chins, fashion models in cowboy hats, black disco divas with flattops, cabana boys in short-shorts, sorority sisters in pink and green, construction workers in white jockstraps, Puerto Ricans with cocaine mustaches, albino artists with platinum wigs, bare-chested centurions in golden helmets, shirtless ballet stars straight from a performance, drag queens with towering pink hairdos, tuxedoed Englishmen in red feather boas, policemen with leather truncheons, Arab princes in bejeweled masks, teenage hustlers in tie-dyed shirts, Navy officers in summer whites, debutantes in rhinestone tiaras, Cleopatras with pythons around their shoulders, celebrity authors with Chinese fans, Carmen Mirandas with fruit piled on their heads, near-naked gymnasts rolled in glitter—an overkill of bare shoulders and arms with cigarette burns, the savage smell of perfume in their hair, women's breasts bouncing through open blouses, men's designer jeans unzipped to the crotch, jagged jewelry, fingernails in day-glow polish, big red lips parted to reveal hungry teeth, connoisseurs of cocaine and poppers, hard lean bodies pounding hard lean bodies, men kissing men and women kissing women, indecipherable combinations of lovemaking on low couches, and constellations of sexual need in side lounges.

And all the beautiful people were dancing as their radiant faces and dreamy half-closed eyes floated in the darkness. No hunk was a stranger. Every beautiful nobody was Morgan's next conquest. He wanted them all, every single one of them!

In this alternative universe where celebrities were the only royalty, Morgan caught sight of the elderly queen bee nicknamed Disco Sally, decked out in gold spangles and puffing on a cigarette, as she zoomed past on roller skates. One night she had cornered him at the bar and shouted in his ear, "Tonight I thought about staying home, but then I came to my senses!" Always in a different pair of sunglasses, the granddame arrived with an entourage of musclemen and danced with the cutest boys, always the first to take their shirts off. She left when they left, near dawn, heading to an after party.

"That's what I want to do when I'm eighty," Morgan thought. "I want to grow up and become the next Disco Sally." But he was kidding himself and he knew it. The last thing any gay man wants to imagine is being eighty and still haunting the clubs. Everyone has seen the old geezer at the end of the bar chatting up the boys who let him sneak gropes only because he is buying their drinks. Morgan's permanent nightmare was waking up one day and realizing he had become the old geezer at the end of the bar. He harbored the notion that he would avoid this fate by finding a lover, or maybe he would die before getting too old for sex without money changing hands.

Morgan was drenched in sweat and needed another drink. On his way to the bar, he jostled past a couple of celebrities mugging for the cameras. He was ashamed to admit it, but he loved celebrity-sightings and always phoned Claire the next morning to tell her who was at the disco, only to hear her bitch about his namedropping, "You're just a pair of binoculars away from becoming a stalker!" But Morgan slipped past the photographers. He came to Studio 54 not to be seen but to disappear.

The granddaughter of a famous American novelist asked him to dance, but he replied, "No thanks." A woman married to a famous rock star invited him downstairs to the VIP lounge, and he said, "No thanks." A man calling himself a prince offered him some cocaine, and he said, "No thanks!" Morgan envied titles and wished he had one, even a professional title like Doctor or Professor, but he brushed aside the invitation because he liked his sex in dark places, invisible and anonymous, not the sort that required paying attention and looking interested.

He pressed through the hot bodies as he headed to the bar, enjoying the crush of muscle-hard torsos against his own. He paused when a gymnast in leather chaps reached through the tangle to caress his crotch before continuing toward his next vodka tonic.

As he tried catching the bartender's eye, Morgan glanced across to the far side of the bar—and saw *him*—and everything changed.

Morgan froze and stared. He watched as he took the highball from the bartender and slapped money on the counter. His hands were large and powerful-looking as if they had been carved by Michelangelo. Morgan followed him to the dance floor and kept his distance. A frightening sensation took hold as he dimly suspected this man with his dark eyes, broad shoulders, and dramatically slender waist might be the one, his opposite equal. What would Nietzsche say? What would Nietzsche do? Suddenly sober from this gut-level threat, Morgan knew he would need another vodka tonic to cope.

Drink in hand, safe in the fantasy world where he regained a sense of power and control, Morgan did not know how long he had been gazing at the Armani man. He only knew he felt frustrated. His need was overwhelming. As if to punish him for not paying attention from the dance floor, Morgan climbed to the balcony where a hunky guy in a lumberjack shirt was quick to give him what he wanted, but the easy orgasm brought no relief.

Oscar Wilde was right, Morgan thought as he came down the staircase, checking the front of his khakis for cum spots. Sex makes even the best of us a little sad. He always got what he was looking for but still he felt something was missing. The real fun was always somewhere else. Even now as he readied himself to flee into the night—to escape the Armani man who might end his freedom to do what he wanted, when he wanted, as often as he wanted—he realized sadly the only sexual conquest he really ever craved was the next one.

The last sight Morgan had of him, the man in the designer suit was dancing with a famous movie star, the daughter of an even more famous movie star, so drunk she could hardly stand up, much less dance. Yes, sir, definitely a star-fucker, Morgan thought as he pushed his way through the crowd.

After pounding down his last drink in the lobby, Morgan remembered what Cary Grant asked Marlene Dietrich in one of his favorite old movies, "Are you happy? Are you in love with anybody?" And he remembered what Dietrich replied, "I'm not in love with anybody, and I'm completely happy. Funny, isn't it?"

Outside on the sidewalk, Morgan also recalled what Dietrich wrote on her dressing room mirror. *He travels fastest who travels alone.* The Armani man was just another heart-breaker, definitely not marriage material, and the last thing Morgan wanted was his soul battered by some disco-dancing fashion plate like him.

Yellow taxis were always lined up outside Studio 54. He jumped in the backseat of one and headed uptown to Central Park.

Now Morgan was at the boathouse long after midnight, and the Armani man had also arrived beside the lake. They stood next to each other and had not moved, still not saying a word, still not touching.

Boots crunched over the carpet of fallen leaves, and a young man approached from the bushes, a muscleman with huge arms and massive shoulders in a tanktop. Morgan always thought that people looked like other people, usually in the movies and on television. This blond hulk looked like the Austrian bodybuilder with the funny-sounding last name as he kneeled down in front of the Armani man, reaching to unbuckle his belt and unzip the designer trousers. The Armani man, already rock-hard, bulged inside his tight underwear. The Mr. Universe lookalike pulled down the waistband, grasped him in both hands, and gave an admiring squeeze before stuffing his mouth.

The Armani man glanced down and gave a lopsided smile. The streetlamp dappled light across his face as his eyes returned to Morgan's, looking straight into the face of this tall preppy with his blond hair and classic good looks. Staring back, Morgan felt staggered by the smile dawning upon the face so remote and mask-like at the disco.

With all the natural ease that he displayed on the dance floor, he reached over and stroked Morgan's arm. Morgan drew a quick breath as he felt electricity course through him. Gooseflesh rose where the hand caressed him. Their bodies leaned into each other while down in the darkness at their feet, the man with the mop of black hair and the man with the big-muscled shoulders were busy on their knees.

Morgan reached over and his fingertips traced the line of his jaw, gently, down to his chin where the small white crescent of a scar shown faintly in the dim light. An imperfection! He has an imperfection, Morgan thought as his hand molded itself to the sleek architecture of the man's skull. His partner closed his eyes and sighed.

Then the Armani man turned slightly and stroked Morgan's head, smoothing the sun-bleached hair under the weight of his palm. Morgan shut his eyes and sank into the pressure of the touch. As his knees weakened, Morgan leaned harder into his partner's body. He drew Morgan closer as his hand moved along his backside, tracing the trench of his spine until the touch reached his bare ass. Morgan tensed.

Twisting at his waist so he would not disturb the two men down below, Morgan slid his hand into the man's unbuttoned shirt and felt its starched crispness. He caught the scent of cologne mingled with the pungent smell of cigarette smoke from the disco. The Armani man's body had its own sharp aroma. Inside the open shirt, Morgan's fingers glided slowly along the smooth chest. He liked his men hairless.

Morgan's hand cupped the roundness of the pec muscle. The nipple felt like a small button, round and flat and hard to the touch. Morgan stroked the nipple with his thumb as his partner drew a deep breath. Then a small pinch. The man arched his spine and his head fell back as his jacket slid down his shoulders. He uttered a sigh like pain as he savored Morgan's rough touch.

Now their arms were looped around each other. How long? Morgan had no idea. Only one thought kept running in his mind, *Your eyes have shot their arrows into my heart!*

Then they were kissing. Kissing with eyes wide open at first, then with eyes closed. It was like nothing Morgan had experienced before. His tongue traced his partner's lips. He tasted like he just ate an apple. Their embrace tightened with all the muscularity of two strong men.

Suddenly a great surge overtook Morgan with a spasm that knocked the breath out of him. At exactly the same moment, his partner shouted "Oh, God!" and caved forward and pressed his face into Morgan's shoulder. They clutched each other as the sexual waves slowed, and they were still holding each other after the other two men, the swimmer and the bodybuilder, swallowed hard and struggled to their feet and disappeared into the darkness.

Finally their embrace ended. Nothing perfect lasts, Morgan began thinking. They drew back and struggled with their pants. Slowly they zipped their flies and buckled their belts, the metallic clink of buckles the only sound beneath the branches. Morgan wondered if this perfect lover would disappear back into the darkness, too. The thought hurt him with a pain that was almost physical. He almost felt like crying.

But then they started walking together, still shoulder to shoulder. Morgan reached out and took him by the hand, knitting their fingers. Immediately he realized it was a dumb thing to do. But his partner gave a squeeze back and Morgan tightened his grip. As they exchanged glances, there was a glint, a spark, *something* that passed between the two men as they walked along the gravel path.

"I'm Eddy," the young man said finally. "That was wild back there. I didn't follow you here, you know."

"My name is Morgan."

"That's easy to remember, different," he said. "I would have followed you if you hadn't disappeared from Studio in such a hurry."

"You saw me?"

"Sure I saw you, just thought you were one of those guys into standing and modeling. Great-looking guys like you are usually a total waste of time."

Morgan looked down. "I'm nothing special."

"Yeah, right! You're what my people call an Aryan god. Like Robert Redford, only bigger."

"You haven't seen me in daylight. I'm completely beige—beige hair, beige skin, no-color eyes. That's why I'm invisible in a disco. I just blend into the background."

"What makes you think you were invisible? All the guys were cruising you, only you looked stuck up, or stoned."

"I don't do drugs."

"Yeah, I know, kept watching to see whether you snorted anything. You didn't even take the free blow from Prince Ego. I don't get involved with cokeheads."

"You don't smoke. There was no cigarette taste on your breath."

"Tried a cigar when I was twelve. Got sick and puked. That was the end of my smoking career. Guess I'm an all-around failure as a Cuban man."

"Cuban? You don't have any accent. Are they all as handsome as you?"

"Catalan originally, but my family went to Cuba for a couple hundred years, then ended up in New Jersey." Eddy gave a sideways look. "Handsome? Didn't notice the beak?"

"Big nose, big hands, big feet. You know the rest of that old saying."

"So we don't smoke and don't snort coke," Eddy said. "Think we might be boring?"

"My biggest problem is that I talk too much, except for small talk in a bar."

"You weren't dancing and you weren't talking to any guys, so I figured you were straight. You look straight. Studio is confusing that way."

"The way you're dressed, I guessed you were an actor and couldn't risk being gay in public."

"Like the hotty from *Looking for Mr. Goodbar*? No way! I just like dressing up when I go dancing. My parents were like that when I was a kid and they went salsa dancing. Your parents dance?"

"My parents attend dinner dances at the country club and don't dance. It runs in the family, not dancing, something in our DNA."

"Know what I'd love? Some night I'd love showing up at Studio dressed in a gorilla outfit and come out in a platinum Afro wig."

"Like Marlene Dietrich in *Blonde Venus*. You really are a card-carrying homosexual."

"You know *Blonde Venus*? Can't believe you know one of my favorite films."

"I know all of Dietrich's films. My all-time favorite is *Destry Rides Again*."

"Me too! Didn't you think Jimmy Stewart was sexy as the sheriff? I got a thing for cowboys. Jeez, I hope you don't have a boyfriend. Never met anyone our age who likes old movies."

"I know what you mean," Morgan sighed. "It's easy finding someone to have sex with, hard finding someone to see a film with."

They continued slowly down the pathway bordered with late-summer roses, saying nothing until Morgan broke the silence. "Do you realize it's one chance in a million we met twice?"

"I can see myself going back to Studio every night waiting for you to show up again."

"I'd probably have gone back there tomorrow night, too, looking for you. I'm really persistent about things."

"Could be Providence that we kept meeting."

"Coincidences happen. Aristotle was wrong, I mean, about logic and probability," Morgan muttered. "Maybe there *is* a destiny that shapes our ends, roughhew them how we may. Besides, everybody shows up at Studio 54 eventually, everybody who counts."

Eddy cocked his head. "First Aristotle, then Shakespeare. Sound like an Ivy Leaguer."

"Yes, sir, Princeton. Just like Jimmy Stewart."

"Know what your biggest problem is?"

"I talk too much?"

Eddy steered them to the edge of the gravel trail. He reached for the yellow roses, grabbed a fistful of blossoms and pulled hard, tearing them loose in his hand. He scattered the petals over Morgan's head. Morgan laughed softly as he brushed the petals from his hair with his free hand, realizing it was the most romantic thing anyone had ever done to him. "I'll always remember tonight if we never see each other again."

Eddy pulled him closer, "It *is* Providence we kept meeting, but call it Studio 54 if you need to." He kissed Morgan on the neck.

There was no talk about whose place. Morgan took the lead and Eddy followed. He was not breaking any rules for his sublet because he already knew Eddy was more than an overnight guest.

4

What the River Doesn't Know

King's Old Boys—Cambridge, 1960

Robert Branch Cabell was once heavyweight boxing champion at Princeton. Still the youthful athlete and striking in his summer whites, he stood alone near the river, enjoying the sunshine and his third glass of claret. The breeze tousled the blond hair about his forehead. His one overwhelming desire, once the garden party broke up, was to walk along the river and visit the college boathouse where he had trained as a rower.

As the only American and only old boy back less than ten years after matriculating, thanks to an assignment from the Treasury Department, Robert felt out of place at the reunion luncheon. He had chosen King's because it was the college of Keynes, who died four years before he arrived, and now he knew nobody except his own former tutor in economics. While mustering courage to introduce himself to the celebrity attendees Sir Adrian Fortescue and E. M. Forster—Robert hated making small talk—he contented himself with the memories prompted by his return among the ancient buildings and quadrangles. Like so many other Virginians, he had a powerful affection for places steeped in antiquity.

Already his reputation as the oarsman who rowed stroke when they beat Oxford by ten lengths was fading as a distant recollection, except for Gilmartin, the college steward, who had a prodigious memory for such things. This was the downside of nostalgia, Robert reflected, that some special experiences are vividly recalled while others slip away into darkness and are forgotten. Memories of his first term at Cambridge had this darkling quality. A studious, serious-minded grind, Robert studied late into the night and rose before dawn so he could bicycle down to the boathouse and practice in a one-man scull. His two fellowship years might have passed in this gloom of hard work and strenuous sports, if not for Brian O'Koren.

College friends had ousted him from the library one night at closing and forced him to have a pint at The Eagle, where even lab scientists took a break from searching for the double helix structure of the DNA molecule. At a crowded table in the front room, he was introduced to Brian O'Koren of Peterhouse. Another American, from Harvard where he lettered in basketball, Brian was an aspiring novelist studying English literature, a nonstop talker full of jokes and wordplays, fascinated in everything, an enthusiast for movies and symphony concerts, a showoff comedian addicted to laughter, but with a touch of sadness in his rowdiness. Along with his Black Irish good-looks, an air of melancholy hung about him.

Robert's rowing buddy Michael was there, and years later as a career diplomat at the State Department, he still remembered exactly what happened at The Eagle. "As soon as we introduced you to Brian, it was as if the rest of the gang disappeared. It was just you and Brian, talking, talking, talking. The same for the rest of the academic year. We never saw the one without seeing the other. And you were always talking, talking, talking."

After that first night, they wore a path between King's and Peterhouse, where Brian had palatial rooms previously belonging to a don, a stark contrast to Robert's shabby bed-sitter up the wrong staircase. Robert took his new friend to the river and taught him to row in a two-man scull. Brian was a natural. He had so much strength and stamina he could recite lines from his favorite poet Yeats between strokes—"All is changed . . . changed utterly . . . A terrible beauty is born"—without losing his rhythm or his breath. Swans darted out of their way, sometimes taking to the air with loud slaps of their wings as the boat shot past.

The two men lifted weights together and ran together for miles through parsley meadows crisscrossed by canals. And always they could be spotted by sleepy college servants as they headed off at dawn to train together when the river belonged only to moorhens. Sometimes the sunrise came so dazzling Robert lost concentration and caught a crab, as he did one morning when his oar butt knocked him backward between Brian's legs.

"You okay?" Brian asked as he gave his partner a gentle shove to recover his seat.

"Never better," Robert replied, embarrassed, hating to accept help even from a friend.

One morning they took a break from rowing and rode their bicycles on an all-day trip to Norwich where Brian wanted to visit the hermit cell of the mystic Dame Julian. "Would you know God's meaning?" he recited from the saint's writings inside the dimness of her medieval shrine, newly rebuilt after German bombers wrecked it. "Love was his meaning, and all shall be well, and all manner of things shall be well."

Riding home through black plowland, they raced each other along willow lanes between rows of dog roses. Then early the next morning, hobbling down to the boathouse, both men complained about legs cramped and sore from hours of peddling. On their way back from the river, they passed some Italian tourists who had been sightseeing in the Chapel, young men probably students, walking arm in arm, some with arms looped around each other's shoulders. Brian stared down at the pavement. "Glad we're not queer."

Robert replied under his breath, "Yes, sir," drawing closer and bumping elbows as they cut across the lawn.

Late into the night in his rooms on the front quad, Brian played him a recording of Furtwängler conducting *Tristan und Isolde*. The next month as a present for his birthday, he took Robert down to London to hear the opera performed at Covent Garden. "It's about impossible love," Brian kept saying afterwards as Robert hailed a taxi so they would not miss the last train back to Cambridge. "Only the saddest story in the world is worth writing an opera about, worth writing *anything* about, and impossible love is the saddest story in the world."

Robert read the novels Brian recommended, *The Sun Also Rises* and *Charterhouse of Parma* and *Room with a View*, and in return he took Brian to lectures by visiting politicians and economists. They taught each other to play squash with a muscular, hard-driving style that appalled the English students who looked on. There was always some new event on the calendar, a concert or poetry reading or punting on the river, and always something new to talk about late into the night, over port or whisky, as if feeding off each other's energy and intellectual zeal, until the end of Easter term 1951.

Late in the academic year when summer sunshine turned Cambridge into one lush garden, Robert's fiancée came for a visit. Leslie Carr stayed at a bed-and-breakfast near the rail station, and everything changed between the two rowing buddies. Brian was courteous, inviting the couple to dinner at Peterhouse. Miss Carr was scrupulous about social engagements and informed Robert the very next day, "Now we owe him."

So Brian received a return invitation to dine with them at the best restaurant in Cambridge. The wines were plentiful and the food was excellent by English standards. Robert laughed so hard when Brian told the old Catholic schoolboy joke—"What's black and white, black and white, black and white?"—he spilled claret down his boat club tie. But everything else went sour. Leslie cared nothing about Hemingway's new novel *The Old Man and the Sea*, not interested in Cuba or people who came from there. For his part, Brian was visibly bored by talk of sorority dances and debutante cotillions at the country club. Robert grew depressed, minute by minute, realizing no common ground could be found between his best friend and the woman he was marrying at the beginning of August.

Leslie turned sulky when he walked her back to the guesthouse after their second dinner together. Robert did not know what to say. He felt it was wrong to ask her about what she was thinking, what she was feeling. Besides, he knew what she would say because he had heard her say it so many times already: "I'd prefer not to discuss that."

So they never talked about it. He kissed her under a yellow porch light, confirming plans for cycling to a country inn the next day for lunch, just the two of them. Never did they mention the awkwardness of the expensive dinner hosted for his friend Brian O'Koren.

After the university's summer vacation when he returned with Ladybug— her family nickname because she was "cute as a little ladybug" when she was born—they moved into married-student accommodations in the nearby village of Trumpington. Their tiny flat overlooked the stretch of river where legend held that Lord Byron went swimming as an undergraduate at King's.

Robert almost never saw Brian now. When they bumped into each other at the university library and he suggested lunch, Brian always begged off, claiming he was busy studying for his examinations. "I need to master the Anglo-Saxon language in the next two weeks," he explained. "The external examiner is coming from Oxford, a professor named Tolkien, who surely expects me to know something about *Beowulf*."

Their easy, fast-paced conversation was the same as before, but Brian seemed remote and wounded when they spoke briefly on the steps of the library, as if his whole Irish heritage had awakened in him with the instinct for withdrawal in defeat. His ancestors knew humiliation in battle. Starvation drove whole families to other shores. The strongest suffered the most, and their inwardness took root in sadness and silence. His was a race long schooled in loss.

Robert too felt a deep sense of loss. Late at night when the library closed, he sometimes peddled his bicycle past The Eagle, pausing to look through the window to see if Brian was there with friends. He never was. Brian had abandoned the pub where they met, just as he managed to create a new life for himself without two-man sculling on the river. As the term ended in the bleakness of an English winter, Ladybug was overjoyed to discover from her doctor that she was expecting—their firstborn in 1952 would be a boy—and Robert never felt sadder in his whole life.

Years later he understood what he only half knew when he and Brian enjoyed their months together in Cambridge. He understood what Brian was and vaguely understood what he was, too, partly anyway. It was deep-dark secret he never discussed with another human being.

Particularly he remembered one summer afternoon when he and Brian were alone at the boathouse, changing from their street clothes to go rowing on the river. He looked over from his locker and saw Brian, completely naked, standing in a shaft of sunlight that poured through the upstairs windows. He was powerfully built with broad shoulders and long arms, a natural rower, with the striking good looks of the Black Irish and eyes that flashed in strong light. Brian stood motionless, looking back where Robert was rooted without shirt and trousers, just his stocking feet. Nothing was said. The two men simply stood there.

They looked at each other.

The moment passed, and the rowers dressed and went downstairs to carry the two-man scull on their shoulders the short distance to the water. There was no conversation during their hour-long session on the river, no reciting poetry by Yeats, and almost no talk when they returned and changed for dinner. In Robert's memories, though, it was the one day that stood out vividly among all the days of his life.

In the middle of a Cambridge winter when he thought he could not feel more depressed about his parting with Brian, Robert received a letter. A former Rhodes Scholar, a champion oarsman at Oxford in the 1940s, had visited during the previous spring and spotted them rowing. He was struck by their strength, their form, and their amazing speed. He clocked them. The two strapping Americans were naturals together. After finding out Robert's name and college, he had written a friend at the Olympics Committee with an enthusiastic recommendation. Now Robert received the official invitation to the time trials, along with his partner, to qualify for the next Summer Games. But it was too late now that everything had changed in his life. He was a husband and expectant father. He had a government job waiting for him back in Washington when he completed his degree. He had adult responsibilities. And of course he and Brian had abandoned their sculling together.

The next spring, Robert rowed stroke for the Cambridge Eight that triumphed by ten lengths over Oxford. There was a bump supper followed by a bonfire when the boat was burned in the middle of the quad. Crispin the cox was debagged and rode a bicycle around the flaming pyre while singing the Eton Boating Song. Robert made a point of wearing his club tie with the claret stain and looked for Brian in the crowd, scanning the faces illuminated by the flames, but his friend had not come to the celebration. Sunk in desolation, Robert kept the official letter inviting them to the time trials, along with the gnawing regret they could have been Olympic athletes together, he and Brian, maybe even medal winners, if only things had been different.

Memories of his friendship with Brian remained powerful over the years, though they saw each other only once back in the United States, by coincidence at a performance of *Ariadne auf Naxos* by a touring company at Constitution Hall.

Brian was by himself. He had been drinking and reeked of whiskey. Still, they fell back naturally into their animated talk, complaining about the conductor's slow tempi—"Did that guy fall asleep on the podium *or what?*" Brian burst out—before the lights flickered and they returned to their seats for the second half of the opera. Neither man suggested meeting later, with Ladybug, for drinks after the concert.

His relationship with Brian had been an awakening which Robert honored in his silent, stoic way, rereading the novels that his friend had recommended, with a growing fondness for Stendhal, and always searching the *Post* for any German operas scheduled in Washington. Every year at the beginning of June, rowing season, he sat down again with his well-worn copy of *A Room with a View*.

Brian O'Koren's name remained in their address book, so Ladybug did her wifely duty and sent Christmas cards with photographs of the two boys, Morgan and T. J., as they grew taller, lost teeth, changed haircuts, and went from clip-on bowties to long neckties with their dark Sunday suits. Brian sent back large Renaissance Nativity scenes purchased at museum gift shops, always enclosing a photograph of himself from some foreign travel—straddling a toppled obelisk at Karnack, leaning against a broken column in the quarry at Syracuse, wearing a sleek leather jacket on an azalea terrace overlooking Lake Como—but he never included a note. Robert kept all these photographs in his desk drawer, tied in a red ribbon saved from Christmas, but he never wrote back. What could he say?

Even now in early spring, when the sunshine turned warm and the air was still, Robert drove by himself to take a one-man scull out on the Potomac. It was his one time to be completely alone and remember. His memories were always the same as he put his shoulders into deep strokes and pulled hard against the water. He recalled the one perfect summer afternoon, with sunlight so fiery it was almost blinding, when he and Brian went rowing through the intense greenness of the English countryside. Maybe there was nothing that could equal the recollection of having been young together. Was it his loss of Brian, or was it Robert's sense of his own lost youth—both had slipped away together to be replaced by a wife, two sons, and a government career that would take him from the Treasury Department to the Federal Reserve—that moved him almost to tears as he rowed alone in his scull?

"What the river doesn't have isn't worth having," he remembered Brian saying while resting on his oar, as mists lifted from the water and a kingfisher caught fire in the sunlight. "What the river doesn't know isn't worth knowing."

Such were the thoughts that played through the mind of Robert Branch Cabell, the brilliant young economist and legendary oarsman of King's—his American friends dubbed him Big Bob—as he stood beside the river and finished his third glass of claret. Automatically he took the comb from his pocket and slicked back his hair, combing straight the blond curls that had tousled over his forehead.

He had not been staring into empty space, Robert realized. Though he had lost track of time, he was gazing unwittingly at the elderly man seated by himself against the gray wall. He recognized the famous writer E. M. Forster whose novels had been recommended by Brian. Their favorite was *A Room with a View* with the happy ending where nobody dies.

Robert felt sorry for the old man with the rabbit face who had never been attractive even when young, pitying also the writer who had not published a novel since the 1920s. How thwarted he must have felt over the decades! His reputation would probably decline after his death, certainly wouldn't improve, since the critics had already spent forty years sorting out his literary achievements. He hoped Brian would not face the same sad destiny of this old man, neglected and alone at the end of his life. Brian had not become a successful novelist, only an English professor moving from one university to the next. He lived alone and traveled the globe alone. He drank too much.

Robert realized that his sad thoughts took the form of a prayer. He found himself praying for Brian, and praying also for his son Morgan, almost eight, but already showing all of the signs that caused worry. He kept his room neat. He did not like team sports. Last Halloween, he dressed for trick-or-treat as a gypsy with one of his mother's hoop earrings, and neighbors mistook him for a girl when they opened their doors to drop candy in the children's bags. He kept to himself. He liked reading.

Robert did not pray that his son would change or turn into somebody he wasn't. Good Presbyterians, he thought, were supposed to believe in predestination. Damned if you do, damned if you don't. He prayed only that his son would find happiness whatever his lot in life. Even if he did become like Brian, never married and never had sons of his own, Robert hoped Morgan would find his own special resources of happiness.

"God," Robert found himself saying inwardly in the ancient language that linked man and maker, "please don't let Morgan end up like this old man, all alone on a park bench."

Well, well, Forster thought, the champagne was delicious and the solitude was sweet. It had been a special treat during the garden party to have young Evans as an object of admiration, the young man growing more intensely good-looking as he stood gazing at the river, no doubt lost in his own fond musings. Or perhaps it was the wine. Strange how he looked so sad just now, perhaps lonely because he had nobody to talk with. Such a pity to be so masculine and athletic but look so terribly unhappy. Such a pity, too, all of the trouble he took combing back his perfectly beautiful curls.

For himself, there was only one sad thing to fret about now, the ending of his life's story that Sutherland was sharpening his pencil to write, the moment he popped off. This slow dying was a lonely business, Forster reflected as he lowered his glass, empty. He studied the blue veins on his pale hand. Friends leave. Connections fail. The three men he loved most passionately—Masood, Meredith, Mohammed—had all gone down into the undergloom.

He had always felt like a propped-up dummy whose real life had been withheld. More and more strongly now, the feeling came that he no longer quite belonged to this world but lingered anyway. He was not renewing life, merely continuing it, until every minute became a weariness. He had become the old Oedipus tugged along the road to Colonus by some destiny, understanding only that humanity endured sadness without help from above. Was this the final voyage into solitude which man was born for?

Perhaps there was some divinity that shaped his end, roughhew it though he had. Tomorrow or ten years from tomorrow, he had a good idea how the final scenes would play out. Already he had suffered some little strokes. Finally there would be a big explosion in his brain and he would find himself falling, aware only of his face pressed against the Persian carpet before he lapsed into unconsciousness beside his upright piano.

Somebody, probably Sutherland in the rooms below, would hear his body hit the floor with a thud. There would be a great commotion, and running in and out, and a doctor summoned. He would not be dead yet. No fear! He would die as he had lived, lingeringly. Bob and May Buckingham would take him into their home one last time, caring for him until the end. It was comforting to know one man loved him all of these years, a policeman, big and boyish. When we meet them young, we always see them young. Forster hoped never to forget, even as he lay dying, that one man and possibly two had loved him.

Thus he would return to the suburbs after these many years, with geraniums in window boxes and wives walking their corgis. Clocks ticked away the hours in those empty rooms, like the room where he would lie dying. Forster knew for a certainty that Bob would sit on the edge of his bed holding his hand while the darkness closed in, perhaps reading from *A Room with a View* inscribed to him in a first edition: ONLY CONNECT! Hadn't he and Bob connected in their own muddled way? Already lasting half a lifetime, theirs was a friendship which would endure until the end.

Then all that would remain, after the doctors and the undertakers, was for May to scatter his ashes among her roses and make an end. Strachey long ago described him as a mole, drab-colored and clumsy above ground, but digging wonderful caves of imagination in his novels. "You never know where he will pop up, in what odd places and unexpected circles." Soon he would disappear among

May's roses, not a phoenix ready to rise majestically from the ashes, but just a mole burrowing. And pop up where? If not in this life, perhaps in the life to come.

Not an appalling ending, he thought, not an appalling ending at all.

Then *Maurice* would be published. It became another leave-taking, Forster thought, to set loose this novel upon the reading public.

His whole life felt like a series of leave-takings. First school, which he hated. Then university, which he loved. England failed him, so he went to Egypt. India failed him, so he returned to England. His old college gave him sanctuary but never guessed how long he would linger in his gray decrepitude, dithering, bone-idle, pottering about nowhere in particular, then disappearing for weeks in his vague travels, seen and half-seen like the Scholar Gypsy. He did some tutoring, and prided himself on never getting pervy with the boys, but mostly he dithered.

He always joked that *Maurice* could not be published until his death, or England's. His final exit meant a huge surprise because it spelled release for Maurice and Alec. The couple would proclaim a happy ending, life-affirming in its own queer way, though surely not what Sir Adrian and Lady Fortescue would consider charming.

Then the questions would come again after the first shock subsided. Who were the models for his two characters? Would anyone guess the lovely young couple met during his weekend at Carpenter's, the gentleman and his working-class friend, who disappeared from all good society, nobody knew where? Did these two handsome men stick together over a lifetime after vanishing from England?

As fictional creations, would *his* two lovers have stuck together? Strachey diagnosed Maurice as a case of lust and curiosity, his attachment to Alec a wobbly affair that would rupture within six months. This prophecy haunted Forster. What would survive of the young men's passion after six months? After six years? Could Maurice and Alec, different in every other way, preserve their friendship over a lifetime? Or would they wreck upon some crisis, or merely the daily boredom of showing up at breakfast with nothing new to talk about?

Permanence is the chief excuse for a work of art. Readers want books to endure and a novel's characters to remain always the same. After giving them the book they never suspected he had written, would they vex his ghost, summon him from the great beyond, and demand continuing the story he could never properly imagine? What did Alec do with Maurice after climbing the ladder to his bedroom? What did Maurice do with Alec in the hotel in London? What did they do in bed, and what *all* did they say with each other on that final night in the boathouse, while in the manor house Clive devised some method of concealing the truth from his wife? Isherwood never quit insisting upon a continuation. He wondered about their travels and troubles.

Very well, he gave all that he had to offer from the still-empty grave, his blessing for their untold story. Isherwood would get the royalties and King's would get the rights, but future homosexuals would get something far more precious—the romance of Maurice and Alec played out, in constantly varying sequels, in their own faraway nations and generations. Forever young in the pages of his book, his two characters would arrive as messengers from Edwardian England and harbingers of some wonderful new age. His lovely boys would never die, but gain and gain.

Like Tolkien with his interminable trilogy, Forster always felt that England deserved a great mythology and not just a silly folklore of ghosts, water witches, and pixies with their crocks of gold. Somewhere, far beyond the suburbs with their tidy back gardens, beckoned a heroic landscape of great poets and a thousand lesser poets who sang of these strong men, godlike and youthful till the twilight of their years, dwelling in a greenwood more ancient than memory, among groves made enchanted by their lovemaking and lakes sanctified by naked swimmers.

The descendants of Alec and Maurice will embark upon this heroic landscape, where there will be sex and sunshine. In other lands and other times, male lovers will cast off their clothes to brave the beauty of their bodies in the fullness of day. They will swim in these sacred lakes and stretch out in the grass, in the warmth of summer breezes, careless whether parson or policeman passes by. Men will love differently then, openly in the light of day. Love will be born there in forest or desert, of what quality and into what worlds, only the future would decide. And some bright spark of Maurice and Alec will remain aglow like white heat somewhere deep inside those men's hearts and loins. Story without end.

"And more sex," Forster muttered as he leaned unsteadily upon the arm of the bench to rise. The college cat rolled onto its back and clawed at the leg of his trousers. "With these young men and their silky erections, naturally there will be more sex."

When the Provost's wife spied the novelist struggling to his feet, she was emboldened to try again for an introduction and handshake. Her white glove gripped the arm of beefy young Evans as they headed his way. Forster decided he would oblige them gladly. "Come here, you beautiful boy," he whispered, "Come here." Even the college steward noticed he seemed uncommonly cheerful today.

5

All Madly Gay

Martin and Alan—Santa Fe, 1924

The train was two hours early when Katherine St. John Howell arrived at the Lamy station in the heat of August. She took a cab rather than waiting for her brother, on the deserted platform in the middle of nowhere, her only diversion the unopened magazine *Milady's Boudoir* given by her sister at Southampton. The jalopy was driven by the local taxista Amarante, who spoke no English because he came from the northern village of Milagro. Sneaking swigs from a half-pint bottle, he smoked hand-rolled cigarettes and coughed on the steering wheel as he drove, but his rattletrap was the only conveyance not horse-drawn, and Kitty considered herself a thoroughly modern woman.

She recited the Santa Fe address slowly and loud. When the driver heard the name Martin Howell, he brightened up. "English?"

"Yes, I am English."

Then he knew exactly where to drive.

After turning their backs on England's middle-class prejudices and smug cruelties, Martin and his friend Alan Sutton had come halfway around the world only to be cast in the role of the local Englishmen. No portrait of Queen Victoria hung in the dining room, but instead landscapes by their artist friends John Sloan and Randall Davey, but still they were the expatriates with the charming accents. Martin minded more than Alan his status as the local Englishmen, and Alan minded hardly at all. Yanks thought a British accent was posh and could not distinguish a Dorset gamekeeper from a Cambridge scholar. He actually enjoyed laying it on thick with folksy expressions from his grandmother's parlor. Doing what was expected, they served tea at four and always had Earl Grey on offer, as well as gin and chokecherry wine. Sometimes when local painters came, teatime lasted past midnight.

When Kitty's taxi arrived in a cloud of dust with three barking dogs following behind, the two men were cutting wood beside the acequia. Martin shouted, "Look who's here!"

"The train was unbelievably early," Kitty said as the driver hurried to open her door.

"How ghastly!" Martin wiped the sweat from his forehead. "I don't know why they bother posting such ridiculously precise times. Imagine eleven-o-eight! Usually two hours late, not early, but *never* eleven-o-eight. Not at all British. Isn't it wonderful?"

Kitty walked up the little hill and made the first tentative gesture, offering her cheek for a kiss. The brother and sister had exchanged gossipy letters back and forth across the Atlantic, until suddenly she fired off a telegram on her thirtieth birthday in response to Martin's sweet card from New Mexico: WOULD LOVE TO VISIT THIS SUMMER. SO DULL HERE. Martin had replied at once: DO COME. AUGUST BEST. But now seeing each other face to face after ten years, he leaner and suntanned, she plumper with short-bobbed hair, brought back a stiff formality almost as if their mother were invisibly watching.

Martin hung back. "My clothes are filthy dirty, I'm afraid. Need to wash up. We've hot and cold laid on, when you've unpacked. Then you'll be wanting tea."

Kitty felt awkward and changed the subject. "What in the world are you doing?"

"Making a coyote fence." Alan, hatchet in hand, rose from where he had been hunched over his work. He grinned as he sidled close to Martin.

Stirred from odd nooks where the two men were digging, seeds from Chinese elms planted a decade earlier had taken flight and gathered in the former gamekeeper's hair. Kitty had not met Alan before her brother took him for a holiday in Italy, never to return, and she always remembered this first vision of him with these white seed flakes in his hair. Suddenly self-conscious, she dropped her gaze. "Forgive me. I must be gawking as if I'd just seen a unicorn."

Alan continued about the fence, "Martin roughhews the cedars, and I shape their ends."

Kitty turned again to her brother, "I thought today was the big party."

"Next Saturday."

"I had the date marked on my calendar."

"It's what we call a movable feast."

Martin had written to his sister that they were hosting a party for their friends, but neglected to explain he was celebrating his tenth anniversary with Alan.

The date needed amending because a minor disagreement persisted exactly which day to observe. Alan cared little for birthdays and anniversaries, never even wore a watch, but if pressed, he was absolute that their life together began when he climbed into the bedroom at Pendersley. Martin, though, calculated from the night in the boathouse following Alan's courageous decision not to emigrate to Argentina. So they alternated. Only after posting his letter did Martin realize it was his year for the later date.

Martin showed his sister to a bedroom furnished in the eclectic manner that ran throughout the home. There were very old-looking tables and chests carved in an ornate Spanish style, but also modern couches and armchairs shipped in by rail. Navajo blankets were draped over the backs of chairs and painted Indian pots lined the tops of bookcases. The hodgepodge made Kitty realize what a very great distance she had traveled from their garden suburb in England. She was also struck by the snugness of the rooms. Ceilings were low. Windows were small. Thick adobe-brick walls muffled all outside noise with only a cricket chirping somewhere on the stairway. And books were everywhere. Bookcases lined the walls in nearly every room, stocked mostly with histories and novels, even some poetry. Her brother had become a great reader during the slow days and long nights of New Mexico.

After Martin excused himself to bathe, Alan took over the tour of their rambling household. Kitty puzzled over how differently the two men had adapted to their new homeland. Martin still seemed very much the English gentleman as if stationed in some colonial outpost where he smoked his pipe, wore wing collars, and chuckled over *Punch* cartoons. But Alan had become almost indistinguishable from other Americans she had encountered in her travels. Dressed in his corduroys and open shirt, he had no elaborate manners and engaged in little idle chitchat. Aside for keeping up his countrified speech, she thought, Mr. Sutton had gone native.

The tour ended in a kitchen equipped with modern icebox and stove, which surprised Kitty in such primitive surroundings. Alan grew suddenly quite formal when introducing her to their housekeeper Léona Baca, a handsome woman her own age, maybe younger, whose family lived downhill beside the Acequia Madre, the town's main irrigation ditch. Alan switched easily between English and Spanish when introducing her to the housekeeper—called simply Tía Léona—whose fine dress and silver jewelry, clearly worn from the occasion, made her seem even more imposing, almost regal. Kitty was impressed that Alan had learned the local language, which Martin apparently never even tried.

The housekeeper's bright-eyed niece Sara was curious about meeting her first English lady. Kitty very sweetly made conversation with the little girl, asking her to name the dried herbs hanging from the vigas overhead, then reaching into her purse to offer some chewing gum as a treat.

Recovering after her rail journey, Kitty spent several days reading a Thomas Hardy novel found in her bedroom, while Martin nervously bombarded her with details of local history in order to avoid more awkward topics, all very British. Meanwhile Alan wanted to show off the country beyond the plaza. The Palace of the Governors where Indians sold their pots and jewelry, he huffed, was strictly for tourists. At the crack of dawn on her fourth day in town, he whistled loudly to rouse the household. His hair was still wet from his morning bath as Alan loaded the motorcar for an all-day adventure.

Alan's automobile had already become a local legend. For trekking into the northern mountains and staying overnight wherever he wanted, he had taken a Model-T touring car and cut off the back seat and trunk, replacing them with a flatbed wide enough for a mattress. To improvise a shelter, he took the bows and canvas from a covered wagon. When trout fishing during summers, he learned about seasoning his stews with saltweed and juniper berries, just the way his guide Pina-yo-Pi showed him. The Tesuque Indian spoke little, but sitting beside their lucky stream one evening, he announced the Towa-é spirits had come in a dream, playful and unpredictable as ever, and they wanted him to paint pictures, just like the Anglo artists for money from tourists.

Looking like a colonial sahib going to shoot tigers, Martin fussed about packing provisions for their day trip. Tucked in Alan's belt was a pistol that he deposited on the floorboard between Kitty's feet. "Good heavens!" she exclaimed. "This *is* the Wild West!"

"There's rough characters up north. I know I'd want my Colt if I hadn't brung it. Now everyone get a finger out!"

The three of them squeezed into the front seat, and Alan drove at alarming speed, barely missing a burro loaded with firewood, as they headed north on the bumpy road. Their destination was the mountain village of Cañada de Chimayó.

After miles of heat through dusty highlands, Alan stopped the car in the middle of nowhere beyond the Nambé pueblo and switched off the motor. A herd of white-faced cattle ranged on either side of the road, some with half-grown calves, grazing in an orchard of chollas ablaze with the remnants of their magenta blossoms. The cows stared at them like dumb, bewildered ghosts. "Call of nature," Alan announced as he hopped from the driver's seat and legged it across the road. He scrambled up the sandy slope and disappeared behind a clump of junipers.

At her brother's suggestion, Kitty went in the opposite direction and found her own large cluster of junipers. She had been warned to dress comfortably in loose knickers. Stones of pink, green and creamy white were strewn everywhere on the dry earth. She walked carefully to avoid low-growing cactuses.

When she paused behind the tallest of the junipers, Kitty found herself staring at the ground nearest her feet. A cow's skull lay among a jumble of bones bleached by the sun and scattered among purple thistles. Looking up, Kitty gazed at gray-green bushes spreading across the arroyo that led downhill toward the distant Rio Grande. Faraway in the opposite direction, the high mountains shifted colors where the dark green of ponderosa forests gave way to the light green of aspens. On the summits, alpine pastures were parched yellow by summer drought.

Kitty suddenly became aware of the profound stillness of the desert. Wisps of cloud-drift streaked the sky above sienna hills and black mesas. Overhead a raven wheeled, turned, and then wheeled again before passing on. An orange butterfly fluttered around the fuzzy branches at her feet, while a blue-tail lizard darted along the shade side of a rock. Big ants scurried across the sandy earth. But with all of this commotion, the only sound was the breeze stirring in the hollow of her ear. She was beginning to understand what drew her brother to this desolate landscape, yet also felt stirring in her breast some unfamiliar, painful sense of her own aloneness in this vast, empty desert.

As the threesome returned to the motorcar, Kitty carried the cow skull by its horns and deposited it carefully in the back. It became a macabre souvenir of her first visit to the New Mexican badlands.

After a few more miles, Alan's Model-T crested a hill and followed the rutted road down along a network of gulches and gullies. Below was a scattering of one-storey dwellings. The glint of tin roofs showed a few sheep sheds. Kitty smelled water at the bottom of the hill. They had entered a valley of chile and bean fields, each farmhouse with a flower garden in front and corral in the back, and farther on the apple and cherry orchards. Horses grazed along the river. There was no road sign, but Alan knew his way to the sanctuary chapel that was the first stop for any visitor to Chimayó. Chickens scattered before them on the dusty road.

Martin played tour guide after Alan disappeared with his camera. Escorting his sister into the small church with its massive mud-brick walls, he named the saints painted in bold colors by native artists, dwelling at length upon the crucifix of the Black Christ. When Kitty admitted she had never heard the legend of the Santo Niño de Atocha, he explained how the Christ Child was said to run errands of mercy around the countryside. In front of his statue, pilgrims left baby shoes to replace the ones worn out by running from household to household during the night. Kitty teased, "You'd make a good verger, dotty and sputtering, taking sightseers around some old cathedral and getting all the history wrong, just to make a good story."

Martin remained undaunted as he had explained the miraculous discovery of the chapel's healing soil. "The natives believe that if you mix some sacred earth with water and drink it, you will enjoy prosperity and live to great old age."

As he spoke, three dark-eyed children, two boys and a girl, followed shyly at a distance. Martin whispered, "The natives are fascinated by my fair hair. They're always staring, giggling, even reaching out to touch it sometimes when I'm sitting down. I feel like a Viking at the Byzantine court, adored and spoiled."

Outside as they waited for Alan beside the acequia, Kitty asked some of the questions weighing on her mind since her arrival. "How do you get by?"

"Get by?"

"Manage, I mean." Kitty pursued the euphemisms of the middle class for whom money was a distasteful subject, while behind the genteel evasions, it remained the one subject that truly mattered.

"What are you on about? The dolly? The dough? The pelf? The cabbage? The meed? The moolah? The dinero? The filthy lucre?" Martin had always enjoyed ragging his sister. "For God's sake, Kitty, surely you don't think we're professional woodcutters."

"Don't be tiresome. You know what I mean."

Seating himself on the embankment besides the fast-running waterway, Martin sketched events after their passage from Palermo. "I had considered selling out the business, but Alan convinced me that made bad sense. He likes to boss the show, you've noticed. When we got ourselves sorted out in New York, I found another small firm of stockbrokers on Wall Street, about the same size as us, chaps named Merrill. We discussed a partnership to handle both sides of the Atlantic and came to terms."

"So you remain a partner of Howard and Howell. We didn't know if you had thrown everything over when you left England. Mother hates asking unpleasant questions, you know."

"You can say your brother is an outcast, even a criminal, but you cannot say he's bad at business. Even when I was off my head, when everything was moving toward some turning point with Alan, I still managed my business affairs. *Young Howell's all right* was the verdict in the railway carriage back and forth from Richmond. *He'll never lose a single client, not he.*"

Kitty looked baffled. "Living here, how do you conduct your business in New York and London?"

"With the telegraph and postal service, I manage things quite nicely. The *Wall Street Journal* arrives next day, the *Financial Times* a week later. Not many friends in the local arts colony have money for investing, but they've attracted the rich bohemians who live on family investments, trust funds, those sorts of assets. You'll meet Lady Brett at our party, with her ear trumpet and her ten-gallon hat, and her remittance from Viscount Somebody back in England. The father is rotto with money, and she paints rainbows! Quite obviously such an artist needs all of the financial advice that only I can provide."

"Have you invested everything in these stocks for yourself?"

"Do you take me for a loony? The truest thing I heard about Wall Street was that the market will vacillate. Who can predict what will happen in just five years? Real estate is my principal investment here in New Mexico."

She looked around at the empty expanses of high desert surrounding the valley. Only junipers, piñon pines, and prickly pear cactus dotted the red hills. "Land speculation here? Have you a screw loose?"

"Land, Kitty, the one thing a man could hardly dream of owning back in England. Here you have to navigate a quagmire of old Spanish land grants, but you can actually acquire land in New Mexico. I have been buying property east of downtown Santa Fe and farther to the north."

"But the place is such a wasteland."

"Little girls don't understand a good deal. Just a short drive above Santa Fe, there is a green valley more beautiful than this one. It has rushing streams and fields for planting peach and apple trees, also pasturing horses. A place they call Tesuque."

"People live there?"

"Old Archbishop Latour retired there among his orchards, even built a little RC chapel, pretty as any place you ever saw in Surrey. There's one stretch of the valley I call my own little spot of heaven, at the foot of a sandstone cliff and just above the river. Alan and I talk about building a summer cottage there among the catalpa trees. We motor out on hot summer evenings, in that infernal jalopy of his, and spend the night under the stars, lulled by the sound of the stream. Nighthawks swoop. Coyotes yowl far off. Sometimes a family of skunks frolics in the moonlight. People will *love* living where they can build their houses, then listen to the water flowing beneath their windows as they lie in bed at night."

"Do you have an office?"

"I run the whole affair out of my study at home, just like the painters in their studios. I put in a good day's work before lunch and never change out of my dressing gown. I can even work in bed."

"He does some of his best work in bed." Alan surprised them with his silent return. He sat down next to Martin, pulled off his shoes, and dangled his feet in the rushing water of the acequia.

Kitty reddened, shocked to take Alan's meaning. "You're quite the will-o-the-wisp, Mr. Sutton."

"I make my rounds."

"You have business here?"

"Pictures."

"You buy paintings from the villagers?"

"If you're Spanish, you weave frazadas or carve santos. Only Anglos paint pictures but I can't paint, so I use my camera."

"Oh, photography. You take pictures of . . . ?"

"Landscapes, houses, people. Mostly people. Chimayó is like a country village in Dorset. Nobody ever leaves."

"The sense of tradition feels complete here," Martin continued. "This yeoman breed has followed the movements of the sun generation after generation. These families farm during the summer, they weave during the winter, and they light candles in their mud churches."

"Also drink beer, pull knives, and send their amigos to the camposanto," Alan added.

"Still, it's like nowhere else in America."

"I do portraits, the same people every time we come. Here and Truchas, Milagro, Corazón Sagrado. The Spanish like posing for the camera, especially the men, none modest."

"Alan has the advantage over the professional portrait-takers who come through."

"I bring back the pictures in person, don't use the mails."

"But he's always giving away his photographs, gratis, to perfect strangers."

Alan shrugged. "I like knowing the families."

"And whose kitchen door were you knocking on today?"

"Time for another photo of Epifano Jaramillo."

"I imagine we're invited for lunch."

"Doña Trinidad was stirring her stew when I left, adding a few special herbs. I've a private notion she's a curandera."

"That's a native woman who uses charms to cure people," Martin explained.

"And cast spells to hex people and drive away witches."

"You're superstitious?" asked Kitty. "Witches indeed!"

"See this?" Alan pulled a toffee tin from his pocket. "Dirt I dug from the church the first time we came here. I carry it when I drive, never had an accident, never had a breakdown far from town, not even a flat tyre. Call it what you want, I call it good luck."

"You're a brilliant mechanic, that's why you don't have breakdowns, not because your pockets are filled with good luck charms like your crooked six-pence."

"*And* I've never got nabbed for running moonshine, or anything else." From another pocket Alan took a tobacco tin and shook it. "This stuff's not for cigarette smoking—a nasty habit that I gave up, which is more than I can say for Mr. St. John Howell. There'll be guests at your party who enjoy their locoweed, especially a certain rich lady from Boston. Whatever's necessary to keep his clients happy, I'm only too willing."

Martin smiled at his sister. "Alan is a caution!"

Kitty was warned that the anniversary party would be on the wild side, and the drinking heroic, but she was utterly taken aback by the much-anticipated celebration. "All tarted up!" was Alan's description of their household, including himself as he stood on the front steps in formal attire with white tie, waiting to welcome their first guests.

A luminaria blazed in the middle of the driveway as cars arrived, and farolitos flickered along the entire front of the house. The revelry went late into the night with heavy drinking, rude jokes, and loud laughter. Everyone "got a bit illuminated" as Martin politely described the collective descent into drunkenness. Alan characterized the guests more bluntly: "A passel of piss artists!"

Gin was the principal liquor consumed in the fruit punch and tall glasses, straight. Kitty had been alerted that alcohol was illegal in America, but there seemed no difficulty in obtaining large quantities. Alan enjoyed a reputation for manufacturing the best bootleg gin in Santa Fe. His distilling operation was hidden among the willow bosques in Tesuque, and his covered wagon Model-T delivered his cargo home without detection. Kitty was impressed by the resourcefulness of her brother's friend.

She was also fascinated by the odd assortment of party guests. Artists in Navajo blouses with concha belts, poets in Chinese gowns with jade cigarette holders, and society matrons in bejeweled turbans, all mingled easily with Spanish ladies wearing lacy mantillas and Indians sporting pigtails and brightly colored chaparajos. Someone was strumming a guitar in one room, and someone else playing polkas on an accordion in the next. Beside the bar, two writers were exchanging limericks—"There was a young man from Nantucket . . . "—while in the dining room, a couple of artists challenged each other to a duel of painting each other's portraits across the same studio at high noon the next day. One young man was dressed as a French fisherman while a young woman showed up in a Hawaiian grass skirt.

Over and over without success, Kitty tried the small talk that would have passed admirably with the waxwork guests at an English house party. One tall woman was costumed in a Hopi wedding dress with her hair done up in the tribal fashion, with two buns like twin towers on either side of her head. This Boston heiress produced the first of the evening's many shockers when she announced, "I was told at a séance that the angels would protect me only if I moved to Santa Fe." The lady was smoking a cigarette Kitty knew was not tobacco.

"There's people sleeping with people," Martin explained when he found that his sister had taken refuge in the kitchen, where little Sara helped her aunt putting ten candles on the anniversary cake. "There's people feuding with people they used to sleep with. Witter Bynner and Mabel Dodge Luhan just feud for the sake of feuding. He fancies himself Jesus Christ on a bicycle—as the old saying goes—so he just might be jealous of Mabel's success at attracting celebrities to her place in Taos. Right now they are having a tug-of-war over that bearded novelist with the dreadful German wife. Best for you to view the whole evening as madly gay, like pure Restoration comedy."

"Perhaps if I had a thimbleful of gin?"

"A drop or two of something sustaining? I could use a bracer myself. We'll have the good stuff, imported, not the burro piss from Alan's still." He poured them both doubles in their best Waterford tumblers. "Happy days!"

The only other Englishman at the party was the novelist with the German wife, D. H. Lawrence. "Of course I'm using Alan as model for the gamekeeper in my new novel *Lady Chatterley's Lover*. Only my gamekeeper will be the version of Alan if he had not escaped England in the company of Mr. St. John Howell. He fights in the Great War, he marries and fails as a husband after returning from military service, and he retreats into his solitary life as a gamekeeper once again, a hardened and embittered man. My gamekeeper remains cynical about love until he discovers the pure sexual union that shatters his shell of loneliness, though the book will doubtless be banned for what tight-arsed vicars call obscenity."

"For all your talk of obscenity, Lorenzo, you don't fool me. You're really a complete Puritan yourself." Bynner was dressed as a Chinese mandarin with artificial fingernails so long that he could hardly hold his cocktail and his cigarette. "That's why you feel at home in America, because you're such a Puritan at heart."

"If by Puritan you mean someone obsessed with his darker passions, delving into the deeper wellsprings of his spiritual life to uncover the full fervor of what it means to be human, I make no argument, I surrender."

"So you acknowledge that forbidden passions remain the Puritan's lifeblood?"

Lawrence downed his moonshine with lemon. "The passions are not forbidden, never. They remain the true beginning and end of all good writing. When Odysseus hears the minstrel reciting the story of the Trojan War, he weeps for his fallen comrades in arms. That moment marks the beginning of Western literature, when Odysseus weeps. Sadness over loss, indignation over injustice, sexual arousal—especially sexual arousal—whatever powerful emotions stir men's most primitive feelings, great literature must never shy away from, it must embrace, it must dive deeper, ever deeper. The future's great novels will combine eroticism and spirituality. That's one thing my world travels have quested for, the bringing back together of the mind and the heart and the loins, in places on the map where that vital union never entirely disappeared, here in New Mexico, in the Indian pueblos. I want to write something as tremendous as the constellations circling overhead in the desert's silence. And its people! I can live so intensely with my characters that I get lost in their lives, disappearing here, emerging there, completely happy and contented in that other world. Not them and not me, my stories, but the strong wind that blows through me."

Kitty asked politely, "You have grown very fond of New Mexico, then, Mr. Lawrence?"

The novelist's reddish beard scarcely concealed the sunken cheeks of a consumptive, but his eyes flashed as he began again his monologue. "I think New Mexico is the greatest experience from the outside world I have ever known. It is the new continent of the soul. I spent years in Sicily among the Greek paganism that still survives on the slopes of Mount Aetna. But the moment I saw the brilliant, proud morning shine high up over the deserts of Santa Fe, something stood still in my soul and I started to attend. So soft, so utterly pure in its softness. In the magnificent fierce morning of New Mexico, a new part of my soul woke up suddenly, and the old world gave way to the new. And so beautiful, God! So beautiful!"

Kitty was fascinated by the man whose body exuded the sweetness of dried grass, but unnerved by the voice that gave no sign of pausing in its torrent of loud talk. She excused herself to freshen up.

Her own bedroom had been converted to a cloakroom, where guests locked the door so they could sniff a white powder they called *naughty salt*. Looking for another loo, Kitty ventured farther into the rambling house and tried a door. Inside she saw Alan. She saw the angel lady from Boston. She saw the bed they were lying on. Closing the door, Kitty backed into the hallway and retreated.

After topping up her tumbler of gin, she went outdoors and sat on the terrace steps, pondering everything that she had witnessed in this extremely irregular household. Nearby in the garden, her cow skull was mounted where Alan nailed it to an elm tree, its bleached whiteness shining in the midnight shadows. Playing nervously with her turquoise bracelet, a belated thirtieth birthday present from her brother, Kitty stared at her curious souvenir of the badlands and continued thinking. Did Martin have a clue?

She was still musing with an empty glass when she heard strange music. A mariachi band had materialized on the balcony above the front porch. These musicians in their sombreros traditionally played at Mexican weddings, but tonight they provided the music for the anniversary dance. Guests streamed out of the house and into the courtyard. Bynner stood on a chair and announced that the anniversary couple would lead off the first dance. The crowd parted as her brother and Alan walked hand in hand into the center of the flagstone court. Martin was always one for ceremonies. Dashing in his dinner jacket with gardenia as a boutonniere, Alan had reassembled himself neatly after the scene in the bedroom.

The mariachi band began a slow waltz, and Kitty recalled that her brother, no fan of loud Wagnerian opera, had always said, "A good waltz is more my style." Though she understood none of the words, she was surprised at the beauty of the melody, also struck deeply as she watched her brother and his friend, the two most handsome men at the party, leading the other dancers. When they exchanged glances, there was a glint, a spark, *something* that passed between the two men. Kitty felt a strange sensation and realized she was on the verge of crying. Suddenly she realized how lonely she felt, the only young woman at the party without a date. *And not so young, either,* a frump in the offing, she thought as she fingered the turquoise bracelet. As other couples joined Martin and Alan in the waltz, she retreated inside the house for another glass of something bracing. Soon Bynner's younger boyfriend, completely sozzled, had taken off his clothes and was striking poses in the fountain on the lower terrace.

Most of the guests left after sunrise when Tía Léona served a vast English breakfast of gammon, scrambled eggs, and fried tomatoes. Finally the novelist Lawrence decided that the remaining guests needed to pile into cars and go have their fortunes told by the gypsies whose caravan wagons, painted canary yellow with red wheels, had arrived at the edge of town for their yearly visit to Santa Fe.

"Ripping, absolutely topping, like pure Restoration comedy," Martin teased his little sister, quite nicely pinching her ear before he hopped into the last car. "All madly gay!"

Kitty waited until breakfast on the morning of her departure six weeks later, when she and her brother were alone, to share her misgivings about his relationship with Alan Sutton. The Howells always hated a row. "During the anniversary party, I discovered your friend in a bedroom with that woman, the one who moved here for the protections of angels, in a very compromising position."

Her brother took a bite of toast loaded with marmalade, seemingly unphased. "When I first met Alan, he bragged that he could marry whenever he wanted. He's normal plus, not minus. He finds it completely natural to care for both men and women. I don't but he does. Alan was honest with me going in, so nothing comes as a surprise."

"Doesn't it bother you? Has it never caused a falling out?"

"What's the good of a scene? Ours is a special friendship unlike a church marriage. It doesn't include the necessity to possess. I know Alan will remain at my side for the rest of my life. He didn't sign a contract, simply promised that we would never be parted. I always asked myself what was the point if we merely copied old-fashioned wedded couples. So we've invented our own ways of doing things, not exactly holy wedlock."

"You simply look the other way?"

"Not possible really. You know Tía Léona's little niece who helps in the kitchen? The lovely child with the bright brown eyes? Léona is actually her mother, and her father is Alan. So it's no good pretending things are different than they are. Christ Almighty, my randy gamekeeper even indulged in a shipboard romance with a very pretty Italian girl from Palermo, leaving her, for all I know, in the family way to raise their lovechild by herself after reaching America."

Stunned, Kitty stared down at her bowl of porridge a long while before continuing. "Do you imagine you'll remain here? Never mind what the wicked novelist said about the beauty of the morning and the Indian religion and the soul waking up. It's so primitive, a wasteland really."

"Santa Fe seems a good enough place to grow old. Living here is like the railroad. It's the end of the line. The town may be the backend of nowhere, but we have colorful, artistic friends. We enjoy all the necessities, many of the luxuries, and we aren't bothered. Can any man ask for more?"

Kitty disappeared into her own thoughts before speaking again. "I have seen you miserable at home, with me and Eva and mother trying to make you happy and failing. It was too, too sad-making. Now I've seen you happy here, as you understand happiness, with Alan and your artistic friends. I shall not judge the morality and I don't know the law, but I am truly gratified you have got beyond the wretchedness that I saw in your eyes every day after Cambridge."

Martin rose and gave Kitty the brotherly hug that he had hesitated to bestow when she first arrived.

"Unless you strenuously object," she continued, "I shall report your happiness to those who still care about you in England."

Martin asked Alan when he arrived for breakfast, and neither of them objected.

Later that night when undressing for bed, Martin was still thinking about Kitty sharing news with old friends. "Colin was not really such a bad lot." He picked up the corduroys that Alan left in a heap on the floor, folding and laying them on the chair. "I give him some credit, beastly as he was about me and you, because he might have turned out entirely useless like my school chum Worcester. He married respectably enough, never straying from Adela as far as I know, and he's been attentive to their boys. He entered politics when he didn't need to. He gets good mention in the newspapers for always having the welfare of his constituents at heart. Colin's sense of duty strikes me as admirable."

Alan made a vinegar face. "He wasn't exactly Father Christmas back at bloody Pendersley," he replied bluntly from where he lay naked on his side of the bed, a spearhead of tan at his throat where he wore his shirt open to the sun. "He was always running my feet off with *do this* and *go there*, not remembering my name half the time, boot up the bum if I looked sideways. Welfare of his constituents? Balls! Your wanker chum's just acting English."

～～～

Later that winter back in London, Kitty was invited for a quiet family dinner with the Dunbars at their home in town, making a fine report of Martin's happiness with their former gamekeeper in the wilds of New Mexico. She began so casually and was done so quickly, Colin had no chance to send the boys from the table.

"Deuced indecent of Kitty," he kept muttering later as he sat on the bedside untying his shoes. "Fundamentally unsound, like everyone in that rummy family. Did you never hear about the father's shameful scene in Monte Carlo? Imagine everyone fancying Martin the blue-eyed boy. We were entirely taken in, myself included. Deuced indecent, that's what I say."

"What could the boys have understood?" Adela consoled him as she latched the shutters.

"Let's talk no more about those two men and their colossal impertinence," Colin said as he switched off the lights before undressing. His wife had never seen him naked. "They have vanished off the face of the earth as far as we are concerned, just as they have disappeared from all good society."

But Martin was not the only member of the St. John Howell family to harbor secrets and spring surprises. At the dinner table of the Dunbars in town, Kitty was accompanied by her friend from the Domestic Institute. Lydia Tansy had become her inseparable companion since Kitty's return from America. They attended lectures on modern psychology, queued for tickets to Tchaikovsky concerts, and visited picture galleries displaying the bold paintings by women artists. They even enjoyed a long holiday together in Italy. Everyone knew they had always been great friends.

The next spring Kitty and Lydia arrived in Santa Fe together. At first Martin feared his sister had gotten herself in the family way and needed some obscure place to disappear until the baby arrived. Alan ragged him, "Kitty's not stuffed. Your head's screwed on so wrong-ways, you'll always be the last to catch on."

"Little boys don't understand a good deal, you noodle!" Kitty pinched his ear before kissing him.

While Martin welcomed his sister and her friend tentatively at first, Alan thought it would be a jolly idea for English women to take charge of the kitchen, women who knew how to make a proper steak and kidney pie. Martin conceded that he always treated his sisters beastly, unkind and brutal, and owed something back as a decent chappie ought.

"Maybe it's something chemical," Kitty speculated about her attachment with Lydia. "Father, after all, took comfort on the other side of the sheets in Monte Carlo when he was young."

Martin reddened when he took his sister's meaning.

"I have news from home that will gladden you," Kitty said to divert her brother from his embarrassment. "Colin Dunbar's hair is falling out. Bald as an egg before forty. If you saw his comb-over, you'd laugh yourself into a permanent state of hiccoughs."

Plans were made for expanding their warren-like home into a true compound. A separate casita with a bedroom, a sitting room, and a bath was completed before Thanksgiving, a new holiday that the expatriates very gladly celebrated. Snug inside their mud-brick cottage in later years, Lydia sat beside Kitty reading aloud from novels by Miss Austen and Miss Woolf, also their friend Willa Cather's *Death Comes for the Archbishop*, their favorite. The cottage was separated from the main house by a courtyard where the two women cultivated their dahlias, peonies and purple irises, just like home.

In the kitchen beneath hanging herbs, the English ladies taught their cook's pretty niece to make a very fine steak and kidney pie as well as a traditional Christmas pudding. Alan lapsed into his rustic dialect, exclaiming, "My ma never maked a yummier figged pudden!"

To become useful in their adopted homeland, Kitty and Lydia sought work at the local hospital with the Presbyterian doctors. In a matter of months they went from volunteers to fulltime nurses, eventually traveling as midwives whenever there were difficult births in mountain villages. They smuggled bootleg gin to sanitize their instruments, as well as ease the women's pains and keep the men in the kitchen. Tía Léona came along to translate, sometimes bringing little Sara so she could learn about birthing babies.

Some years later when finishing high school, Sara Baca spotted an advertisement in a magazine at the beauty parlor and filled out an application. She was accepted to attend school to become a stewardess with Pan American Airways. She had always been restless and spoke two languages, even knew how to deliver a baby if there was an emergency onboard. Alan paid the girl's tuition and all her other expenses. After graduating at the top of her class, she flew clippers on Pacific routes halfway around the world. In Hawaii she met a Japanese man who became her husband. She and Jimmy Hamahiga returned to Santa Fe to raise their family, and in the course of time she opened a restaurant famous for the most authentic New Mexican cooking in town. She named the restaurant after the aunt who taught her all the old native recipes. Its walls were decorated with photographs by Alan Sutton.

After D. H. Lawrence died at a sanatorium in France, his body was cremated and his ashes shipped back to New Mexico for burial. There are many legends about what happened next. One version of the story tells how Mabel Dodge Luhan placed the urn for safekeeping on a shelf above her stove, but it fell over and spilled his ashes into the pancakes frying on a griddle below.

But here is the true end of the story. After arriving by railway, the package with the author's ashes was left behind at the house of the two Englishmen. Everyone who traveled down from Taos drank so much gin by the time they piled back into Mabel's Cadillac for the long drive home, they forgot what they had come for. A great believer in good-luck charms, Alan was sure he could absorb the writer's creativity if he consumed some of his physical remains. All by himself with curtains drawn, he took a spoonful of the ashes and mixed it with his afternoon tea. For extra measure, he added the tiniest pinch of the church-dirt from Chimayó. From that time onward, Alan claimed that he always gained extra vigor for his photographic work whenever he drank a piping hot cup of Earl Grey.

But that was not the end of the story for the English exiles.

One more refugee arrived ten years after Kitty and Lydia. It was Colin's older son Adam. Weedy as a lad and shambling too-tall by sixteen, he had grown into a striking young man taking more after his mother, dark-haired, fair-skinned, and addicted to entertaining. He had also become an outlaw of the Oscar Wilde sort infected with "the unspeakable vice of the Greeks," as the Provost described his crime when sending him down from Cambridge. One of the Dunbar boys had been listening at the dinner table when Kitty described her brother's friendship with their former gamekeeper, and the lad began eagerly taking these strange thoughts to heart, finally making sense of his own fascination with the gardener's son George. There was talk of packing Adam off to Kenya where the dipsomaniacs went to live on a monthly remittance, but America would serve just as well.

Adam arrived at the station with two enormous steamer trunks and no immediate plans. Martin and Alan welcomed him because he was exceptionally good-looking, and Colin's son. Martin took secret satisfaction at "winning over" the elder son and the heir of Pendersley. The next year, they converted the photographic studio into a bedroom and extra bath. The camera equipment and chemical bottles went to Alan's new studio up a nearby dirt road, quiet and secluded, where tourists seldom wandered.

Adam lingered. For years Martin called him their godson, without the blessings of parents at the church fount, then later simply their son. The young man had a good head for business, especially real estate, and he became a great help as Martin became more interested in reading his books, as well as entertaining the writers and artists passing through town.

Aside from the Catholic feast days and processions, the favorite holiday for this band of exiles was the autumn fiesta invented by some local artist friends. The Zozobra Festival became an exuberant celebration when the townsfolk burned a giant image of Old Man Gloom embodying the uneasiness, uncertainty, and sadness of the coming winter.

Early in the day's merrymaking, Alan made his annual contribution by captaining a cricket match on the plaza with wickets, batting pads and gloves, just as they had done back in Dorsetshire. Adam organized the opposing team of Indian boys captained by their best batsman, Jorge from Pecos, an Apache as swift-footed as he was strong, and very striking with his long hair and lean muscular body. To guarantee the best athletes, Adam rewarded his youngsters with a café dinner after their practices, with pitchers of beer, so he always had his pick of boys eager to learn bowling and batting. Other local Indians, peddling their pots and jewelry, watched the cricketers with blank-faced curiosity from the portál of the Palace of the Governors, while storeowners stood in front of their windows to prevent breakage from stray balls.

Later that night, the Englishmen came together with the rest of the community watching as black-hooded figures encircled the great papier-mâché figure of Zozobra. Thirty feet tall, the monstrous marionette had cables lifting his arms while his huge head turned ominously left and right, his eyes flashing, and everything illuminated by weird green lights. The gong rang out and the tom-toms beat the funeral cadence for Old Man Gloom. Hundreds of onlookers chanted "Burn him! Burn him! Burn him!" Drunken cowboys fired pistols at the evil-looking eyes as the giant effigy's robes caught fire and masses of shredded paper inside—the tax notices, divorce degrees, traffic tickets, paid-off mortgages—sent flames leaping higher and higher into the night sky. Kitty and Lydia stood with their handkerchiefs covering their mouths to keep from coughing when smoke blew in their direction.

It was a rare occasion when Alan thought back nostalgically about England. "Reminds me of the Guy Fawkes bonfire set ablaze on Blackbarrow when I was a kid. Gramfer Venn, who'd drove his wagon selling red dye for the sheep before settling down in his butcher shop, he always brung me with him for lighting the beacon."

Even after the mock funeral pyre collapsed into cinders, Martin stood shoulder to shoulder with Alan awaiting the very end. Sheltered beneath a Navajo blanket against the chill of the autumn night, the two men sported the same cricket flannels they wore after their first night of lovemaking, with some alteration in their waistlines over the years. Heedless of the soot and ash, they wore their summer whites as they stood together keeping vigil until the last flames died down, signaling another year free of sadness, while Adam searched the shadows for any pueblo boys who drank too much and were left behind by their friends. Alan waited till the gigantic figure was no more than a smoldering heap to give his customary pronouncement, "Now that's settled and done with."

The years passed with the seasons. After Prohibition was repealed, Alan shut down his still and quit running bootleg gin. When Wall Street crashed and banks folded, the Great Depression deepened the poverty of a region which had never known real prosperity. Only prairie dogs made their homes in the alfalfa fields Martin had bought as his real estate investments north of town.

When the world went to war again, young men from the villages and pueblos disappeared into military service. The colossal Zozobra puppet was given the faces of Hitler, Mussolini and Hirohito during successive fiestas, but the cricket matches were suspended because there were not enough young players to make up two full teams. Martin and Alan joined the rest of the locals keeping mum about the odd assortment of scientists arriving in town and then disappearing out the back of an office on East Palace, secretly spirited away to the windy mesa at Los Alamos. They made the same joke as the other men about the "secret submarine base" hidden among ponderosa pines where the Japanese would never find it.

Calling himself Mr. Bradley for security reasons, the chief physicist in his cowboy boots and porkpie hat, rakishly cocked, showed up unexpectedly one afternoon for tea and sat late into the night, switching to Scotch along with the painters. After hearing that Martin owned the finest collection of books in town, the scientist seemed intent upon discussing Baudelaire, John Donne, and even the *Bhagavad Gita*, volumes which Martin kept jumping up and grabbing from nearby shelves, while never a word was said about the project on the plateau west of Otowi Bridge. Alan did his patriotic duty by keeping their tumblers topped up.

The local community followed Alan's lead by closing ranks, hunkering down, and turning a blind eye to the presence of Jimmy Hamahiga. "He's Navajo. I knew his father. They made beautiful silver belts, both of them, and turquoise bracelets too." That was the story everyone told whenever the Feds came snooping. Thus Sara Baca's husband never ended up in the internment facility that everybody called the Jap Camp in the dry hills west of town, where more than four thousand American lawyers, teachers, grocers, journalists, farmers, and insurance salesmen whose parents happened to be Japanese were imprisoned during the years immediately after Pearl Harbor.

Finally the world came back from war again when so many local boys, including Adam's best batsman Jorge, were laid to rest in the military cemetery with its white stone markers, stretching for acres along the north road toward Taos. The physicists scattered. The plaza turned sleepy again. The little English family lingered, as they had for so many year, in their adobe compound on the Old Santa Fe Trail.

Tia Léona cooked.

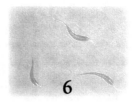

6

Only Connecting

Morgan and Eddy—Santa Fe, 1979

Morgan remembered birthdays and anniversaries. Eddy felt slightly irritated by all the fuss unless it involved travel, as when they celebrated their second anniversary with a getaway to Santa Fe. The plan involved matching Morgan's annual leave with Eddy's vacation time. They also organized with Morgan's old Princeton friend Ethan Rees and his wife Meredith, who made equally complicated arrangements to join them with their six-month-old son Josh. Grandparents would babysit their daughter Meghan, aged three, at the old family home in Westport. The year was 1979, and Ethan had finished his M.D. but was just beginning his long years as a medical resident specializing in virology.

"Jeez, you professional men and your schedules!" Eddy remarked after the third try at getting a common date for their vacation. "When a waiter wants a break, he just quits and looks for another job when he comes back."

"Know how to tell you're getting middle-aged? It's when your friends are all doctors and lawyers."

"Ouch!"

When they did arrive in Santa Fe, Morgan had something else on his mind during their stay in the historic capital. He started his professional life as an attorney specializing in corporate mergers and acquisitions with a reputation for some of the best-firing synapses on Wall Street, and so he knew the value of contracts. Also he kept reading about *spelling out the terms of your relationship* when flipping through the gay self-help manuals in his favorite West Village bookshop which also sold lube, poppers, cock rings, and leather collars. The bookstore's manager Gene, another transplanted Virginian like himself, stocked the shelves with the latest publications. Experts agreed that gay couples needed some written agreement so there were no misunderstandings about boundaries and expectations. He and Eddy had spent two whole years together. It was high time, Morgan decided, to spell things out in black and white.

How did their relationship survive for the two years after their first encounter at the boathouse in Central Park? Morgan had always been the master of the one-night stand and quick sex in backrooms, and even his best friend Claire declared, "You're not the marrying kind!" So the real question is how he and Eddy reached their *first* anniversary?

It was going to be a real scorcher in August 1977 when Eddy awoke for the first time beside him. Usually Morgan hated making conversation first thing in the morning, but not this morning, actually early afternoon by the time the two men roused themselves. He hurried for coffee and bagels from the Jewish bakery downstairs, and dashed back upstairs dreading that Eddy had left as so many other men had left, as he actually wanted them to leave, just slipping away without leaving a name or number.

But Eddy was still there in bed, propped up on the pillows, waiting for Morgan to return and afraid he might not. They had spent the night exploring each other's bodies, and now each was curious about the other's life. "Gay men fuck first and ask questions later," as Claire began observing back in law school.

Eddy greeted him with a big smile and scooted over as Morgan slid back into bed. They drank coffee and chewed bagels and settled into conversation. Morgan asked, "What line of work are you in?"

"I'm a waiter."

"An actor/waiter/model?"

"I started as a busboy and now I'm a waiter, just a waiter. End of story."

Morgan fell silent as he lay back staring at the ceiling. His pelvis felt bruised where he had pounded Eddy's tailbone really hard the second time around. Now he felt emotionally bruised because the reply *end of story* sounded rude. As he focused on a big crack in the plaster, Morgan knew his own life was a work in progress and Eddy's life, in his early twenties, also remained in Act I of some ongoing story. Fitzgerald was wrong about no second acts in American lives, except his own boozy descent into a dark night of the soul. Just as Morgan could not look at a lake or mountain without transforming it into a comment on his life, he was almost incapable of having an experience without fitting it into a plotline. Already he sketched out the unfolding drama:

Act I: Lawyer Enjoys Wild Sex Life
Act II: He Finds Lover and Settles Down
Act III: He Makes Partner in Major Firm
Act IV: Couple Shares Fun and Adventures
Act V: They Live Happily Ever After

With so many plans and ambitions he wanted to share with another man, Morgan felt that he deserved a better answer than *end of story* as he lay in bed, chewing a poppy-seed bagel as he tasted Eddy's lingering saltiness and the aftertaste of mouthwash. Morgan was squeamish about oral sex. While he made an exception for this incredibly sexy man, he always sprang from bed, spit in the sink, and gargled with mint-flavored mouthwash. His motto remained, "If you can't cope, use Scope."

"What are you thinking," Eddy asked when his bed partner went silent for a whole minute.

"Nothing." This was the first real lie he had told Eddy. Technically it was the second. Morgan's first lie was his confession that he talked too much, because really he did not talk nearly enough. He would go silent, start thinking, grow sullen, get sulks, and never explain what was bothering him. There were *many* things, Eddy soon learned, Morgan simply did not talk about.

On their first morning lying in bed together with the window air conditioner providing the only background noise, Eddy was already sore behind where Morgan pounded him twice, really hard the second time. Now he grew irritated that he needed to ask questions about his lover's moodiness—because they became lovers from their first night together—and extract the whole story. "Is it about me being a waiter?" Eddy asked with tough-guy defensiveness. "You gotta problem with that? Huh?"

But Eddy had been lying, too, despite his brief flare-up of anger. His job as a waiter was not the end of his story and he knew it even then. Eddy was smart. He had dreams that he was afraid to share with the good-looking preppy he just met in the park. He had moved from the restaurant in the old neighborhood where his parents lived in North Bergen, New Jersey, and started working his way up the job ladder in Manhattan restaurants. All the time he was waiting tables, he was learning the business. He took cooking classes and business classes in his spare time. While he never sat down with pencil and paper to sketch a storyline, he had goals and took actions. In the years to come he opened his own restaurant, a popular eatery that would make a very comfortable livelihood for its hardworking owner.

All these things would happen, but not for a couple of years. Now, on their first morning after meeting beside the lake, Eddy curled up in a double bed with its box spring on cinderblocks, in a tiny walkup above a Jewish bakery which sold orange bagels on Halloween and green bagels on St. Patrick's Day, licking Morgan's nipple and feeling him get hard again where his hand stroked beneath the sheet. "You're insatiable, mister," Eddy said in a voice husky with fatigue, "impossible to satisfy, you know that?"

He had gotten over his brief anger, and Morgan had gotten over his pique, too, as he relaxed into the sensation of Eddy's tongue on his nipple. Morgan actually felt relieved that his partner did not have some long, well-rehearsed autobiography ready to rattle off at the first opportunity.

"Blue," Eddy said as he took a break and rested his head on Morgan's chest, listening to the strong steady beating of his heart. "You said your eyes have no color, but they're blue. Pale blue."

It was the way Hemingway described bankruptcy happening, first gradually and then suddenly. Morgan never knew when Eddy moved in. One morning there was a toothbrush in the bathroom. Next, food in takeout containers from the Italian bistro where he waited tables began appearing in the refrigerator. Then white work shirts were hanging in the closet. Everything felt so strange because Morgan never realistically imagined a lover. Even back in Charlottesville when he first came out, he hated going through the motions of making coffee and exchanging phone numbers. Usually he did not even want the guy's number, just wanted to know his name before hurrying him out the door. He agreed with his friend Claire's oft-quoted remark: "Tricks should never be left lying around the house where grownups might trip over them."

But he wanted Eddy in his bed the next night, and Eddy was there the next night. And the next night and the next. In later years they had bigger beds, but even when they slept on a super-king mattress the size of a baseball diamond, they always awoke pressed close and tangled in each other's arms. Their bodies sought out each other while they slumbered.

Summer went into autumn. All their friends came back from Fire Island and Duchess County. At the boathouse in the park, the leaves turned colors in the softening light. Morgan arranged his daily five-mile jog to pause halfway beside the lake. He loved running among the tall trees where he felt removed from the city itself, as if magically transported back to the horse country of Albemarle County with the smell of green living things.

Morgan always wanted to live exactly where he was, minus one. When he went off to Princeton, he was homesick for the Virginia countryside of his youth. When he went to law school, he missed his undergraduate campus with its gray medieval quadrangles. Now in Manhattan, he yearned for Mr. Jefferson's redbrick university and the rolling hills around Charlottesville where he enjoyed his earliest sex with scruffy boys, sweet hillbillies most of them, with slim hips and knobby shoulders beneath their sleeveless shirts. Their long messy hair drove him wild as he pulled it back while riding them from behind.

At least Central Park offered a quiet retreat for New Yorkers who sacrificed so many creature comforts, including solitude itself, for the opportunity of advancing high-powered careers, meeting interesting people, and enjoying the movable feast of spontaneous sex. The gray boulder remained on the lake's shoreline beneath the branches of the beech tree, his trysting place, just as before, but everything else in Morgan's life was changing at a velocity that left him feeling dazed and curious.

With his Princeton t-shirt dark with patches of sweat, Morgan sat atop the rock and rested a few minutes. He liked sitting quietly upon this small promontory, gazing across the algae-covered water where sometimes a single swan glided along. He looked at the ground to see if any white feathers were lying nearby as evidence of some fall from the sky. Lately he started feeling like a latter-day Icarus who desired too much and soared too high and now came tumbling to earth, not some tragic victim of overweening ambition, but someone who had plummeted downward into, well, *normalcy*. He commuted to work. He ran five miles. He went home to his lover. Boring, boring, boring. The Old Masters were never wrong about suffering.

Beside the lake now, Morgan imagined how Jay Gatsby looked across to the green light, small and faraway, burning all night at the end of the dock. This had been another image that played in his mind when he came cruising late at night, looking for anonymous sex but telling himself that he was enjoying the orgiastic future prophesied by Fitzgerald's gay narrator. But when he gazed across in full daylight, Morgan saw instead the green roof of the boathouse on the opposite side, and he no longer felt the same yearning for those sexual marathons that ended with getting his rocks off just once more before heading home. Something had happened.

As he sat un-tying and re-tying his running shoes so no passerby would think he was a sissy for resting, Morgan noticed the hunks in cutoff jeans beckoning from the pathway. They cast backward glances as they crossed the pedestrian bridge toward the Ramble. Nothing if not disciplined, Morgan did not follow, feeling triumphant about passing a major test, maybe the biggest. Because he had come to realize while sitting on the shoreline that Eddy was the one he had been seeking during all those long nights of cruising. His lover's touch, his unexpected smiles, the sound of his voice on the telephone—"What are you doing?"—and even the funny noise that his nose made when he slept, not quite snoring, still made Morgan want to write love sonnets.

Gatsby believed in the green light. Every Princetonian chanted that line like a sacred mantra. As he readied himself to slide off the boulder and resume his five-mile course, Morgan thought how their freshman English teacher made the whole class write an essay on the meaning of the green light. Groaning, he and Ethan complained that it was exactly the lame assignment they expected from a professor who came back from two years at Cambridge with a phony British accent, always making a point of reminding the class that one of his degree examiners had been J. R. R. Tolkien.

The light was supposed to signify some impossible love, the unattainable, the ideal, the thing that was so beautiful and so precious precisely because it slipped through a man's fingers even as he grasped it. The colossal significance of the green light seemed to vanish for Morgan, now, as grownup realities suffused his daily routines and his collection of enchanted objects diminished one by one. But did the ideal really need to be something remote and unattainable, he wondered, a love impossible to embrace and hold for a lifetime?

Morgan shook out his legs before starting to run. Careful not to tread on stray cock rings dropped along the trail, he quickened his pace toward West 76th Street where he knew Eddy, who already had his own key, was waiting to surprise him with some new recipe for dinner. Not altogether boring, boring, boring.

A Halloween party was marked on the kitchen calendar. Eddy had given Morgan fair warning that he liked dressing up and going out. With their friends Lawrence, Gary and Frankie—Eddy's gay cousin studying interior design at Pratt—they were going dressed as the hot new disco group the Village People. Cousin Frankie even wanted them to lip-sync the hit single *Go West* until Morgan put his foot down. He did not dance, he did not like dressing up in weird-looking outfits, and he certainly did not intend performing some totally queer skit in front of a bunch of strangers.

Always a red-letter celebration for gay men, Halloween also meant the beginning of the holiday season. As Morgan contemplated the prospect of Thanksgiving and Christmas, he wondered how far he and Eddy had become officially a *couple*. Also he wondered what it meant to become a *gay* couple in hip Manhattan culture where most men considered it unfashionable to sleep with the same partner twice. What does a summer romance become when leaves are turning yellow?

Everything in Morgan's life felt like a graded assignment. All his energies went toward earning the next A, getting the next gold star, and adding another line to his résumé. What he knew best were exams. So he knew he was testing Eddy one morning after having sex—they had a knack for simultaneous orgasms, mostly because they came so quickly with each other—and they were lying in bed, drowsy and content, when Morgan broke the silence, "So what's next?" He had planned the answer, having mentally rehearsed the whole conversation in advance. "I think we need to get ourselves organized. If this is a merger, we need to rid ourselves of duplicate assets."

"Roll over, and I'll duplicate your assets."

"In your dreams!" Morgan was a total top, a pitcher and never yet a catcher.

"So what are you talking about?" Eddy sounded irritated. "You never just say what's on your mind. Drives me crazy!"

"This apartment is too crowded. We should go through our stuff and get rid of extra clutter. How many typewriters do we need? How many crock pots?"

Though his idea, actually merging their books and records struck Morgan as a drastic sign of commitment. The LP albums were easier. What gay household needs two copies of *The Divine Miss M*? But thinning out the books proved tougher. Eddy had memorized one-liners from the Marx Brothers, never missed a Preston Sturges festival, and could recite plot summaries from nearly every film starring Bette Davis and Katharine Hepburn, even quote dialogue from *All About Eve* and *The Philadelphia Story*. But movies were not his only passion.

Like many men who never went to college, Eddy compensated by reading books that he heard other people talk about. He loved his novels and lugged them in cardboard boxes from one rental to another. When he moved into Morgan's place, Eddy's only other treasure was a large unframed painting, a riot of electric oranges and greens with two men, more like gigantic stick-figures, dancing so furiously that their movements bounced off their bodies likes waves of color. A graffiti-style inscription ran across the bottom of the canvas: EDDY—HAVEN'T STOPPED DANCING YET—KEITH. So when Morgan suggested jettisoning duplicate copies of their books, Eddy felt the sacrifice acutely.

Some decisions were easier than others. They kept Eddy's copy of *Women in Love* because it was hardcover and Morgan's *The City and the Pillar* because it was a first edition. Morgan held up two identical paperbacks of *Pride and Prejudice*. "Lesbianism, cross-dressing, sexual humiliation, and a strong hint of incest. No wonder we never get tired of Jane Austen." They sold both copies of *Giovanni's Room* because the story was a total downer, but one book caused a major snag. Eddy wanted to keep his copy of *Maurice* and Morgan insisted on keeping his. "I've got all the juicy parts underlined," Eddy said. "It's my favorite gay love story. How many others can you name with happy endings?"

"I received my copy for Christmas from my father."

"Your father gave you this novel? So your family can't be completely clueless you're queer."

"My father actually met Forster when he was at Cambridge, drank champagne together and talked about rowing, even got the author to tell a story about John Maynard Keynes that he used in his economics textbook. He rereads *A Room with a View* every year in June, really disciplined about his annual rituals. When a new novel was published the year after Forster's death, my father just bought it. I don't think he read it or even knew what it was about. He's always super-busy working. Besides, my father doesn't talk about things like that."

"Junior high was when I got my copy, shoplifted it actually, too scared to take it to the checkout counter. Maurice and Alec saved my life or helped. Thought I was the only teenager with these feelings about men."

Finally they shrugged and agreed without further discussion—the first of many such compromises—their one-bedroom apartment was big enough for two copies of *Maurice*.

With the 1977 holidays coming on, Eddy turned the tables and subjected Morgan to his first big test. They were working on their Village People costumes for the Halloween party at their friend Geoff's place in the West Village, and Morgan was grumpy about the queer-looking outfits, complaining, "Can't we just go as Scott and Zelda?"

Eddy said, "I have a son."

Morgan looked stunned. He was dressed as a cowboy in tight Wrangler jeans, a rawhide vest, and a close-fitting denim shirt unbuttoned to reveal his chest hair. He had been trying to decide if a red bandana made him look like a total fruitcake. "When were you going to tell me?"

"I'm telling you now. His name is Tony."

Morgan just stared.

"I was married and now I'm not," said Eddy. "Maybe I watched *Cabaret* one too many times. What, you never took a Quaalude and knocked up your girlfriend?"

"But you're a total bottom."

"Technically a Kinsey Four. You know what Woody Allen says. The best thing about being bisexual is it immediately doubles your chances for a date on Saturday night."

"It's a big deal."

"Tony is three now, and I have him for a month during the summer. His mother Tara lives in LA. Tara the Bitch as she is affectionately known. She remarried. Her new husband Dave is an asshole but he's okay with Tony. It's not something I tell a man on a first date."

"It's a big, *big* deal," Morgan repeated, "and for the record, we have gone pretty far beyond the first date."

"Have him for Christmas vacation, too, which is why we're having this conversation." When Eddy spoke again—he was wearing his Indian costume with feathered headdress, his bare torso smooth and hairless—his eyes had a doleful look that his lover had never seen before. "Deal-breaker?"

"Let me think about it."

"If Cousin Frankie and the others flake out, we can always show up as the

Lone Ranger and Tonto." Eddy tried to lighten the mood. "I think cowboys are hot. Montgomery Clift really rattled my spurs in *Red River*."

So Morgan thought about Eddy's son as they continued their lives as before, making a huge hit at the costume party as the Village People.

An associate in Morgan's law firm was transferred to the London office and had a rent-controlled apartment with two bedrooms to sublet. That night, Morgan came home and told Eddy that Tony would have his own bedroom when he came for Christmas. Everything was settled. For the rest of the year, Morgan could use the room as a home office. Usually he brought paperwork home on weekends, sometimes during the week, but he was very careful about not bringing home the stresses of the workplace. Princeton instilled an iron-clad belief it was bad form to talk about work, even be seen working, instead accomplishing the most grueling assignments with effortless ease. Morgan loathed whiners who mistook complaining for making conversation. Eddy managed the same, never bringing home gripes from the restaurant, only funny things they could laugh about as they crawled into bed. Both men were highly competitive, even aggressive in their pursuits of success, but never competitive with each other.

They moved apartments during Thanksgiving weekend—which became a perfect excuse for not visiting their families—but remained on the Upper West Side.

What about their families?

All their other friends were big drama queens, even the straight women like Claire, but not Morgan and Eddy. As an undergraduate, Morgan went through a period when haunted by a morbid dread that he would never have a great adventure. He would become one of those boring suburban neurotics in *New Yorker* short stories who did something not very important, then realized something not very interesting. He found himself fantasizing about some heroic escapade worthy of a front-page story in the *Times*. As he grew older, Morgan changed his attitude and aimed instead at a quiet, unspectacular existence without the high drama that regularly convulsed the lives of their gay friends. So Morgan and Eddy never staged the sort of family coming-out dramas which inspired so many Off Off Broadway plays.

"Are you going to tell your mother and father about us?" Morgan asked while driving to a friend's place outside Rhinebeck. He let go of Eddy's hand when reaching for the turn signal. They liked holding hands while driving.

"Can't." Cuban families operated in a state of denial so profound that it eliminated a whole universe of moral possibilities. Eddy's father routinely asked if he had a new girlfriend. His mother bragged about Tony and wanted to know when she could expect more grandchildren. In matters of sexual conduct, Aunt Lourdes summarized the verdict repeated on many occasions: "The worst thing for a family is a daughter who is a whore or a son who is a *maricón*."

"Ever gonna tell your parents?" Eddy asked one evening while giving Morgan a backrub.

"Don't need to." Southern families operated in a different realm of avoidance, knowing about things but never actually talking about them. "My people have made three great contributions to American culture. One, we buy retail. Two, we make a really terrific gin and tonic. Three, we don't talk about things like that. We can live with a rhinoceros in the living room and call it a credenza."

He elaborated. "When I introduce you to Big Bob and Ladybug—those *are* my parents' nicknames, swear to God—my mother will ask how we met. You can give her any story you want, short of the truth, and it will be fine. It's just her ritual. They will know we live together but never want to know why two grown men are still roommates. The day will come when we visit them in Falls Church, and they will give you the guest room and put me in my old room. I call it The Museum with all my awards and swimming trophies. But they will never ask precisely why I am bringing home this incredibly handsome, sexy single man. Even if we tried explaining, my mother would cut us off with the statement *I'd prefer not to discuss that*. I've heard her say it a million times. That way, she keeps her little world neat and orderly, nothing ugly, nothing unpleasant."

"I saw the movie *Ordinary People*," Eddy said as he rubbed massage oil between the cheeks of Morgan's ass.

"Then you've already met my parents, if you also saw *Cat on a Hot Tin Roof*." Morgan closed his eyes and relaxed, feeling maybe this was finally the Big Night when he would let himself get topped for the first time. "When you grow up in the South, you realize that Tennessee Williams wrote documentaries."

"They ever bring up the subject of marriage?"

"I tell them that I would rather be with no one than with the wrong one. Big Bob and Ladybug hardly ever mention marriage, though, not directly. I told you, my people don't talk about things like that. My younger brother T. J. is the breeder. The big galoot and his wife Josie already have one son and another baby on the way. So I'm off the hook for maintaining the bloodline."

"Your father gave you a copy of *Maurice* for Christmas, right? So Big Bob isn't totally in the dark." Eddy slid his crotch up and down Morgan's backside, now slippery with the warm oil, as he continued massaging. "Most parents just want their kids to be happy. Maybe he was trying to help, you know, giving you a gay love story by a famous writer with a happy ending."

Morgan's whole body hardened like a dead weight under Eddy's hands. "No, the thought never occurred to me," he said finally. "I might need a year of therapy to begin considering that possibility."

"Relax," Eddy said as he tried rubbing the tension out of Morgan's back. "This is gonna feel really, really good. Better than therapy and a lot less expensive."

"First get a rubber," Morgan said as he lay spread eagle. "It makes the cleanup easier."

"Okay, okay!" Eddy reached to the bedside table and opened the drawer. "Anything for my preppy prince."

By the time he tore open the wrapper and unfurled the condom, Morgan's body had tightened so much that Eddy knew this was not the Big Night. They would enjoy some other form of lovemaking, maybe just the Princeton rub, as the votive candle flickered nearby.

Morgan and his parents did not talk very often on the phone. His mother sent a letter every week recounting their lives in the Washington suburbs with concerts, church events, dinner dances at the country club, and the daily routines of her household. She always ended with a sentence like "I just put laundry in the dryer and had better finish this letter before the mailman comes. I don't know where the time goes."

Morgan sent back a letter every week with reports of his legal work, opera performances, gallery openings, local politics, and celebrity-sightings, as long as they were stars like Katherine Hepburn his mother had actually heard of. Not even spotting Greta Garbo at a street market earned him a call from Ladybug, who believed strongly that long distance should be reserved for something drastic, like a death in the family. "My mother doesn't like bad news," he explained to Eddy. "Everything is always fine in my weekly letters. Everything is always *fine* in the Cabell household. Fine, fine, fine."

Unlike Morgan, Eddy spent several hours every week on the phone with his mother, sometimes twice a day, usually speaking the Spanish language that Morgan liked to eavesdrop upon without understanding. His second language was Latin. He caught only the occasional word and proper name, including his own, but he remained fascinated by the musicality of his lover's language when he switched to the Cuban dialect, a singsong lilt completely missing from his English.

Morgan sometimes teased Eddy while he was on the telephone, kneeling between his legs and unzipping his pants, stroking and nibbling through his tighty-whities until he got hard inside, then pulling him out and giving him a slow sex, even bringing him to climax while Eddy kept talking casually to his mother in North Bergen. Morgan horsed around with sex because he learned that he could. Teasing back, Eddy closed his legs and caught Morgan's head between his thighs until he heard the ocean ringing in his ears. Gradually each man discovered the boundaries of his partner's sexual preference, giving and taking erotic pleasures which most of their gay friends with tastes for handcuffs around headboards, harnesses from ceilings, and golden showers in basement bars described as "vanilla sex" despite the frequency that Morgan and Eddy went at each other.

One night someone at a party gave them a bottle of amyl nitrate, but the next morning Eddy complained it gave him a headache, so they stopped snorting poppers. When Morgan finally allowed a VCR into their home, Eddy bought a porn video entitled *Ivy Blues* from a sidewalk vendor near Times Square. The film starred a young Tom Cruise lookalike arriving home from Princeton and lusting after the family chauffeur, ending up in a three-way with the driver and his well-hung brother. But they could never watch more than five minutes before they got so involved in their own lovemaking they completely ignored the video. Once, Eddy asked him to perform some foreplay, and said exactly how much he enjoyed it, but Morgan absolutely refused, even when drunk, to rim him with his tongue before screwing him. "That's *not* going to happen!" A boundary had been set.

On other days, usually overcast days with wind whistling in the window air conditioner, they simply cuddled. Morgan sat reading at one end of the sofa under the pole lamp, maybe listening to some favorite recording like the Adagio from Schumann's Second Symphony or Schwarzkopf singing *The Four Last Songs*. Eddy crossed the shag carpet in stocking feet and joined him, curling up and laying his head in his lover's lap, saying nothing as he closed his eyes and rested beside him. Eddy did not want to talk. He did not want to start a round of lovemaking. He wanted only to lie with his head in his lover's lap. Morgan stroked his hair with his free hand as he kept reading and the stereo kept playing.

Usually the sofa was Morgan's time machine where he traveled mentally into his life's yesteryears where he found grudges and regrets, or into the future where he fretted about nameless dreads, already worrying about Tony's holiday visit and then his summer visit, and even whether the boy, not yet four, would apply for colleges in the New York area, maybe Princeton – and whether he would get admitted, or end up on the waiting list, or get rejected and need to attend UCLA instead. But when Eddy's head rested in his lap, their sofa was world enough. They remained in this cozy stillness for a whole hour perhaps, not chatting and not getting frisky, just quiet in each other's company, until Morgan complained about his leg going to sleep or Eddy jumped up to pee.

When Tony arrived for his first Christmas visit, the youngster was given the spare bedroom, which they pretended was Eddy's bedroom. His father made a great show of sleeping on the foldout sofa in the living room, then sneaked into Morgan's bed every night after his son was asleep with his ragged *nighty*, the faded blue remnant of his baby blanket. Eddy made sure that he was back in the foldout before Tony woke up wanting the sugar-frosted flakes, with the tiger also named Tony on the box, which he demanded for breakfast every morning.

"Boss, boss, boss, just like his mother," Eddy complained as he dragged himself from beneath the covers to set the table. "Must be something in the DNA."

Of course Tony was only three and would not have understood, much less been upset, if Daddy was having a sleepover with Uncle Morgan. On Christmas Eve when he was too excited to sleep, Tony went looking for his father and discovered the empty sofa bed. He kept searching until he found Eddy in bed with Morgan. The boy crawled under the covers and fell asleep beside his papa, clutching his blue nighty and waiting for Santa Claus to arrive with his bag of toys. He was sleeping so quietly, just a little bump under the comforter on the other side of the bed, that Morgan did not notice him when he rose, groggy, in the middle of the night to fetch presents from the hall closet.

At first light, Tony was jumping up and down at the foot of their bed, screaming for them to wake up so they could unwrap presents. Eddy looked embarrassed. Morgan laughed out loud. He loved Christmas and could hardly wait to watch Tony tearing into the gifts under the tree. He had made three separate trips to FAO Schwarz to buy a Lego set, a soccer ball, an Etch-a-Sketch, a GI Joe doll, every toy he thought a boy ought to have. On his last trip, Morgan made an impulse purchase and carried home a gigantic stuffed tiger, so large that it could never travel by airplane back to California. The tiger remained a permanent fixture in their Manhattan apartment, migrating back and forth from the living room to the bedroom, in and out of the hall closet, always a source of minor irritation for Eddy. Morgan defended the practicality of the stuffed tiger. "It's not too soon for Tony to start thinking about Princeton."

So making a home for themselves on the Upper West Side, with their fumbling efforts at parenthood with Tony, filled up their first year until summer arrived and their anniversary approached.

In 1978, Morgan and Eddy celebrated their first anniversary in Santa Fe by accident. They did not know it then, but Santa Fe was a place where people simply ended up. There was a story about how it happened with them. Later they discovered everyone had a story about ending up there.

Morgan never completely outgrew his addiction to exams and graded projects. Early on, he needed to discover whether Eddy would like *Rosenkavalier*, his favorite opera. While Morgan's parents exposed him to German opera from an early age, he never became an opera queen who argued the relative merits of Maria Callas and Renata Tebaldi. He idolized *Parsifal* but thought *La Boheme* was also a musical masterpiece. *My Fair Lady* was alphabetized in his record collection next to *Meistersinger von Nürnberg.* Morgan's whereabouts in their apartment could always be pinpointed by the aria he was whistling, though he was so tone-deaf, one melody sounded pretty much like any other. Whenever he wanted to escape the blues, he whistled Gilbert and Sullivan and knew all the lyrics from *Pinafore.* When put to the test, Eddy earned an A+ when he recognized the *Rosenkavalier* waltz used in the film *Carnal Knowledge.*

As the ultimate test of their ability to survive as a couple, Morgan decided they should spend their first vacation driving across country together. "Why not?" Eddy was ready to take a break from waiting tables when his summer hours got cut and tips were lousy.

Heading west in their rental car with an eight-track tape deck, taking turns listening to Wagner and Village People, they followed the northern route that brought them to San Francisco after speeding almost nonstop through the boring square states. The summer of love from the 1960s had turned into the gay liberation of the 1970s, and the whole community was mobilized against gay-bashers like Anita Bryant, led by Harvey Milk out of his camera shop. Just walking down Castro Street provided an exhilaration which Morgan described as a contact high.

Heading south, they drove the old Pacific Coast Highway to visit Carmel, Big Sur and other fabled places like San Simeon—which thrilled Eddy as the model for Xanadu in *Citizen Kane*—until they reached Los Angeles.

Eddy expected to love LA but hated it. He had spent a month there working as a waiter when Tony was born, but the previous visit did not count because he had no car and never left West Hollywood. "You drive and drive, and when you get there, you can't park!" On this trip, he needed to negotiate with Tara the Bitch—and "make nice" now that she was going through her second divorce and taking back her maiden name, Palermo—so he could spend some extra time with Tony.

Morgan expected to hate LA but was dazzled by the Getty Museum, built as a replica of the Villa dei Papiri in Herculaneum, perched on a slope overlooking the ocean in Malibu. In one gallery he was studying a black-figure calyx with two young men enjoying anal sex, pondering how the young models had been dead for two thousand years, when Morgan was treated to his first Hollywood sighting. Oscar-winner Shelley Winters, too heavyset to walk, was pushed past him in a wheelchair while bitching to her attendant, "I've had it with art. I want a drink!"

The next day he and Eddy explored farther south along the coastline, and Morgan discovered the seaside communities of Venice and Santa Monica. They made a special pilgrimage to the all-male beach nicknamed the Gay Bay, just a stone's throw off the boardwalk, where gym-hardened bodies were spread out on beach towels and tanned hunks sold cocktails from coolers, their blond hair cropped short, military style. A steady breeze blew off the ocean while muscle boys tossed Frisbees in the surf.

Lying back with his third gin and tonic, Morgan watched the jumbo jets taking off from LAX heading for Hawaii or Japan or some other exotic destination. He thought as he watched the airliners sailing high into the blue Pacific sky, he did not want to be anywhere else on the planet. Drinking his iced cocktail, with Eddy stretched out beside him turning pink as he always did when sunning, Morgan felt completely, wholly, entirely content.

Squinting against the glare off the waves, Morgan gazed at Eddy lying on the sand beside him, his back smeared white with sunscreen, regretting that he could not read a history behind a face. To him, these musclemen were like cardboard cutouts, just like the gay men on the sidewalks of New York. His gaze stopped with the face, handsome or at least cute, but he could penetrate no further into the human being behind it. Much as he knew the facts of Eddy's life, much as he knew his body's smells and tastes and movements, awake and asleep, Morgan felt he ought to be able to read beneath the features, the evasive smile, and the sudden set of his jaw when he was surprised or upset.

Eddy had two basic expressions he showed the world. One was a broad smile with super-white teeth, and the other was a blankness so stoically severe that it defeated Morgan's attempts at guessing what his lover was thinking. Both expressions were masks, including the wide grin he bestowed upon restaurant patrons, behind which he could retreat to someplace remote and safe. Some secrets Eddy kept out of pure cussedness. When he went on vacation and stopped shaving for a few days, a small white crescent appeared in the stubble underneath his chin. When asked about the scar, Eddy only teased—"It happened in the wilds of Transylvania!"—as if a sinister mystery instead of some stupid childhood accident, like falling off a bicycle or running with scissors.

So Eddy, never a big talker, was full of surprises. Morgan recalled the evening after six months together when he discovered his lover could play the piano. They were invited to a dinner party at a townhouse in the West Village by a young friend with old money. The home was filled with antiques and artworks wholly at odds with the blond twinkie who owned the showplace, plus a summer home in the Hamptons and a winter retreat in Key West. Eddy was admiring the Steinway when their host Geoff asked if he could play.

"A little."

When Geoff would not stop insisting, Eddy seated himself at the keyboard and paused before launching into a flashy showpiece, his large hands flying over the most difficult octave passages. His performance halted conversation and drew other guests into the living room to listen. "Chopin's Etude No. 12 in C Minor," remarked a dermatologist who had minored in music at Yale, loud enough for everyone to hear.

When Eddy finished and the guests applauded—"Bravo! Bravo!"—Morgan was so astonished that he could only say, "I never knew you could play. I never knew."

"Took lessons when I was a kid. I don't play show tunes, so nobody ask for *Some Enchanted Evening.*"

"You are very, very good."

"My mother made me enter competitions," Eddy replied, closing the keyboard. "Senior year in high school, one competition was in Carnegie Hall."

"My lover performed at Carnegie Hall," Morgan exclaimed, turning to the dermatologist. "Not just another pretty face!"

"Just a student competition, which I didn't win."

Morgan drew Eddy into the library to continue their conversation in private. "Failed as a pianist," Eddy said gloomily. "Hated the pressure of the competitions and hated the sense of being a performing pet, a freak. Then there were these ball-busting pieces by Liszt I could never play, not in a million years, so I just walked away. Tonight's the first time I've touched a keyboard in years. My parents expected lots from me, like the gymnastics."

"You were a gymnast?"

"I told you that."

"No, you didn't."

"Weren't paying attention. I told you about the pommel horse and the parallel bars, my specialties. Taped my wrists, and dusted my palms, and did all that macho he-man stuff. Come on, you watch the muscle boys in the Summer Olympics."

"So what happened?"

"Couldn't do flips. Anything that involved a somersault, I balked, couldn't even try. Some things, I don't know why, I just have blocks about. Like that thing about going to college, just felt blocked."

"My father almost competed in the Summer Olympics in 1952."

"You never told me that. The only Olympics you ever talk about were the Nude Olympics at Princeton, when you and your doctor friend got naked in the snow."

"Big Bob was a champion oarsman. Two-man scull was his specialty, what's officially called Coxless Pairs. Swear to God, I'm not making it up. Are you sure we never talked about this before?"

"I lose track of all the family stuff you *don't* talk about. What kept your pop from competing?"

"Me," Morgan said. "I was born and Big Bob had a family to support, but he kept the letter from the Olympics Committee inviting him to the time trials. A couple of times, I caught him reading it in his study. He keeps it locked in a drawer with other personal papers. I fantasize it's where he hides love letters from some old boyfriend."

"Not Big Bob!"

"No, not Big Bob."

Though not quite a musical prodigy or medal-winning gymnast, Eddy was born a prodigy of sorts in Cuba, a milk-white baby with bright red hair. His family gathered around the crib to marvel at him—this became the mythology that followed him into later life—their admiration mixed with a sense of reproach for a boy so completely different from birth. At school, the nuns singled him out partly because he was quick and bright, passionate about old movies, but so completely unlike other boys, handsome almost to the point of beauty, crazy about clothes and dancing, full of mischief. Once, Sister Mary Martha punished him for writing a four-letter word on the bathroom wall, and later he was caught shoplifting a book from the chapel's gift shop, *The Poetry of St. John of the Cross*. When a Jesuit came to lecture the boys about sexual abstinence before marriage, the white-haired priest ended by asking for questions. Eddy raised his hand, "How does a penis get hard?"

The Sisters of Loretto treated him with a baffling mixture of suspicion and encouragement that left Eddy feeling isolated, confused, and anxious over the whole school experience. He was never given permission to fail, even to be less than perfect. They expected him to attend Fordham because he had top SAT scores— he tested well—but he became a waiter instead, saddening the nuns and angering his parents. The Mallafré men had always been lawyers, journalists, priests, and university professors before Castro took over, and his parents were obsessed with rebuilding their former lives after arriving in America.

After sharing a bed almost every night for a year, Morgan felt Eddy opening up about his New Jersey childhood and trusting that every deep-dark secret would be respected. For all his height and powerful physique, Eddy preserved the quality of a little boy in his nakedness, smooth and cool-skinned, not with shyness or unfamiliarity with the sex act, but with the heart of a child who has been hurt too often. Just as he guarded the secret of the scar on his chin, the little boy learned to conceal his psychic wounds beneath a show of toughness and hot temper.

Still gazing intently at his lover stretched on the towel, Morgan liked this special feeling on Venice Beach, warmed by the sun and cooled by the ocean breeze and iced gin, alone together even though surrounded by scores of other gay men. He even enjoyed getting his hands greasy as he rubbed Eddy's back with sun-block lotion, his lover's body relaxing under his touch until both men got erections that showed through their swimsuits.

Heading back to New York on the return leg of their cross-country odyssey, they took the southern route and ended the first day's journey in Albuquerque. It was late at night when they checked into a motel just off the interstate in the middle of a pelting rainstorm. As he filled out the registration form, Morgan made conversation with the desk clerk, a young Latino man with glistening black hair. "Okay, we're in New Mexico. Are we anywhere near Santa Fe?"

"Santa Fe is an hour north. I can make you a reservation at our hotel there for tomorrow night."

Eddy, hungry and crabby for the past two hours, suddenly perked up. "Why not?"

"Why not!" Morgan was not savoring the long, boring drive across Texas. The desk clerk picked up the phone and made their reservation.

The next morning after a breakfast of green chile omelets, Morgan headed the car northward while Eddy studied the map and translated place names from Spanish. Leaving behind the river valley with its cottonwoods, the highway climbed into dry hill country with dark mesas stretching in the distance. Farther on, their route passed between red outcrops and black volcanic cliffs. Sandy hills were dotted with the dark green of junipers and the lavender green of sagebrush.

"The shrubs are so evenly spaced, probably how desert plants share scarce water," Morgan said. "Neat, tidy, and well-organized. My kind of world."

As Eddy fiddled with the radio to find local stations, thunderheads moved from the west across the whole landscape, lashing out with lightning and trailing purple veils of rainfall. The wind blew dust from surrounding ridges as the storm's course intercepted their own. Then came the sudden downpour. The windshield wipers could hardly keep up as rivulets of rainwater slithered down the side windows. After a cloudburst that lasted only a minute, the summer storm moved off as quickly as it had overtaken them. Thunder grew distant. The sun came out again. Morgan turned off the air conditioning and Eddy, holding tight to his sunglasses, hung his head out his window like a dog riding in a car, repeating over and over, "Smell the air!"

The hill country fell away behind and the mountains drew closer. A broad plateau forced the highway to ascend at a steep angle taxing the Volvo's horsepower. Then they crested the last ridge and saw two rainbows arching over Santa Fe. "Don't tell me it's an omen," Morgan said. "There was a storm and now there is sunshine. Rainbows happen."

Exiting the highway, they followed the Old Santa Fe Trail curving its way to the center of town. The whole world turned brown adobe, every building a slightly different earth tone, nowhere a right angle. Their hotel's architecture was modeled after a famous pueblo with its flat roofs and rising terraces. Beside the hotel stood a medieval-looking church built in imitation of Sainte Chapelle in Paris. "Beautiful and strange, on the verge of surrealistic," Morgan said as he steered into the parking lot. "We like surrealistic, don't we?"

"Doesn't this place remind you of Bedrock from *The Flintstones?* You expect to see Fred and Barney coming around the corner. Yabba-dabba-doo!"

"You really know how to ruin a guy's bliss."

The desk clerk asked as they registered, "Are you here for the opera?"

"Opera?" Morgan replied with astonishment. "There's opera here?"

"I can get two tickets for tonight's performance. We have a shuttle running directly to the opera north of town."

"Why not?" Eddy piped up.

"Why not!" Then Morgan asked as an afterthought, "What's playing tonight?"

The clerk checked his schedule. "*Rosenkavalier.*"

Eddy leaned over and whispered, "Don't tell me it's an omen. Strauss happens."

Once in their room, Morgan checked his address book and found that he had a law school classmate living in Santa Fe. When he called the office, Joel answered his own phone. He said that he was really glad to hear from Morgan. His office was only a couple of blocks away. He would reschedule an appointment so they could have lunch together.

"I don't know who I was just talking to," Morgan said when he hung up. "The man I just talked to is *not* the same power-driven, work-obsessed jerk I knew at Virginia, never someone to reschedule a business appointment for anything or anybody. Living in Santa Fe must have done something to him."

Joel already had a table when they joined him for lunch in the courtyard of the old hacienda in the heart of town. A stone fountain gushed in the center of the plazuela, and a massive cottonwood shaded the secluded garden of pink peonies, yellow snapdragons, and lavender. When Joel was halfway through his salad—he had become a vegetarian, too—he nodded at the tree. "The cottonwood is named Bill." Eddy gave Morgan his deadpan look with eyes opened wide in disbelief.

Instead of rushing back to his office after lunch, Joel took them on a walking tour of the downtown plaza, Eddy disappearing whenever they passed a restaurant and coming back with another menu for his collection. As a Virginian, Morgan loved old things and felt most comfortable in places rich in human history. Starved for antiquity after California, he trailed behind Joel, the former jerk who now provided legal services *pro bono* to three Indian pueblos, thinking how many astonishing things must have happened in this town over the centuries, and how many men had lived hard, heroic lives here.

After an early dinner that evening, Morgan and Eddy sat on the third-floor terrace outside their hotel room, just the two of them, drinking margaritas before dressing for the opera. Westward, the sunset turned fiery gold before shading toward purple. Two great ravens, soaring against the breeze, seemed suspended above the tree-lined river. The town's hush was disturbed only by the tolling of the cathedral bells. The air was dry and thin, almost as intoxicating as the tequila. When the cathedral's twin towers finished chiming the hour, Morgan interrupted the lull in their conversation. He had a strange look when he turned to his lover, "I think we belong here."

Eddy also looked dazed when he replied, "I think we *do* belong here."

Morgan reached across and took his hand. "Let's stay an extra day. Let's celebrate our first anniversary here tomorrow night."

"Today *is* our first anniversary," Eddy corrected him, giving his hand a hard squeeze.

"I thought it was tomorrow. I had the desk clerk make a reservation at the restaurant he swears has the most authentic New Mexican food in town, a place called Tía Léona's."

"Depends how you mark your calendar. You probably calculate from meeting in Central Park after midnight, which was a Sunday. Wrong! I figure from when I spotted you at Studio before midnight, which was a Saturday, exactly one year ago today."

"So we discovered Santa Fe on our first anniversary. What are the odds?"

Later that evening during the opera's first act while the Marschallin bade her bittersweet farewell to love and youth—"*Die Zeit, die ist ein sonderbar Ding!*"— the audience watched through the wide-open back of the stage as a gigantic orange moon rose into the night sky above the desert. Morgan gripped Eddy's arm and whispered, "We've got to come back here."

"Shhh! We're here now. Listen to the fat lady."

The same full moon hung high among the stars when they toppled into bed, long after midnight, and made love in the silver light streaming through open windows.

A year later, they were back with Ethan and his wife Meredith to celebrate their second anniversary. Morgan had fixated on Santa Fe as the one place they needed to keep coming back, also the place where he needed to have a serious discussion with Eddy about their relationship.

Their hotel room was connected with the Rees family's suite by the same terrace. Here in the morning, the two couples took their coffee and enjoyed the sunshine. Before bedtime, they shared nightcaps while marveling at the million stars flickering in the New Mexican sky. "Truly the land of enchantment," Ethan remarked as he finished his bourbon.

"Always the great phrasemaker, old sport. You should write the Great American Novel," Morgan teased. "I have the perfect title—*A Cry of Seagulls*—about a bunch of pirates tumbling through a crack in the time-space continuum."

"Now I understand why the vote wasn't unanimous when they elected you captain of the swim team."

On their first evening in Santa Fe, two days before, Eddy had started wondering about their dinner reservation. Morgan made these bookings weeks ahead of time, but he had disappeared. So Eddy walked across the terrace and through the French doors looking for Ethan and Meredith. "Knock, knock! Is my Aunt Minnie in here?"

Inside, he found Morgan lying with Ethan, side by side, propped up on their elbows facing each other, only a couple of feet apart on the large bed. In between them, on his blue blanket decorated with *Star Wars* characters, slept Baby Josh. Morgan and Ethan were simply laughing quietly over some joke they just shared, while the infant napped peacefully between them. In years to come, Joshua Rees would grow into an athletic six-footer, he would become a documentary filmmaker and recovering cocaine addict, and he would marry the daughter of a famous Japanese novelist, but he would always remained "Baby Josh" to Morgan and Eddy.

Slumping in the doorway, Eddy thought that he ought to feel jealous and actually did experience a throb of hurt somewhere in his gut. But he knew there was nothing to feel jealous about, except Morgan shared prior history with Ethan when they got drunk one night and had sex in a dorm room, long before the two of them first met at Studio 54. He felt permanently excluded from the four years they shared together as undergraduates at Princeton. Ethan had taught Morgan to play squash. Morgan taught him about classical music and made him into a big fan of Wagner's operas. Ethan's favorite remained *Parsifal*. Eddy was painfully aware how far away he was at the time, working his first job as a waiter at a neighborhood Cuban restaurant in a completely different part of New Jersey.

Morgan glanced over, "Hungry?"

"You bet."

Ethan said, "As soon as Meredith finishes putting on her makeup, which can take forever, we can head out."

Eddy sat on the sofa. "Morgan can shower, dress, and get out the door in five minutes."

"I'm famous for being quick in the bathroom, also in the bedroom."

Ethan stifled a snicker. Eddy was already upset by the sight of his lover on the bed with the object of his early romantic obsession and could not help a wiseass remark. "Do you know how to tell you're getting middle-aged?"

He was going to say, "It's when your lover's ex-boyfriends are all doctors and lawyers." But he paused, caught himself, and weighed the remark. Sometimes he had the presence of mind to ask himself before opening his mouth: Is it true? Is it kind? Is it necessary? This was a restraint that Sister Mary Martha drummed into the kids in junior high.

So he said instead, "It's when you start having dinner at 5:30."

Strange for someone trained as a lawyer, Morgan hated arguments, and so did Eddy. They never shouted even when drunk. Nobody ever slammed a door or smashed a dish. The little things they got out and got over. When Eddy felt some grievance was true and necessary, he said what was on his mind. Not Morgan. He brooded over hurt feelings so his lover needed to ask questions and guess why.

On those occasions when Eddy did become furious about something—always Eddy—they would inflict each other with the silent treatment for maybe a whole day. The spat was usually caused by something completely trivial—in Morgan's opinion—such as the time that he referred to Eddy's parents as *immigrants*. Or he told a cruel joke about nuns: "What's black and white, black and white, black and white?" Or he kidded about their relationship as a *mixed marriage*. Or he asked Eddy to translate what Ricky Ricardo was saying when "that crazy Cuban" started ranting during an episode of *I Love Lucy*.

After the initial explosion, Eddy became angry-silent and ran the vacuum, while Morgan was hurt-silent and sat reading under his pole lamp, sometimes so upset he locked himself in the bathroom and threw up. They persisted in stony silence all through dinner and all through an evening of *M*A*S*H* reruns on television, until it was bedtime and they crawled between the covers. Then they turned to each other without talking and made love, waking the next morning almost as if nothing had happened, a little awkward at first, maybe making love again, and then started the day as they always did with a kiss.

Later during the day Morgan would get around to apologizing—always Morgan—and everything was smoothed over and forgotten and never mentioned again. Soon, both men were talking excitedly as they caught up on the conversation stored up from the night before. Each of Eddy's blowups gave Morgan some new insight into his lover's sensitive points, such as the reference to *that crazy Cuban*, which he could later use to tease and needle him.

Something tremendous had happened with their first kiss beside the lake in Central Park. Maybe somehow Eddy's DNA had been imprinted upon his own, Morgan theorized, and they were no longer disconnected men, their two lives like a double helix binding in elegant arcs, separate but together. Not that they clung to each other like Velcro. They never wore matching shirts. Though almost the same size, Eddy shorter by a couple of inches, they never traded each other's coats or slacks and always needed separate closets.

Eddy never said anything, but he hated all the Princeton orange in Morgan's wardrobe. His lover owned orange-striped ties, orange polo shirts, orange socks, even a pair of orange boxer shorts. He also wore monogrammed shirts and packed madras shorts when staying with friends at the beach. Fortunately Morgan believed grown men should wear shorts only at the beach and the gym, but he did own a seersucker jacket and thought mallards made good ornaments. He even wore paisley! He didn't owned a single pair of Italian shoes, only wingtips, topsiders, saddle bucks, penny loafers, weejuns with tassels, and a really ugly pair of something called duck boots from L. L. Bean.

Once as a gag, Eddy bought him *The Official Preppy Handbook* and was horrified when Morgan treated it as a lifestyle Bible confirming that he went to the right universities and had the right career. Eau Sauvage was the right cologne, Tanqueray was the right gin, Brooks Brothers sold the right men's clothes, and a Volvo was the right foreign car. The paperback became dog-eared over the years as Morgan kept it beside the toilet for ready reference.

Their relationship was like a Venn diagram. At least that is how Claire described them one night when she drank too many Long Island iced teas, got sloppy sentimental, and needed to be poured into a taxi for a safe trip home. The two men had a one big area of overlap, mostly in the sex department, but otherwise they did not coincide—which would have meant lopping off spare parts—which would have meant diminishing as individuals.

Typically they went their separate ways. If Morgan wanted to attend an opera and Eddy didn't, he went anyway. If Eddy wanted to go dancing with friends after work and Morgan was too tired, he went anyway. Once their friend Mark phoned to say he was not meeting them at Lincoln Center because his new boyfriend did not like opera. "I don't want to see *La Boheme* if I can't share the experience with Roger." Morgan clutched the receiver and cringed. Later when he reported the conversation, Eddy cringed.

The same when they attended the holy union for two lesbian friends at the MCC Church. The women held two candles which they used to light a third. Then they blew out their separate candles while the minister explained they had merged their lives into a single union, represented by the flame of the single candle. Eddy turned to Morgan and made his deadpan expression with brown eyes opening wide with disapproval.

Besides their secret looks, the two men developed a shorthand in their conversations and could share a laugh by repeating only the punch line of a favorite joke. Eddy could say something completely out of the blue—"If Princess Margaret had been here, we could have saved the Rolls Royce!"—and Morgan would crack up while nobody else understood why.

They shared a love for Edward Gorey's cartoons and could recite the whole *Gashlycrumb Tinies* by trading off the lines. Eddy would begin, "A is for Amy who fell down the stair." Then Morgan followed suit until they reached the end, "Z is for Zillah who drank too much gin."

They went through a period during the early 1980s addicted to recordings of Ruth Draper's comic monologues. Eddy could hardly speak three sentences without lifting a line from one of her routines, like *Don't make me laugh—'cuz I'm on my way to a funeral*. It was a line he had far too many opportunities to recall as their generation of gay men drew further into the 1980s.

So they went their separate ways and almost never argued. But if something really bothered Eddy, he got it out, which he did later that night in Santa Fe after discovering Morgan and Ethan lying side by side on the bed with Baby Josh napping between them.

"So tell me," Eddy said as he slipped between the sheets, "how many times did you and the good doctor have sex?"

"Just once."

"How'd it happen?"

"The way Princetonians always have sex. First we got drunk."

"I never understood how you ended up at Princeton in the arms of the good doctor. You're such a Southerner, you should have gone to Duke."

"Princeton is the northernmost Southern university. It's a well-known true fact. Besides, Big Bob went there so it was expected."

"You talk about the South all the time, but you never go home, like you hate it or something."

"I don't hate the South, only it's boring and a tough place to be gay. No opera, no art galleries, and hardly any ethnic restaurants."

"Back to the good doctor. Did he bottom for you?"

"Don't get gross."

"I like details."

"I never asked for details about your first sex with Cousin Frankie."

"It was an overnighter with two fourteen-year-olds in the same double bed. We jerked each other off. End of story. Now we're talking about Ethan Rees, lacrosse hunk and super-stud, God's gift to women, except for that one night. Enquiring minds want to know."

"He was really curious, experimental, even wanted to try poppers. It's the scientist in him."

"Did you talk about it later? Did Ethan like sucking cock?"

"You know my people don't talk about things like that."

"Come on, you and Ethan never talked about fucking?"

"No, sir, we talked about Nietzsche. The closest he ever came to mentioning it was on the squash court, when he mumbled something about *an aroused penis has no conscience.*"

"He still loves you."

"Does not."

"Does too! The two of you always end up walking ahead of me and Meredith—yak yak yak yak—in your own private world. Anyone watching the four of us would guess that you and Ethan were lovers, and I was Meredith's hubby pushing the stroller."

"We're just catching up," Morgan muttered before falling silent.

"What bugs me a little, just a little, is that you were in love with Ethan. You still are."

"Am not."

"Are too! You're the sort of man who never falls *out* of love."

"You're right," Morgan said at last. "I do everything for the rest of my life. I'm going to the gym for the rest of my life. I'm watching calories for the rest of my life. *And* I'm going to love you and stay with you for the rest of my life."

Morgan rolled over on his stomach. "Got any massage oil?"

"The Big Night at last?"

"I never fantasize about sex with any other man," he whispered as Eddy grabbed a rubber from the suitcase. "Not even Ethan."

Next day, they had a reservation for dinner at Tía Léona's because Eddy had decided the year before that the restaurant did serve the most authentic New Mexican food in Santa Fe. It became their favorite local eatery, not pretentious for the tourists, a place that felt old-fashioned and authentic, its walls hung with photographs of the old Spanish families. Meredith nodded to the two framed photographs showing the same Spanish man, first as a teenager and then a father with his four small sons, both posed beside the same gnarled tree. "Anything is an excuse for art in Santa Fe."

Morgan said, "Gays always know the right places."

Eddy added, "But we don't always know where the right places are."

"Comedy of Errors. That's the story of our lives, how we found each other and how we discovered Santa Fe last summer."

Officially they were celebrating the second anniversary of Morgan and Eddy. After another round of margaritas, they were celebrating the arrival of Ethan's firstborn son. Morgan had stood at the font during his baptism at Holy Trinity Episcopal, the venerable old church on Lower Broadway, and accepted responsibility as Baby Josh's godfather. With his unerring sense of timing, Eddy made the whole company laugh when he leaned over and said in a loud stage whisper, "Always a godfather, never a god."

"I've got a question," Ethan said after losing count of the number of rounds. "We know our anniversary because it's the date of our wedding."

"Morgan was best man," Meredith said to Eddy, "and so handsome in his tux, I wondered if I was marrying the wrong Princetonian as I came down the aisle and saw the two of them standing side by side at the altar."

"Where I come from, it's the groom who runs off with the best man."

Ethan tried sounding serious. "Okay, I've got a really important question. I want to know is how gay couples know when to celebrate *their* anniversary?"

Morgan and Eddy volleyed replies.

"It was the day we met."

"It was the first time we had sex."

"It was the day we fell in love."

"It was the day Eddy decided to move in."

"It was when Morgan wanted us to live together."

"Yes, sir," Morgan concluded, "and it was all the same twenty-four hour period."

"Just need to decide which side of midnight."

"So we take turns, alternating years."

"It's what the nuns called a movable feast."

Later while finishing desserts, Ethan stole off to settle the bill so there would be no argument over who paid. Eddy excused himself for the men's room and took a detour to compliment the chef. The owner, Sara Baca, young-looking at sixty, sat at the counter sorting orders as her bright brown eyes kept close watch on every activity in her kitchen. They had a nice talk.

Speaking Spanish, Eddy asked about a couple of recipes, and she explained some of her special ingredients, but was very secretive about her famous *mole* sauce. "I'm not telling, so you're gonna die wondering." When she switched abruptly to English, Eddy detected the trace of a British accent, something as unexpected as the jar of Marmite above the stove. They took an instant liking to each other, and not many years later, an item called Tía Sara's Piñon Nut Pie appeared on the dessert menu of the restaurant Eddy opened on West 76th Street.

When Eddy and Ethan had left the table, Morgan found himself alone with Meredith for the first time during all the years they had known each other. As he ran his finger along the rim of his glass to collect the salt, Morgan thought what a striking woman she was, already reclaiming the figure of an avid tennis player after her pregnancy. He recalled her legendary self-control, how she kept a bowl of M&Ms on her kitchen counter to have *just one or two* whenever she felt like a treat. He could not imagine that degree of self-restraint, taking just one or two of anything that tasted good.

Wandering in his private thoughts, Morgan was jerked back to the present moment when Meredith started talking in an intimate tone that he had never heard before. "When I met Ethan in high school, he was so intense. All that he ever thought about was lacrosse and science labs. I was relieved we went to different colleges because our parents considered us practically engaged already. What happened at Princeton made Ethan into the man I really wanted to marry. He loosened up. He had more interests. He learned about classical music. He read *The New Yorker*. He became, well, more fun to be around."

"The whole point of a Princeton education is to produce intelligent readers of *The New Yorker*. It's a well-known true fact."

"The classroom didn't change him. He didn't learn to love *Parsifal* from a professor. I know you could be a bad influence, too, the night of the Nude Olympics when you dragged him out of bed to streak the campus. Did you think he didn't tell me how you made him romp around naked in the snow? I just wanted to say I'm grateful for *everything* that happened at Princeton to make Ethan a better husband."

Morgan grew uncomfortable with this conversation as he stared down at his sundae, muttering, "I leave them better than I found them."

"Did you know I experimented sexually at Wellesley? Her name was Nona. We met in a senior seminar on Virginia Woolf. I hate the expression LUG—lesbian until graduation—but I can hardly point the finger, blaming you for getting Ethan drunk and taking advantage of him."

Back from the kitchen, Eddy seated himself beside Morgan and tried catching the waiter's eye for more hot water for his tea. Ethan returned and took his time finishing his piñon nut pie. Morgan stared glumly at his melting ice-cream, pondering Ethan's version of their one-night stand, probably the same version he told himself by casting *him* as the seducer, while Meredith talked excitedly about visiting the flea market north of town at Tesuque.

But they did not visit the flea market the next afternoon. Baby Josh was cranky, so Meredith stayed with him at the hotel. Ethan spent the afternoon beside the pool, getting a little sun while catching up on back issues of *The New Yorker*. His rotations as an intern kept him so busy he had trouble keeping up.

Morgan and Eddy struck out on their own in the morning, driving their rental car up the high road to Taos, past the Nambé pueblo and into the badlands farther north. In the middle of nowhere, where a red metal gate opened onto an old ranch road, Morgan pulled over so they could walk through the juniper range.

Wearing the brand-new cowboy hat Eddy gave him as an anniversary present, Morgan felt drawn to a landscape that lacked clutter and reduced detail. There were ridges and gullies and piñon slopes, then more ridges and gullies and piñon slopes. The dry hillsides were so stark every living thing stood out. It was a clean place, unpeopled. White-faced cattle grazed among the chamisa bushes and cholla cactus. The men's pathway rose through arroyos dotted with yellow scruff. Small holes concealed the burrows where pocket mice and kangaroo rats slept away the heat of the day. Everywhere there were signs of water, with deep gulches and sandy washes littered with the debris of flashfloods, but for miles around the arid earth stretched away without sign of stream or pond, not a drop of water.

When Morgan turned around to see how high they had ascended into the hills, he gazed across the Rio Grande where he spotted buildings stretching across the far-off plateau beneath volcanic peaks. Puffy clouds cast shadows on the mesas. He did not realize that he was looking at the Los Alamos Lab. If he had known, Morgan would have begun explaining about Robert Oppenheimer's work on the atomic bomb in the top-secret facility, then recalling lines from the *Bhagavad Gita* as he watched the mushroom cloud rising above the desert, "Now I am become death, the destroyer of worlds."

The two hikers continued wandering through shades of yellowness. A dust devil whipped along the gully before disappearing over the ridge. Further on, a meadowlark perched on the gatepost as they approached a barbed wire fence. Only its singing intruded upon the monotone of the desert. When Eddy complained about his face getting burned without his sun-block lotion—really a ploy for preventing his partner from walking endlessly into the scrub oaks of the foothills— Morgan took the hint.

"The desert is the loveliest and saddest landscape in the world," Eddy said as they walked back down the ranch road beneath wisps of cloud drift. "It's where the Little Prince appeared on earth, then disappeared."

Morgan turned to him with a wistful look.

"Gotcha!" Eddy exclaimed. "You're way too easy to psyche out, no street smarts, not enough common sense to leave a burning building. It's a miracle you never got mugged."

"Ha ha. You're so far behind the curve, you think you're first."

Back in the car, they drove northward until the road descended into the red-flaked valley of Chimayó where fast-running rivers converged among farm fields and cottonwood groves. The young men enjoyed a lunch of green chile stew and sopaipías at an old hacienda converted into a restaurant popular with tourists. Their table was nestled in a corner beneath an old photograph of the family matriarch, operatic-looking with her dark eyes and black rebozo, identified with a handwritten label as Trinidad Jaramillo.

Further down the roadway, they visited the Sanctuary Chapel, sometimes called the Lourdes of the Americas because of the miracle-working earth. The church's twin towers of brown stucco leaned at odd angles. Pigeons roosted, cooing, in the rafters above the old bronze bell. Inside, discarded crutches lined the wall of the tiny chapel where pilgrims dug the healing soil from a pit in the floor. Leaving the dank-smelling room with its gaudy religious paintings and plaster saints, Morgan forgot to stoop—"Son of a bitch!"—and banged his head on the low doorway.

Morgan pressed his handkerchief to his forehead because he knew from Boy Scout first aid that even small head wounds were notorious bleeders. He found some shade where he could sit down beside a fast-flowing acequia in front of the church. Settling beside him, Eddy took off his shoes and dangled his feet in the water. While Morgan thumbed the guidebook with his free hand, Eddy turned and gave a strange look. "I have this weird feeling we've been here together before. Think maybe we came here in a previous lifetime?"

"Another *gotcha*? You must think I'm totally retarded to fall for another psyche-out."

"No kidding, I think we sat in this same place before. I had my feet in the stream, and you were lecturing me about the church. Like an old movie you sit halfway through before realizing you've seen it before."

"Fool me once, shame on you. Fool me twice. . . Any moron can finish *that* old saying." Morgan returned to his guidebook to read aloud about the Black Christ hanging above the altar.

Later in the gift shop, Eddy bought a silver crucifix hollowed out to contain some of the healing soil. From that day on, he always wore this cross with the church-dirt inside whenever he flew in an airplane or had an important business meeting. "You're so superstitious, muchacho, you'd make a good sailor," Morgan remarked as he helped fasten the silver chain around Eddy's neck.

"You grow up Catholic, it's hard to know where religion stops and superstition starts, especially if you're educated by the nuns."

Driving back to Santa Fe, they arrived in time to shop for a painting by some local artist. They moved from one gallery to the next, advancing by stages to Canyon Road where painters were opening their studios to the public. Morgan liked these informal galleries better. With no tolerance for ugliness, he felt a visceral disgust at the clichéd paintings churned out for tourists from Texas, landscapes with mauve sages and aqua-blue junipers, or coyotes in bandanas howling at crescent moons. He wanted something old and authentic, not Southwest schlock.

Somewhere on the far side of the river, Morgan folded the city map and they began drifting. Eddy liked exploring dirt roads where local men, repairing their old cars, bickered with each other in Spanish under the hoods. Soon the sightseers found themselves at an intersection where five roads converged at odd angles, and the town's main irrigation ditch, lined by knotted elms, disappeared beneath the pavement. Morgan asked, "Well, muchacho, shall we take the road less traveled?"

"I've trusted you this far. But if you don't stop calling me *muchacho*, you're gonna be really sorry tonight."

So they turned down the dirt road. No street sign marked this empty byway that curved back and forth with the contour of the hills, past low-slung houses untouched by renovation, their yards shaded by cottonwoods and feathery tamarisks. After the first bend, they were already far off the tourist track. Morgan had an eerie sense of stepping through some mysterious portal, as if they were walking backward in time where everything modern disappeared. Giant sunflowers peeked over the tops of cedar fences. A cat lapped from a puddle left by the previous evening's downpour. The window frames were painted blue, in shades from indigo and turquoise to a deep sky-blue, the color of the Virgin's mantle, to keep evil spirits from entering these simple homes. Even the mailboxes were painted blue. A hummingbird whirred overhead for a moment before darting off.

"It's as if," Morgan muttered, "we've stepped over a bridge into some corner of the Elder Days and are walking into a world that isn't anymore."

They found only one art gallery down this lone dirt road. Its sign was weathered and faded. The outside walls were overgrown with honeysuckle and climbing roses, and the yard had become a forest of hollyhocks waving in the afternoon breeze. "Why not?" asked Morgan.

"Why not!"

Morgan opened the wooden gate and walked toward the door of the old adobe house. Inside, something happened that altered their lives together in the years to come. Inside, something was said that saved their lives more than two decades in the future. . .

Though located next to their hotel, the Loretto Chapel was the last place they visited as tourists with Ethan and Meredith in 1979. The church was famous for its spiral staircase that had no visible supports, just steps swirling upward into the sanctuary's interior space. Their guidebook told the story how a mysterious man in black, a carpenter by trade, built the staircase without using any nails, then disappeared without accepting payment from the nuns who ran the school nearby. When the mother superior went to the lumberyard to settle the account, she was informed that no planks had been supplied. Later, scientific tests indicated the wood came from a species of fir tree not even native to New Mexico.

It was the design, though, that visitors marveled at. The staircase should have collapsed because no central pillar provided support. Its sturdiness was impossible from an engineering viewpoint but it had remained strong for more than a century. "I love it," Morgan whispered in the hush of the chapel, "when something stands the test of time that shouldn't."

"That's how Sister Mary Martha explained a miracle—when it's impossible for something to happen, until it does."

"That's the official Catholic definition of a miracle?"

"My old math teacher used to say *you can phone the Pope if you don't believe me.*"

"William James was right. Mankind benefits from a practical belief in God even if God doesn't really exist. Hence we need the *idea* of miracles whether or not we actually believe in them. The story of the staircase doesn't need to be true, like jackalopes. Everybody knows what they are. There are photographs on postcards. Jackalopes don't actually exist, of course, and the same gimmickry applies to the church-dirt in your crucifix. If you believe that the soil gives you good luck and good health, it probably will, not because the dirt itself is miraculous but because you *believe.*"

"Putting up with a pompous lover for two whole years, now *that's* what I call miraculous. You deserve to be smacked hard and sent back to Sunday school."

Morgan imitated Eddy's tough-guy voice. "You wanna see a miracle? Huh? I got your miracle right here!"

Later that evening when they said goodnight to Ethan and Meredith, after nightcaps on the hotel terrace beneath a sky electrical with starlight, Morgan had changed his mind about a formal relationship contract. What was said in the old art gallery down the dirt road altered the way he understood his friendship with Eddy. After spending weeks rehearsing the conversation about spelling out the terms of their love affair in black and white, Morgan ripped into little pieces the elaborate "partnership agreement" concealed at the bottom of his suitcase.

With no explanation, Morgan took a sheet of hotel stationery and wrote down only two sentences. He signed his full name at the bottom of the page the way he did with other legal documents—Morgan Carr Cabell—and passed it across the table.

Morgan watched and waited, sitting back in the rawhide chair in tense silence while his lover, with his blankest expression, stared at the piece of paper. Finally Eddy broke the silence, "No problem." He took the pen and signed his full name—Eduardo Blas Toboro D'Ainadamar Mallafré-Corrasco.

This small page of hotel stationery became an heirloom they kept in the drawer of their bedside table, along with photographs of Tony at ages three, four, five and six, as well as their lubricant and condoms. Walking quietly into the bedroom on stocking feet in the years to come, Eddy sometimes found Morgan sitting on the edge of the bed, looking at the single page. Not that he was reviewing the contract with a lawyer's eye. It was the world's easiest agreement to understand in only two sentences:

Whatever I do, I will never leave you.
Whatever you do, I will never leave you.

7

Never Leaving You

Morgan and Eddy—New York, 1987

Eddy had grown accustomed to Morgan's obsession with birthdays and anniversaries. The calendar read July 1987, which meant they were marking ten years together in one more month. Morgan planned parties far ahead of time and already was mailing out invitations. They were celebrating with a champagne brunch, which meant that Eddy's restaurant would cater.

Years before when the Italian bistro down the block closed, Eddy asked Morgan's advice on financing and took over the lease. Morgan said it sounded like a terrific idea and long overdue. Because Eddy was too proud to ask his own parents, Morgan borrowed money from Big Bob to bankroll the opening and cover expenses for the first year of operation. It was a small restaurant with only fifteen tables, most of them doubles, a tiny kitchen, and just enough room for five stools at a bar. Eddy decided the neighborhood needed a place for people to eat after work, stylish but not pretentious, nothing expensive, very friendly, with a simple menu, fast service, and quick turnover. He began with a combination of American and Continental items, as well as a few Cuban dishes passed along from Aunt Lourdes, such as yuca con mojo, lechón asado, ropa vieja and flan diplomático, appearing from time to time as daily specials on the chalkboard.

The restaurant became a new focus for the two men's lives together. Every night after work Morgan dined at the corner table always reserved for him, and Eddy took a break from the kitchen so he could share the meal. He had been a waiter long enough to have an unerring instinct who would be a good food server, who not, and who showed up stoned on drugs. He knew how to cook and manage, but hired capable assistants, so the business would not take over the life he shared with Morgan.

"Your food is always great, with interesting recipes, large portions and super service," Morgan said regularly as encouragement. "I'd eat here even if my meal wasn't free and I wasn't having red-hot sex with the owner. You're so talented, hardworking and passionate about cooking, not to mention you work the room like a Kennedy, you're a natural for success in the restaurant business."

Eddy stared down at his plate. "Not like I'm a big shot Wall Street attorney."

"Your work makes many more people happy than mine." Morgan reached under the table and grabbed Eddy by the knee. "If it wasn't for the money thing, and the fact I can't boil water except for making coffee, I'd quit my job as a pettifogging shyster and join you in the kitchen."

"Then maybe *Gourmet* would review my greasy spoon."

On a slow evening with rain or snow, Morgan lingered over his wine and Eddy brought out the backgammon board for a few quick games. Though Morgan was competitive, he became so easily distracted by conversation that his partner usually won. Eddy needled him, "You're such a left-brain thinker, no wonder you can't play this game worth shit. You've got no street smarts, either, and not sense enough to leave a burning building."

"If being right-brained means forgetting appointments and never balancing your checkbook, like a certain crazy Cuban I know, maybe it's fortunate that one of us is left-brained. Besides, maybe I have *un*common sense. Ever think of that?"

While Eddy became more successful over the years, Morgan tempered his professional ambitions and revised the script of his life's story so that he no longer aimed at making partner in his law firm. He refused fourteen-hour days, determined to safeguard his personal life for enjoying movies and opera performances and five-mile runs in the park—and letting his lover beat him at backgammon.

Every day he looked forward to a "date" with Eddy, if only for their evening meal together, while the restaurant owner kept jumping up to handle problems in the kitchen and greet regular customers. Even if Eddy was pressed into service as a waiter when one of the staff phoned in sick, Morgan liked sitting quietly at their corner table, nursing his wine and smiling at what they had become together.

But Morgan and Eddy were not like most other gay couples in Manhattan. They remained sexually faithful to each other without ever once discussing whether theirs was a monogamous relationship. They were large men, athletic and straight-acting, yet they were openly affectionate in public. On Fire Island during their first vacation late in the summer of 1977, Morgan and Eddy started holding hands in broad daylight when walking on the beach. It just happened.

"I'm glad we don't need to discuss every little thing," Morgan said one rainy night while finishing his flan diplomático before breaking out the backgammon board.

"I know a waitress who stopped being a lesbian because she got tired of always discussing Our Relationship with her girlfriend."

"Marxists are worse. They need to discuss the whole socioeconomic meaning of homosexuality in the political context of bourgeois American culture in the postmodern era. They went from the *love that dare not speak its name* to the *love that won't shut up about it.*"

Back in the city after their first beach vacation, they held hands when strolling the sidewalks in the West Village. But their boundary for hand-holding extended to Washington Square, not beyond.

Meanwhile Tony showed every sign of turning out straight for real. Even as a little boy, he liked watching baseball on television but showed no interest in men's gymnastics. Dirty jeans remained on the bedroom floor where he dropped them.

When he was twelve, Tony went on his first real date, escorting Ethan's daughter Meghan to a dance at her school. The boy was self-conscious about his new braces for closing the gap in his front teeth. His mother, bossy as ever, had insisted upon Eddy paying the orthodontist bills, even though he pointed out that the teeth-gap ran on her side of the family, not his.

Eddy stood in the doorway of his restaurant, nursing a cup of tea while waiting for the hour to arrive when he would catch a cab to pick up the preteen couple. "Where did I go wrong as a father?"

"You're just upset because your son is out on his first date, and you're feeling old."

"No, I feel middle-aged—which is a whole lot worse."

Morgan gave his ass a squeeze. "You're the sweet bird of youth and always will be."

But all was not utopia.

Much as he loved Eddy and loved the life they shared together, Morgan felt unhappy at some very deep emotional level. He grieved how much of his old life's freedom among bushes in Central Park had been left behind forever, and he grew restless with the feeling that *something* was missing, something that would keep his life from becoming boring, boring, boring.

While on their cross-country odyssey to California during their first full summer together, Eddy detected the main differences between their temperaments. "I'm energetic and you're nervous. I'm excited about stuff but you're driven," he remarked somewhere in Wyoming. "Everything is black or white in your world. I always wonder whether new people can be useful, funny or at least ornamental, but you hurry up and make them right or wrong. Usually wrong."

The differences ran even deeper. Morgan brought with him some vast discontent, an oceanic ache deep at his emotional core, and this sad restlessness was something no man's love could reach. Eddy filled an emotional void starting from their first night together, but as the years passed and Morgan's illusions about life dropped away, the great psychological void grew bigger. His world seemed covered with a thin layer of ash, like a landscape after the eruption of a volcano, stealing color and smothering life. He was plagued with the narcissism of a man staring obsessively at his own reflection, and hating what he saw. Sometimes he felt like Blanche DuBois. He didn't want reality, he wanted magic.

So Morgan drank. His parents drank, his Princeton classmates drank, his colleagues drank after work, and all their gay friends drank in the bars. It was their culture. He had a cocktail or two after work "to take the edge off"—and then at some point in the mid-1980s switched from vodka tonics to vodka martinis. He had a few glasses of wine every night at Eddy's restaurant "because it is civilized"— and then started ordering bottles. He drank a bourbon or two at bedtime "to help me sleep"—and then it became three or four large tumblers.

When he drank, he felt a huge sense of relief all the way down to his fingertips and further down, to wherever the oceanic ache lurked deep inside. The world looked mean and ugly when he saw it through sober eyes, but the world started looking beautiful after three vodka martinis. The grayness was replaced by Technicolor, and he wondered why Dorothy wanted to leave the Emerald City and return to boring, colorless Kansas. How did drinking become so indispensable to his daily existence that martinis, bottles of wine, and whiskey nightcaps crowded out almost everything else? Again it was how Hemingway described going bankrupt – first gradually and then suddenly.

In July when the streets were full of people shopping after work, Eddy started disappearing during the dinner rush at the restaurant. Morgan asked, "Where are you going?"

"Out."

"When are you coming back?"

"Later."

Morgan poured himself another glass of wine, then another and another until he finished the bottle, feeling abandoned and hurt as he sat alone at his corner table.

Eddy had a bisexual hunk named Ken who managed the restaurant whenever he took time away. The two of them joked and fought in the kitchen and generally got along great. Ken had been an Idaho farm boy drafted at age nineteen and sent to Vietnam. After two tours of duty, he returned with a serious alcohol and drug problem, marrying and divorcing three times, with kids scattered from Montana to Alaska. He even got a vasectomy because he hated paying for abortions when he got women pregnant—which is highly unusual for a man who actually preferred screwing other men. Sober on and off for years, Ken was blond and solidly built and retained the scruffy farm boy handsomeness that Morgan found such a turn-on.

Here is what Morgan noticed. On the nights when Eddy disappeared from the restaurant during the busiest part of the dinner hour, Ken also disappeared. Before, the two of them were never gone at the same time. When Eddy returned and Morgan asked where they had gone so long, he replied only, "My troika was chased by wolves." Nothing more. Morgan felt excluded, abandoned, and jealous of whatever the two men were doing so mysteriously behind his back.

As he sat feeling sorry for himself, Morgan devised two plans. Plan A was to remain at the restaurant until Eddy came back and confront him, maybe ordering a second bottle of wine to bolster his courage. He never liked an argument. Plan B called for going back to their apartment and waiting for Eddy to come home, where he could sip some bourbon to strengthen his resolve for demanding an explanation. Morgan decided on Plan B.

Eddy arrived home before ten o'clock, much earlier than usual. To Morgan's surprised, Eddy poured another big tumbler of bourbon for him and then he filled a second tumbler for himself. His behavior was strange in every way.

Eddy was never a big drinker. He was one of those infuriating men who nursed a single glass of wine throughout an entire meal. At parties he lost cocktails because he put them down and walked away, forgetting where he left them. Once, Morgan even caught him pouring an unfinished martini down the sink, remarking as he stood in the kitchen doorway, "Now *that* is what I call alcohol abuse. I'd rather see a church burn."

Morgan was prepared for a big showdown but Eddy was the combative one. He sat down in the wingback chair, leaned forward over the coffee table, and began the conversation abruptly. "Morgan, you're an alcoholic."

"No, sir, not me."

Eddy did not miss a beat. "Ken took me to some A.A. meetings and I know what your problem is. You're an alcoholic who needs to get sober."

"I never drink in the morning and never drink during the work day."

"An after-five alcoholic is still an alcoholic."

"Maybe I have been hitting the Jack Daniels a little hard lately. No problem. I'll go on the wagon."

"You went on the wagon last summer, only you called it a diet, and you were a total bitch the whole time. Your real problem is you can't *stay* on the wagon. When an alcoholic falls off, he only gets worse, probably because he feels guilty and drinks to forget the shame. Remember the Tippler in *The Little Prince?* That's exactly what you're like when you've been drinking, isolated and miserable on your own little planet."

"There's therapy."

"No."

"No?"

"No."

"My secretary Scott loves his sessions with this woman named Gabrielle."

"No," Eddy repeated. "A psychiatrist will put you on valium, switching from one chemical to another."

"Maybe if I went with Ken to his A.A. classes, I could find out what's wrong and fix it."

Eddy held his ground. "Listen, mister, I've made all the arrangements. You're going to rehab, and you're going first thing tomorrow."

"Let me explain in words of one syllable. I'm not going. I've got work."

"You've got medical leave. I talked with the office manager and you're completely covered. And it's totally fashionable now that Liz and Liza are checking themselves into the Betty Ford Clinic."

"I'm not going. I have a big case."

"You just finished your big case. I checked with Scott. Your calendar is almost empty. *And* you're got the full support of Mr. Satterfield. He noticed you were a heavy hitter when he took you to Five Oaks to observe your drinking habits. He was impressed how you knocked back the cognacs, but you looked like you could handle your liquor, back then anyway."

"You talked to a senior partner at my firm? My God, what were you thinking? Maybe I've been over-served sometimes, but I've never been arrested, never even missed a day of work. I don't get into any trouble from drinking."

Eddy raised his voice, "Listen up. You don't get into *anything* because of the drinking. Look at what your life has become. Every night you come to the restaurant and drink. Then you come home and drink. End of story. You stopped scheduling vacations. We never go to movies anymore. When was the last time you even went to the opera?"

"The Met wasn't doing anything I wanted to hear last season."

"They did *Ariadne*. Right? That's one of your favorite Strauss operas. Right? You didn't even try getting a ticket."

Morgan knew it was true. He had seen advertisements for *Ariadne auf Naxos* week after week in the newspaper. He even clipped the review of opening night and put it on the bedside table, but he never picked up the phone to order tickets. He had stopped living life to the fullest. What was happening to him? "I need some time to think about this rehab thing."

"No, I've done the thinking, I've made the decision. You *are* going to rehab in the morning, far enough outside the city you won't know anyone. You'll like it. It's called Princeton House. With all the actors and rockers getting detoxed, you'll probably have a celebrity-sighting."

When Morgan got there, he did see someone he recognized, the professor who taught his freshman English class. The teacher with his phony British accent had collapsed in the middle of a lecture on *Pride and Prejudice*. They thought he had suffered a heart attack, until he was rushed to the emergency room and the doctor determined he had a .32 blood alcohol content.

For the first time in Morgan's ten years with Eddy, there was no compromise, no finding some middle ground, and no letting things slide. Morgan surrendered to his lover's decision, the first of many surrenders, as he sprawled on the sofa without even bothering to remove his wingtips, feeling thoroughly miserable and depressed as he finished the last of his bourbon.

"Enjoy it. It's the last highball for the rest of your life."

"One day at a time," Morgan replied. "Don't we need to speak in slogans now that my life is being reduced to a made-for-television movie?"

"You do *everything* for the rest of your life. Not drinking becomes one more thing you do for the rest of your life."

Slumped back in his chair and emotionally drained from the confrontation, Eddy sat watching his lover stretched out on the sofa. He thought back over their years together while remembering all the evenings they curled up on that same sofa, not talking and not making love, just lying together comfortably in each other's arms. Morgan had always been the one who arranged things. He planned vacations, scheduled flights, and juggled their social engagements so there were never conflicts. Orderliness gave him a sense of control. He kept his record albums in alphabetical order and lined his books up evenly on their shelves. He even kept count of the number of times they had sex since the first two times in the walkup above the bagel bakery.

During their first year together, Eddy needed to bite his tongue, making every effort not criticize his lover's mania for neatness. "You're not much of a bargain," Eddy remembered saying one Sunday morning when he prepared fantastic omelets, and Morgan spent the whole meal reading the newspaper. "You're conceited and thoughtless and messy."

"Thank you, Margo Channing." Morgan recognized the lines from *All About Eve*.

"Actually you're not messy. You're pathologically neat, so neat it's hard living around you. You compensate by being doubly conceited and thoughtless."

Acceptance of Morgan's fastidiousness had become second nature for Eddy over time. He realized Morgan could not help himself. His passion for order was part of who he was, his identity, something inherited from Big Bob and Ladybug and generations of up-tight Virginians, their proud and stubborn determination that everything should be done properly, nothing unpleasant, nothing unsightly.

Morgan never even got dirty, not after jogging for miles on muggy summer afternoons, not even after long hikes in the New Mexican badlands scrambling through dusty arroyos. Once, he was helping Geoff clean out the basement in his townhouse and came upstairs with cobwebs tangled in his hair, but still looked fabulous, as if the cobwebs were artfully applied by their favorite stylist. The orderliness of his life was almost genetic, something encoded in his DNA like his perfectly even teeth, the perfectly symmetrical T of hair across his chest and down his stomach, and the four perfectly round moles spaced to form a perfect diamond-shape in the center of his back.

Morgan was never neurotic about his neatness, certainly not some fussy queen or obsessive-compulsive freak. Things simply fell into place for him. Maybe that's why he never appreciated his accomplishments, Eddy thought, because everything came so easily for him.

Morgan got out of bed in the morning and shook his head and his hair fell into place, with no product and no blow drying, just some quick finger-combing on his way to the bathroom. He took an un-ironed shirt and khakis from the dryer, gave them a couple of shakes, and his outfit was ready and he looked great. He bought his suits off the rack at Brooks Brothers and they looked custom-tailored. He did a few push-ups and sit-ups in the morning and looked as if he worked out daily with a trainer. *Sprezzatura* was his favorite word learned at Princeton. His whole world maintained this effortless order and attractiveness. He wanted everything to turn out right. He hated ugliness.

Now for the first time in his life, Morgan confronted something hopelessly messy in himself that he could not fix, arrange, replace, alphabetize, smooth over, or sort into folders. He was not comfortable letting go of the controls, not used to being taken care of.

Without realizing clearly until this night, Eddy had long ago taken charge of one whole area of their lives together. After rescuing him from a loneliness no other man could reach, he stood sentinel over Morgan's sorrows. His lover was witty and loved jokes and had such an explosive laugh that friends always knew when he was in a movie theater. But for all of his enthusiasm for *New Yorker* cartoons and Ruth Draper's comic monologues, some look of profound sadness always returned to Morgan's eyes. Making love, planning an elaborate dinner party, kidding about the orange boxer shorts, threatening to get his nipples pierced, playing dumb so that Morgan would launch into one of his lecture on opera or local history or gay novels: Eddy learned a dozen different ways to distract his lover and make that look temporarily leave his pale blue eyes.

Sometimes Eddy deliberately started an argument over something trivial, like the time Morgan referred to their relationship as a *mixed marriage* or told the dumb joke Catholic schoolboys have been telling for a million years about the nun falling down the stairs—"What's black and white, black and white, black and white?"—just to draw his lover out of whatever gloomy mood he was sinking into. Sometimes Eddy just kicked his foot, socked him on the shoulder, or cuffed him playfully on the chin, anything to bring him back to present reality. Morgan wasn't crazy in the sense of being out of his mind, but living too much *inside* his mind, forever thinking, thinking, thinking.

Yet Eddy had never seen his lover's sadness any deeper than on this night when he stretched out on the sofa, all six-three of him, without even bothering to slip off his wingtips. He rose from his chair and lay down beside Morgan, who made room for him on the sofa without saying a word and without opening his eyes. He took shelter in his lover's arms. Kissing Morgan on the tip of his nose, Eddy held him loosely until both men, still fully dressed, dozed off into restless slumber.

Early the next morning Morgan's bags were packed. Eddy had booked a car and driver. Later Morgan discovered he had been the victim of a one-man intervention. He also learned that Eddy had done everything wrong by handling the whole process by himself without the assistance of an alcoholism counselor, an addiction therapist, and a group of concerned friends, coworkers and family members. The evening should have been a fiasco. The intervention worked only because Morgan completely trusted the lover who promised on hotel stationery, *Whatever you do, I will never leave you.*

The twenty-eight days Morgan spent in rehab coincided with the month that Tony came for his summer visit. Father and son drove down to attend the family sessions, although Morgan's parents and brother never even knew he went away. The doctor's insistence that alcoholism was a disease did nothing to lessen Morgan's humiliation. He always felt that sickness was a mark of weakness, just as he believed that obesity was a sign of stupidity. Even getting the flu made him feel guilty. Morgan phoned his parents a couple of times during his stay at Princeton House, and he continued sending weekly letters to his mother with fabricated stories of celebrity-sightings—"Did I mention seeing Jimmy Stewart at the Café Carlyle?"—because everything was always *fine fine fine* when communicating with Ladybug and Big Bob.

Scott's official story at work was that Morgan had a four-week assignment at the firm's London office. Eddy's official story in case the family actually showed up in Manhattan was that Morgan had gone to New Mexico to help an Indian casino with IRS troubles. Tony had a completely different reaction to Morgan's recovery, announcing enthusiastically—he was thirteen now—"I can attend AlaTeen meetings where there's cute girls!"

The day Morgan celebrated thirty days clean and sober, his mind so clear he felt like doing calculus, was the day they celebrated their tenth anniversary. "What are the chances of that?" Eddy asked when they woke up together and kissed and prepared to have sex, with no reference to the intense conversation that had taken place the night before, no hint that anything momentous had changed in their lives together.

"One in a million," Morgan replied as he rummaged through the bedside drawer. "Those have always been our odds."

"Sure you'll be okay with the drinking tonight? Claire's coming."

"Don't worry about the booze. I've got a plan."

Morgan survived the party by eating gigantic helpings of everything on the table, plus two huge slices of anniversary cake, washed down by glass after glass of Diet Pepsi. He drank sugar-free sodas alcoholically the same way he began drinking coffee alcoholically.

Claire compensated, coming early and staying late. She snubbed the prissy little champagne glasses and headed straight to the kitchen for a tall iced tea glass, which she filled so full that the sparkling wine spilled onto their best linen tablecloth. Never once, Morgan thought, had he witnessed Claire filling a glass without overfilling it. "That girl," he concluded with the medical information gained from a month in rehab, "is clearly an alcoholic and needs A.A."

Shit, shit, shit, Claire thought to herself as she lingered in the kitchen doorway watching Morgan and Eddy opening their presents. Ten-year anniversary? Give me a fucking break! They haven't got one goddam thing in common. They don't even look like cocksuckers, more like frat brothers or teammates on the lacrosse squad. They don't even own a goddam cat!

Ten years earlier when Morgan phoned on a Monday morning to say he met this really wonderful man, Claire was convinced that hot sex would keep him banging Eddy maybe a week, a month at the outside. Horniness and novelty meant a limited run because Morgan just wasn't the marrying kind. "You're infatuated," she told him over the phone. "Remember that you're Passion's plaything, always have been, always will be. Just go back to bed—and don't sign anything."

What kept them together for a whole decade completely baffled Claire. They didn't listen to the same music. Morgan wouldn't go dancing with Eddy. She was positive Eddy only pretended liking *Rosenkavalier*. When it came to eating, Morgan was a steak and potatoes man while Eddy was becoming a borderline vegetarian. Eddy enjoyed a cup of tea in the middle of the afternoon, but Morgan needed two cups of coffee just to get out the door in the morning. They almost never worked out together at the gym. Eddy catered fundraisers for the Stonewall

Democrats while Morgan, she knew for a fact, once reached for his checkbook to make a donation to the Log Cabin Republicans.

Smart, good-looking and successful in their careers, men like Morgan and Eddy don't have a problem in the world. They're immune. Maybe that's what ticked her off the most. They could stride through life with the goddam world by the balls, a latter-day Tom Sawyer and Huck Finn all grown up at the end of the twentieth century and living the American dream to the max. First, they were men, and men always have the advantage over women. Second, they were butch and could "pass" in the mainstream professional world, right up to the point where they held hands in public.

Maybe that was the thing most shocking about them as a couple. Completely straight-looking, they go and do something incredibly queer like kissing goodbye on a subway platform. Kissing each other right on the lips! And they didn't even have the apologetic stoop that tall men have from bending to hear what the rest of the human race is saying. *And* they didn't seem to age like everyone else. That was one more thing that really ticked her off. Big men are supposed to age faster but—fuck!—it's like Morgan and Eddy had two really old-looking pictures of themselves stashed in a closet somewhere.

There were other things she noticed, though, sweet things. They could sit incredibly close to each other, like now, opening presents, taking turns reading the cards out loud, discarding the ribbons and wrapping paper, not getting in each other's way and not getting on each other's nerves. How the hell do they do that? When they walk together down a crowded sidewalk, Eddy always ends up a little ahead because he is shorter, and when there is a sudden movement, something to see, they look in the same direction at the same instant. As if fucking synchronized, for Christ's sake! It drove her crazy and she felt like another glass of champagne as she waited impatiently for them to open her present. She had cadged tickets to the American premiere of the film *Maurice*—because she knew they loved the novel—and an invitation to the reception afterwards to meet the stars, including the drop-dead gorgeous newcomer Hugh Grant. Any man *that* good-looking can't be that straight. Shit, shit, shit!

Claire and their friends were so busy drinking that nobody realized Morgan was not. He was relieved to avoid some big scene. Early sobriety was no excuse for turning into a drama queen.

Nothing if not disciplined, Morgan attended regular meetings of Alcoholics Anonymous as soon as he arrived home. He started with a cadre of rehab alumni and then watched with alarm as one by one they fell away, relapsed, came back, disappeared again, and sometimes died of overdose or suicide. His disco favorite *I*

Will Survive came back to him as he grew determined to beat the odds.

Working a recovery program felt like attending school where getting straight A's became the minimum for success. He kept a running total of the number of days that he had been sober, carefully noted in the upper margin of his daily meditation book, as if his existence was now reckoned on completely new principles, like the Aztec calendar. Everyone in A.A. offered their phone number to new members. Morgan never came away from gay meetings without two or three numbers scribbled on scraps of paper, which he dutifully deposited in the kitchen drawer nearest the telephone, only dimly aware that most men offering their numbers really wanted to have sex with him.

On Sundays when his restaurant was closed for dinner, Eddy came with him to Perry Street and enjoyed what he heard shared around the meeting room. He was fascinated by the funny and tragic stories told by people from all backgrounds, all walks of life, people they would never have encountered in any other way. "A.A. is the best show in town for a buck," Eddy told the kitchen staff on Mondays.

When Morgan was sober for a whole year, he was invited to tell his story from the podium at his regular meeting in the West Village. He obsessed for two weeks about his drunkalogue because Father Michael Finnegan said that he would definitely be sitting in the front row. Father Mike was the jovial white-haired friar who always gave him a pat on the back, offering a few simple words of encouragement whenever they saw each other at meetings downtown. "You have a disease that makes you think you're a bad man," the gay priest was famous for saying, "and it's going to fuck you up without a strong program."

Prepping for the talk, Morgan had studied the latest recovery books by experts like John Bradshaw and Wayne Dyer. Though he did not show it, Eddy felt just as nervous as he sat in the front row of the church's fellowship hall beside Father Mike. He knew how important the night was for Morgan, but knew also that intimate secrets would tumble out, even secrets never shared with him during years of pillow talk. Eddy's dread went into overdrive when his lover introduced himself and a room full of the ex-drunks shouted back, "Hi, Morgan!"

As a little kid—Morgan began—he was always afraid of failing and being humiliated. When he found out that he was good at school, the classroom became the place where he concentrated his energies even though he didn't enjoy it. He was just running scared. Morgan confessed that straight A's on report cards never convinced him that he was smart enough, even though he was the first student to learn the multiplication tables and the only one to memorize all the presidents *and* vice presidents.

Attending an Ivy League university did not make him feel smart enough. Though elected captain of the swim team, he still resented the fact that the vote was not unanimous, as if some teammates knew the secret truth about him. He just didn't measure up. Morgan admitted that he didn't feel vindicated by whatever honors he achieved. Not when he won as freestyle champion at Princeton and stood on the center riser to have the medal hung around his neck as spectators cheered. Not after winning a Rhodes Scholarship to study at Oxford, which he declined. Not after winning a Marshall Scholarship to follow in his father's footsteps at Cambridge, which he deferred, permanently as things turned out, so that he could proceed directly to law school. The prestigious scholarships were just two more lines on the résumé, just two more things he had won. He was always in such a hurry. He needed to make Law Review and then he needed a job with a top law firm in New York. The more he excelled in his pursuit of success, the lonelier he felt.

Eddy was not surprised to hear Morgan admit that he was afraid of being late and getting left behind, because his lover was pathologically punctual, always in a panic about getting places on time, usually making them the first couple to arrive at any social event. But he had never heard his lover mention his first taste of alcohol. From the podium Morgan recounted how it happened when he was five and ordered a *crème de menthe* parfait at some fancy restaurant. "How queer was that?"

A late starter, Morgan said his first real drinking experience came only during the summer after high school at a debutante party at the country club. He was shy about talking to people and nervous about dancing. After a few gin and tonics, he could talk to anyone and dance with every deb. Gin worked. "What made me an alcoholic was what alcohol did *for me* from the beginning, not only what alcohol did *to me* later on."

Leaning forward on his folding chair, Eddy understood exactly what Morgan meant about always trying to be the best little boy in the world. Of course the best little boy in the world would never drink alcohol—and then he did. Thank God! Morgan felt certain that he would have committed suicide if he had not found relief in drinking, because the burden of being the best little boy in the world was just too crushing.

Eddy knew it was true when Morgan described the gradual progression of his alcoholism. Problem drinking overtook him only when everything else in his life looked perfect. He had a world-class education. He had an interesting and high-paying job. He had a fabulous co-op apartment on the Upper West Side and a wonderful lover to share it with. And still he was not happy.

"I always thought that I would be happy when I got promoted or owned a bigger apartment or lost five pounds. I was always going to be happy in the future and couldn't figure out why I always felt unhappy. I never realized that I can't be happy in the future. Nothing ever happens in the future. Everything happens now. Abraham Lincoln was probably right. Most people *are* as happy as they make up their minds to be."

Achieving everything left Morgan feeling empty, as if all the promises of his life had been broken and nothing mattered anymore. As he valued his present life less and less, he dwelled more and more on memories of his youth, drinking to reach back. The more he tried filling up this emptiness with vodka and bourbon, the bigger the void grew and the more alcohol he needed to fill it. Only when he landed in rehab did he realize how far down he had gone. Wearing Brooks Brothers should have meant his life was more together.

"I never felt that I was loved, either. Now I realize I was right. I can't feel anyone else's love. I can only feel my love for another person. It's like ice-cream. I love Haagen-Dazs, but Haagen-Dazs doesn't love me back—and doesn't need to."

Eddy was stunned to hear Morgan say he never felt loved. He had spent more than a decade loving this man, doing and saying loving things, even performing gross duties like cleaning up the vomit when he had food poisoning and didn't reach the toilet in time. Now Morgan stood at the podium and announced over the PA system that he never felt loved. Inwardly Eddy winced at many of the things he heard openly confessed to a bunch of strangers, mostly saggy-assed old leather queens that Morgan would never have drunk beer with at a kegger. Morgan even acknowledged one of his most deep-dark secrets: "I can't piss if anyone's watching."

As he drew near the end, Morgan said that he went to a meeting every day. He phoned his sponsor. He read the Big Book. He was working the Twelve Steps. He read spiritual books like *The Road Less Traveled*. (Etcetera.) He did not want to work a perfect program of recovery, just better than anyone else's. (Laughter) Occasionally he had little spiritual awakenings and eye-opening realizations. "I always felt frustrated because I wasn't getting everything I deserved. Now I ask myself the simple question. *What at this moment is missing?* The answer always comes back the same. *Nothing.* I've always been a very lucky guy."

After Morgan talked for exactly forty-five minutes as instructed by his sponsor, everybody held hands and said the Lord's Prayer. Some people lined up beside the podium to thank him and give him hugs, while others hurried outside to smoke cigarettes. Eddy, who had grown increasingly fidgety as he sat in the front row, now stood patiently at the end of the line of well-wishers.

Standing just in front of him was Father Mike, who shook Morgan's hand so that he could look him in the eye as he spoke. "Those were fine words that you delivered from the podium. You're a very articulate, well-educated man. I bet that you've done a lot of studying over the past year. But you shouldn't be reading books like *I'm Okay – You're Okay.*"

"Why not?"

"Because you're not okay! You're still operating on superior brainpower. You may think you've had epiphanies and realizations, but they're all intellectual.

Do you know the longest journey a man travels in this life? It's the journey from his head to his heart."

When his turn came Eddy whispered, "You *are* the best little boy in the world!" as he embraced Morgan, who looked puzzled and annoyed by what Father Mike said to him.

Back when Morgan entered rehab in New Jersey and the nurses searched his luggage, removing his Scope mouthwash according to regulations, the doctors did all the routine blood work, which included an HIV test.

The year was 1987. He and Eddy had lived together in Manhattan for an entire decade while the AIDS plague raged around them. Nearly every week they attended the funeral of some friend who had died from complications. Tom was the first, when the doctors were calling the disease "gay cancer" maybe caused by poppers. Hospitals did not have a clue how the mysterious illness was transmitted or how to protect their own workers. Nurses would not touch gay patients. Orderlies left meal trays on the floors outside their rooms.

While celebrities like Rock Hudson, Steve Rubell, and Perry Ellis got all the media attention, other gay men quietly dropped from sight at the gym, the bars, and the discos. Few people knew what had become of them until their names appeared on the obituary page. After Tom went into the hospital, Lawrence and Lenny got sick. Then Michael and Ron and Peter. Then Chris and Vito and Gary and Gordon. The next man and the next and the next: Todd, Brett, Ryan, Jimmy, Chip, Bill, Louie, Ariel, Pedro, Brad, Marcus, Craig, Myles, Barry, Jake, Mario, Rich, Avery, Russ, Marcel, Daniel, Barry, James, Manfred, Wes, Thommy, Jorge, Cliff, Bem-Ho, Lee, Vince, Levy, Marc, Glen, Taylor, Jody, Walter, Guthrie, Skipper, Blake, Ruskin, Wayne, Joey, Walter, Jean-Paul, Michael, Clay, Philip, André, Morris, Alex, Chad, Bruce, Peregrine, Jacques, Kyle, Ted, Kirk, Lincoln, George, Tad, Geoff, William, Ben, Gordon, Perry, Stuart, Chaz, Patrick, Gayle, Nick, Paul, Steven, and Mark.

Keith, Kelvin, Kevin: Morgan's address book became a mess of black ink as names were cross through, crossed through, crossed through.

Some deaths were hideous. Their friend Max, who worked his way up to an executive position at Bloomingdale's, went through the torments of the damned as he grew sicker and sicker. Near the end, he had so few T-cells that he gave them names. When he was reduced to a human skeleton with concentration-camp thinness, things still kept getting worse. Before he lapsed into dementia, he joked feebly about being attacked by the alphabet—KS, CMV, MAC, HPV, TB, and PSP. When Max could no longer recognize them, Morgan and Eddy stopped visiting him in the hospital. They waited for the memorial service. In the early

1980s, funerals provided public recognition that a whole generation of gay men was vanishing one by one.

Then one morning while having his second cup of coffee and reading the *Times*, Morgan came upon the obituary for Jacques Morali. The genius behind the Village People and composer of hits like *YMCA* and *Go West* had died of AIDS-related complications. After so many deaths and so many memorial services, Morgan finally hit some emotional wall. Slumping in the kitchen chair, he felt overwhelmed by the cumulative sense of loss, as if suddenly realizing that the entire culture of wild clubs and loud discos had died along with Jacques Morali. Morgan still went to the office that day, and later in the afternoon he had a strenuous workout at the gym followed by dinner with Eddy at the restaurant. But if anyone asked when being gay stopped being fun, Morgan knew the exact date.

All the while during their first ten years together, he and Eddy enjoyed a frequency of sex that astonished other gay men and certainly their straight friends. Even Ethan once complained on the squash court, "It sounds like Eddy puts out a lot more than Meredith. I wish I had your sex life."

Morgan patted him on the ass with his racquet. "You had your chance, old sport."

Yet throughout this decade of marathon sex play in the bedroom, on the sofa, on the heirloom Turkish carpet, in the shower where they lathered each other's erections, even in the front seat of the Volvo if they were certain nobody was watching, Morgan and Eddy had never once discussed the question of their own HIV status. They attended AIDS benefits starring Bette Midler and Joan Rivers, they schmoozed at fundraisers with celebrities wearing red ribbons on their lapels, and then they went home and ripped each other's tuxedos off on the way to the bedroom. Never once did they discuss the disease as anything touching their own lives directly. While they observed the rituals of grief and leave-taking for dead friends, their refusal to discuss their own health status became part of an unspoken covenant, like their monogamy, that they scrupulously guarded.

This is how Morgan rationalized not getting tested in the early 1980s. Since there was no effective treatment, what was the benefit of knowing? It could only cause stress, which would hurt more than it would help. He knew a young man named Gene who managed his favorite bookstore in the West Village, another transplanted Virginian, with a sexy lean body, gimlet-green eyes, and a broad smile that almost melted Morgan's heart every time they saw each other. Gene freaked out when he was diagnosed HIV positive and jumped off the Williamsburg Bridge later that same night. Better, Morgan decided, to take precautions and eat right and exercise and do everything that a gay man does to stay fit and healthy, without the stress of knowing for sure.

What is more—Morgan rationalized—he had always used condoms. At the very beginning of his sex life, he decided that cleaning up afterwards was not nearly so gross. This way, he just flushed the rubber down the toilet and splashed a little water, toweled off, and jumped back into bed. Eddy remarked on their first night together when Morgan used a rubber, "It feels different." Otherwise he did not make a big deal about it, and they never discussed the unusual degree of fussiness that Morgan imposed upon their sexual rituals.

Once they were in bed watching a rerun of a *M*A*S*H* episode—when Hawkeye falls in love with a nurse so highly cultivated that she quoted poetry—and Morgan started getting frisky and Eddy joked as he paused for a condom first, "There's an old Cuban superstition about not dipping a banana in chocolate. Sounds pretty Freudian to me."

"You don't really believe all those voodoo legends, you crazy Cuban."

"Don't call me a crazy Cuban, and don't tell me *you* don't have any superstitions."

"No, sir, not one."

"What about your belief the world becomes a safe place if your books are lined up evenly on their shelves? Isn't that superstitious?"

"Neatness isn't superstition. It's chaos theory in reverse. Order begets order, hence spreading out in every direction in a ripple effect until everything falls naturally into its proper place."

"You always have a goddam theory, only your goddam theories never make sense. You may be highly educated but only sound intelligent. *Hence, hence, hence*—just like a Jesuit. You totally lack street smarts. Let's hope the building never catches fire."

"You're so full of bullshit, your eyes are brown."

"Not that I'm complaining. I like my men big and stupid." Eddy reached inside Morgan's boxer shorts. "At least you're got good luck. Know how lucky you are? You got me."

"And being lucky is better than being smart."

Eddy took Morgan's erection in his fist and squeezed. "Are we done talking yet? Can we turn off the television?"

Morgan switched off the *M*A*S*H* rerun just before the surgeon's classy girlfriend quoted a line of poetry she claimed was Dante—"Your eyes have shot their arrows into my heart!"—while Eddy pulled open the drawer of the bedside table.

Morgan did not realize that he had been tested for HIV when entering Princeton House in the summer of 1987, sleepy and confused and ashamed as he was about everything. He signed a consent form. He signed whatever paperwork they put in front of him, which a good lawyer knows he should never do. He found out about the blood work only several days later when the doctor sat him down and closed his office door to review the results. "Your liver functions are pretty good. And you're non-reactive."

"What does that mean?"

"Your test was negative. Congratulations. You don't have AIDS."

Now Morgan knew. Yet he grew painfully aware that he did not know about Eddy. The next weekend when the wives and parents came for family sessions, he took Eddy for a walk around the grounds and told him. "They gave me an HIV test, and it came back negative."

Eddy said "Great!' but nothing more. They simply kept walking among the willow trees beside the lake. Morgan broke the silence, "What are you thinking?"

"That's my line. In ten years together, you never once asked me what I was thinking."

"I never need to. You blurt out whatever is on your mind, except for this rehab conspiracy."

"Want to know what I'm thinking? I bottomed in New York and I bottomed in West Hollywood, there's no way I couldn't be positive. I never even touched a condom before I met you, didn't know if I was supposed to unfold it, unroll it, or blow it up like a balloon."

"Hence Tony."

"Yeah, hence Tony. At least Tara the Bitch got him tested after making a big fuss about me paying the doctor's bill, still bossing me around as if we were married, but the results came back negative so the kid is in the clear."

"Okay, if Tony is negative and I'm negative, how in the world could you keep from being negative? Look, we've had sex hundreds of times over the past ten years and haven't always been a hundred-percent safe. There's no way that you could be positive if I'm not infected."

"You're probably right."

Both men fell silent. Finally Eddy gave him a sideways look and smiled. "The piano arrived yesterday. It's a beauty, just as nice as Geoff's Steinway."

"It *is* Geoff's Steinway. I bought it at the estate sale. Poor Geoff, I thought it'd be good to have something to remember him by." Morgan stared down at the flagstone path. "It was supposed to be a surprise for our anniversary. I didn't plan on being padlocked in this spin-dry joint when the delivery men brought it. I thought you might try playing again after all these years. Otherwise it becomes a very expensive piece of furniture."

"You are my Rosenkavalier!" Eddy imitated Blanche from *Streetcar Named Desire*. "I love that the piano was Geoff's. Maybe I'll learn something new for your homecoming. Practicing will be different if my mother isn't standing over my shoulder."

Eddy waited a week after he got back to the city, thinking and anguishing and tossing around sleeplessly in their big empty bed, before he decided to get tested. The results would take another week to come back.

While he waited and tried not to obsess about the results, he followed through on his promise by learning some new pieces by Chopin, all in minor keys, not because he felt depressed over the outcome of the lab work, but because Morgan's favorite musical compositions from Mozart's *Requiem* to *The Four Last Songs*, even Broadway favorites like *Memories* and *September Song*, were always sad-sounding. Eddy had no trouble finding three minor-key waltzes to practice while he passed the interminable days and nights waiting.

When he went back to the clinic, Eddy was correct. He tested positive.

He waited for Morgan to arrive home from rehab to tell him. They were lying face to face on a single pillow while a candle burned on the bedside table. "I love you so much," Morgan said.

"I love you, too," Eddy said. "I got tested."

"And?"

"Positive."

"And?"

"I'm scared."

Morgan gathered him into his arms. "I think I knew you got yourself tested. I think I knew you'd be positive."

"You didn't sign up for this nightmare," Eddy whispered as tears welled in his eyes. "The disease feels like a bomb ticking inside me. You saw what happened to Max. Others were just as gruesome. For all his millions and millions, Geoff couldn't save himself from the blindness, the incontinence, the dementia. I don't want you changing my diapers when I don't even recognize your face anymore."

Morgan put his hand over Eddy's mouth. "I don't want to have this conversation. I told you I'd never leave no matter what. Right? We'll handle whatever happens and not worry about it until it does. Every day is a bonus day from now on."

"We've always had bonus time, when you think about it. How many other men do you know who've enjoyed ten good years together?" Eddy slid closer and cradled himself in Morgan's embrace. "You've always made me feel important."

"Because you *are* the most important thing in my life, you crazy Cuban." Morgan smiled as he kissed him on his chin. "I loved you on our first night together, and I'll love you on our last. Now we're done with this conversation."

Eddy rested his head on Morgan's chest, listening to the strong steady beating of his heart. "End of story?"

"End of story."

So here Morgan and Eddy were in 1987 in their middle thirties, a high-powered Wall Street attorney and a successful restaurant owner, just when they thought they were secure and their lives would become smooth-running, an alcoholic in early recovery and gay man tested positive for HIV.

These were the new realities that loomed over the August afternoon as they celebrated their tenth anniversary with a champagne brunch which had already been planned and the invitations mailed out, the new realities withheld from friends like Claire who saw only the two athletic-looking men more like teammates or frat brothers. These two successful men were totally immune to problems, she thought resentfully, as they sat close together on the sofa opening their presents.

One friend was not kept in the dark about Eddy's diagnosis. Dr. Ethan Rees had completed his long years of medical school and residence programs in virology, and he joined the staff at St. Vincent's Hospital at the height of the gay men's health crisis. He followed the grant funding, and soon his laboratory found itself on the forefront of international AIDS research. He took charge of Eddy's case.

Eddy always harbored a quiet resentment toward "the good doctor" because he had been the great love of Morgan's life at college, but he accepted Ethan's help without any fuss. Morgan felt a great sense of relief.

After his first appointment with Eddy and Morgan at the hospital, Ethan went home and told his wife Meredith, who burst into tears. Baby Josh, who did not understand at age eight, started crying because his mommy was crying. Finally Ethan, who kept up a brave front for the whole afternoon, could not keep back the tears and started sobbing along with his wife and son. So while the two gay men were stoic and resumed their daily routines, their longtime friends went to bed with eyes red from weeping.

Only when Ethan wanted to prescribe a regime of AZT did Eddy show his stubborn streak. "Those pills are toxic. They'll definitely make me sick. I may be dying, but I'm not gonna look bad doing it." Agreeing that AZT had severe side effects, Ethan suggested monitoring his patient's T-cell count for the time being, remaining alert for any sign of opportunistic infection.

Like most every other gay man in the 1980s, Morgan and Eddy went to the gym religiously. Eddy had always belonged to a health club, even when he could hardly afford it. His motto was "no pecs, no sex" in the days when the gym was gay church and the hardbodies formed its priesthood. If these men shared any common devotion, it was worshiping the naked gods of the locker room. After he was diagnosed, Eddy continued his regular workouts with a grim determination that bordered on panic, obsessed with looking good.

As the years passed and he did not get sick, Eddy enjoyed his visits to the gym as he tried enjoying everything that he did, even running his restaurant. He attended HIV support groups and read spiritual books, giving away copies of *Man's Search for Meaning* to everyone he knew. He meditated first thing in the morning and again before bedtime. While Morgan started reading thicker novels until he was plowing his way through *Dance to the Music of Time*, Eddy liked to read and reread simple books like *The Little Prince*. He went wild for Raymond Chandler. "About as inconspicuous as a tarantula on a slice of angel food!" Rumi became his favorite poet, and Eddy dropped hints that he would really love a vacation in Turkey to visit the mystic's hometown and sit in his rose garden.

Lingering in the aisles of bookstores, Eddy read books on dying by Raymond Moody and Elisabeth Kübler-Ross, but never purchased any, because he knew Morgan would be upset finding them around the house. When leafing through the *Tibetan Book of the Dead*, he came upon an account of Tara the Lady Savior, a female bodhisattva who rescued men's souls from falling into eternal shadows in the afterlife. From that day onward he stopped calling his ex-wife Tara the Bitch—which he never did in front of Tony anyway—and he used instead the maiden name that she resumed after the breakup of her second marriage. Palermo was the surname taken by her grandmother Rosalia, the iron-willed matriarch famous for her independence, after arriving from Sicily in 1914.

One morning Eddy made an announcement over breakfast as Morgan was only halfway through his first cup of coffee. "I'm going to A.A. meetings with you all the time, not just Sundays."

"What about your AIDS support groups?"

"All those guys talk about is dying. In your meetings, the men have a fatal disease, too, but they talk about living and having fun while they're in remission. That's what sobriety is, remission, right?"

"I never thought about it that way."

"AIDS guys are always hoping for some miracle drug. Remember the Chinese cucumber treatment? A.A. guys already have a miracle cure. I see the results every night in a church basement."

Morgan shrugged. "Why not?"

The months turned into years as Eddy sat silently beside Morgan in his A.A. meetings, listening and laughing along with the recovering alcoholics, and he did not get sick.

In the meantime Morgan read books like Susan Sontag's *AIDS And Its Metaphors*, which he kept at his office so Eddy would not know how much the diagnosis weighed upon him. His family had taught him how to keep a rhinoceros in the living room and call it a credenza.

Partly a fine-tuning of his fitness program, partly something spiritual, Eddy expanded his workout routine to include yoga. At first he felt awkward and klutzy, even though he was in great physical condition, and he almost quit until one afternoon his hunky young instructor Sean T. described to his students the Warrior Dance. Immediately Eddy understood the rhythms of their movements and finally the pleasure that was the true arrival point of these yoga sessions. In time he could almost feel his spine's thirty-three vertebrae moving individually, while his ribs opened and closed like a tiger's claws.

He adopted the new motto "no flex, no sex" after starting yoga. Almost every weekend as his body grew suppler, he introduced Morgan to some improbable new position, all open and sweaty and loose, very experimental for a couple accustomed to vanilla sex. After leafing through *Light on Yoga* on Eddy's bedside table, Morgan began noticing that men at the gym, who otherwise looked like perfectly normal all-American homosexuals, were using yoga postures to tone their muscle groups. For stretching their glutes, they were using the pigeon pose. For glutes and hams, they went into down-dog pose on all fours with ass in the air, extremely sexy if the man had a cute bubble butt.

"I'm practicing Shavasana. It means corpse pose," Eddy said early one morning when Morgan, on his way to the kitchen for his coffee, almost stumbled over him lying motionless on the Turkish carpet. Eddy started every morning with a series of Sun Salutations in the middle of the living room. "Reclining the way a body is laid out for a funeral, feet splayed and palms open upward."

"Morbid, don't you think?"

The spiritual point—Eddy explained—involved seeing the whole world of material things from the vantage point of a dead person, realizing how little anything mattered from the viewpoint of a corpse, freed from the earthly body to attain an essential selfhood, becoming the inner seer at the core of being, completely centered in the present moment in the immediate experience, an emptiness that creates radiance at the heart's center. Sometimes men sleep. Sometimes men weep. Unexpected emotions well up when the body contacts fully with the earth, surrendering to the peaceful splendor, melting and being granted a glimpse of the soul's unknown, on the edge of a great mystery, the only really safe place.

"Here and now, nothing else is," Eddy muttered as a stick of incense emitted a thin ribbon of sweet-smelling smoke. "Jeez, I'm starting to sound like *you*, explain explain explain."

"Does this mean we can't fuck on the Turkish carpet anymore?"

"Lie down, we'll breathe together." Eddy scooted over to make room for him. "Sad to think you only love me for my body."

Morgan blew in his ear. "That's not true. I love you for your cooking, too." Again he blew into Eddy's ear.

No longer in their twenties, eating right became another part of their new lifestyle as each man had his own challenge for maintaining good health. They took tons of vitamins and tried every new supplement recommended by trainers, yoga instructors, and bodybuilders at the gym. Eventually each man had a multi-compartment pill dispenser, like old people for their medications, just to keep all their vitamins and supplements organized.

Once Morgan tried ginkgo biloba as a memory enhancer, but it gave him headaches. Eddy tried creatine as a muscle builder but it gave him diarrhea, which was sometimes a symptom of an AIDS-related illness. He phoned for an emergency appointment with Ethan, who recommended he stop taking the creatine. The doctor discovered his cholesterol was high, however, so he wrote a prescription for lowering Eddy's LDL. The statin drug became one more pill in his daily cycle.

They had a kitchen drawer solely for protein bars and a shelf in the refrigerator for quick-energy drinks. In a novelty shop, Eddy bought a nutritional snack called "Nietzsche's Will to Power Bar" and sneaked it into the drawer with the other soy and whey products. When Morgan discovered it, he laughed so hard he got the hiccups.

Healthy nutrition proved tougher for Morgan. When he sobered up, he immediately developed a huge craving for ice-cream. Instead of bourbon at bedtime, he wanted Haagen-Dazs. He was convinced St. Augustine knew what he was talking about when he wrote "it is easier to abstain than moderate."

Chocolate became a whole other addiction in a class by itself. Morgan hopefully scanned the *Times* for news that medical researchers had discovered the health-giving properties of ground cocoa seeds. One Sunday at the restaurant's corner table where he was having brunch with his Eddy and his A.A. sponsor—and discussing the newcomer's obsession with desserts during early recovery—Morgan blurted out, "I'd eat pussy if you put chocolate on it!"

Instead of taking fistfuls of AIDS medications every day, Eddy went to the hospital regularly for Ethan to monitor his T-cell count, and waited.

The months passed and his T-cell levels remained normal. More years passed, and his T-cells remained abundant and Eddy took no drugs. "When I start going downhill, I'll take the new cocktail of protease inhibitors," he assured Morgan. "Promise!"

One afternoon—the year was 1999—Ethan looked up from the latest lab results and began reflecting out loud. "The latest research among people of European descent indicates a tiny percentage of individuals with special CD-eight

T-cells which inhibit HIV cells from replicating. Some individuals have no CCR-five gene and therefore HIV can't enter their cells. Europeans whose ancestors survived the Black Death probably inherited this genetic anomaly in their DNA."

"Catalans have really rich, complicated gene pools," Morgan spoke up. "I googled your people, Eddy. Originally they were freckled-faced Celts, and then the region was settled by Carthaginians before the Greeks arrived, according to Herodotus. Next came the Roman legions. The emperors Trajan, Hadrian and Marcus Aurelius were Catalans, know that?"

"Yeah, and don't forget Dalí and Miró and Gaudí."

Morgan hardly missed a beat. "Jews arrived in larger numbers in the second century during the Diaspora. When the Roman Empire collapsed, then came the blue-eyed Goths, the Visigoths, and even a few blond Huns. The Moslem invasions brought swarthy Arabs, Berbers, Egyptians, Bedouins, and everyone else as far as Baghdad. Moroccan traders and Viking raiders came ashore adding their DNA to the mix. Not mentioning the two centuries your family lived in Cuba, the Mallafrés inherited enough genetic material to explain any medical anomaly."

"Some people get hysterical when they're nervous," Ethan said when his old friend wound down. "Not you, Morgan, you get *historical*."

"It's like being married to the *Encyclopedia Britannica*," said Eddy. "So I got the mutant gene and special T-cells?"

"Beats the hell out of me! I'm still guessing, still in the dark why you're so healthy. Maybe your original HIV strain was so weak your immune system fought it off. Who knows? Definitely you're one in a thousand, Eddy, maybe one in a million, still my star patient. That's probably why you never got infected, either, Morgan."

"Just as I suspected, life is just one big crapshoot where it's better to be lucky than careful."

"Not that I want anyone thinking I'm superstitious," Eddy spoke up, "but I believe the Chimayó church-dirt that I wear in my crucifix helped. I'm the only man from my original HIV support group still alive. Call it a weird DNA if you like. I call it miraculous."

"I'm the only man from my rehab group still sober after a dozen years. Half the rest are dead, I know for a fact, probably including my old English professor. The last I heard, they found him unconscious in some dingy apartment lying in a puddle of his own shit and vomit. But I don't wear any voodoo charm around my neck."

"So neither of us should be alive."

With tears brimming in his eyes, Ethan rushed from the examining room while mumbling, "I've got to talk to my research assistant about something."

"Great bedside manner," Eddy said, giving Morgan a quizzical look. "How come you never cry? Ethan's a rough-tough jock, almost completely straight, a doctor who deals with gruesome deaths nearly every day, but he's the one who bursts into tears at the drop of a hat."

"My people don't cry." Morgan pondered for a moment. "Actually I saw Big Bob cry once, just once. I was about twelve. The newsletter from his Cambridge college said they were tearing down the old boathouse to build a new one. He started sobbing and closed the door to his study, with me standing there in the hallway, watching. It was creepy. I knew he loved rowing, but never understood why he got so broken-hearted about his college's old boathouse."

"Your people are really weird. Somebody ought to write a book."

"So how about celebrating your test results with ice-cream sundaes at our favorite lakeside restaurant? It's been a long time since we took a walk in Central Park."

8

The Two Towers

Morgan and Eddy—New York, 2001

Morgan made fun of people who moved to Brooklyn. Then in 1991 they did.

Eddy knew somebody who knew somebody, and they bought a brownstone on Park Slope, a neighborhood of tree-lined streets, gracious old homes, and church bells. Dating from the 1870s, the address looked like move-in condition when the realtor showed them around, but turned out to be a real fixer-upper. The mantelpieces and wainscoting were beautiful, but the plumbing became a nightmare after leaks from the upstairs bathroom stained the ceiling in the drawing room where the movers put the Steinway, at exactly the right angle so Eddy could look up from the keyboard into the back garden. When the dripping started, he and Morgan hurried to shift the heavy instrument themselves, pushing shoulder to shoulder and grunting and cursing.

Morgan resigned himself to settling amid the faded nineteenth-century refinement that he called Gilded Age Gothic—"Can't you feel the ghosts of Newland Archer and Countess Olenska?"—while Eddy could hardly wait to rip out old appliances. He did not stop until he had a restaurant-quality kitchen downstairs, warmed by the lolling aroma of saffron and fresh-baked bread, with a home office for his ever-growing library of cookbooks. He himself was compiling favorite recipes, mostly traditional Cuban dishes passed down from Aunt Lourdes, but he didn't tell Morgan until he finished the manuscript and found a publisher. Next came the bathrooms, with such a radical makeover of pipes and drains that the two men spent weeks going to the gym for hot showers.

Claire pitched a fit when they announced the move, as if Brooklyn were a planet in a far-flung galaxy. Morgan replied that the subway commute to Lower Manhattan, where his law offices had moved to the World Trade Center, was actually shorter than his commute from the Upper West Side. *Even in the wilds of Transylvania* became Eddy's deadpan response when anyone implied that their lives had dropped into some barbaric hinterland. From time to time they talked about moving back into the city, maybe Tribeca or Chelsea, but the more they renovated their brownstone and got accustomed to its eccentricities, like the old staircases that creaked no matter how much they oiled the wood, the more comfortable the house felt and the harder to consider leaving.

No longer just for show when Tony came for visits, Eddy had his own bedroom next to Morgan's, connected by a large walk-through closet, where he collapsed after some late-night crisis at the restaurant for a good night's sleep without disturbing his lover. They also slept separately whenever Morgan left for early-morning meetings with clients, or one of them was sick with flu and spent the whole night coughing, wheezing, and tossing back and forth with fever. The gigantic stuffed tiger from FAO Schwarz found a permanent home atop the dresser in this spare bedroom, and the large canvas of electric oranges and greens which Keith Haring inscribed HAVEN'T STOPPED DANCING YET had a place of honor over Eddy's bed.

After he stopped drinking nightcaps, Morgan often had trouble sleeping, and now he could move to the empty bed and catch up on back issues of *The New Yorker* in the middle of the night without waking Eddy. He developed a fondness for Virginia Woolf and found that novels like *To the Lighthouse* provided ideal reading after midnight. When he and Eddy did curl up in the same bed—which was still most nights—sleeping together became more of a special experience, not just domestic routine. Still they awoke pressed close together and tangled in each other's arms, just as they did during their first year, sharing the bed propped up on cinderblocks.

The brownstone had a garden in the back, and Eddy discovered he loved working the soil. His manager Ken had grown up on a farm outside Boise and had a knack for growing things, helping on his days off and taking charge when his boss spent summer months in New Mexico. Ken laid out the flower beds, taught Eddy when to plant and water, and wrote careful instructions for applying fertilizers. His obsession for drugs and alcohol had turned into an obsession for gardening. The Vietnam vet usually took his shirt off to get some sunshine, and Morgan sneaked a peek from his fourth-floor study, sometimes lingering longer than he planned, enjoying the blond scruffiness of the country boy. Ken's longsuffering boyfriend called him "a hunk and a handful," and now Morgan understood why. Later he would tell friends he enjoyed a great view from his home office, smiling slyly, because he meant more than the sight of the Twin Towers rising above the neighborhood rooftops, his law offices just visible on the eighty-ninth floor.

Eddy was not very interested in flowers, only herbs and vegetables, and his specialty heirloom tomatoes. He made one exception for flower seeds taken from the historic bed-and-breakfast where they stayed during vacations in Santa Fe. He planted these seeds in the back corner of the garden where they got the most sunlight and soon had own patch of black hollyhocks.

Eddy liked standing downstairs at the kitchen window where morning glories entwined the security bars, admiring the wisteria bower where they read the Sunday *Times* while the carillon chimed from a nearby church. Whenever Eddy spotted odd bits of masonry, stone corbels, or discarded pillars from old buildings being demolished anywhere in Brooklyn, he loaded the stonework into the trunk of the Volvo, even in broad daylight, and brought these treasures home to furnish the back garden. His proudest haul was an Art Deco panel from the liner *Normandie* which had burned and sunk in the Hudson. Morgan never felt comfortable when he spotted more junk stacked against the fence. "It's stealing."

"It's not stealing. It's recycling, it's good ecology."

"This from the guy caught shoplifting *The Poetry of St. John of the Cross.*"

One morning as Eddy stood at the kitchen window looking out through the morning glories, Morgan came up quietly behind and slid his arms around his waist. He hooked his chin over Eddy's shoulder, and they watched together while a gray squirrel bounded along the top of the fence before disappearing into the tallest of the hollyhocks.

"Know how tough it is getting seeds that haven't been cross-pollinated?" Eddy asked. "Usually hollyhocks come out pink or scarlet, never pure black. Forget about Tribeca. We're settled here. End of story."

Before he turned forty, Eddy sold his restaurant on the Upper West Side and could have retired, but instead opened a new restaurant on Flatbush Avenue near their brownstone. Keeping pace with the times, his menu featured organic meats and produce from a collective of farms from Vermont and northern California. He could still walk to work in five minutes and hurry home for a quick break whenever he needed it.

After their move to Brooklyn, he and Morgan worked hard at finding new friends locally, which became more difficult now that they were older. After working around people all day at his restaurant, Eddy was happy to come home and cocoon in his comfort zone, watching videos or playing the piano or simply curled up on the sofa while Morgan read.

Basically Morgan was a high-functioning hermit content listening to recordings, as his opera collection made the transition from vinyl to compact discs. He was a runner and a swimmer who never liked team sports, never someone comfortable in the common herd, even in his reading preferences. He returned to favorites like *Age of Innocence* and *The Great Gatsby* over and over, and eagerly purchased each new novel by Tom Wolfe, another transplanted Virginian, always hoping for something as good as *The Right Stuff*. He made a point of reading every Santa Fe novel he could find, even *Ben Hur*, written while its author served as territorial governor of New Mexico during the 1870s, just when their brownstone was built in Brooklyn.

Blocking off a hundred days at the beginning of 2000, Morgan finally settled down with a facing-page translation of the *Divine Comedy*, committing himself to one canto every night at bedtime, but baffled when he never found his favorite Dante line. Back at Princeton, Ethan had coaxed him in starting *The Lord of the Rings*, but Morgan bogged down halfway through *The Two Towers* and never got around to finishing Tolkien's trilogy until the blockbuster movies came out. True to form, his favorite chapter was one omitted from the film adaptations. He returned again and again to "The House of Tom Bombadil" with its description of the enchanted valley, sheltered and protected from the world's troubles, where the household was safe and nobody grew old.

Eddy noticed his partner bought CD releases of the same recordings that he already owned on 33⅓ albums, so that the Broadway production of *My Fair Lady* was again alphabetized next to *Meistersinger von Nürnberg* on the shelf where his discs were neatly lined up. Eddy teased him for adding only one new pop group to his collection because Pet Shop Boys recorded disco tunes like their version of *Go West*. Shooting back, Morgan said he had a theory that listening to the Village People's original recording, on the eight-track during their epic drive across America in 1978, planted subliminal messages bringing them to New Mexico and making them come back. He recited the lines, not singing them really, because he was so tone-deaf:

> *There where the air is free, we'll be what we want to be.*
> *Now if we make a stand, we'll find our own promised land.*

Eddy gave back his deadpan expression with eyes wide with disbelief, meaning he thought Morgan was talking bullshit as usual.

Not stuck in a rut for vacations, they treated themselves to a getaway to Las Vegas where they stayed at the Bellagio. Eddy was comped tickets to a show by one of the hotel's celebrity chefs after publishing his own cookbook and getting several write-ups for his Brooklyn restaurant. So they spent their first night in Sin City not playing poker or blackjack, not even dining at a three-star bistro, but attending a splashy stage performance by Cher.

Psyching himself for the big night, Morgan whistled *If I Could Turn Back*

Time as he gazed from their hotel suite down at the plumes of dancing water, ten stories below, amid a simulated Lake Como so voluptuously beautiful, only better than the original, against the surreal backdrop of the Paris skyline illuminated by neon lights flashing and shimmering weirdly across the water show. Morgan had flown separately after a business trip to Los Angeles. On his last day there, he had taken time to drive to Venice Beach so that he could revisit the sun-drenched paradise that he remembered from 1978, where rainbow kites fluttered overheard, gym-hardened bodies stretched for acres, and tanned surfer boys tossed Frisbees back and forth where the waves rolled ashore.

But when he arrived at the stretch of beach just off the boardwalk, Morgan found nobody on beach towels, no gay jocks playing volleyball, and no bodybuilders selling cocktails from coolers, just an empty expanse of windblown sand and a single Mexican family eating sandwiches in the shade beneath a lifeguard station. Out beyond the breakers, a single kite-surfer skimmed at incredible speed along the shoreline.

Where were they now? Where had all the beautiful boys gone?

So Morgan was already brooding nostalgically over some great loss as he stood in his Las Vegas hotel suite, whistling *If I Could Turn Back Time* while gazing down at the dancing fountains in the make-believe Lake Como.

When they arrived at the indoor arena and Morgan opened his souvenir program, he discovered that Cher's opening act was none other than the Village People.

Eddy asked, "Were you expecting the Mormon Tabernacle Choir?"

As they sat in front-row seats watching a live performance of *San Francisco* by members of the original group, a deeper sadness stole upon Morgan when he realized how this exuberant paean to gay freedom, practically a marching song for the liberation movement of the 1970s, had degenerated over the years into musical kitsch. Drifting away, he recollected the night when he almost collided with Cher outside Studio 54 back in the days when he drank one vodka tonic after another, and anonymous sex was his life's biggest thrill. And he recalled the heartbreak when he read the obituary for the composer who wrote the catchy tune *YMCA* which teenagers still danced to, raising their arms to form the letters spelling out the title. Yet these youngsters knew nothing about the plague years. They were spared the hospital sickrooms with the smell of dying mopped over with disinfectant, the fear of touching infected men and even breathing the same air, and the memorial services with receptions afterwards, when everyone stood around gloomily wondering who would be next.

The First World War had wiped out a whole generation of England's best and brightest young men at the beginning of the century—Morgan brooded— leaving the emotionally scarred survivors like Tolkien, invalided home from the

Somme, with the horrific experiences which grew into his vision of lifeless faces in the Dead Marshes and the corpses piled up like cordwood at Helm's Deep. But at the end of the twentieth century, the great mortality of HIV had erased some of the most amazing men of his own generation, with no writer yet emerging among the survivors, except maybe the author of *The Farewell Symphony*, to publish the great American AIDS novel commemorating the legions of the lost.

This profoundly sad moment first came upon Morgan as a little epiphany over his morning coffee, years before, as he sat hunched over Jacques Morali's obituary in the *Times* and realized on some bleak emotional level how the AIDS epidemic transformed the world in which he came of age in the 1970s, taking away so many friends full of youth and promise and wicked fun, as well as strangers seen regularly in the bars and discos, their faces floating in the dim light of backrooms and among the bushes beside the lake, their eyes eerily illuminated by lamplight filtered through leaves, eyes that came back in his memory now as ghostly reminders of the men who had died. So many strong bodies were laid in dark places, and so many handsome men had become the dust the wind blew away.

When he and Eddy drove to Washington to see the AIDS Quilt displayed on the Mall, he wandered off by himself, row after row, looking at all the young faces smiling in the stitch-work panels, with small mementoes, along with their wise or wiseass sayings, all the while thinking that each man had his own square of remembrance, a small fragment of his individuality joined with thousands of other men, their lives sewn together on the grass as their actual lives had touched and overlapped and warmed one another's, generation upon generation, the older passing along something to the younger, an opera anecdote or title of a much-beloved novel, or maybe some homely advice like *stop and smell the roses*, bits and pieces of many lifetimes not completely lost.

No writer of elegies, Morgan came away feeling almost a sacred duty to fulfill some of the dreams on behalf of these men who had fallen into darkness before the fullness of their years. So from time to time he did totally queer things like attending a Cher concert, not because he really wanted to, but because he knew *they* would have wanted some totally queer thrill like witnessing a live performance of *Strong Enough*.

And of course the virus still lived inside Eddy, lurking deep within every cell of blood and bone. Any day something could go haywire activating its lethal power and unleashing the medical horrors witnessed among their friends, the wasting away of muscles, the disfigurement of skin, the loss of control in bowels and bladder, and the blindness followed by dementia and a slow strangling death. Sometimes when Morgan could not sleep, he rolled over and watched Eddy, gazing at his profile against the window and listening to Eddy's slow breathing. Morgan smiled at the funny noise he made that was not quite snoring and counted the breaths—ten ... eleven ... twelve—as one way to become intensely aware of Eddy's stubborn hold on life. A few times in the middle of the night, Morgan drew close enough that he could inhale Eddy's breath, strangely comforted tasting the air that had already passed deep inside his lover's body. If he had known how to pray, Morgan would have given thanks for all the bonus time shared with this man who lay slumbering beside him.

In Las Vegas when the Village People finished their first song and the audience was cheering wildly, Eddy leaned over and said above the roar, "These guys don't have the same dance moves they used to."

"That's because they're really old. They're my age."

Eddy elbowed him. "*Our* age! You gotta problem with that? Huh?"

It was not long before they were on their feet with the rest of the audience, Morgan clapping a... laughing out loud while Eddy joined the teenagers bogeying in the aisles.

During the ... months after moving to Brooklyn, they launched themselves upon a campaign of giving dinner parties and ho... ing fundraisers for food deliveries to AIDS patients (Eddy's charity) and a halfway house for gay alcoholics in early recovery (Morgan's charity) until they discovered their niche on the other side of the East River. Eddy found a yoga studio run by a Russian woman who went every year to study with Iyengar in India. Morgan knew a lot about foundations and fundraising, and he wrangled an invitation to join the board of the Brooklyn Museum. He enjoyed the VIP treatment whenever he arrived unexpectedly to look at O'Keeffe's painting of the Brooklyn Bridge, always lingering an extra minute to recall that curly-haired art student in the tattered jean jacket in front of *Black Hollyhock Blue Larkspur* at the Met.

Morgan established a new line-up of weekly A.A. meetings, the only places where he really felt connected with the rest of the human race. Every time he sat in a church basement with a cup of coffee and a chocolate chip cookie, he felt something deep-down awaken in his ancestral memory, something hardwired into his DNA, from when warriors sat around the campfire, ate, drank something warm, and shared stories as they looked into the eyes of their brothers.

They acquired different friends generally after Morgan quit drinking, owners of art galleries, English professors at NYU, old money and new money with showplaces in the Hamptons, sometimes Eddy's high-class customers and sometimes Morgan's non-drinking friends from meetings. Values had shifted and they got invited to tonier parties. "Is Susan Sontag here yet?" became Morgan's standard question when arriving, always anxious to eavesdrop on the high priestess of bohemia, but afraid he might get snapped at, so usually just smiled and nodded, and never expressed an opinion on the latest play, novel, or political controversy. All the while he kept a careful reckoning of social engagements, just as his mother used to, always reminding Eddy when they left for the evening, "They owe us" or "Now we'll owe them."

The move to Brooklyn occasioned much personal stock-taking after disrupting the comfortable rhythms of their lives on the Upper West Side. Morgan could not remember exactly when he quit running outdoors, for example. He knew he took a break during the frigid winter when there was too much ice on the jogging paths, and he remembered taking time off during the brutal summer when it was too humid, even if he rested midway on the gray boulder across from the boathouse. "Do you remember exactly when I stopped running in Central Park?" he asked Eddy one autumn evening, sweater-weather, when they were sitting on the front steps.

Their brownstone had marble steps where they chatted with neighbors about mutual problems like water in their basements. Pigeons roosting in the eves provided a ready-made topic of complaint with the lesbian couple across the street, both gynecologists, when Morgan and Eddy were not engrossed in their own conversation. "Wasn't it the summer Jim Fixx dropped dead while jogging?"

"That's right. On a country road in New Hampshire."

"Another senior moment? Memory is the *second* thing to go."

"As if!"

In the 1980s when aerobics classes became popular, there was never any excuse for getting lazy. At the gym on Lower Broadway on his way to work, some aerobics classes were taught by a black drag queen in high heels and a blonde wig who shouted, "Come on, girls! If you don't squeeze your asses, nobody else will want to!" Though never one for team sports, Morgan swallowed his pride and started with high-impact aerobics, then bench-step classes easier on the knees, and ended up in bicycle spin classes as the fashion in cardiovascular exercise shifted along with the styles in men's jackets, from two-button to double-breasted to three-button. Once in a while, he enjoyed a game of squash with Ethan, even though they spent more time talking than chasing the ball around the court. But with his hospital duties and family obligations, his old Princeton partner had little time for racket sports. Morgan swam whenever he had a chance but found the indoor pools too small, too skuzzy, so finally he settled for pounding out his five-mile runs on the treadmill.

As an extra reward for regular workouts, his local gym was full of masculine eye-candy in shorts and tank tops. Young hotties half his age asked Morgan to spot them for bench presses. Hunky trainers touched him on the shoulders and thighs, a trick of their trade, when showing him how to use the newest machines. The weight room was an all-male Versailles with its hall of mirrors, where professional men could cast romantic glances at bodybuilders without risking rejection, even without making eye-contact with the objects of their erotic longings, and then turn away quickly, if caught, and fix their attentions on a barbell rack.

When tattoos became the new fad, Eddy talked about getting ink on his upper arm, an Egyptian ankh or a circle of barbed wire, or maybe the Chinese ideogram meaning *Health*. He never did. "How do I know the tattoo artist really knows Chinese? Maybe I'd walk around for the rest of my life with *Fuck Me* inked on my shoulder."

Morgan's response was simple: "My people don't get tattoos." Then one night when they were crawling into bed, he noticed that Eddy had trimmed his pubic hair. "What the fuck is that?"

"Just neatening up."

"Without asking me first? What if I shaved my chest to show off my pecs. I used to shave my whole body when I swam competitively at Princeton."

"You'll ruin the perfect T of your chest hair."

"Okay, so no more trimming or shaving."

Always supportive of his partner's A.A. recovery, Eddy never mentioned the increase of profanity in their conversations. Even after years of sobriety, Morgan came home from meetings using every four-letter word the nuns punished eighth graders for writing on the bathroom walls.

Eddy never intended to mention Morgan's weight gain, either, until he slipped and referred to his lower belly as his *overhang*. So when he turned forty, Morgan joined Weight Watchers to lose the ten pounds gained when he stopped drinking and started eating Haagen-Dazs at bedtime. These were the stubborn ten pounds he could not work off by running his five miles on the treadmill. Nothing if not disciplined, Morgan dropped fifteen pounds during the first month. The obese women at his neighborhood group envied him and hated him and gave him dirty looks when he showed up for weekly weigh-ins.

Eddy did nothing new with diet or exercise after turning forty, although yoga had gradually given his body new definition, increasing the shoulders while lessening his biceps, like a ballet dancer whose strength went entirely to his legs and upper arms. Then one night Morgan thought he noticed something about Eddy's body that filled him with tremendous sorrow. It was a small patch of loose flesh on his lower back, a slack area just over the kidneys where the skin seemed to sag a little. Morgan had noticed this problem area on older men at the gym. To his horror he thought that he discovered the same crumple on his own lower back when he aligned all the bathroom mirrors at just the right angles to check.

"You're still an Aryan god from the front," Eddy said when Morgan modeled naked for him in the bedroom, "but your days as a Speedo model are numbered. Your backside is starting to look like . . ."

"Like Brian Wimmer in *Late for Dinner?*"

"I was gonna say Clint Eastwood in *Bridges of Madison County*. Also suggest you phone Kyan's salon to start back waxing."

"If you really love me, you'd say Brian Wimmer."

Their all-time favorite Santa Fe movie was an independent film about two cute guys who get cryogenically frozen and come back twenty-nine years later, not aged a bit, searching for the loved ones they had left behind. The villain was played by Peter Gallagher with his crazy black eyebrows. The sidekick was played by Peter Berg who became a successful director. The hero's wife was played by Marcia Gay Harden who later won an Oscar. Even the minor role of the bitchy counter girl was played by Janeane Garofalo. But the star of *Late for Dinner* never made the big time, but had the cutest, firmest, and most well-rounded butt Morgan ever saw. Brian Wimmer's rump set their gold standard for cute asses.

Confronting the prospect of this minor sag on Eddy's backside upset Morgan deeply, because in his mind Eddy never changed from the gorgeous man first spotted at Studio 54. When you meet them young—as the old saying goes—you always remember them young. Whenever Morgan touched his lover's body and ran his hand along his back, he still thrilled at the physique of the teenage gymnast.

One night after Morgan had been working late, he came home and found Eddy curled up in bed, watching *Duck Soup* on the VCR and sobbing. At first Morgan feared his T-cell count had dropped and Ethan diagnosed something hideous, but actually Eddy's ophthalmologist had told him he needed reading glasses. Shocked and depressed, he slept until noon and spent the rest of the day watching Marx Brothers videos, his favorite *Night at the Opera* twice, rewinding so that he could watch the Stateroom Scene a grand total of five times, while Morgan wandered in and out of the bedroom asking, "Is my Aunt Minnie in here?"

When Morgan's hair started turning gray, it blended so naturally with his wheat-colored blondness that nobody noticed for a long time, including Morgan himself. The truth hit one Saturday morning when he was getting a haircut at their favorite salon in SoHo. Staring at the clippings fallen in his lap, he suddenly realized how much silver was mixed with the blond. He felt so upset he almost threw up. It was far worse than the day his stylist suggested getting an electric trimmer for his ear hair. When did this happen? At first Morgan quipped that a man in his professional position needed to look distinguished, but two weeks later, he asked Kyan to begin coloring his hair when he came for weekly trims.

Eddy found out that he was developing crown baldness when Kyan asked if he had ever thought about minoxidil treatments. The stylist used the term *thinning hair* because he had long experience with middle-aged gay men and their horror over going bald. When he angled the hand mirror for his client to see, Eddy nearly cried in the middle of the busy salon. Immediately he joined the other men wearing baseball caps at the gym and in the kitchen.

"Why should you be the last gay male wearing his Yankees cap backwards?" Then Morgan moved closer and lowered his voice so nobody else in the restaurant would hear. "Remember how long your hair was when we first met? When you would lie on top of me, your hair tumbled down over my face like a tent, brushing across my forehead and making the whole world go away. I could smell your cologne, and your mouth tasted like you just ate an apple. I loved disappearing under that tent of long hair while you lay on top kissing me."

The next morning, Eddy started using minoxidil twice daily as directed, and decided to let his hair grow longer again.

In 1997 when they celebrated twenty years together, Eddy forced his partner to confront the "dancing issue" that had troubled their relationship since the first night at Studio 54 when Eddy danced with the movie star and Morgan hovered on the sidelines, watching. He made a reservation at the Rainbow Room and invited some other couples—Ethan and Meredith, Baby Josh and his girlfriend Akiko, and Tony and his fiancée Rachel—to join them for dinner and dancing. Claire brought her latest boyfriend Bobby, a jumpy A.A. newcomer who resembled the movie star Colin Farrell, Morgan thought, only not as ragged-looking and not chain-smoking. Their table was served by a tall young Russian who introduced himself as Peter. "I understand there is a very special dinner tonight. The pastry chef has been working all day on the cake."

Morgan replied, "Nothing is too good for the man I love most in the whole world."

Eddy's timing was flawless. "He means *himself!*"

To make sure that Morgan would not balk, Eddy arranged in advance for the orchestra to play a medley of waltz tunes from *Rosenkavalier*. "If you danced with the debutantes, you can dance with me," Eddy said as he led Morgan reluctantly onto the revolving dance floor, both men in tuxedos with gardenia boutonnieres. "They're playing our song."

"We can't dance to opera."

"We can dance to anything."

Nearby an older couple stared and whispered to each other. Eddy got his tough-guy expression and looked ready for a fight when they drew nearer, smiled again, and offered compliments. The wife said how much they looked like Tom Hanks and that good-looking Spanish actor in *Philadelphia*.

"Do you realize," Morgan said as he followed Eddy's footwork, "we belong to the first generation of gay men not living in secret, not like those two cowboys in *The New Yorker* short story? We never needed to whisper in bed."

"Does it matter, I mean, as long as we had each other?"

"Absolutely! I want a world where two men can love each other, and rednecks be damned."

"Who are you kidding? You're so old-fashioned, you care what every stranger thinks, rednecks included."

It was only a short time before Morgan slowed to a two-step and they were simply embracing, rocking back and forth in the middle of the floor. Dancing nearby with his wife, Ethan caught Morgan's eye and gave a wink. Morgan looked back at Eddy. Among all the couples in the Rainbow Room, there was a glint, a spark, *something* that still passed between the two men after twenty years. When Morgan laughed out loud, his lover knew why. The orchestra was playing the same waltz tune that Eddy recognized from *Carnal Knowledge* when Morgan first tested him about opera.

The week before the tenth anniversary of their move to Brooklyn, he and Eddy had one of their rare tiffs. Earlier in the day while Morgan was eating lunch at his desk, his usual peanut butter sandwich, he had been googling "Schwarzenegger 1977" for images of the bodybuilder from the summer when he *might* have been in Central Park. Certainly Mr. Universe was in New York then, because Morgan found homoerotic portraits of him by '70s artists like Warhol, Mapplethorpe, and Jamie Wyeth, really quite a beautiful man when young, and Claire had never proved wrong about any man that good-looking—when his secretary Scott, also on lunch break, took over the keyboard and showed him an online website for gay dating. "Tell me about your ideal man. Just for fun."

Morgan mused. To help him with the game, Scott went from question to question in the profile, filling in the lifestyle preferences (nonsmoker) and sexual preferences (top seeking bottom). Morgan hesitated when it came to the question of age. "Online, Mr. Cabell, men lose years and gain inches."

After deciding on 35-50 for the men's ages, Scott searched only for profiles with pictures. He hit the enter key, and in seconds all the profiles matching Morgan's ideal man came flashing up. When he leaned forward to look at the monitor, the first picture he spotted was Eddy's.

"Well," Scott said awkwardly as he shut down the internet browser, "I guess the system works. It found your perfect match."

Morgan felt crazed for the rest of the day. He sat at his desk but could not focus on paperwork. He paced the office. He stared out the window of the World Trade Center, always unsettled to look down upon a helicopter flying hundreds of feet below. He drank a double cappuccino and ate three of the Krispy Kreme doughnuts that Scott always kept handy. Then he swallowed two aspirins, the only pills still "legal" in recovery, and leaned against his desk waiting to feel better.

Finally he phoned his A.A. sponsor and was told to pray about it. After slamming down the receiver and saying "Shit!" a dozen times, Morgan closed his office door and got down on his knees. Always skeptical about prayer, Morgan had long ago decided that the mass sobriety of millions of alcoholics offered objective evidence that God existed, or consolation if He did not. But he felt crazier than ever when he rose from kneeling. He knew the words by rote after memorizing all of the standard A.A. prayers, even the complicated St. Francis Prayer letter perfect, but could not focus. All that he could think about was finding Eddy's profile on the gay dating website.

Sexual preference: "Bottom seeking top."

Relationship status: "Shh! Don't ask."

Of course over a lifetime together, each man had faced his moment of weakness and strayed. One evening in Sean T.'s crowded yoga class in Santa Fe, Eddy brushed fingers with a Coyote Café waitress on the next mat while doing their last round of Sun Salutations. He felt an erotic surge and the woman felt it, too. While lying in corpse pose at the end of class, the young blonde's fingers extended and grazed Eddy's palm where it lay open upward. Eddy should have inched away to break the contact, but he did not, as their fingertips continued lightly touching. Afterward the waitress lingered in the parking lot and said directly when Eddy stared down at the ground and kicked gravel into the acequia, "I have a partner, too, but she's in San Francisco on business. You know the hundred-mile rule." Later that night when he had showered and was slipping into bed beside Morgan after lights-out, he mumbled only, "My troika was chased by wolves." But he knew where home was.

And one afternoon in his office at NYU where he taught part-time, Morgan looked up and saw a third-year law student loitering outside in the hallway. He never had this young man in any classes, but noticed him in the library and on the stairs. Morgan retained an acute sense of male beauty wherever he spotted it, casting enough curious looks he set off the young man's gaydar. Even as the professor looked up from the pile of bluebooks, his gaze lingered until the young man took courage and stepped slowly into the office, turned and closed the door. He fiddled with the knob to make sure it was locked. "I want to suck your cock," the student said as he turned again to face him. Startled by his directness, Morgan did not move, said nothing in reply, and next he found himself reclining in his chair as the student kneeled between his legs and unbuckled his belt. Morgan kept repeating silently with his eyes closed, "He's not my student, he's not my student."

The world did not explode afterwards. Nothing worse happened except

Morgan brooded guiltily, lost sleep, ate too much ice-cream, blamed the student, and finally resolved the moral impasse by reminding himself of his simple contract with Eddy: *Whatever I do, I will never leave you.* He too knew where home was. But this online hook-up advertisement felt like a huge public betrayal for the whole world to see. Scott knew. Anyone could know.

So when Morgan got to the restaurant at dinner time, he went straight to the kitchen. "Let's take a walk around the corner," he said. Eddy had not heard this line in a long time, but knew that it meant Morgan was upset about something, and he would ask a bunch of questions before finding out why. Turning his Yankees cap around, brim forward, he followed Morgan outside and down the sidewalk.

When he discovered the reason, Eddy shot back, "So why were *you* looking at a dating website?"

Calming down a little, Morgan explained. Then Eddy explained. "You know my waiter Stephen, the actor/waiter/model from Ohio?"

"Iowa."

"Whatever! One of those square states. He did it for a joke. When things got slow after lunch on Friday, we went through the list of questions online. He took pictures with his digital camera, headshots only, nothing X-rated. He wrote down the website and said my profile would be posted over the weekend. The email address is Stephen's. Look it up if you don't believe me. I never got around to it. Too fucking busy."

"And vice versa?"

Eddy gave him a hard glance under the brim of his cap.

No longer angry, Morgan went red with embarrassment, slumped forward, and stood silently staring down at the sidewalk, working his jaw muscles as he moped. Eddy took off his baseball cap and swiped him across the head with it. Then he leaned forward and kissed Morgan on the tip of his nose. "Careful, Old Man, or those furrows in your brow will cause more wrinkles."

Soon laughing, the two men began jostling playfully and having a tickle war. Morgan never checked the website to see if the email address was Stephen's. There were things these two men never discussed with each other—what exactly Morgan did in bed with Ethan, for example, or why Keith Haring dedicated a painting to Eddy—but they never intentionally lied to each other.

The evening ended in the usual way when Morgan apologized for getting upset.

The next morning promised a gorgeous late-summer day in New York. Morgan and Eddy rode together on the subway into Lower Manhattan. This was rare. Every weekday Morgan took the subway to work while reading his pocket-sized A.A. meditation book, scrupulously marking the upper margins with a running tabulation of the number of days he had been sober. On September 11, 2001, Morgan had gone without a tumbler of bourbon for exactly 5,140 days.

Today Eddy rode with him because he had an appointment with a design firm at Ninety West, near Morgan's offices at the World Trade Center. He was moving his restaurant to a larger space on Fifth Avenue, the latest hip-and-cool boulevard in Brooklyn, and he wanted a major makeover of the entire space. The chief designer for the project was Cousin Frankie, Aunt Lourdes's son and the other *maricón* in the family. "It's not just about the food anymore," Eddy kept explaining as he did when nervous. "The failure rate for new restaurants is nearly a hundred percent. Know that?"

"Only because you told me a million times already. Since when did we worry about the odds?" He brushed a speck of dandruff from the shoulder of Eddy's black Armani suit. "Donald Trump is wrong. You don't need to be paranoid to succeed in business."

Morgan decided to get off at Bowling Green, the first subway station on the other side of the river. It was such a beautiful day he wanted to walk the rest of the way to work. "Remember the old saying about taking time to smell the roses? I'll phone Scott and tell him I'm running behind today."

"Be sure to tell him you're smelling the fucking roses! I'd join you but I'd be late for Cousin Frankie."

"Ha, you're just afraid of scuffing your new Gucci loafers."

Morgan gave Eddy a quick kiss—"Good luck!"—before he squeezed out of the crowded subway car and disappeared beyond the sliding doors. Before the train left the station, the electricity flickered on and off, creating an eerie glow against the red-glazed tiles on the tunnel walls. Eddy felt a sinking feeling in his gut like a foreboding, an alien sensation that caught at his breath. His scalp prickled. He touched his chest beneath his crisp starched shirt, making sure he put on the silver cross from Chimayó that he always wore for business meetings. When he found it fastened on its sturdy chain, the crucifix with the church-dirt calmed his nerves.

All major events in Morgan's life occurred during summers, but autumn remained his favorite season in New York. The air was clearer, the sky seemed bluer, and the sunshine gave the city a cleaner, richer look. He looked forward to the elegant Custom House as he climbed the stairs from the subway stop. Vendors had set up booths around the grass ellipse. In case Scott forgot the doughnuts, Morgan stopped and bought a bag of chocolate chip cookies from a cute guy who said he baked them himself. Chatting about the nice weather as he fell further behind in his morning schedule, Morgan lingered because the young man had such a bright smile and gimlet-green eyes. He was reminded of Gene, the transplanted Virginian who managed his favorite gay bookstore and had jumped off the Williamsburg Bridge when diagnosed HIV positive, almost twenty years before.

There was definitely a hint of autumn in the air as he hitched his leather bag over his shoulder and walked up Broadway. He kept gazing at the cloudless blue sky, never failing to feel a little awe-struck when he turned a corner anywhere in Manhattan and caught sight of the World Trade Center looming at unexpected angles. The Twin Towers belonged to the air and light, Morgan thought as he ambled, catching the moods of the weather, the times of day, constantly changing colors, solid as earth and high as heaven. In the gray dawn, the towers were gray. At sunset on a clear day, they glowed golden. But on foggy winter mornings, their tops disappeared into the clouds and seaborne mists, becoming as otherworldly as some sacred mountain in Japan. Their pewter surfaces did not glare like glass but reflected back, gently, with a softness that belied their immense sizes. Whenever he and Eddy strolled along the esplanade in Brooklyn Heights, the twin campaniles of some crazy postmodern Venice seemed to float above the river like a great lagoon.

Eddy was right, Morgan thought as he dropped his gaze to the sidewalk where three pigeons were pecking at a discarded pretzel. His mind always likened something to something else, always reaching for weird comparisons, the more esoteric the better. But there *was* something Moorish about the Twin Towers at street level, how the columns converged in rows of arches across their facades, something intended as historical allusion by the architects. On rainy winter mornings when he trudged across the plaza to the North Tower, he imagined the awe of Ferdinand and Isabella, conquerors of Granada, when they first stepped inside the wonderland of the Alhambra Palace, with its forest of pillars and walls alive with gold inscriptions, and gaped in amazement.

It was fashionable to dismiss the Twin Towers as ugly, useless even as office space, but Morgan never agreed with majority opinions. These were buildings that even a child could love because they were so easy to draw: two upright rectangles and some puffy clouds with maybe an airplane flying by. Whenever he drove into the city, they drew him like some prehistoric monument, a glass and steel Stonehenge with the enchantment of those long-dead architects stored in their colossal masses. Like an astronomer before the dawn of human history, Morgan plotted the movements of the moon by the two pylons as he gazed from his fourth-floor study at home, these primordial giants forever defining the Manhattan skyline. He could always close his eyes and see Cher, still in her opera dress from the night before, kicking the tin can down the street in *Moonstruck* with these two towers sparkling in the early-morning light across the river behind her.

As Morgan reached Trinity Church and paused across the street from the old cemetery with its weathered gravestones, the air's clarity had a whiskey-zing that made him yearn for cool autumn mornings back in New Mexico. There, wild sunflowers would be blossoming, and soon the fields would be lined with bales of alfalfa ready to be stacked in barns. Pueblo boys were selling apples and raspberries from roadside stands, while downtown the air grew pungent with green chiles roasted for sale in parking lots. A west wind blew dry off the mesas where snakeweed bloomed in yellow clumps. Milkweed pods were splitting open, their silky puffs lodging in thistles bordering the horse pastures. Their neighbor Demian, the old hippie with his silver ponytail, would be burning dead hollyhocks cut along his driveway, the pall of smoke hanging above stubble fields.

Soon chilly gusts would rattle corn stalks in Eddy's garden now that their caretaker José shut off the acequia water for the winter months. Willows would glow scarlet along the rivers, while aspens turned golden at the higher elevations where marmots whistled to each other among lichen boulders. Deer would sniff frost on the air and move silently along the edges of alpine meadows. A sugary sprinkling of snow would soon cap the tallest mountains. The sky turned a thin blue after a snowfall. From Park Slope to Tesuque, it was eight hours door to door, very doable, even on a whim. Yet he and Eddy almost never witnessed the autumn glories in their sandstone valley, when migrating doves flocked the cottonwoods and white cranes glided down the Rio Grande flyway. Never once had they attended the Zozobra Fiesta with the burning of Old Man Gloom. It came too late for summer vacationers. Checking his watch—it was 8:46 a.m.—Morgan felt that his well-regulated habits meant he was always missing out on *something*.

As he stood on the curbstone waiting for the traffic light to change, his eyes played along the old church's reddish spires, and he recalled another autumn morning, years before, when Baby Josh was christened and Eddy made him burst out laughing in the solemnity of the medieval chapel when he whispered, just loud enough for everyone to hear, "Always a godfather, never a god."

Morgan was still looking up into the blue sky above these spires when suddenly the jetliner shot into view. He was amazed how low it was flying. He had never seen an aircraft flying so low over Manhattan. Maybe they were filming a TV commercial? The plane soared so close, he felt the vibrations, its turbines making a whistling noise as if descending to land. The pilot began gunning the engines. "Pull up! Pull up!" Morgan repeated out loud.

The airliner flew directly into the North Tower, which Morgan could hardly see from where he was lingering across the street from the churchyard. The South Tower was in the way. But he saw with terrifying clarity the flames that burst from the building, then a white mushroom cloud rising high into the sky. Enough jet fuel for a transcontinental flight ignited on impact. A moment later, he heard the explosion. The shockwave sent a flock of pigeons scattering into the air from the cemetery lawn where they were feeding. After that, everything moved in slow-motion for Morgan. Everything felt unreal.

Morgan couldn't move as he sensed intensely the solidness of the building nearest him, the sunshine glinting in its windows, and the large FedEx truck with orange and blue lettering that slowed to a halt on Broadway. Morgan would never tell anyone what he really thought when the aircraft plunged into the tower and the orange fireball exploded against the sky, with a blizzard of papers showering down like confetti on a tickertape parade, because he thought it was the most spectacularly beautiful sight he ever witnessed. Lines from the poem his father used to quote popped into his mind: *All is changed, changed utterly. A terrible beauty is born.*

After several moments of almost mystical clarity, Morgan's brain went into overdrive. His office was located in that tower with all his colleagues and staff. Scott was already at his desk. Morgan had spoken to him on his mobile phone maybe ten minutes earlier. But he could not think about that now. All he could think about was Eddy riding the subway into the heart of the disaster. Ninety West was in the shadow of the explosion.

Morgan dug his cell phone from his shoulder bag and pressed the speed-dial button. He got a recorded message saying the call could not go through. He dialed again and got the same message. He dialed a third time, but the circuits were overloaded and he got only dead air. He dropped the useless mobile back into his leather satchel.

Morgan did not spend another moment thinking. His mind went into some white arctic zone of pure alertness, and he headed in the direction of West Street where he knew Eddy had been going. There was no time, only movement forward.

Everyone was looking up and pointing as Morgan ran past. The impact's concussion had triggered car alarms. A workman in a hardhat shouted "What the fuck!" over and over. A fat black woman held tight to a mailbox, moaning loudly and wailing as she rocked back and forth. Men in dark suits walked quickstep in every direction.

People backed up against buildings and stared up, their hands shielding their eyes against the slant of morning light as Morgan dashed past. A stockbroker was yelling into his cell phone, "Turn on your fucking TV!" A young man in a white shirt and dark tie, with a student knapsack on his back, sprinted past him in the opposite direction. His face was visible for only a second. A mask of horror.

Thousands of papers had been blown from the higher floors and a paper trail of international commerce was suddenly airborne. Scraps of office memos, purchase forms, and stock orders began reaching the sidewalk near him, some on fire as they fluttered to earth. Higher above the narrow street a flock of seagulls, beating their wings and crying warning calls, flew seaward for safety.

In the next block Morgan encountered a familiar face in the crowd. It was Father Mike from his old A.A. meetings, the white-haired friar always offering a word of advice and a pat on the back. Father Mike was wearing his FDNY jacket and chaplain's cap as he hurried toward of the burning building, dodging people not watching where they were going as they ran down the sidewalk. Morgan shouted, "Have you seen Eddy anywhere?"

"No, but he's a good Catholic boy so he's in God's hands."

"I don't know what to do to find him."

"Go where God wants you to, Morgan, and do what He wants you to do— and pray." He gave his arm a quick squeeze before rushing to join his firefighters. "God likes hearing from strangers!"

A photographer with three cameras slung around his neck zoomed past on rollerblades, slammed into a parking meter and fell backwards on the pavement, stunned with the wind knocked out of him. Father Mike paused just long enough to help the young man to his feet before continuing toward the lobby of the North Tower.

Papers were still falling from the sky like ghostly snowflakes when Morgan arrived at Ninety West. He bolted through the lobby to check the directory board, and then bounded up the stairwell two and three steps at a time until he reached the design offices five flights up. But Eddy was not there. He never arrived. At least that's what Morgan gathered from the one frantic secretary leaving just when he arrived. Cousin Frankie had been one of the first to evacuate the building. Morgan decided to wait, slipping off his shoulder bag and depositing it along with his laptop on the sofa in Frankie's office. The bag of chocolate chip cookies fell out. Most were broken now. He left them where they lay on the cushions.

Morgan checked his watch—it was 9:02 a.m.—as he stood at the window watching Tower One burning high above him. From the gaping hole in the skyscraper's side, a huge cloud of black smoke trailed for miles across the river toward Brooklyn, when another screaming came across the sky.

Something like a shadow passed overhead, and a second airliner streaked into view, banked sharply and smashed into the corner of the South Tower. The window where Morgan was standing rattled when the waves of impact hit. The explosion rolled from one side of the massive structure to the other as an orange fireball erupted and shards of metal flew into the air. Fiery debris rained down toward the street below. One of the airliner's engines broke off and flew away on its own, gliding in a wide curve, its contrail streaming behind like a comet as a black mushroom cloud rose, shrouding the whole upper half of the tower.

Morgan suddenly understood that the first collision had been no accident. These were suicide attacks. Men had killed themselves in order to kill many others. Wobbly in the legs, Morgan sat back against the desk to steady himself. What else could he do? Where else could he go?

The office suites were deserted now. Morgan did not panic because he did not grasp the danger. He did not know that jet fuel had fallen on the roof and the building's top stories had caught fire. People had been killed in the elevators several floors above while he leaned against the desk, still staring out the window and hoping that Eddy would show up.

Flames were pouring from great gashes in both skyscrapers. Smaller plumes streamed from broken windows, and thermals made the bigger smoke clouds billow violently between the two towers. Morgan watched the smoke merge into one monster cloud, blocking light and dimming the office where he stood. Faraway a crescent moon, strangely serene, hung pale on the horizon.

On the street below, a hook-and-ladder truck with flashing yellow lights speeded in the direction of Tower Two. The windows muffled its siren. Papers like white butterflies continued fluttering down.

Morgan spotted other objects falling at steady intervals now, strange moving objects, human beings jumping from the upper floors where the fires raged out of control. Near the impact zone, office workers were throwing chairs, fire extinguishers, computer monitors, anything to break the glass and let fresh air inside. First these desperate people clustered at the windows in groups, four and five pressed on top of each other, waving white cloths as distress flags. Then they crawled out, or were squeezed out, hanging in the breeze to avoid the burning jet fuel inside, desperate to breathe.

Now they were jumping, forced by toxic smoke to leap from those impossible heights. At such a great distance, just more falling debris, Morgan thought, some tumbling while others plummeted, rigid, all the way to the ground. Four, five, six seconds—gone.

What did these people think and feel, he wondered, in these unimaginably long seconds as they fell while still alive? Did this man concentrate on the pain of the hand, cut by broken glass as he perched briefly on the ledge until the final desperate decision, not jumping really but releasing himself into the air? Did that man look up into the blue sky and black billows as he fell, thinking nothing? Did another decide to make a quick end by plunging headfirst like a diver, looking straight down at the same plaza he had viewed hundreds of times behind protective glass, now rushing up at him at amazing speed. The velocity meant no time in the micro-second when the body hit and the skull exploded to feel any pain.

The Old Masters were wrong about suffering, thought Morgan. At least the boy Icarus had some dignity left when he fell from the sky, hallowed by a private death instead of being gawked at. Was his secretary Scott one of the faraway specks with flailing arms and legs, plummeting from the eighty-ninth floor? Or was Scott inside being burned alive by the flames? When Morgan craned his neck to see the topmost floors belching smoke, he saw people leaning from windows and waving for help that would never come. A sudden wave of nausea overwhelmed him and he stumbled into the executive washroom—which turned out to be a storage closet—where he threw up into a box of architectural blueprints.

When he finished and began searching his pockets for a handkerchief, Morgan heard a series of loud snapping noises. Nearby the South Tower was cracking at its seams. Floors gave way as steel supports melted, sagged, and buckled. Then the vast downward movement began amid billowing smoke as the skyscraper's geometry dissolved, and the gigantic structure imploded in a white avalanche, its upper floors pan-caking one on top of the other, like a freight train rumbling loudly overhead. The lethal snowball of panels and girders tumbled down in instant freefall.

On the fifth floor of Ninety West, a sudden rush of wind slammed the door behind Morgan in the storage closet, just before windows shattered and shards of glass were blown inward with the force of a bomb exploding. Crouching down, Morgan shut his eyes tight and clasped his hands over his ears. His mind raced and he thought if he survived, he would become a better lover, a better brother, a better lawyer, and a better human being. Then his mind focused and he had only one thought. He hoped for a quick and painless death.

The room went pitch-black as the electricity failed and the air filled with dust. When he realized he was still alive, strange memories and long-buried images flooded Morgan's mind. Beneath the busy brainwork and randomly firing synapses, Morgan was filled with the fear of dying and especially dying alone. Desperately he longed to embrace Eddy one last time.

When the rumbling stopped and he emerged from the closet, the room swirled with thick dust. His eyes stung, hazed over with tears whenever he tried opening them. He held his handkerchief over his mouth to keep from choking as he groped for the door and lurched into the hallway. Emergency lighting guided him toward the stairwell and downward, floor after floor, until he found his way out. When he reached the street and looked up, he saw the upper stories of Ninety West engulfed in flames. Only then did he realize that he left behind his shoulder bag with laptop and mobile phone. "Big fucking deal!" he cried out loud. His voice sounded strange in the profound hush of the street. "Where's Eddy? Where the hell is that crazy Cuban?"

Dust from pulverized drywall continued pouring through the streets as Morgan plodded ankle-deep through layers of debris. Parked cars were covered in white. Other vehicles were crushed by twisted girders. The Marriott looked split open, the lobby collapsed so completely, nobody inside could have survived. He could see upper rooms with beds hanging out the windows.

Morgan lost track of time as he trudged forward. He crawled over rubble, stumbled, struggled to his feet again, and then staggered forward to the next tangle of rubble, his movements robotic. His mouth felt dry and his throat burned. The world looked submerged in black water. Breathing became more difficult. Dizziness came over him, wave after wave, as he peered through the soot-clogged air at every moving figure that came within sight, rushing toward anyone plodding through the buried street, hoping one of these phantoms might be Eddy. "This is what hell must look like," he kept repeating to himself. "This is what hell must look like."

Morgan felt weak. His whole body trembled uncontrollably and he sensed utter isolation, never thinking that people on rooftops throughout the city were training their binoculars on the disaster, while television cameras sent images of the catastrophe across oceans and continents. People all over the globe were focusing their attention on the very spot where Morgan felt so deserted and alone.

He forced himself to focus. "I am standing. I am walking. I am breathing through my handkerchief." When he paused for a coughing fit, Morgan looked down and saw a hand, a woman's hand, with fingernails painted bright red and rings on every finger. In that instant he realized that the dust everywhere, even the filthy air he breathed through his handkerchief, was loaded with physical remains of the people vaporized when the tower came down. Groaning, he turned and stumbled away.

Morgan was somewhere near Vesey Street when a figure emerged through the dim air and staggered in his direction, collapsing on his knees in front of him. It was a young fireman who had lost his helmet and his FDNY jacket, his whole face covered with blood. His nose was bleeding and he had a gash in his forehead. "Are you okay?" Morgan asked.

"Don't know. How bad does it look?"

Morgan took his handkerchief and pressed it over the head wound to stop the bleeding. The young firefighter had lost almost everything else but still clutched a bottle of water. Caked in white powder, hacking and bleeding, the young man did not realize the one thing that he still possessed was water. Morgan took the plastic bottle from his clinched fingers and raised it to the young man's lips. Then he took a deep swallow himself. Even his teeth felt gritty.

After several drinks, Morgan poured water over the gash on the fireman's forehead to see how deep it went. "What caused the cut?"

"Don't know, sir. Something falling, I guess."

Morgan shook out his handkerchief, rolled and furled it, tying it around the fireman's head to stop the bleeding. As he was helping the injured man to his feet and steadying him, there was a loud noise overhead.

Morgan had heard this sound before, a rumble like a freight train. The North Tower was collapsing far above them, its ceilings sagging and pipes bursting as the last supports gave way. Each floor emitted a whoosh of wind as it crashed down, pan-caking one on top of the next – boom! boom! boom! boom! boom! – showering the streets below with more glass and twisted steel. The pavement started vibrating. The vast structure standing half a mile in the sky was coming down, threatening to overtake the two men.

Spotting a subway entrance, Morgan grabbed the fireman and hustled them down the stairs. One floor below the street level, Morgan spotted an open entryway. A bearded man in a white turban held the heavy glass door wide as they fell inside his shoe repair shop. The owner bolted the door behind them.

Though weak from loss of blood and close to fainting from exhaustion, the young fireman sprang into action as his training kicked in. He pushed Morgan flat against the floor and fell on top of him, covering his rescuer's body with his own. Morgan closed his eyes and cringed at the noise of debris thundering overhead. One of the shop's windows blew out but the door held strong. Morgan felt the fireman's heart beating through their clothes, pounding fast from fear and adrenaline rush. Morgan was gripped with terror at the thought of being buried alive, trapped beneath the tons of rubble and slowly suffocating underground in total blackness. Only the hard pounding of the young man's heart steadied him to wait out the firestorm.

When the long shower of debris stopped falling, cinder-filled smoke flooded the subterranean space and blotted out all light. The air felt like a solid mass. Finally succumbing to exhaustion and blood loss, the fireman loosened his grip and rolled onto the floor now covered with gritty dust. Rising and turning quickly around, Morgan caught the fireman's body up in his arms and pulled him into a seated position, grabbing some white athletic socks from a display rack to cover the young man's mouth so he would not suffocate.

Gradually the emergency lights illuminated the room swirling with powdery clouds. The bearded man in the turban emerged from beneath the counter where he had taken shelter, looking like a warrior saint out of ancient myth, his brown skin turned white by the fine-grained dust. "Thanks!" Morgan shouted to their Sikh savior and then gasped for air. The owner of the shop nodded but said nothing, disappearing once again beneath the counter.

Morgan turned his attention to the firefighter, conscious again but dazed. "We need to get out of here."

"I need to get back to my buddies."

Morgan tried sounding street-tough. "You need a doctor! Gotta problem with that? Huh?"

"Whatever you say. You're my guardian angel. No lie!"

"I know where there's a hospital. Can you walk?"

"Yes, sir, I think so."

Morgan forced a smile to reassure him. "Make sure the handkerchief stays tight around your forehead, doesn't shake off. Think you can keep up with an old man?"

"Yes, sir."

"Then hold on. We're getting the hell out of here!"

They stumbled together up the subway stairs now cluttered and partly buried in debris. Near the street exit, their way was blocked by a large chunk of twisted bronze that had been Rodin's statue of a nude athlete mounted in the boardroom of a bond-trading firm. Strong after years of lifting weights, Morgan stooped down and gripped the crushed metalwork, pulling with all his might until it fell from their path. Stumbling behind, the fireman crawled the rest of the way up the stairs on his hands and knees.

Above, the scene was ghostly empty. The gigantic buildings had completely disintegrated, leaving behind no desks, no computers, no cubicle partitions, nothing but dust and twisted steel. Morgan felt disoriented as he tried deciding which way to head. His ears rang with the force of the concussion. Small pelting fragments were still falling. The smell was thick and toxic. In the distance, the gasoline tank in a burning car exploded, and the fireball briefly illuminated the scene with an eerie glow.

The streets looked like they were covered with new-fallen snow. When they agreed which way was north, they trudged in that direction. With Morgan's arm around his waist, the fireman did a brave job of keeping pace, his heavy boots plodding through the debris. "Hey, man, what's your name? I'm Ray—Ray Rodriguez."

Without answering, Morgan glanced over his shoulder. The Twin Towers were gone, erased from the landscape, an entire zip code vanished. All that he could make out was a row of Moorish arches topped with a ragged checkerboard of empty windows, vague in the distance where smoke billowed from underground fires, the only remnant of the colossal structure that had disappeared.

With so much destruction in every direction—police cars crushed, the hulk of a fire engine, an ambulance upside down with its lights still flashing, nearby buildings belching black smoke—Morgan looked down and saw empty shoes everywhere, mostly sandals and flip-flops, a few expensive high heels. Had people literally run out of their shoes while fleeing for their lives? A terrible feeling seized him when he spotted a single Gucci loafer in the dust.

People died here, lots of people, Morgan thought as he returned his attention to the fireman. "You still with me?"

"Let's roll!"

With arms around each other's shoulders, they quickened their pace, staggering away from ground zero.

Ethan's research assistant Carmen had turned on the television so he saw the events unfolding on CNN, the World Trade Center spewing smoke, the second airliner plowing in, and Tower Two collapsing. Thinking fast, he rushed downstairs to join other doctors in their green scrubs preparing for triage in the Emergency Room. St. Vincent's was one of the closest medical centers.

He was in the ER checking on the blood supply for transfusions and bandages for burn victims when Morgan arrived with his firefighter. Ethan hardly recognized him. Morgan's face was plastered white and his eyes were ringed with red. "Jesus Christ!" Ethan said. "There's blood all over your shirt."

"It's the fireman's. His name is Ray Rodriguez. He is with Ladder 1, Engine 7 of the Fire Department of New York. He's a proby, which means he's a rooky in the nine-month probationary period. His favorite food is some Puerto Rican pork roast his grandmother made when he was a kid. He grew up in Queens. He used to be a Marine. I've gotten to know him pretty well over the past hour."

Fireman Rodriguez was quickly surrounded by two doctors and three nurses. They lay him on a gurney and began rolling him down the hallway, but Ray grasped Morgan's hand as the gurney moved away. "¡Gracias por mi vida!" he cried before disappearing through the swinging doors. "You're my guardian angel. You're gonna to be in my prayers every night. No lie!"

Later in the day when the television crews arrived at the hospital, Ray Rodriguez told them how he was rescued by a stranger and he didn't even know the man's name. But Ethan gave the reporters his identity so that by the end of the week, Morgan Cabell had become one of the official heroes of 9/11. Some weeks afterwards, the mayor gave him a citation and wristwatch engraved with an inscription expressing the city's appreciation for his valor. He was even invited to a reception at the White House, but did not make the trip to Washington, having long ago stopped writing checks to the Log Cabin Republicans. Best of all, Ray Rodriguez's fellow firemen held a ceremony making Morgan an honorary member of Ladder 1. As a sign that he was one of their own, they gave him a FDNY t-shirt that Morgan wore at the gym until the lettering faded and the armpits wore out. Whenever people praised his actions, though, Morgan always gave credit to Fireman Rodriguez for the quick thinking that saved their lives when Tower One collapsed. Ray became a regular visitor to the Brooklyn home of his *Ángel de la Guardia*, as he never stopped calling Morgan, with more and more tough-guy teasing as the years went by. He was Tony's age, and the young men enjoyed attending Yankees games together with Tony's two sons.

But none of these future events were known to Morgan, even as vague possibilities, to distract him from his urgent business on September 11. "I'm looking for Eddy," he said to Ethan as he watched the fireman wheeled down the hall. "He had an appointment at Ninety West, but never arrived. Has he turned up here?"

Ethan shook his head. "He hasn't turned up here. Hardly anyone has. That's not a good sign."

Morgan slumped in the nearest chair. "Those that got out, they got out. Those that didn't, they died."

Ethan turned and leaned into the wall, his eyes staring blankly at the white surface.

"My cell phone didn't work," Morgan continued as he struggled to his feet. "I can't get home because the subways aren't running. Somebody told me the police had closed the bridges. Is there a landline I can use?"

Ethan gathered himself together and led Morgan to a nurses' station. He got only the answering machine. Then Morgan called the restaurant. Ken said that Eddy had not come back, had not phoned to check in.

"You can stay here," Ethan said when Morgan hung up. "Eddy might come looking for you here."

Morgan thought for a moment. "Is there anything I can do to help?"

"You're already done a hero's work," Ethan replied gravely, looking around at the edgy doctors standing outside on the dock where the ambulances were supposed to arrive, but had not.

"Then I'll keep looking."

"At least let me clean out your eyes." Ethan sent an intern searching for an empty examining room.

"I want to tell you something." Morgan came to a halt in the middle of the hospital corridor, reaching out to the wall to steady himself as a wave of dizziness came and went. "I'm so proud of what you've made of your life, your commitments to helping people. You didn't need to work with AIDS patients. I just wanted to say I'm grateful you stayed my friend."

"I'm proud of you, too, your loyalty, the men you help in A.A. recovery, your passion for the things you care about. I'm glad we didn't drift apart after Princeton."

"You have your lacrosse buddies."

"It's not the same. You and me, we've got something those other guys don't. We're lifers, friends for the long haul."

"Yes, sir, for the long haul."

"But now I'm worried about Eddy." Ethan dried some tears with a knotted kleenex he found in his lab jacket. "He's my star patient. After beating HIV for so many years, I can't believe anything else awful could happen to him. Not today, not this way."

"He knows how to take care of himself. He's got street smarts."

The intern returned with the saline solution and Ethan washed out his friend's eyes, using the damp cloth to scrub away as much grime as he could from

Morgan's face. When he finished, he grasped Morgan's arm and squeezed tight. "Go get 'em, tiger!"

Outside on the sidewalk, Morgan lost the sense of bravado about Eddy's street smarts, his trick of survival. A lone ambulance arrived with a burn victim, a woman with her hair scorched off. Not far away, Morgan looked into the hospital's plate glass window and saw his own ghastly figure, his suit covered in ash and hair plastered white with dust.

Moving unsteadily along a wall that would soon be covered with pictures of the missing, Morgan lurched to a halt, stood still for several moments, and then kneeled down beside a large trash barrel so that he would not look so conspicuous. He remembered what Father Mike said. He began searching his frantic brain for a prayer.

Far-off sirens wailed at different pitches through the canyons of Lower Manhattan. Police helicopters hovered overhead. Motorcycles with swirling red lights wove in and out between trucks parked in the middle of the street. Otherwise an eerie quiet descended on the city. Crouching on the sidewalk, Morgan's sense of embarrassment was overwhelming. Even in the privacy of their bedroom whenever Eddy walked in and found him on his knees, Morgan always felt awkward, as if he had been caught masturbating or reading porn.

But what else could he do? After hundreds of meetings in church basements, his cliché-ridden A.A. training clicked in. Before, he merely went through the motions, hit his knees, mouthed the words silently to himself, always the same set prayers, and then went about his day. Now he found his words without any forethought. "God," he whispered, "Father Mike says you like hearing from strangers."

After this halting start, Morgan paused, concentrated on quieting his mind, and asked some spiritual power that he never really called upon before— that he had no name for—to help him find Eddy safe and sound. He remembered Father Mike's favorite prayer repeated so many times in A.A. meetings:

> Lord, take me where you want me to go,
> Let me meet who you want me to meet,
> Tell me what you want me to say,
> And keep me out of your way.

A sense came over Morgan as he knelt on the sidewalk, where small bits of gravel hurt his knees, that he had always been guided places. On this one single day he should have been killed three times over. Instead of sitting at his desk on the eighty-ninth floor, he had gotten off the subway two stops early so he could smell the roses. Instead of standing at the windows when they exploded and strafed the room with glass, he was in the closet where the door slammed behind him. He and the young fireman just happened to find an open entryway and safe haven down the subway stairs when Tower One collapsed. And this was only one day!

His whole life suddenly materialized before him as a long series of close calls and near misses. Every bit of good fortune had depended upon inches and seconds, totally defying the laws of probability and beating the odds to deliver him here, safe on the sidewalk, where he had the extraordinary privilege of feeling the gravel hurting his knees. Morgan felt like the cartoon character Mr. Magoo stumbling blindly through life and never really aware of the disasters he narrowly missed. For all his worrying and scheduling and careful planning, Morgan had never really controlled his life. So how could he doubt that Eddy, a good Catholic boy who really *did* know how to pray, was also being taken cared of?

Morgan experienced a profound sense of letting go. Like releasing a window ledge and sliding out into clear air, his surrender to life's uncertainties felt like floating, like Icarus soaring so near the sun that he connected fully with the sky, but not falling, instead with a sense of lightness as if tumbling through some crack in time.

When the speeding stopped, his mind went quiet and some deep tranquility settled upon him. Morgan had entered a place of inexpressible stillness, passing into a zone where he felt intensely his own presence while feeling some other presence just as strongly. Inspiration came as the words of an old man. Not some grim old man on the ceiling of the Sistine Chapel wagging his finger in disgust and disapproval. Not even the white-haired Franciscan priest smiling and offering a word of encouragement. They were the words of another old man, met years before, talking about *a crock of gold* in an odd British accent that now Morgan heard somewhere deep in the nucleus of memory.

When the old man's words came back to him, without a moment's hesitation Morgan sprang to his feet. Brushing away the pebbles that clung to his knees, he knew exactly where to go for finding Eddy.

9

Black Hollyhocks

Morgan and Eddy—Santa Fe, 1979

While vacationing in Santa Fe to celebrate their second anniversary in 1979, Morgan and Eddy had one whole day completely to themselves when they left Meredith tending Baby Josh, who was cranky, and Ethan catching up on his back issues of *The New Yorker* while sunning beside the hotel pool. They wandered and explored.

Somewhere beyond the art galleries on Canyon Road, they found themselves far off the tourist track where flat-roof homes bordered snugly the dirt roadway. There were no cars passing and no sound of traffic. The earth was dry. A sparrow was cleaning itself in the powdery dust. Somewhere a cook fire added the tang of piñon smoke to the warm air. All the doors and windows were painted blue to keep witches from entering these native households. "It's as if," Morgan muttered after they crossed the old acequia, "we're stepping over a bridge into some corner of the Elder Days, walking into a world that isn't anymore."

The moon hung pale in the afternoon sky. A calico cat, skittish at their approach, lapped from a puddle left by the previous evening's rainstorm. The young men found only one gallery down this narrow road. Its sign was weathered and faded, its front yard taken over by a forest of hollyhocks—including some striking black blossoms—and its mud-brick walls overrun with banks of climbing roses. The door was open.

"Why not, muchacho?" asked Morgan.

"Why not!"

Inside, they found the plain walls completely covered with framed photographs, old by the look of them. Some were pictures of mountain villages and native houses, but most were portraits of families and individuals, the Spanish, not in fiesta costumes or Sunday suits but in their everyday clothes, caught in the midst of their work in fields and kitchens. There was a luminous quality to the stark, proud faces of the young men and the worn, sun-etched faces of the old women. "I really like these," Morgan said as he moved from one picture to the next. "Not a single coyote in a bandana."

"We've seen these before."

"Where?"

"At the restaurant."

"Are you sure?"

"I notice stuff like that in restaurants. *And* I wasn't hitting the margaritas as hard as you and Ethan."

A voice came from the room behind the main gallery. "It must have been Tía Léona's. Here's more pictures if you fancy what you've seen. I wager you've been walking your feet off, and feel nearly done in, the heat and all." It was an old man's voice with an odd-sounding British accent.

Eddy led the way. "You always liked backrooms." He stifled a laugh as they passed into the rear room where walls were crowded with more black-and-white photographs.

In the corner beneath the only window, there was a desk piled high with papers, books, mail, folders and ledgers. Behind the desk sat an old man who looked in his eighties. His weather-beaten face was deeply wrinkled, his craggy features now the vague recollection of a man who had once been fine-looking, still with a full head of hair, white and thickly matted. His bright brown eyes fixed upon the young men as they made their way into his office. "Would you take some tea?" he asked, not bothering with formal introductions. "It's nearly four. I always have a cup myself. Nice to have company."

There was a pot of Earl Grey steeping on the corner of the cluttered desk. The green tea cozy looked ragged from years of use. "I don't have milk," he apologized. "Yanks never took their tea white. Or perhaps would you prefer a thimbleful of gin?"

"Tea would be great," Eddy replied.

The old man motioned for them to sit down on the bench against the wall.

"Are these yours?" Eddy asked, nodding to the photographs.

"All mine," the old man replied. "My name is Sutton—Alan Sutton. You won't know my work so don't be embarrassed."

"The accent," Morgan remarked. "You're English. How long have you been in Santa Fe?"

"Me and Martin arrived during the Great War," he began as he bustled about the ritual of pouring and serving the tea. He was only partly paying attention as he rattled off the basics facts—how he had been a gamekeeper back in England, how he met a gentleman who had been his employer's friend at Cambridge, then a stockbroker, and how they had decided in the estate's boathouse to leave England so they could stay together—without the least reluctance to share the whole story with these uncommonly good-looking young men.

"A gamekeeper with a Cambridge-educated stockbroker?" Morgan exclaimed. "In the boathouse on a country estate? You're just like Alex Scudder in E. M. Forster's *Maurice*"

"Did the old sod write his book and put me in it? Go on, pull the other one!"

"Yes, sir, it was published just a few years ago, after Forster's death, because he was afraid of legal action," Morgan said. "I thought he was worried about being prosecuted for obscenity, and never imagined he couldn't publish because he wrote about real people. English libel laws are much stricter than ours."

Alan Sutton settled back in his chair. "We were at a country weekend, men only, our host by name Carpenter, who kept saying we should call ourselves Uranians and make our own sandals and become Socialists. The writer watched us close, I know, and invited us for a long sit-down and asked a lot of questions that Martin answered, mostly. We found benches in the garden and drank wine. Later when we went in to dinner, I touched Forster on the backside, friendly-like, and the old bugger started like he'd never been touched by a man before, not that way."

"He wrote down your whole story how you first met Maurice—Martin, I mean."

"Couldn't have known much, leastways the parts behind closed doors, if you take my meaning. And nobody knew how we ended up in Santa Fe, a place I'd never heard of."

The three men sat in silence, each pondering Forester's decision, made decades before, to base his homosexual novel on what he learned from this real, flesh-and-blood couple. As Eddy peered into the Alan Sutton's eyes, they struck him as strangely familiar, a little unnerving, like eyes that he had seen before, looking at him from other faces.

"Now you've found me out, I'd take it as a great favor if you wouldn't tell anyone," said Alan Sutton at last. "I enjoy my quiet life and shan't want people coming to gawk because a writer made a character after me in a book."

"Promise," Morgan said. "We'll say nothing more about it. End of story."

Eddy nodded. "Besides, you made your own name for yourself. You became a photographer. It's nothing Forster predicted."

Meanwhile Morgan kept saying to himself, "This is Alec Scudder!" He felt as if Greta Garbo had just stopped him at the Farmers Market and invited him for cocktails. His jaw locked so tightly he was almost grinding his teeth. Here was a major celebrity-sighting that he could never share with a single soul, not even Claire, all the while thinking, "This is the original, real-life Alec Scudder!"

"Sorry we don't know your work, don't know much about any New Mexican artists," Eddy apologized. "Just yesterday I saw my first painting by Georgia O'Keeffe."

Alan Sutton gave a loud laugh. "I stole her tubes of black paint!"

"_____?"

"The pictures she made in New York were so dark, I stole her black paint when she came to stay with us. She *had* to paint brighter pictures then, all reds and oranges and blues."

"She stayed with you?"

"With me and Martin. Everyone stayed with us when they first arrived in Santa Fe," he explained. "Georgia came with her friend Rebecca, somebody's wife in New York, the same summer Kitty and Lydia spent beside the sea at Carmel. Martin fussed that his life was never free from womenfolk, especially the day the two girls stripped naked and sunbathed in the courtyard. He was always the proper English gentleman, John Bull to the backbone, more as time went by. He always wore a collar stud and never quit reckoning his weight in stones, though he'd never admit he was old-fashioned."

"And Martin now?" asked Morgan.

"The next year Georgia came on her own. I drove her to the caves around Blue Lake, her very first week, in the mountains above Taos. The plums were in blossom and wild roses were everywhere. Right then she had to have her own car. *Nobody told me,* she kept repeating—*Nobody ever told me how wonderful it is!* She had money, you know, and bought a Ford and wanted me to teach her how to drive. Martin laughed, oh, how he laughed. He thought I was the world's most dangerous driver, and there I was teaching a woman how to clutch and shift gears. For her first real outing at the steering wheel, we drove north beyond the Rio Grande until she caught sight of her special mountain, the Pedernal, rising above those red hills. I knew while she sat gazing at the queer old mesa, she was never leaving us, she was here to stay. Martin gave her a house key, told her the meal times, and turned her loose. Georgia had something special about her, not a meanness like people said, but an aloneness. She didn't bother us and we didn't bother her."

"And Martin now?" Eddy asked again.

"Then Georgia foxed me about the black paint. She wanted to do a picture of the hollyhocks in our garden, very rare, imported from Turkey."

"I saw that picture," Morgan said with surprise. "*Black Hollyhock Blue Larkspur* was hanging in the Metropolitan."

"She always told people she found her black hollyhocks at Mabel's place in

Taos, because she knew we liked our privacy and wouldn't want tourists looking for seeds."

Alan Sutton pulled open a drawer and began burrowing through its contents—"Hullo!"—until he found what he was searching for. He came up with an unframed photograph he handed across the desk to Eddy. It was O'Keeffe herself, a smiling younger woman and not the parchment-skinned icon of the desert, standing among the hollyhocks. She held a cow's skull by its horns. The great white skull had been the whimsical souvenir of a trip to the badlands, made years before by her hosts, which caught the artist's eye where it hung nearby on an elm tree. Beside her stood a tall gentleman in tweed jacket and striped college tie, a pipe dangling from the corner of his mouth. He was good-looking in a very English sort of way, with broad forehead, clear eyes, and well-combed blond hair with one lock out of place, fallen across his fine brow. Overhead, frozen above the highest cluster of flowers, hovered a hummingbird.

"That's Martin beside her," said Alan Sutton. "He was always a looker. I remember the first time I saw him, I said to myself, wouldn't I like to have that one! He seemed like the hero from a boy's adventure book, you know the color picture that's always in the front, him shooting a tiger or harpooning a shark. You can't tell from the photograph but Georgia was ragging him. She was threatening to kiss him, because she knew it made him squirm and he'd turn his head. Martin had a certain way he held his head when I took his picture. He thought his ears looked odd, the way they stood out, so she was ragging him to make him turn his head."

"And now? Is he still . . . ?"

"No, gone more than ten years. He smoked his gaspers and couldn't quit. There was morphine at the end. Martin never went gaga, thank God, just slipped away while I was sitting on the bedside, gripping his arm and hoping I could keep him here somehow, if I just held tight enough. *Don't nanny me.* Those were his last words, he was so angry with his illness and the pain and feeling helpless—*Don't nanny me.*"

Alan Sutton stared at the floor. "Once you've got a man in your blood, it's terrible when you lose him."

Morgan leaned hard against the wall while Eddy edged closer on the bench.

The old man wiped his eyes with his shirt cuff. "Now I'm on my own to sort through my pictures, the storeroom chockablock with boxes. Martin bought me my first camera in Rome. It was a beauty. He said I had a gift, said I could be professional if I worked hard. Him a gentleman that'd been at university, but always making me feel like the important one."

Alan Sutton had worked hard. He possessed a quick eye and natural talent, but was clever enough to know there was always more to learn, so never shy about asking questions from professionals who passed through New Mexico and stayed at their home. Ansel Adams taught him about improving his silver gelatin prints. In return Sutton helped the landscape photographer explore human subjects and produce some portrait masterpieces like *Trailer Camp Children.* "Martin fussed at me to take notes with my pictures. He ran offices and knew to keep records. Good thing. It's easier sorting what's here. There's hundreds lying about."

Morgan and Eddy sat spellbound, hardly sipping their tea as the white-haired man rambled on and on, telling his stories of old-time Santa Fe. The notebooks piled everywhere on the desk and floor chronicled the decades of his travels in northern New Mexico, preserving haphazardly the old legends that were fading even then, whatever struck him as interesting and strange, the customs and superstitions now lost to the natives themselves, here and there scribbled in his schoolboy handwriting that grew more clumsy as the years passed. He had an ear for language and learned the local dialect of Spanish said to descend from Castilian, the language of Cervantes, full of funny old words not even in the dictionary. He visited the people, returned again and again, and got to know the old families— Ortega, Martínez, Medina—now scattered from California to Montana.

Gradually Alan Sutton was accepted, and even won the trust of the Penitentes who had their chapel above Abiquiu, after providing gin to fortify the cherry brandy for their rituals. Their morada was a long windowless structure with no steeple, only three large crosses out front for commemorating Good Friday. He became the only photographer allowed to take pictures of their ceremonies. Among all his Penitentes pictures, his most famous portrait showed the man honored with the role of Christo, bleeding profusely from a cross carved in his back while lashing himself with a whip studded with cactus thorns, torch-glow casting shadows across the stony earth. Sutton had caught the light at just the right angle to show the self-inflicted wounds while keeping the man's hooded face shrouded in shadow, his identity secret.

Alan Sutton also sought out the curanderas who healed with herbs and charms. His notebooks recorded their stories about the brujas, witches who traveled the night sky as fireballs and turned themselves into owls and coyotes. They put the evil eye on people who got sick and died. They stole babies from their cradles and ate them to prolong their own lives, then used the bones to cast spells that made streams go dry and beanfields wither.

But especially he loved taking pictures of the young men of the northern villages. His photographs captured their fleeting masculine beauty, their wildness and feral energy, yet also the ancientness of a race that had dwelled apart for centuries. They were the proud descendants of the Conquistadores who left their homeland, some of them secret Jews escaping the threat of burning at the stake, to settle as exiles in these remote valleys.

He took pictures of these youths when they were just boys, scribbling the dates and locations—on a bench beneath a portál, under a cottonwood by an acequia—wherever the subject himself chose his special place to be photographed. When he came back years later, he posed the young man, now a teenager, on the same bench or under the same tree. More years later he returned and took another portrait of the man, now a husband and father. Critics later praised the elegiac quality of these sequences showing the juvenile beauty which faded over the years into sunburnt, crinkled countenances. One critic likened these sad, lovely images to the poetry of Cavafy, another to the natural sensuality of D. H. Lawrence's stories, and yet another to the frank homoeroticism of Baron von Gloeden's pictures of Sicilian boys.

Now an old man himself, Alan Sutton was grouping these photographs and writing down the names and places as he sorted them into folders. Already he had many of them framed as diptychs, the two pictures side by side, the bashful little boy and the proud young man. If the men escaped knifings and tuberculosis, their lives could be charted from childhood to old age, which came early in the harsh northern valleys. Alan Sutton had assembled a whole series of triptychs showing three photographs over the years, the beaming boy, the good-looking young man, and the withered old farmer. His pictures were not frozen moments but told stories.

Other triptychs told different stories. For Reuben Martínez, one photograph showed the lean ranch hand with a devilish smile, while the next showed the weathered husband with missing teeth and a beer belly hanging over his belt. The third showed simply the wooden cross of his descanso, surrounded by plastic no-fade flowers, beside the road to Nambé where his pickup rolled over and crushed him in an arroyo. For Sebastián Montoya, he did a portrait of the bright-eyed little boy with bangs tumbling over his forehead and, next, the surly wrangler with his first mustache. Shirtless to show off his muscular shoulders, Sebastián possessed a twitchy energy that almost jumped out at the viewer. With none of the roundness that came with Indian blood, his long eagle-face looked as if it belonged inside a helmet worn by Coronado's soldiers in a bygone age of adventure, when explorers came searching for the seven cities of gold. The third and final picture showed the marker in the Veterans Cemetery where Sergeant Montoya, a haunted man with body ravaged by malaria and dysentery after the horrors of Bataan death camps, was buried with full military honors within weeks of returning home. The dates on the tombstone told the end of this wickedly good-looking vaquero's story.

Alan Sutton's work was recognized during his earlier career. He did projects for the WPA during the 1930s. O'Keeffe's husband even arranged for a one-man show in New York. But interest in his photographs waned after World War II, and his reputation faded so completely that almost nobody, even in Santa Fe, now remembered his striking native portraits.

As the old photographer paused in his monologue and took a sip of tea,

Eddy glanced over and noticed something strange, almost frightened in his lover's eyes. Morgan had been seized by the dreadful realization. *They are all dead now.* Not only Reuben and Sebastián, but all the handsome young men in the photographs were long dead. They stared like ghosts from these pictures as after-images of human lives. Once so intensely alive when they posed for the camera, these men no longer breathed mountain air, no longer snuggled under wool blankets with wives and lovers on snowy nights. Never again on summer mornings would they hear children laughing at their games beneath tamarisk trees. The sum total of each lifetime had disappeared into the undergloom.

The young lawyer, who had always imagined himself bullet-proof and eternally young, suddenly felt overwhelmed by the desperate shortness of a man's life, including his own.

On some profound level in the dimness of the gallery's back room, Morgan began changing his attitudes toward his professional ambitions and his relationship with Eddy. Later that evening he would throw away the complicated relationship contract hidden in the bottom of his suitcase and substitute two simple lines handwritten on hotel stationery:

Whatever I do, I will never leave you.
Whatever you do, I will never leave you.

This deep seismic displacement of life-values had begun as he gazed into those ghostly faces on the walls. The young men with their dark eyes, like specters staring from another world, seemed to proclaim the grim reality that no man endures forever, no material possession or high-priced toy lasts, and his own impressive résumé was only some phony, makeshift image of himself. What was the future except Time coming to swallow up whatever we accomplish? The way life is, life ends. Even artistic preservation was little more than a counterfeit reprieve. Morgan could almost visualize the skulls beneath these youthful faces. He had no idea how long he would live, but now he realized how long he would be dead—*forever!*

They were all gone now, these young men gazing at him from the photographs, and what was the lesson that they offered to the living? All of us must lie down in the darkness someday, Morgan thought as he slumped back against the wall, but maybe what really matters is how much life, how much *fully lived* life, we trail behind us when we go.

Cocking his head, Eddy nudged his foot under the bench so that his lover turned with a faint smile, as the dread and sadness faded from his eyes.

"Just thinking," said Morgan softly.

The mist-like tatters of Morgan's grim thoughts evaporated in the warm air of a summer afternoon, drifting like wisps of ghost-smoke out the window where a single lace curtain, drawn aside to let sunlight in, rustled on a breeze that brought indoors the scent of dry grass. The ghoulish fantasy was gone. These had been passing thoughts. Morgan spent so much time thinking that even his most penetrating insights became merely passing thoughts. Back in the present moment, Morgan leaned to the side and rested his head against Eddy's, allowing these bleak questions to drift away in the immediacy of his lover's touch and the power of the old photographer's story.

Lucky enough to find one another, the two Englishmen had loved and endured for a lifetime, winning against the odds. Alan Sutton taught the one great lesson for lovers everywhere, the one that Forester only dimly hoped for Alec Scudder when he wrote the conclusion to *Maurice*. The restless gamekeeper had stayed put and never left. Hence something lifelong was possible, too, for him and Eddy.

After pouring more tea and talking more about his photographs, Alan Sutton's weather-hardened features relaxed into a crooked smile as he gazed at the two young men. The gap in his grin showed that he still had his own teeth, not dentures. "How long have you been together?"

"Two years," Eddy replied.

"Two years as of yesterday. We're here celebrating our anniversary."

"Jeminey! Two years is a long time."

"Not as long as you and your friend Martin were together."

"We had our two years, too, before we had twenty and thirty. May I take your picture? We ought to mark the occasion."

"If it isn't too much trouble," Morgan said.

"A piping hot cup of Earl Grey always fills me with a burst of energy," Alan Sutton said as he shuffled to his darkroom, quickly returning with his camera and tripod. "Let's step outside for better light."

Out front Morgan and Eddy allowed themselves to be posed among the tallest of the hollyhocks. "Just like Martin and Georgia," Eddy said excitedly as Alan Sutton adjusted his camera.

Morgan and Eddy put their arms around each other and leaned their heads together. They stood in profile, gazing into each other's eyes. They kissed. Alan Sutton snapped several pictures.

Morgan felt they ought to buy something from the gallery. Instead as a gift, Sutton gave them the unframed photograph of Georgia O'Keeffe among the hollyhocks with Martin. Seating himself on an elm stump, he signed and dated the back of the photograph, pulling from his pocket an old pair of reading glasses. Scratched and smudged, the glasses had frames so badly bent they sat crooked on his nose; they had once been Martin's.

"Where did you first meet?" Sutton asked after presenting them with the photograph. "Where did you know, really know for sure, you wanted to be friends for the rest of your lives?"

"What do you mean?" Morgan asked.

The old man's hands were spread upon his knees, and his brown eyes twinkled as he spoke. "Perhaps my old grammer told too many stories of pixie markets and green men of the forest. Her father had seen the elf riders of Bottlebrush Down, and she went there herself, when she was a girl, and sat atop the hillock at noontide to hear the fairy music deep inside their barrow. All her life after, Grammer Venn told her tales of sprites and goblins, always saying by the parlor fire, *Many ghosts were azeed and ahierd!* So, one thing and another, I have a superstition."

"What's that?" Eddy asked.

"The place where friends first meet I believe is a magic place where's buried a crock of gold. This is fairy gold, boys, and a place known only to those who first meet there. I believe we can always go back there, too, when there's need. When we are old and sad and afeard, we can dig up that crock of gold. And there, in that special place, we have back every joy we knew from a lifetime."

"Where we first met, you mean, and fell in love?" Morgan asked.

"Don't tell me!" the white-haired photographer exclaimed as sprang to his feet and began folding his tripod, his hands still strong and nimble. "It needs to stay a secret only the two of you share. Tell someone else and the magic fades away— poof!—like the vanishing of the last elf." Then he laughed softly. "Will you listen to me yammering on and on, like some old gramfer."

Morgan paused at the gate and offered his business card to Alan Sutton, who fumbled in his pockets before finding a yellowed card with his home address on the Old Santa Fe Trail.

"An' don't you forget to smell the roses," Alan Sutton shouted after them as they walked away, hand in hand, down the same dirt road that had brought them to his door. "If my mother said it once, she said it a thousand times—*stop and smell the roses*. My God but life can be rich!"

Back in New York, Morgan and Eddy sent separate letters thanking Sutton for the photograph. But they kept their promise and told nobody the identity of the old man met down the lone roadway in Santa Fe, not even years later when the story was widely known. A promise is a promise. It wasn't long before they received back the whole series of portraits taken of them in the front of his gallery.

The hollyhocks were the connection backward in time. Their seeds descended with careful selection from the blossoms in the garden where, five decades before, the flowers grew head-high when the original photograph was taken in the one place where Alan and his friend felt truly settled in their mud brick home, some of its rooms built with their own hands. Martin had a single lock of his carefully combed hair, the width of a blade of grass, fallen over this wide forehead as he stood beside O'Keeffe, beaming and beautiful before her face succumbed to age, becoming as parched and runneled as the sandy hills which she loved painting in her faraway desert. The hummingbird hovered.

Eddy framed the entire series of portraits showing him and Morgan among these same black flowers in front of Alan Sutton's studio. Later these photographs hung in their bedroom in Brooklyn. As the years passed, the two men never tired of admiring the precious silver images as they lay together. "We were certainly a good-looking couple," Morgan said one night after Eddy finished meditating and was sliding into bed.

"What do you mean *were*? Just look at you—still what my people call an Aryan god."

"And look at *you*—still the cutest trick I ever picked up in Central Park," Morgan said. "Ever wonder why we still love each other?"

Eddy rolled over on his back, looking puzzled. "Stubborn," he said finally. "Too stubborn to admit maybe we made a mistake, might have found someone better."

"And why do you reckon we still lust after each other? Most couples grow so comfortable together, they forget to have sex anymore."

Eddy paused from stroking his lover's thigh. "Don't know. You're the one who thinks weird stuff like that."

"I have a theory. I think it's because we never got too comfortable. We never stopped growing. It's the unexpected dividend of my being emotionally retarded and having no common sense. Hence there's always something new to learn." Morgan continued gazing at the photographs on the opposite wall. "I always wanted sex with a different man every day. That's why I played Lord Byron in the bushes by the boathouse. Now I do have a different man every day. It's you, Eddy Mallafré. You aren't the same man you were last night. You're always changing. You can't notice it, the small ways you grow and transform, but I do, all the time. Hence I *do* get sex with a different man every night."

"Hence hence hence, sex sex sex, just like a Jesuit."

After Thanksgiving of 1979 when preparing for the holidays, Morgan sent a Christmas card to the photographer at his home on the Old Santa Fe Trail, but there was no card in return. Some weeks after the first of the year, they received a form letter from someone who signed himself Adam Dunbar, saying simply that Alan Sutton had passed away and apologizing that it took so long to contact everyone. "Alan had addresses scattered in the strangest places." He gave no details about how the old man died.

"They were the real pioneers," Morgan said after Eddy finished reading the note. "They deserve a monument like the one for Kit Carson in front of the courthouse inscribed PIONEERS AND TRAILBLAZERS – THEY LED THE WAY. And I always thought we invented homosexuality after Stonewall."

"That's what you get for thinking too much. Ever realize how much you're like Jimmy Stewart in *Harvey*, always having conversations with a giant rabbit the rest of us can't see?"

What Adam Dunbar did not explain in his note—because the English do not like talking about unpleasant things—was that Alan Sutton died quite suddenly. He was walking across the dining room and just fell down beneath the landscape paintings by their long-ago friends John Sloan and Randall Davey. He was dead by the time he hit the floor, the doctor speculated.

His body was cremated. Ten years earlier, Martin's remains had been burned to ashes and kept in a mesquite box on the mantelpiece above the fireplace, where D. H. Lawrence's urn had once rested, in the living room amid the Spanish tables and Indian pots.

The following summer Adam flew back to England for a furtive trip to his old family home of Pendersley. After only five generations as lords of the manor, the Dunbars had left hardly any trace of remembrance in the village except for some stone monuments in the church and a stained-glass window in the guildhall. For his part, Adam's only souvenir had been the Broadwood pianoforte his agent had bought at auction and shipped overseas to New Mexico. The estate was now owned by a German industrialist who had restored the place to something of its former charm and made it again a working farm, famous for some rare breed of cattle, not the Alderney cows that Adam remembered from boyhood. The grounds were open to the public on Sundays for £2.50.

Adam took the train from London and arrived late in the afternoon at the station in East Egdon, walking the rest of the way along once-familiar country lanes. No longer an unenclosed wilderness, the heath was now carpeted with council housing and industrial parks. He paid the entrance fee, carrying his secret cargo in a plastic Oddbins sack. He avoided the manor house with its wide lawns striped by the mower, noticing only that the wych elm had disappeared from the place where once it grew outside his bedroom window, his sleeping tree. He squeezed through a gap in the hedge and made his way through the pasture, a mass of bluebells in springtime, until he stood beside the lake which struck him as much smaller than he remembered as a lad. Welshnut trees still lined the far shore.

While walking down the pathway, Adam brushed against a stinging nettle and felt a burning sensation on the back of his hand. The pain brought back a sudden flood of boyhood memories from the first time he missed a tennis service from the gardener's son George, his secret playmate, and he chased the ball into the high weeds where the nettles grew. Spider webs, beaded with dewdrops, had sparkled in the early-morning sunshine as he ran crying to his mother. Now an old man on the wrong side of sixty, he paused on the path for a few moments as all the long Sundays of his youth materialized with amazing vividness in his remembrance. Adam smiled faintly as he recalled those bygone days, filled with loneliness and sad yearnings, when his hand was first stung by nettles while searching the weeds for a lost tennis ball—and he wondered whatever became of rough, beautiful George.

Midges swarmed toward dusk. As he had been directed many years earlier, Adam emptied the mesquite box and deposited the ashes of Martin and Alan, already mingled with one another, among the willow herbs nearest the boathouse. The two men's earthly remains would return to the soil and nourish the evening primroses which still grew nearby, filling the air with their scents on a summer's eve. The spot lay close to the shoreline where grey squirrels came down to drink at twilight. Adam lingered on the overgrown trail long enough to find a stone to skip over the surface of the pond. He heard owls.

"They'll never be parted again," he muttered as he replaced the lid on the empty box and prepared to make his retreat down the laurel avenue. "Now that's settled and done with."

But it was not really the end of things.

After his death, Alan Sutton's pictures gained recognition for their historical significance as well as their beauty. Galleries specialized in them. Prices soared. The notoriety of Forster's *Maurice* only enhanced their market value as it became widely known that the photographer was the real-life model for Alec Scudder. Along with other coffee table books, an art professor at the University of New Mexico published a *catalogue raisonné* with all the photographs arranged in chronological order. The volume's last page showed a series of portraits of two handsome young men ("Identities Unknown") standing among black hollyhocks and looking already settled in their partnership, committed never to leave one another, no matter what.

What the photographer Edward Curtis was to the American Indians, Alan Sutton became for the Hispanic natives. He had produced a pictorial record of the people whose ancestors had arrived in the seventeenth century and settled the mountain villages of northern New Mexico. They had come when the threat from marauding Indians was so real that settlers at Chimayó, his favorite village, constructed their homes around a defensive plaza, the first in the region. They raised large families, tended their orchards, and practiced the arts of weaving. They attended Mass when the priest came to their mud churches, and they left baby shoes as offerings before the statue of the Santo Niño de Atocha. In the end, these families buried their loved ones in the small walled cemetery in front the Santuario

Chapel, beside the fast-flowing acequia where summer pilgrims cooled their tired feet. Nobody bothered them.

Alan Sutton liked this best about the people of Chimayó. Nobody bothered them.

Their first visits in 1978 and 1979 made an annual vacation in Santa Fe one of the most important routines in the life shared by the two New Yorkers. Eddy phoned ahead to make reservations at their favorite restaurants, and Morgan threw his copy of *Death Comes for the Archbishop* in his suitcase to reread this classic gay novel. They seldom felt the need to venture south to Albuquerque or north to Taos, unless to visit D. H. Lawrence's phoenix tomb at his ranch north of town. But they did become hiking enthusiasts with a passion for the area around Abiquiu. Early in their vacation, Morgan booked them a room at the monastery of Christ in the Desert for their treks around the valley. Eddy became fast friends with the oldest monk who ran the kitchen and filled the courtyard with the aroma of fresh-baked bread.

Morgan took special pride in the strenuous day-long ascent of the Pedernal. Parking where the dirt road ended at the foot of the mesa, they climbed up steep talus slopes studded with piñons and scrub oaks, over boulder fields and along basalt cliffs where the wind sang in the spruces. Morgan wore the well broken-in cowboy hat Eddy had given him for their second anniversary, and Eddy carried an aspen walking stick and watched for rattlers. Sweaty and almost gasping for air, they finally stood atop the flint ridge which O'Keeffe so often painted from faraway at her Ghost Ranch. There always seemed to be one lone raven flying above them, squawking. Morgan took comfort in mapping his life with extraordinary places like this one, standing high on the windy summit where only the great black ravens soared, while Eddy walked apart on the flinty crest after arriving, unbuttoning his jeans and pissing over the edge.

Morgan came to specialize in obscure trails like this one, mapped in no guidebooks and visited by no tourists. At Otowi Bridge sat the crumbling adobe structures that had been the tearoom of Helen Chalmers. The renegade socialite from back East built her house beside the river in 1928 and later found herself in a strange double world between the puebloans at San Ildefonso and the physicists at Los Alamos. First Robert Oppenheimer in his porkpie hat came knocking on her door, and soon her dining room became the mealtime retreat of Max Plank, Enrico Fermi, Edward Teller, and her favorite Niels Bohr, hard-working scientists who never talked about their secret work up on the Hill, but always swore how much they looked forward to her famous chocolate cake as a reward at the end of a long week. By the time the two New Yorkers found it, the old house had become the studio for a young clay artist, descendant of the famous Maria Martínez, who had surrounded the compound with a chain-link fence to keep out vandals.

All these years later at the river's bend, which Indians called Where the Water Speaks, they crossed the old wooden bridge, now hidden in the shadow of the highway overpass, its underside crowded with the mud nests of cliff swallows. There they could hike for miles the overgrown rail bed of the old Chile Line along the Rio Grande, its wooden ties and narrow-gauge tracks long gone as nature reclaimed its own. The shadows of tall grasses swayed beside the river, where tiny animals left their tracks in the sand, while blue herons fed on minnows in the shallows. Sometimes a carp with golden scales broke the surface where it swam upstream against the early summer run-off. High above, buzzards on outstretched wings soared on the thermals where the gorge narrowed and the river twisted between volcanic cliffs.

Along some stretches of the trail, the two hikers needed to weave their way among boulders that had tumbled from the slopes above. The stillness drew Morgan, while Eddy scanned the lower banks for wild asparagus. Often along the pathway, his sharp eyes spotted pottery shards and broken flint, the remains of the ancient peoples who had lived in these canyons and hunted deer on the ponderosa plateau. Sometimes on summer afternoons a mile below the bridge, they stripped and stepped naked into the water where the current sucked sand from beneath their feet. The first time that they went skinny-dipping below the old rail bed, Morgan discovered another one of his lover's deep-dark secrets. Eddy couldn't swim.

"How can you *not* swim?"

"The same reason you can't play the piano. Your mother never made you take lessons."

So in a lagoon where the river widened and the current slowed, the former captain of the Princeton swim team gave him a lesson on the basics of stroking and kicking, until Eddy could at least keep his head above the water. An egret stood motionless on the far side, watching, as waves lapped the bank.

Then they stretched out on a flat boulder facing the sunshine. Doves came to drink and their cries were mournful. When Eddy's skin started turning red and Morgan decided they were dry enough to get dressed, they hoisted their knapsacks and hiked upstream where the car was parked. Late afternoon light made the brown currents glow like tawny silk.

After several summers at the hotel where they celebrated their first two anniversaries, they found a more authentic place—another one of Morgan's special places—to lodge for their yearly getaways to Santa Fe and the mountains beyond.

After Alan Sutton died, his estate was divided between Adam Dunbar and

Sara Baca. In addition to his gallery started with Martin's New Mexican paintings, mostly by friends in the local arts colony, Adam had taken charge of the real estate holdings along Canyon Road and Bishop's Lodge Road. Having no children of his own, Adam used his inheritance to establish the Alan Sutton Foundation providing scholarships for pueblo boys who wanted to train as artists and later, as the endowment grew, for other local students who wanted to major in art at the university in Albuquerque. Their longtime attorney Joshua Arnold, an Alabama native who grew up in Corazón Sagrado, drew up the trust documents and served as the board's first director.

Sara already had a legacy from Martin and used the money to open her restaurant. Always her *Ángel de la Guardia* since she was a little girl, Alan Sutton provided Sara with a generous inheritance which allowed her to modernize the kitchen, hire more staff, and pay off her children's college loans. The original compound was sold.

For many years, nobody lived in the rambling residence on the Old Santa Fe Trail. Every summer when Morgan and Eddy arrived on vacation, they took a walk on their first evening in town to see what had become of it.

"If only those walls could talk." Morgan sounded dismayed.

"I wonder if there are ghosts."

"Nothing *but* ghosts! Hence the place's beauty. Stravinsky stayed here during the first season of the opera back in the 1950s, and now it's starting to look like Miss Haversham's house."

Eddy quoted from one of his favorite old movies, *Sunset Boulevard.* "A neglected house gets an unhappy look. This one has it in spades."

The house did have an unhappy look. Patches of mud stucco crumbled from the walls. The coyote fence that Martin and Alan were constructing when Kitty first arrived had rotted to pieces. The fountain where the poet's outrageous boyfriend frolicked in the nude had gone dry and filled with dead leaves. A local college bought it, administrators turned it into a dorm, and the students trashed it. Next a widow from Dallas, with big hair and big money, tried turning it into a guesthouse catering to tourists from Texas. She furnished the bedrooms with cowhide sofas and mounted longhorns on the walls, even cut down the old elms so their roots would not clog her sewer lines for the new bathrooms. But the Texans were looking for something grander and more modern, so the project failed as the old adobe residence entered another long period of decay.

Rescue finally came from two men with money, good taste, and time enough to get things right. Louis and Gabriel first met one drunken night at the Blue Parrot in West Hollywood, many years before, and they lived together in Silver Lake until taking early retirements. Then they agreed there were two alternatives. They could tie sweaters around their shoulders and move to Palm Springs, or they could buy cowboy boots and move to Santa Fe. They decided on the cowboy boots along with new careers as innkeepers.

After arranging complicated financing to buy the rundown compound, the two men began the task of transforming its labyrinth of buildings into an historic bed-and-breakfast, using Alan Sutton's own photographs to guide restorations inside and out. Gabriel in particular became obsessed with shopping for the right period furnishings to make the place a duplicate of the original, arranging the living room exactly the way that the old pictures showed with its Spanish tables and Indian pots. Finally Louis, a longtime research librarian at UCLA, did the paperwork to have the house placed on the National Register of Historic Places so that never again could the Sutton-Howell House be ruined.

When the restored guesthouse opened, Morgan and Eddy were among the first visitors, starting their new tradition of spending annual vacations at the historic compound. The rooms were named for the famous authors and artists who had stayed as guests of the original owners—the D. H. Lawrence Room, the Georgia O'Keeffe Room, the Ansel Adams Room, the Christopher Isherwood Room, and so on. "Always book us in the Stravinsky Room," Eddy told the owners over breakfast on their first morning. "I got lucky in the Stravinsky Room last night."

"Which is more than we can say for poor little Igor when he lodged here for the premiere of *The Rake's Progress*," Louis replied.

"Cute as you are, you could get lucky outside in the chamisa bushes," said Gabriel. "And if I'm still here later tonight, you just might!"

"Maybe if you give us some black hollyhock seeds to take home to Brooklyn."

"It's a deal!"

Embarrassed by the banter, Morgan cast an exasperated glance at Louis, who merely tilted back his head and rolled his eyes.

Later that evening behind the coyote fence newly rebuilt along the acequia, Morgan and Eddy sat in the inner courtyard where dahlias still bloomed in early summer, watching in fascination as the compound cat devoured a small wriggling water snake beside the irrigation ditch. "Alan Sutton lived here for more than half a century with his friend Martin," Eddy said. "Think this is where they buried their pot of gold?"

"No, sir, it must have been back in England, maybe behind a cricket pavilion or bicycle shed. Englishmen usually meet for sex behind a cricket pavilion or bicycle shed."

Morgan was wrong. The two, when they were young and full of hope, had buried their crock of gold in some other place entirely. There was a boathouse beside a pond, in a wide green vale above Egdon Heath, on a country estate in bad repair in 1914. The timber was not properly kept, and the manor house became more ramshackle after the First World War. But the boathouse remained for them, in their memories, the place where their special friendship began. It was where Martin and Alan resolved to abandon their jobs and families and even their homeland itself as they took the deep breath before the plunge, two strong men defying the world, almost exactly as Forster described the scene in *Maurice*.

The boathouse beside a shallow lake, where red squirrels came down to drink at twilight, was the place where Martin pulled Alan down to him and forced him to surrender the first of many kisses. It was the place where Alan stretched himself naked on cushions damp with their sweat after wrestling and lovemaking, saying in a voice husky with fatigue, "That's settled and done with. Now we shan't be parted no more."

Some years later Morgan and Eddy bought their own vacation home in Tesuque, closer to the opera and the badlands north of Nambé, with alfalfa fields and orchards that blossomed white in springtime. Running through their property was a stream that flooded with the thaw from the Sangre de Christos and shrank to a trickle during the hot months of summer. By relying upon FedEx, emails, fax transmission, and teleconferencing—and his incredibly efficient secretary Scott back in New York—Morgan stayed on top of his business obligations. When autumn approached and pueblo boys sold raspberries from roadside stands, the New Yorkers packed their bags for home.

The previous owners had modernized the old three-room house but left the gnarled tamarisk tree where it had grown for decades already. Green sprays shaded the portál, and birdhouses were nailed in its higher branches for flickers and bluebirds. It was a good tree for sleeping underneath. Out back among lilac bushes, there was even a beehive-shaped horno which their handyman José repaired so that Eddy could try his hand at baking native bread.

For guests from out of town, they built an adobe casita some distance from the main house. Flagstones led downhill through dandelions and fuzzy foxtails. Separated by a line of poplars, it sat beside the creek high enough to remain safe from spring flooding. Discovered in an antique shop in the railyard, an old Mexican four-poster fit snugly inside the single room. Three white-blossoming catalpas sheltered the cottage with their broad leaves. One tree actually grew up through the porch which had been built around it. During their first summer, Eddy carved a heart in its trunk where a large limb had been sawed off during construction, dyeing the stump bright red. Morgan was impressed: "Are you sure you weren't a professional woodcarver in some previous life?"

Every year when they returned at the beginning of summer, the color had faded and new bark grew back, until only the two men knew what the gnarled scar on the tree trunk originally meant. They called their casita The Boathouse. The nickname remained a mystery to their guests, because the stream was shallow and there were no boats.

When Morgan and Eddy awoke in the casita for the first time in late springtime, testing its comfort for guests, cottonwood seeds came drifting past the open windows. Mountain breezes bore the fluff toward horse pastures on the other side of the creek bed. Eddy had awakened early and gone to the main house to make coffee for Morgan. When he came back with the breakfast tray, some of the white fluff had settled in his hair. Morgan lay back laughing on the four-poster. "Remember how you scattered rose petals in my hair on our first night in Central Park?"

Eddy's parents visited them only once in New Mexico. Morgan expected they would like an area where Spanish was so widely spoken, but the elderly Cuban couple made remarks about the local dialect with c's and z's still pronounced with the old Castilian lisp, and they were openly contemptuous of the newly arrived Mexicans. These were distinctions lost upon Morgan, always a complete Anglo, who let Eddy do all the translating with the locals. He pronounced Spanish words as if they were operatic Italian and regularly confused an empanada with an enchilada when ordering at Tía Léona's. Though he said nothing, Morgan was shocked at Eddy's parents because he never detected any of these Cuban prejudices in their son.

Eddy never staged a big coming-out drama, and his parents simply grew accustomed to his friend Morgan, who was a successful attorney with unusually good manners. Southern gays do well with older women, and Morgan's courtesies completely won over Eddy's mother as well as Aunt Lourdes.

"Mom's got a nickname for you," Eddy confided one day while they were washing the Volvo. "She calls you the Soap Opera Star, or that's a loose translation from the Spanish."

"What about Aunt Lourdes? She always said the worst thing for a family is a *maricón*."

"She must have changed her mind because she calls you the Perfect Specimen, then adds something about wishing she was thirty years younger."

"How about you? Do you have a nickname for me?"

Eddy paused where he was holding the hose. "Nothing worse than the Blond Heathcliff because of your intense brooding, and the staggering resemblance to the young Olivier in *Wuthering Heights*. The jaw muscles, too, the way you work your jaw when you're sulking."

"I always fancied myself more like Mr. Darcy, classy and can't be troubled with dancing and making small talk."

"And sometimes you're just the Old Man."

"A year and ten months older. Big fucking deal."

"In gay years, we practically belong to different generations," Eddy kidded, squirting him with the hose until his khakis were wet through.

Later back in New Jersey when Eddy's father died of a heart attack in his sleep, his mother gave instructions that Morgan should be seated with the rest of the family for the funeral Mass. Afterwards he stood beside Eddy in the reception line accepting condolences from friends and neighbors, though the men's abrazos and open weeping made him uncomfortable. Later he explained to Eddy, "Nobody could accuse my family of being overly emotional. My mother kissed me on the forehead whenever I was sick, but only years later did I realize she was just checking for fever. *A handshake will do.* That's what Big Bob said the two times I tried hugging him and he pushed me away. *A handshake will do.*"

After the graveside service, there was a reception at the Mallafré home where Eddy's mother enacted a ritual that baffled Morgan. Aunt Lourdes tapped a wine glass to get everyone's attention, and Mrs. Mallafré made a speech in Spanish. Eddy was summoned forward and given a small box which he opened with great reverence. Inside was a gold ring which he held high for everyone to see. When he put the ring on his finger, friends and family members applauded. His mother wept.

Afterward while Morgan was chatting with Cousin Frankie and eating a very sweet Cuban pastry, Eddy caught his eye as he slipped out of the living room. Morgan knew to follow. Upstairs, he found his partner in his old bedroom where he was sitting on the single bed. After savoring Morgan's exasperation awhile, Eddy explained what just happened. "My father was a Spanish count in recognition of some military service his forefather performed at the siege of Granada. Even for the past two centuries in Cuba, the title descended from father to son—El Conde D'Ainadamar—along with this gold ring given by Fernando and Isabel. Now my pop is gone, I'm the Count of Ainadamar."

"The things you don't tell me about yourself, it's unbelievable!" Morgan replied as he closed the door and sat down on the bed.

"It's just a title and an old ring. There's no castle or money."

"So you were lying when we first met and you said you were a waiter, just a waiter, end of story. I always suspected that you were the Little Prince dropped into my life from another planet."

"Little Count, you mean."

"*Evil* Count, even better. When we get home, I'm checking to see whether you cast a reflection in the mirror and roses wither in your hands."

"Don't worry, I don't suck blood, *even in the wilds of Transylvania.*"

"Do you realize how many snooty people pretend to be European nobility? You're the real thing and never said a word. From now on, I'll feel like Newland

Archer banging Countess Olenska. But now you're a count and Ethan is a doctor, I'm the only one without a title."

"You'll always be my Rosenkavalier."

Morgan looked around and sighed. "Sad how there's nothing of you left in this room, Count Mallafré, nothing to indicate you ever lived here."

"Wasn't much when I did live here except clothes and records. When I moved into the city, only the old furniture stayed behind."

"So this is the bed where you slept as a kid? The same bed where you masturbated?"

"Hundreds of times."

"North Bergen should hang a plaque out front."

"The first time was in the living room actually. Funny, the things that pop into your head when you return to the house you grew up in. My folks had gone out dancing and I was watching television by myself, a Western called *Laramie*. There were these two hunky cowboys in tight jeans. Sure you never wanted to be buddies with a cowboy?"

"No, sir, scruffy hillbillies were my thing. I had a crush on the farmhand Eb from *Green Acres*."

"I had no idea what had happened. I ran to the bathroom feeling afraid and guilty, like I just exterminated a thousand unborn babies. But I couldn't get over how wonderful it felt and couldn't wait to do it again."

"Can we lock the door?"

Suddenly there was a loud crash and Tony burst into the bedroom, running over to where his father was sitting beside Uncle Morgan.

"Let's see the ring, dude." Tony like talking like a California surfer when he came back East. "And I get to be the count when you wipe out? Most excellent!" Tony ran out as suddenly as he had rushed in.

"Well," Morgan turned with a smile, "there's no doubt who's the perfect father for that boy, always bossing people around."

"What's wrong with being a good talker? Maybe he's destined for Princeton and a career as a petty—what do you call it?

"A pettifogging shyster."

"Yeah, and why not? He'll look good in orange and black."

A gloomy look came over Morgan's face.

"Now what?"

"The ring," Morgan replied. "You and I never exchanged rings."

"For one thing, you hate wearing jewelry except for a watch. I gave you the turquoise bracelet you never wear."

"I wear the gold cufflinks you gave me for my birthday."

"Only if I fasten them for you. If you really need a wedding band, take this one." Eddy slipped the antique ring from his finger.

"No, sir, right of inheritance says Tony gets it next."

"What if I wear it on my left finger? Will that satisfy you?"

"What would satisfy me is locking the bedroom door."

"The lock doesn't work. It never did," Eddy said with a sorry half-smile. "The gizmo was broken when we moved in, and my pop didn't know how to fix stuff, didn't even own a toolbox. Now it's too late because he's gone." Eddy leaned over and rested his forehead against Morgan's, closing his eyes where tears welled up. "I miss my pop."

Eddy's mother did well on her own until she developed Alzheimer's disease and needed to move to an assisted care residence in North Bergen, close to family and old friends. At first she had her good days and she had her bad days. Morgan took turns driving down to visit her, always politely taking her hand and introducing himself as Eddy's friend in case she did not recognize him, which became more and more frequent as the months passed.

She moved quickly past the phase of frustration when she forgot people's names, then their faces. Soon isolated in her own blurred world, she was happy only when she got attention. The nurses dressed her very attractively on the days when a visit was scheduled. If the weather turned warm, Morgan offered his arm and walked her in the garden.

When she grew worse, her conversations lapsed into Spanish so that Morgan did not understand what she was saying. Yet he listened patiently, smiled, nodded, and spoke gently in reply whenever her rambling monologues trailed off. He studied her serenity as the curtain descended on memory, astonished how she could sit absolutely still for long periods of time. When she spoke Spanish to him at the nursing home, he heard the name *Eduardo* over and over. Smiling and nodding, Morgan was never sure if she was talking about Eddy or, in her deepening dementia, she was confusing him with her son.

When the condition worsened so that her monologues ceased altogether, Morgan continued taking turns visiting her in the total care unit where she was transferred. Now the room always smelled faintly of urine underneath the aerosol potpourri. He brought the *Times* and read aloud the latest movie and theater reviews. "Hmm, I see Sondheim has written another musical where you have to go *into* the theater whistling the tunes."

She seemed to respond to the soothing tones of his voice and sometimes smiled slightly as he read to her. Other times settling into the recliner beside the bed, Morgan would simply report on their lives in New York, providing updates on his current caseload, opera performances, gallery openings and dinner parties, all of the social events that filled the weekly letters to his own mother in Virginia. When Morgan ran out of office gossip, like Scott's brief fling with the waiter at Windows on the World, he told her about things around the house, fix-up jobs like the air conditioner that needed to be replaced, evidence of mice living under the sink, and a toilet that kept running unless they jiggled the handle after every flush. He told her how successful her son had become with his restaurant, how disciplined he was with his yoga practices, and how much her son meant to him.

Morgan became so comfortable with her vague half-smiles of motherly approval that one afternoon in the middle of winter, with a low gray sky threatening snow, Morgan shed every inhibition to tell the secrets so carefully concealed for years. As his Piedmont Virginia accent softened with affection, he told Mrs. Mallafré how much he loved her son. He told her that Eddy was the most important person in his life, always would be, and he felt thankful that she and her husband had raised such a fine man, smart and talented, full of fun and thoughtfulness, and very sexy.

"He does have a nasty Cuban temper, you have to admit, but I'm convinced he usually starts a fight just to jolt me out of a bad mood. Sometimes I get the blues, the sulks, whatever you want to call them. I hate the overused term *depression* and think only weaklings pop pills to avoid feeling sad. That's when your son finds some reason to pitch a fit. I've studied his timing. One of Eddy's outbursts means I need to snap out of my gloomy mood. Nobody wants a drip for a boyfriend."

Morgan sat on the bedside and held her cold hand as he continued divulging their deep-dark secrets. He told about his rehab stay for problem drinking and attending A.A. meetings, Eddy's HIV infection and the years of close medical supervision, and even the C that Tony earned in freshman English after submitting his term paper on *The Great Gatsby* two weeks late. While a few small snowflakes began falling outside the window, Mrs. Mallafré continued smiling feebly—"dreaming in Cuban" as Eddy remarked when he reported home—always returning to one memory, deeply buried, of the day on the beach when storm clouds rolled over the waves and rain pelted the cabañas, and she saw the most handsome young man with wavy red-brown hair just as the first raindrops dotted his tight-fitting shirt, her future husband.

When she died, they found that she had left instructions in her will that Morgan should serve as executor of her estate. Eddy shrugged. "I guess she figured it was good having a lawyer in the family."

Two years passed. On another winter night when returning home from a performance of *Elektra* at the Kennedy Center, where the title role was sung by a legendary Danish soprano, both of Morgan's parents were killed in a head-on collision with a drunk driver. Seatbelts and airbags proved useless because the big wheeler was speeding the wrong way on the Beltway.

Only afterwards did Morgan discover that Big Bob had made no arrangements where he and Ladybug would be buried. Besides not discussing such things, Virginians avoided thinking about such things. The decision where to bury his parents, even whether to embalm or cremate them, caused extra stress for Morgan and his brother T. J.

"Don't your people have family cemeteries?" Eddy asked. "You know, some whites-only graveyard in the Virginia countryside?"

"Actually we do. My mother can be buried in the Jefferson family cemetery at Monticello."

"No way! Is that what your brother's initials stand for, Thomas Jefferson?"

"Yes, sir, pretty tacky. But my mother wasn't a Jefferson. She was a Carr, a descendant of Mr. Jefferson's boyfriend Dabney Carr."

"I must've missed the day the nuns covered Gay Founding Fathers."

"Carr and Mr. Jefferson were boyhood buddies who dreamed of living together on the top of their mountain at Monticello. Instead, Carr married Jefferson's sister. Pretty kinky, huh? Dabney Carr died young, Jefferson's wife died young, and Jefferson never remarried."

"Not counting his wild sex thing with Sally Hemings."

"Of all the things that Virginians don't talk about, *that* is number one," Morgan said abruptly. "Mr. Jefferson and Carr agreed as boys they would be buried together beneath an oak tree that grew on the hillside, and they were. Today the burial ground is still reserved for their direct descendants. My mother can go to Monticello but Big Bob can't."

Eddy turned serious. "Can you go there?"

"Sure, with a big tombstone for the fanny-pack tourists to gawk at. But you can't, hence I won't. End of story."

Several weeks after the funeral when he and T. J. were cleaning out the house where their parents lived for forty years, Morgan took charge of the study where his father had written the economics textbook which generated enough royalties to send his two sons to Princeton. Morgan forced open the locked desk because he could find no key, curious to discover what Big Bob kept there for all those years. Inside, he found the letter from the Olympics Committee inviting him to the time trials for the rowing team. There was also his old King's College tie, neatly folded, with a big purple wine stain down the front.

But the big surprise was a bundle of photographs tied in a red ribbon, all of the same good-looking man with black hair and dark eyes, straddling a toppled obelisk in Egypt, standing in some rocky place that looked like a cave or quarry, seated cross-legged beneath a golden Buddha statue, and so on. There were dozens of them, all of the same broad-shouldered man, different ages, from his twenties till maybe his late fifties. Morgan thought that the face seemed vaguely familiar, but he could not place it, and no name was written on the backs of any of these pictures.

Morgan showed one of the photographs to T. J. in a casual manner, careful to say nothing about the secret cache, but his brother knew nothing about the man in the picture. Morgan began wondering whether his father *did* have a secret love life. He theorized that perhaps his own gayness was not some fluke, but something in his DNA inherited from his father, passed down the generations like the alcoholism gene. "If only there was a bundle of letters, too," Morgan thought as this creepy feeling stole over him.

After the upsetting experience of deciding where Big Bob and Ladybug would be buried, Morgan resolved to arrange in advance for him and Eddy so the problem would not fall to Tony. "Same cemetery, adjacent plots?"

"Why not?"

They could not choose between Virginia and New Jersey, and the prospect of disappearing into one of Brooklyn's huge cemeteries proved unacceptable. One Sunday afternoon Eddy had led them on a quest for Mae West's grave in the Green-Wood Cemetery, intending to leave a bunch of red roses, but they could never locate it among the Greek mausoleums and Egyptian obelisks in the sprawling necropolis. They found Samuel Morse, they found Horace Greeley, they found Lola Montez, and they even found the actor who played the Wizard in *The Wizard of Oz*, but they never found Mae West among the granite tombs and marble angels.

"We don't belong here."

"For once we agree," Eddy replied, still holding the roses. "We don't belong here."

They decided New Mexico was the place. Great reverence was shown for the dead in Hispanic culture. Relatives actually visited, sprucing up plots and leaving colorful bouquets beside the white crosses. Families with secret Jewish ancestry placed pebbles on the headstones as a sign to the dead that they were not forgotten. On the Día de los Muertos, newer immigrants from Mexico came with their songs and prayers, and the headstones were illuminated by candles, laden with marigolds, and piled high with tamales and sugar bread. Morgan liked the idea that their graves would be visited, too, not forgotten in an anonymous cemetery somewhere in Brooklyn. But where?

The surest route meant joining a local church with its own burial ground. When Morgan balked at becoming Catholic—"The genuflecting is rough on dress slacks!"—Eddy saw no problem with Morgan's family religion, so they joined El Buen Pastor Presbyterian Church established at Chimayó in 1903. Some of its original members had been old Jewish converts who still lit candles at dinner on Friday nights, abstained from eating pork, and even placed mezuzahs on the doorposts of their earth-brown homes.

Joining these ancient outcasts, Morgan and Eddy came for Sunday services only a few times a year, but put very generous checks in the basket when the offering went around, one year enough for a new coat of stucco on the church's exterior. Once the week before Christmas, Eddy even volunteered to accompany the hymns when the regular pianist, wife of a local heroin addict, failed to show up.

While Eddy pounded out the Old Hundredth on the out-of-tune upright, loud enough to drown the giggles of children chasing each other up and down the aisle, Morgan found himself drifting back to his own childhood when he and his kid brother sat on the hardwood benches between their parents, squirming in their Sunday suits and impatient to get home for *Rocky and Bullwinkle* on television. Morgan could almost smell the scent of the Old Spice aftershave that Big Bob splashed on his face before leaving to join the Frozen Chosen, as his father dubbed their fellow Presbyterians for believing in predestination. "Damned if you do, damned if you don't," Big Bob used to joke in his dry manner. It was one of the few physical remembrances that Morgan carried forward of his father, this scent of aftershave, now as he sat in the wooden pew in the century-old sanctuary with the village congregation singing the Doxology in their native Spanish.

No objection to their burials in the camposanto was raised by the church board, who were mostly old ladies, because Morgan's Southern manners and sweet courtesies never failed to get results. Down a road marked DEAD END off the main highway, he and Eddy secured a double plot on the western edge of the graveyard, dry stony earth among junipers and cholla cactus, but easy to locate if anyone came looking. Morgan commissioned a single granite monument engraved with their names and their dates of births, and Eddy hired David Martínez, a one-armed Iraq War veteran, to pull weeds and pick up beer bottles. Eddy overpaid him for keeping the cemetery spruced up. He always overpaid the locals.

"If I go first, will you promise me something?" Morgan asked one afternoon when hiking in the badlands. They had paused on the highest hilltop where the old ranch road started downhill and disappeared into the arroyo where the cattle had their saltlick. Stillness had settled like a spell over the juniper ridges. Morgan had been turning slowly in every direction. One way where the sun rose, he gazed at the spine of the Sangres that ran along the horizon toward Colorado. In the other direction where the sun set, he looked toward Black Mesa where legend held that witches gathered at midnight along the Rio Grande. The north road headed toward Chimayó, and the south highway led back toward Santa Fe and home. "Will you scatter half of my ashes right here? I love this place so much, its solitude and silence, and I want my ashes caught by the wind and settling where they can nourish living things."

"Anything to make you happy. Want company? I'll show Tony the spot so he can dump half of my ashes here, too."

From that day onward, Morgan always picked up two or three rocks and deposited them on the highest hill, beyond the barbed wire fence and the gatepost where a meadowlark usually sat, to indicate the spot where he wanted his ashes sprinkled. Within just a few years, there was a big cairn of stones circled with desert driftwood as a marker.

Morgan imposed much the same rule of order on their everyday routines. Behind their house in Tesuque there was a sandstone ridge that caught the evening sun, red as embers before shading toward purple. In summertime they walked out in the twilight, threading their way among piñons and climbing plum-colored slopes until they stood beneath the stars. Their neighbor Demian had three beagles that knew their routines and followed, running with their noses down among the sagebrush. Eddy usually remembered to carry a piece of *ochá* in his pocket after Tía Sara told him the dried root warded off rattlers, while in his other pocket he carried a handful of milkbones for the dogs. Nighthawks flew low if rain was coming.

There was a little clearing at the top where Eddy spread an Indian blanket, and they sat gazing out at the sky while the beagles circled them, trying to catch the scent of jackrabbits. The ridge's dark spurs stood out against the horizon. On cloudless nights after the moon set, they found their way down by star glimmer. Some evenings were so still, they could hear the bell of the yellow cathedral ringing, other nights quiet enough to hear a horse peeing in Demian's corral.

On cooler evenings toward autumn when wild geese were honking overhead, Eddy grabbed a sweatshirt and Morgan slipped on his anorak. Moonlight illuminated a ribbon of smoke rising from their chimney below, and the air grew sweet with the spermy aroma of piñon logs. Sometimes while sitting high up on the ridge, Eddy spotted the shadow of a lone coyote moving across the alfalfa field. He stretched his arm for Morgan to see, before the fast-moving shadow disappeared into cottonwoods along the river where moonlight glittered on the pebbles.

As galaxies swirled overhead and the evening star beaconed above faraway mountains, Morgan compared their homestead to the enchanted valley where Tom Bombadil lived. He had read Tolkien's chapter so often that he almost had it memorized. "For nothing passes door and window here save moonlight and starlight and the wind off the hilltop."

Eddy was always kidding Morgan about his rambling monologues about literature and philosophy—"What a nerd!"—and he had almost never described his own feelings about their sandstone valley. But one night when huddled together under the blanket and listening to the barking of the beagles in the distance where they had caught an animal scent, he said something that struck Morgan as very strange. "The stars never die and never change. It's so awesome in the desert at night. You sit down, you see nothing, you hear nothing, and yet something shines, something sings in the silence. It's where I feel the presence of God."

"Cicero was right. Who can stand in a grove of ancient trees and not sense the presence of a god? I've always felt something sacred about trees, the really old ones with character, probably something in my British DNA going back to the age when druids worshiped woodland spirits. I'm a little like Tolkien preferring trees to the company of most people."

Morgan expected a *gotcha!* for getting suckered into lecturing, until he realized Eddy was completely sincere.

Soon afterwards Eddy began attending Mass for the first time since living with Morgan. It started when Sara Baca asked him to drive her to church on Sundays. Her husband Jimmy Hamahiga decided on weekends that he was Buddhist and was not setting foot inside a Catholic church. Eddy preferred the grandeur and anonymity of St. Francis Cathedral downtown. In his suit pocket, he carried the antique rosary beads inherited from his mother.

He even knelt in the side chapel before the venerable image of La Conquistadora in her golden crown, and he lingered on his knees with his eyes closed tight while praying, always thanking the Virgin Mother for good health and asking for many more vigorous years despite his HIV infection. When his manager Ken, the farm boy who came back a heroin addict from Vietnam, died from a lethal combination of antidepressants and painkillers prescribed by Veterans Administration doctors, Eddy made weekly trips to the side chapel and lighted candles for the repose of his friend's soul.

It was while kneeling in the chapel's dim solitude, fingering his rosary beads and wondering why he enjoyed robust health while other men like Ken needed to die, Eddy seemed to hear a voice exactly like his old math teacher Sister Mary Martha speaking sternly to him, *Listen, young man, it's not your time!* Eddy was so startled that he sprang to his feet and looked around, glancing over each shoulder to see if some woman had actually spoken to him. There was nobody. He was completely alone as he settled back, pensive, on the wooden bench in front of the banks of flickering candles.

"Every time I go," Eddy remarked when he met Morgan for brunch afterwards at the restaurant in the plazuela with its fountain and huge cottonwood, "the statue of the Blessed Virgin is dressed in some different outfit, all blue satins and rose silks and cloth of gold. I've lost count of her tiaras. That bitch has a bigger wardrobe than Barbie!" But he said nothing about hearing the woman's voice in the chapel.

When Tía Sara became plagued by varicose veins after years of standing in her kitchen, Eddy pushed his elderly friend in her wheelchair in the Corpus Christi procession through the streets of town, visiting the parish booths with their bright-colored banners of saints. Eddy wore a red ribbon commemorating those who had died of AIDS. Sara pretended not to notice, merely nodding gravely to acknowledge whenever anyone greeted her, "Buenas días le de Dios, Grande."

The following Sunday, he again wheeled her during the annual procession from the Rosario Chapel to return La Conquistadora to her niche above the side altar in the cathedral. This religious festival commemorated the Virgin's intervention in the re-conquest of Santa Fe in 1692, a victory recalling the capture of Granada exactly two hundred years earlier, when Ferdinand and Isabella drove the last Moslem king from his mighty Alhambra fortress. As he looked back in farewell, the Moor's last sigh echoed over his palace garden with its waterways, known forever afterwards in Arabic as *Ainadamar*, the Fountain of Tears.

During La Conquistadora's procession back to the cathedral, Sara Baca wore a red ribbon, too, bigger and brighter than Eddy's. Finally he had confided to his old friend while working together in her kitchen, on the day she passed along the secret recipe for her *mole* sauce, that he himself was infected with the virus. Then Sara told her young friend how she grew up in a household with two men who slept together, in a manner the Pope would never approve, but they were the kindest and most *interesting* men she ever knew, and most generous, treating her more like a daughter than their cook's niece and even leaving her a legacy. That was why she never hesitated marrying a Japanese man, she added, because she grew up in a household where there was never any prejudice. She never heard the words *wog* and *dago* until she started flying with PanAm. Eddy was moved almost to tears by her gesture of wearing the red ribbon, practically flaunting it in the face of the Archbishop himself, even though he kept his deadpan expression and pretended not to notice.

Not many weeks afterwards, when Sara went to make her confession, Eddy slipped into another cubicle and closed the door. The latch made a loud noise that echoed through the large interior spaces of the cathedral. He remained inside for a long time. Afterwards Sara waited patiently on a bench outside, wondering exactly where her good-looking young friend had vanished so mysteriously. When finally Eddy opened the large bronze door and hurried past the stern gaze of Archbishop Latour's statue, he offered his arm to walk her to the car, explaining he had been practicing the sacrament of penance.

Sara gave a rough laugh and replied in English—they usually spoke Spanish when together—"Ha! Pull the other one!"

When Eddy arrived home to fix dinner and said why he was running late, Morgan tried not to act surprised. "I thought maybe your troika was chased by wolves again. Did the priest ask how long since your last confession?"

"Didn't need to, not after I asked why he was using English instead of Latin."

"So what sins did you confess to the good father?"

"The usual pride, envy, sloth, avarice, wrath, and gluttony," Eddy said. "Actually not sloth. Lazy is one thing I'm not."

"What about lust?"

"I don't believe sex counts. Sin should feel wrong deep inside my gut, like the arrogance of wishing my restaurant got written up in *Gourmet*, or the envy I feel for men who don't have HIV infection. I knew that shoplifting was wrong every time I did it, even when I didn't get caught. But sex with you feels like the rightest thing I've ever done." Eddy grinned. "One of the saints said *Love, and do what you will*, but I'm sure Sister Mary Martha wouldn't agree with my interpretation."

On rare occasions usually at Christmas and Easter, Morgan tagged along to the yellow cathedral, sitting rigid in the pew whenever Eddy knelt forward upon his knees during the service. He felt conspicuous as he realized how clueless he was about the act of prayer, but charmed by the elaborate rituals dating back centuries.

"New Mexico is the one place I could be a Catholic," Morgan thought as the choir sang Allegri's sublime *Miserere* and his gaze rose above the high altar to the colorful portraits of saints, the nun with the guitar, the monk with parrots on his shoulders, the dark-skinned priest with loaves of bread in his arms, all of them arrayed around the statue of St. Francis in his faded brown habit, while a thin cloud of incense drifted above the front pews and old women crossed their foreheads, "if I ever became a Christian."

After Eddy was diagnosed with HIV, they began spending longer vacations in New Mexico. They tried arriving early enough for the Corn Dance ceremonies at the Tesuque pueblo, where the Indians still believed that if their hearts were right when they danced, the rains would come. In early June the wind was full of cottonwood fluff, while snow still lingered along the slopes of the tallest Sangres. They remained in their little valley until summer's end, when the green chiles were harvested and houseflies swarmed. When the chamisa bushes bloomed and Eddy's eyes grew itchy from the pollen, it was time to head back to New York.

Morgan changed careers after a year of sobriety, working as legal counsel for charitable foundations and nonprofit organizations. Now he had time to write articles and teach part-time at the NYU Law School, while his classmate Claire won her reputation as the number-one bulldog in the Federal prosecutor's office. A year later, he passed the bar exam in New Mexico and began helping Joel's *pro bono* work with the Indian pueblos.

Morgan also started helping the Hispanic men who were struggling in their A.A. recovery and had legal problems left over from their drinking and drugging days. Eddy came along to translate. To gain these men's trust, Eddy worked hard at the local dialect descended from sixteenth-century Castilian, the language of *Don Quixote*, with obsolete words and archaic forms of address left over from the old caste system to acknowledge who was above, who below. But when he heard nightmare stories from men who slammed heroin in picturesque villages like Milagro, the best that Eddy could manage was "¡*No chite!*"

While Ethan took a wait-and-see approach to his star patient's health, Eddy used his time in New Mexico to consult local herbalists, Chinese acupuncturists, and Tibetan chakra masters. He sat in meditation with the Zen monks in Jemez Springs and attended sweat lodges with a Lakota medicine man down in the Pecos Valley. He attended regular yoga practices with the big, good-looking instructor Sean T., his favorite, who eased him into handstands very gently gripping his ankles and steadying his legs.

Toward the end of one practice, Sean taught him how to fall back into a wheel pose while cradling him in his arms. "Let your head go first, then follow backwards with your arms and hands." Eddy had a false start, paused, then asked to try again. "You're not a bad person if you can't," the teacher said gently. Finally Eddy was given permission to fail at something. He laughed out loud as he arched backward into a perfect pose. Sean whispered in his ear as he lifted Eddy back into the standing position and gave him a hug, "Keep laughing. The warrior is awakening!"

At their next yoga practice, Eddy held his handstand without using the wall for support and without Sean guiding his legs upward. These breakthroughs finally allowed him to get past the psychological block over somersaults lingering from his days as a gymnast in high school. It was a cliché that Santa Fe was the place people came to "get over" something like cancer, a nasty divorce, a business failure, or the death of a partner. So the yoga breakthrough gave Eddy something to drop into the conversation at dinner parties, where guests were so impressed by his Cuban-New Mexican fusion recipes that they were always urging him to open his own restaurant in town. The idea began taking root as Eddy thought back on the Cuban-Chinese restaurant that he discovered on Upper West Side, run by the descendants of Chinese immigrants to the Caribbean island in the 1850s, with a menu of parallel columns for mixing and matching, so he ordered ropa vieja with shrimp chow mein, and nobody laughed.

Morgan established a regular schedule of A.A. meetings in Santa Fe and took friends when visiting from back East. Though basically a cocaine addict, Baby Josh attended meetings with his godfather when he came on vacation, mostly the gay meetings. But nobody ever gossiped that Morgan had found a new younger boyfriend. He and Eddy were solidly established as role models for the stable, monogamous couple throughout the local community. Younger couples, who had often met online, sometimes caught them after meetings and asked their advice on staying together.

"You need to know where home is," Eddy always said, while Morgan mumbled something about sexual compatibility, and laughing at the same jokes, and liking the same hot and spicy food. When asked why they never went to Canada to get legally married, Morgan turned sarcastic, "Gay marriage? Haven't our people suffered enough?"

The truth of the matter was that Morgan felt uncomfortable when younger couples stopped and asked their advice, because having a long-term partnership provided one more reminder that he himself was no longer young. On some level, he retained the belief that growing old was a moral failing, a personal weakness that should have been avoidable, optional, or at least postponable. It was something he should have corrected by eating better, taking more dietary supplements, working harder at the gym, doing *something* to fix the problem that the aging process represented to him. He wanted his body to be forever beautiful and incorruptible, like a saint's, not some broken-down relic of the gay 1970s in New York, practically a museum piece. Mostly he hated the prospect of becoming no longer sexually attractive, just some old geezer that young men in their twenties looked past as if he were invisible. Morgan felt growing old somehow made him a bad person.

Another regular visitor to their Tesuque home was Claire, who finally sobered up after being appointed a U.S. Magistrate Judge, but actually became more cynical after she stopped drinking. "I believe strongly in self-pity," she proclaimed in A.A. meetings. "If I don't feel sorry for myself, who the hell is going to?" In a church basement in New York early in her recovery, she saw Eddy's dance partner at Studio 54, the famous movie star and daughter of an even more famous movie star, who also got sober from time to time. Secretly sharing Morgan's enthusiasm for celerity-sightings, Claire continued attending meetings hoping to see more Hollywood actors and rock musicians.

During these long summer vacations, Morgan fell back into his exercise routines by joining the Taos Road Spa. The weight room provided less eye candy because most men were older, like himself, but incredibly fit and very cruisey, including the ones wearing wedding bands under their weightlifting gloves. Morgan was reminded of his bygone disco days when he had so much trouble deciding who was gay and who was straight, but the homo-hetro categories hardly applied with these gym members clustered at the center of the Kinsey Scale. Morgan began understanding the expression *Santa Fe straight* for describing the bisexual men drawn to the easy freedoms that had prevailed in this very liberal, live-and-let-live community for generations.

At no other time in the entire history of the human race—Morgan realized one afternoon while looking around the weight room—had men his age and older, even into their seventies, been able to exercise and practice good nutrition to preserve their muscular physiques. A sculptor named Ruskin in his late forties, married with a teenage son who sometimes lifted free weights with him, was so attractive with the physical intensity of an artist, his compact body still in peak condition, that Morgan was almost tempted to stray. This rugged sculptor with his steel-gray hair cropped short was so old, pushing fifty, that Morgan would never have given him a second look back in the days when he kept his vigil beside the boathouse. Yet here he was today on the verge of lusting after this virile middle-aged man instead of stoking some secret letch for the adolescent son with his broad shoulders, slender flanks and jet-black hair, a tattoo of serpentine design encircling his biceps with elvish lettering that Morgan guessed was supposed to say *ONE RING TO RULE THEM ALL.*

Many summer nights, he and Eddy retreated to the coolness of the casita for guests from out of town. *For guests* had just been their excuse for building the little adobe house above the stream, where sparrow hawks swooped hunting mice and owls shrieked when feral dogs prowled nearby. On these hot nights after their stroll up the juniper hillside, the sky glimmered above damson trees in the direction of town, while nothing but an ocean of stars stretched toward the great north country. After making love, the two men lay naked on top of the covers before drifting asleep to the sound of water flowing beneath their windows.

If there was ever conversation as they lay together with the yelping of coyotes in the foothills, they might argue about which buff model they liked best on the cover of *Men's Health* magazine, or where they buried the crock of gold Alan Sutton promised would magically reclaim all their past happiness.

"Not at Studio, because you didn't even notice me cruising you."

"I vote for right here," Morgan said as he rolled over on his back, "because I've never felt more contented anywhere in my whole life."

"How about Venice Beach after three cocktails?"

"That's not where we decided to spend the rest of our lives together."

"Not the sublet above the bagel bakery, please, not the dingy walkup with the box springs on cinderblocks."

"It was the first place we slept together."

"The first time I kissed you, I was head over heels."

"And vice versa before the night was over," Morgan kidded. "But what's this business about *deciding.* You and I never spent one minute deciding anything. I just woke up the next morning with you in my bed. You offered your honor, I honored your offer. And we know the rest of that old saying."

"You never pushed me away like the others."

"That's because you never let me push you away."

"Ever wonder what happened to those other guys," Eddy asked as he settled a pillow beneath his head, "you know, the two hotties who sucked us off in the bushes?"

"Dead probably. Most of them died."

"Or became middle-aged—which is a whole lot worse—with sagging bellies and hairy backs."

"I have my own theory why we survived *and* aged so gracefully." Morgan rolled over and pinned Eddy's shoulders to the mattress, planting a kiss on his lips. "From the first night I kissed you, time stood still. It always does. It did just now. Hence you can't grow old and die if time stands still."

"You have the soul of a poet. Now slide down and say a few words in the magic mike."

The location of their crock of gold remained one question that Morgan and Eddy often returned to when lying together in their casita surrounded by catalpa trees, now hung with prayer flags from the local Tibetan center, as they caught up on the day's business, gossiped about friends, traded jokes, bickered, horsed around, tickled each other under the sheets, and ended their pillow talk with one last kiss before drifting off, while listening to the distant barking of coyotes and the murmur of the fast-flowing stream.

They always ended up agreeing on summer nights, as storms rolled over the mesas with the dry crackle of thunder. They knew *exactly* where their crock of gold was buried.

10

End of Story

Morgan and Eddy—New York, 2001

Eddy wasn't at the design offices and he wasn't at the hospital when Morgan delivered the injured fireman. But after he kneeled outside to pray and remembered what Alan Sutton had said about the crock of gold, Morgan knew exactly where to go. Without a moment's hesitation he set out for the boathouse in Central Park.

But Morgan went the wrong way amid all the urban chaos with traffic lights out, gridlocked intersections, some people still running in panic, and a few whitewashed survivors trudging homeward in shock. He only realized where he was heading when he reached Fifth Avenue and looked downtown. The white arch beckoned from Washington Square where he and Eddy had so often kicked their way through autumn leaves. Morgan was yanked back to his senses by a Haitian boy yelling to his buddy, "No more Twin Towers—yo!"

Now there was no more meandering. It was a straight shot uptown. Though Morgan still possessed an uncanny knack for making cabs appear out of nowhere, he took one look at the stalled traffic and decided he would make better time walking.

Jostling hurriedly through the crowds, Morgan felt strangely comforted when passing the city's architectural icons. The Empire State Building, New York Public Library and St. Patrick's Cathedral stood resolutely against the day's attacks. A thin pall of smoke hung over the thoroughfare, wreathing the tops of these buildings and dimming the sunlight. A sour electrical smell seemed to follow, battering his senses with the reminder that terrible things were still happening. Yet he was only an onlooker. Nobody knew his name, not even the young fireman.

Morgan had always sought refuge in the anonymous byways of the metropolis, and this long-familiar sense of invisibility speeded his quest.

Crosswalk after crosswalk, Morgan counted the blocks so he would know how many more were left. He could tell he was approaching the Upper East Side when he spotted well-dressed matrons struggling past him, their arms loaded with bottles of drinking water stockpiled for the emergency.

He broke into a full run when he reached Central Park, sprinting down the pathways, taking shortcuts over lawns and around rocky outcrops, slowing his pace as he went uphill. Behind the bandshell, he raced past a crowded scene of cameras and lights where a famous designer, trailed by wafer-thin models and beautiful Italian boys, was still overseeing a commercial shoot even after he had heard of the attacks. It was Giorgio Armani himself who kept waving his arms theatrically and shouting "*Cinema! Cinema!*" as the latest radio reports were translated to him. But the celebrity-sighting did nothing to distract Morgan.

He dashed toward the lake, and there lying motionless in the grass, his jacket bundled under his head as a pillow, was Eddy stretched out near the spot where they first met on a hot August night beneath the beech tree.

What happened to Eddy during those long hours after Morgan left him in the jam-packed subway car to walk the rest of his way to work?

Late for his appointment with the design staff, Eddy had hurried along Liberty Street, realizing he was actually making up time because he was walking alone, not talking with Morgan and dawdling as his partner thought of one more household project before going their separate ways. He was in the lobby of Ninety West checking the directory when he heard the explosion. Suddenly the elevators quit going up and down. He rushed outside to join the stunned pedestrians looking up at the burning tower of the World Trade Center.

Three young secretaries crouched behind a parked car for safety. Startled, Eddy rushed to the curb and looked down Liberty Street where shattered glass and burning jet fuel were falling to the pavement. He thought how he had passed along that sidewalk only moments before. If Morgan had been with him. If they had still been standing there, discussing the old furnace that needed servicing before winter. Eddy did not want to think what might have happened.

Shaken, he looked up at Tower One where flames and coils of black smoke poured from the impact zone, the section of the skyscraper where Morgan's law offices were located. Huge burning pieces of the building were plummeting to earth. He grabbed his mobile phone from his suit pocket. No connection. He tried phoning Scott. Only dead air. Cell calls were suddenly impossible in the electronic pileup as everyone tried phoning everyone else. Without another thought, only the deep breath before the plunge, Eddy bolted.

Detouring around Tower Two to shield himself from falling rubble, he ran as fast as he could in his new Gucci loafers. Billowing smoke blotted out sunlight as he drew closer. Windows were shattering from the intense heat, showering the streets below with razor-like shards. Using the canopies as protection, Eddy reached the lobby of Tower One just as the first policemen and firemen arrived. Rescue workers were hollering, radios crackled at different frequencies, and the vast atrium echoed with the sirens of fire engines roaring to a halt outside.

The floor inside was covered with water and fallen ceiling tiles. Slabs of marble had toppled from the walls and lay in piles everywhere, blackened with soot where elevator doors were blasted from their frames. Smoke still pumped through shafts where elevators dangled high above, as flames crept in and cables failed. Then there were two loud crashes as elevator cars hurtled to earth.

Then everything grew strangely silent. People were evacuating in double-file down emergency stairwells. Down, down, down—people descended like automatons propelled by the urgent need to reach ground level. Women clutched their purses while men gripped laptops to their chests. Eddy could hardly believe his eyes as a heavy-set executive headed to the underground mall with a golf club over his shoulder. Some officer workers were cut and bleeding, some smudged black with soot. But nobody was screaming, nobody shouting. The only noise came from the firemen's two-way radios and a security guard's repeated order to the people coming down the stairways, "Keep moving, keep moving, keep moving."

Bottlenecks developed at the escalators, but people shuffled forward at a steady pace. Hard to panic, these stoical New Yorkers displayed an eerie calmness as they hurried toward safety. There was a strong sense of order in their movements, almost composure, as debris continued falling from the upper portions of the tower where the airliner had crashed.

Eddy planted himself on the mezzanine overlooking the atrium. He waited and watched. The air reeked. Outside there were sounds like firecrackers every few seconds as bodies hit the ground. Bodies slamming into the building's canopy made louder noises like shotgun blasts.

Eddy's eyes scanned the men emerging from the stairwells, and as he stared at these frightened, soot-blackened faces, he remembered something he said to Morgan maybe a hundred times, a joking insult that now came back to haunt him: "You don't have sense enough to leave a burning building."

Port Authority guards had set up their command post at the master console where all of the emergency lights were flashing red. Men in uniforms clustered around. Directly below Eddy, practically out of sight on the ground floor, someone was barking orders loudly in French. Leaning over the railing, he spotted a man with a camera filming the human drama as it unfolded. The filmmaker stood on top of some ornamental marble torn from the wall by the force of the impact to get a better view, training his lens on a tightly packed group of Japanese bankers who hurried past wearing paper breathing masks.

Eddy spied only two familiar faces from his lookout. There was Scott, Morgan's secretary, carrying a large bag of Krispy Kreme doughnuts. He had forgotten to get them on the way to work and had taken the elevators down to ground level, hurrying to the shop in the underground mall. He did not want his boss getting sulky if he arrived and found no snacks. Stuck in the crush of people in front of the sliding doors, Scott had been waiting for an elevator up to the sky lobby on the seventy-eighth floor, cruising this really cute guy reading *USA Today*, when he heard the explosion and the whole building shook. A burst of flames shot from the elevator shafts on the opposite side of the atrium.

Scott told Eddy that he did not think Morgan had gone up to their offices before the explosion, but he couldn't be sure.

"Get out of here," Eddy ordered. "I'll keep watch for Morgan and anyone else."

Then Eddy turned and recognized at a distance Father Mike, the priest who sat beside him when Morgan spoke on his first A.A. anniversary. Conspicuous in his white cap with gold badge, the FDNY chaplain stood out as a calming figure amid the confusion on the far side of the lobby where firefighters were strapping oxygen tanks on their backs for the long climb to rescue victims trapped above. Even from afar as he leaned on the railing, Eddy could see a remoteness settling into the priest's features, something withdrawn and strangely tranquil. His lips were moving rhythmically in prayer as he stood apart from the other emergency workers.

As Eddy thought about the prayer that Father Mike was probably saying, a young fireman approached and ordered him to leave. "Follow those people. The underground concourse. It's the safest way out."

But Eddy didn't budge. The firefighter was turning angry when his lieutenant hollered to him. "Rodriguez! Get over here!" He scowled at Eddy and rushed back to join his buddies.

The fumes grew stronger now, and the noxious air crept into Eddy's lungs, coated his taste buds and fogged his vision. His nose was running. He wiped it on his jacket sleeve.

As Eddy strained to look through the thickening air, two men emerged together, a bond-trader and a window-cleaner. They did not abandon each other once they reached the lobby. Hand in hand, they ran toward the underground mall and down the stairs past Banana Republic, Border Books, and Ben & Jerry's, through arcades where water was ankle-deep from fire sprinklers and broken pipes, hurrying in the direction of Church Street and safety.

Eddy's attention was so completely focused on the faces of men emerging from the stairwells that he did not grasp what was happening when he felt a jolt. There was the noise of glass shattering and the whole building shuddered, pitching back and forth for several moments. A second aircraft had crashed into the South Tower. A shower of steel and chunks of concrete began smashing into the ground outside. Nearby a policeman shouted, "Holy shit! They hit the other one!"

Eddy glanced out the windows between indoor trees in giant planters and saw sheets of aluminum dropping into the plaza, then a flurry of papers fluttering down and swirling in the crosscurrents. Only distracted for a few moments, he turned back to the faces coming down the stairs. Touching the silver crucifix beneath his shirt, he began silently reciting his rosary in the old Latin the nuns taught him as a boy.

Minutes passed, and Eddy heard people crying, groaning, and screaming. Some had flesh scorched black, others had their skin flaking off in shreds. The intense heat had burned shirt buttons into flesh. Some had eyelids so completely swollen, they needed rescue workers to lead them away. Eddy stared at one woman with her hair completely burned off. The top floors of the building had become a labyrinth of toxic smoke and searing flames where nobody found safe exit.

Security officers used blankets to cover bodies thrown from elevators as smoke continued billowing from the black shafts. Firefighters were using their axes to smash windows and let fresh air into the lobby. Eddy's mind had trouble concentrating now. His throat closed and his chest ached from the acrid fumes. When two stockbrokers emerged from the stairwell carrying a woman in a wheelchair, he realized he was in the presence of some real-life heroes, and the sight helped him focus.

Eddy was still standing sentinel when he heard the rumbling overhead. Again the building shook, more violently than before. The lights went out, and he heard what sounded like a giant vacuum noise and there was a sudden rush of air. Vibrations passed through his whole body, and years of yoga training kicked in as he sank down into a defensive crouch. The sky went dark and windows exploded, sucked from their frames by the tremendous pressure outside. The lobby was instantly flooded with debris and clouds of hot smoke.

Steel girders rained down on the streets outside, and men's voices shouted as a dark tornado of rubble whipped into the lobby. Tower Two had collapsed. Eddy crouched deeper, burying his face inside his suit jacket to keep from smothering.

Suddenly amid the thunder he heard what sounded like a woman's voice. It was the same voice which had spoken sternly to him inside the cathedral in Santa Fe. *Listen, young man, it's not your time!* Eddy guessed his imagination was playing tricks on him, but the Holy Mother herself seemed for a moment to hover above him, with billows of blue satin enveloping her before she disappeared back into a sky ablaze with liquid gold. Maybe it was a hallucination, maybe not, it didn't matter. Before she disappeared Eddy heard the voice saying, *And it's not your friend's time, either.*

In less than a minute everything went quiet. There was nothing else now, nothing but darkness and silence.

As the air cleared somewhat, Eddy eased to his feet and got his first blurry view of the scene below. A monsoon of rubble had inundated the lower level. Flashlights cut through the brown air. Eddy could make out heaps of stonework and, farther on, a row of turnstiles torn from their moorings. Silence gave way to groans, coughs, men calling out the names of friends, weak cries in reply, "I'm over here." Gradually there was more light as the atrium glowed with scattered fires.

Eddy noticed a group of firemen crowded beside the granite desk that had served as their command post. Their uniforms were covered in gray cinders, and they were helping one of their fallen comrades. Although Eddy's eyes were stinging from the swirling dust, he knew the injured man was Father Mike.

Eddy bolted and made his way down the stalled escalator. Layers of pulverized drywall slowed him down before he reached ground level. Climbing over steel supports and slabs of fallen marble, he arrived at the command post just as four firemen were lifting Father Mike on their shoulders. If it was not Morgan's time, there was no reason to stay, and if it was not his own time, either, Eddy knew he needed to leave. Already the building was dying.

With so much grit in his eyes that he could hardly keep them open, Eddy followed the firefighters as they carried Father Mike from the ruined lobby and across a rubble field surrounded by burning buildings. He paused and looked down in horror at a burning arm in a pinstriped sleeve, a Rolex gleaming beneath in the white cuff. Blood was everywhere. Bodies were everywhere, and a dull smell rose about them, like ammonia, leaving an awful taste in Eddy's mouth.

Staggering through litter halfway to his knees, Eddy followed as they carried the priest to the corner of Vesey Street. Some survivors were running past them while others walked like zombies, eyes straight ahead, no expressions. An enormous cylinder of twisted metal sat smoldering in front of a bagel cart plastered with I ❤NY bumper stickers, an engine from one of the airliners. The firemen turned the corner and went directly up the steep steps into St. Peter's Church.

Minutes later only a few blocks south, Tower One collapsed in an eruption of smoking rubble. The tall antenna on the top broke off and hurtled down on its own, like a gigantic spear, piercing the pavement and jutting out of the ground next to the colonial cemetery among weathered headstones buried beneath paper-strewn debris.

"I knew you'd be here, I knew you'd be here," Morgan kept saying as he gripped Eddy in his arms by the lake in Central Park.

"Yeah, I just went on autopilot and ended up here. All covered in this white crap!"

"I must look like an old man."

"A hundred years old."

"I feel middle-aged."

"Which is a whole lot worse," Eddy said, laughing softly. Then he cocked his head and smiled more broadly. "You look terrible. I never saw you really dirty before."

"I went to Ninety West."

"I went to the North Tower lobby."

"We knew the right places."

"Even knew where the right places were."

"We still screwed up. Comedy of Errors, not tragedy," Morgan said. "Let's get cleaned up."

A stillness had descended on Central Park. No joggers ran along the pathways. No brides posed for wedding photos in front of the Bethesda Fountain. No teenagers threw Frisbees back and forth with their dogs in red bandanas chasing after, barking. The weather was perfect but the landscape was empty. Even the restaurant closed early. The only sound came from F15 military jets patrolling high above the parkland.

Slowly, without saying a word, they undressed and lay their clothes in two neat piles on the boulder, the filthy Armani suit and the torn and tattered Brooks Brothers suit. They waded into the lake, careful of the slippery bottom, before gliding into the green water and disappearing beneath its surface. They swam in slow strokes some distance from the shore, their hair now clean of the white dust. Near the center of the lake they paused, facing each other while treading water, saying nothing, till Eddy seemed to have trouble keeping his head above water.

Morgan took the lead swimming back to shore. Washed clean of soot and grime, their bodies were remarkably youthful-looking after all the years of workouts and yoga practices, as they scrambled up the bank.

"Great, now we're covered in algae and swan shit!"

Eddy took the lead, crossing the wide brickwork terrace to the fountain where water tumbled down beneath the angel with outstretched wings. The two waded in the pool where the bottom glinted with coins tossed there for good luck. Standing beneath the falling water, they stood naked as cascades of water splashed like crystals. Eddy went first and Morgan followed, raising their arms outward and their heads upward, facing the sunshine, the Bethesda Angel standing above them.

As water splashed about his shoulders, Eddy seemed to his lover hardly altered by all the years since Morgan spotted him at Studio 54, first standing at the crowded bar and then dancing with the movie star so drunk she could hardly stay upright on her stiletto heels. And Morgan remained in Eddy's eyes the same Aryan god with a natural gift for neatness. He gave his hair a couple of shakes as they stepped out of the fountain and walked across the terrace, and every sandy-blond lock fell automatically into place as it always did.

After all the long years, there was still a glint as they exchanged glances with bloodshot eyes, a spark, *something* passing between the two men soaking wet and chilled by the breeze, leaving behind a trail of water as they walked together across the brickwork. Just as he had done on their first night together beside the lake, Morgan reached out and took Eddy's hand, knitting their fingers and giving a squeeze, as they walked uphill to where someone had left a blanket spread on the lawn opposite the boathouse.

But this was not the end of their story.

Tony turned out just fine. He liked school. He tried marijuana once while hanging with the street kids one summer night on the Santa Fe plaza, but he did not like it. Braces closed the gap in his front teeth for a perfect smile. After going through an awkward period in his early teens when he was just big feet, skinny arms, and a mop of black hair, Tony shot up to his father's height and started tagging along to the gym. Morgan taught him about the machines and spotted him with free weights. So weak at first that he could hardly do ten push-ups, Tony soon discovered a natural ability and determination for power-lifting until he developed vast shoulders and huge arms, resembling a Michelangelo statue of an athlete, but retaining a quiet seriousness in his eyes that sometimes made him look melancholy. With powerful muscles and hands strong and nimble, he chose wrestling as his varsity sport. Antonio Palermo Mallafré ended up the middleweight champion at Princeton.

His teammate Cameron became the best friend he never had while shuttling between the two coasts during high school. The two young men trained together, joined the same eating club, and arranged study carrels nearby on the same floor of the library, with black construction paper taped over the windows so nobody could see how hard they were sweating out the senior thesis.

Cameron taught him to ski in Vermont. Tony invited him to New Mexico where they climbed up steep talus slopes to the summit of the Pedernal and stood together on the windy ridge where the great ravens soared. When hiking up the old ranch road in the badlands and reaching the highest hill, Tony pointed out the descanso of stones encircled by desert driftwood where he was supposed to scatter his father's ashes along with Morgan's. Cameron gazed toward the ridges of the

Sangres, blue beneath banks of cotton clouds, while somewhere a meadowlark was singing. "Tony, I swear, your two dads broke the mold."

"Wrong again, amigo." Tony was picking up rifle shells and kicking cow chips away from the marker. "Tía Sara told me all about two men who came out here almost a hundred years ago. One day I was wheeling her around the O'Keeffe Museum, we stopped in front of *Black Hollyhock Blue Larkspur*, and she just opened up. From Spain or England, outcasts always found safe haven to live their own lives here in New Mexico, it was so remote."

In the end, Tony never did marry Ethan's daughter, although Morgan harbored silent hopes and said to himself on more than one occasion, "If only Jane Austen were writing this story." After graduating with honors in political science— the kid tested well—Tony again followed in Morgan's footsteps and attended law school at the University of Virginia. There on a muggy August night during the first week of classes, in one of the same student hangouts across from the university grounds where Morgan and Claire went searching for good-looking men who could be had in the 1970s, Eddy's son met a beautiful, intense Jewish girl also studying to become an attorney. Tony had a quick eye and spotted her the moment he walked through the door. Mutual friends introduced them. They started talking and never stopped. Her father had buckets of money and no other children, always a great advantage.

After Tony and Rachel graduated from law school, their wedding took place in Palm Beach where her parents kept their winter home. Cameron was best man. Tony's mother flew in from LA with her husband Carlos—introduced to everyone as a professor of Chicano studies at UCLA—but otherwise she remained on her best behavior throughout the weekend, showing off only a little, all blonde and tanned and slender from her years in southern California, the proud mother of the handsome groom. Bossy as ever, she did insist upon sharing a spotlight dance with Eddy at the reception, while Morgan was glad to sit on the sidelines eating a large slice of wedding cake, listening politely as Carlos described the latest rounds his screenplay was making with top Hollywood agents.

Morgan felt satisfied because his work was done. At the rehearsal dinner the night before the wedding, Aunt Lourdes had tapped her wine glass to get everyone's attention and Cousin Frankie had made an announcement, speaking in both Spanish and English. But Morgan already knew what was happening. Eddy came forward and presented the groom with a small box. Inside was the gold ring Tony held high for everyone to see before putting it on his finger. Overseeing the negotiations through the Spanish Consulate, Morgan had worked out the complicated legal details of the settlement so that Eddy could formally abdicate and invest his son with the centuries-old title. When the happy couple left the synagogue under a shower of rose petals, Tony and his new wife were officially the Count and Countess of Ainadamar.

The newlyweds spent their honeymoon in New Mexico during late spring, when the river ran high among willows and orchards buzzed with honeybees across the valley at Tesuque. Tony, nervous to please, hosted a special dinner to introduce his wife to the woman he grew up calling Tía Sara, practically a member of the family. Spry and bright-eyed in her eighties, she still teased him with the nickname Antonito from when he was a little boy—when she showed him how to cross his thumb over his forefinger to ward off evil spirits—even though he was now a grownup towering over her like a hulk. As wedding presents, she gave them a pair of landscapes by John Sloan and Randall Davey. She explained how she had watched these two painters getting drunk on bootleg gin when she was a little girl—"A passel of piss artists!" she exclaimed in English when she remembered back—very handsome men when they were alive, and very famous art figures now that they were long dead.

Rachel Lieberman Mallafré put her career on hold in order to have two children, boys, a year apart, one with red hair and the other with black hair and bright brown eyes. After an entry-level job in Washington, Tony settled his family in Brooklyn Heights, where there were two grandfathers who complained long and loud, but were always glad to juggle busy careers for the privilege of babysitting in nearby Park Slope.

"Know why grandfathers and grandsons get along so well?" Eddy kidded Tony one night when he came to pick up the boys, then ages four and five. "Because they have a common enemy!"

During summer vacations from school, Tony's boys came to New Mexico and learned to ride horses and enrolled in art classes. When old enough, they were taken to tailgate picnics at the opera. Edward liked *Rosenkavalier*. Jonah did not. The two boys were given the guest casita as their own during these visits. Jonah was always bossing his older brother around, Edward still sleeping in retainers to close the gap in his front teeth, and he insisted on keeping the windows wide open even when coyotes yelped in the foothills. Jonah teased his brother that they were really witches who haunted the river bottom and kidnapped little boys to eat. Sometimes at the bottom of the orchard a family of skunks frolicked in the moonlight.

When they grew to manhood and had families of their own – both boys were straight – they told their own sons that the best summers of their lives were spent in New Mexico with their Grandpa Eddy and Grandpa Morgan.

During the years following 9/11, Morgan started attending the Princeton class reunions he had always skipped following the example of his father. Big Bob wrote his checks to the alumni organization but for some reason never returned to visit Old Nassau. These reunions made sense to Morgan now. Memories of his undergraduate years provided one more anchor helping him feel secure in the twenty-first century.

The first time he attended an old-boys weekend was his thirtieth reunion, a big one for him and Ethan, since a large number of classmates attended. They drove down together with Tony and Cameron who were attending their fifth reunion, also a big one, consoling themselves that they were professional men who had not gone bald, not grown fat, and so had nothing to be embarrassed about when meeting classmates.

During the long stop-and-go drive on the New Jersey Turnpike, Morgan glanced over to his classmate and oldest friend, consciously restraining himself from reaching out for Ethan's hand the way he would have automatically held Eddy's. Instead, he enjoyed some quiet satisfaction that the busy doctor had become a little paunchier around his midriff, a little more stooped in the shoulders. Gray now dominated over the blond and red in the famous multicolored hair that had fascinated Morgan when they lay together on the heirloom carpet, drinking whiskey and edging toward their only night of lovemaking together. The Golden Boy was making his slow, dignified transition toward becoming the Silver Fox.

Funny, Morgan thought as he stole another look, how deeply he still loved his friend but felt no sexual attraction for him. And the other way around? Sometimes before dinner when they held hands to say grace, Ethan put real warmth in the connection and gave an extra squeeze before Amen. Morgan had held hands in enough A.A. meetings to know the difference between a casual squeeze and a squeeze that meant *something more*. Yet there he was sitting in the passenger seat and gazing vacantly out the window, the still-handsome Ethan, the squash partner whose bare thighs in gym shorts obsessed Morgan during weeks of sleepless nights during their sophomore year.

Morgan would become the last to know what even Tony was told in hurried whispers while loading suitcases into the trunk. Ethan was in love with his research assistant from Barcelona. "Twenty years younger and beautiful!" Carmen was already pregnant, and he was just waiting for the right time to tell Meredith that he wanted a divorce. Over the years Mrs. Rees had dwindled into matrimony so completely that she hovered in the slipstream of her husband's busy career, his travels to AIDS conferences in Africa, and his widening circle of friends and colleagues. She tended house. She played tennis. She ate chocolate in moderation. She seemed suspended and drifting farther away, until one day Ethan turned around and felt her disappearing like the wife of Orpheus irretrievably into shadows, like a dead thing.

Ethan's immediate problem, as he stared anxiously at traffic on the turnpike, was how to tell his oldest friend, the best man at their wedding and godfather to his son, that his marriage was coming unglued and he was moving his girlfriend into the old family house that he had inherited in Westport. The guy was so goddam judgmental! Maybe, Ethan thought, he would get drunk with his lacrosse buddies and awaken Morgan when he arrived back at the hotel in the wee hours. Then he could blurt out the news when Morgan was too groggy to reprimand him about *an aroused penis has no conscience* and start reminding him how many financial assets could be tied up by a nasty divorce.

When they had arrived at Princeton and settled into their hotel on Palmer Square, a big cocktail party was scheduled in the quadrangle beneath the clock tower. Still angry and disconsolate, his classmates were discussing the demise of the Nude Olympics in the late 1990s as if it happened only yesterday. But their conversation over gin and whiskey got along without Morgan, who slipped away so that he could attend the campus A.A. meeting at the religious life center. He was still dressed in his class outfit, English country house attire with a straw boater inspired by the film *The Great Gatsby*, very dapper, although he envied Tony's sexier black outfit with designer sunglasses inspired by *The Matrix*.

During the Twelve Step meeting as he sipped coffee from a styrofoam cup, Morgan noticed that an old man in a baggy tweed jacket kept staring at him from the other side of the room. His face seemed vaguely familiar. Morgan did not trust his judgments, though, because he always thought that somebody looked like somebody else, usually in the movies and on television.

When the man with the slumped shoulders and gangly legs identified himself as Brian during the sharing, Morgan recognized him as his old English teacher, Professor O'Koren, who was in rehab with him years before. Morgan was amazed to find him still alive. According to rumor, O'Koren had lost his tenured teaching job because he could not stay sober after his third month-long stay in the hospital. The nightmare worsened with more trips to the emergency room, once after he was found unconscious in some rat hole of an apartment off Witherspoon Street.

Then Morgan experienced an even more powerful epiphany when he realized exactly who this old man was. Though florid, wrinkled and blotchy, his was the face of the mystery man in the stack of photographs, bound with an old Christmas ribbon, his father kept locked in his desk for all those long years.

Morgan introduced himself after the meeting, and the two men took a walk together across the quadrangle and sat on the chapel steps, talking late into the night. Brian O'Koren recalled his best friend and rowing partner at Cambridge, while Morgan reminisced about the solitary government bureaucrat and lover of E. M. Forester's novels who had been his father.

"When I heard that Robert had been killed," said Brian, "I went on a bender to end all benders, drinking like there was no tomorrow, because I really didn't care if there was one."

Morgan was dying to inquire whether the two men ever had sex together, even once, but couldn't bring himself to ask.

"We only used first names in rehab, but I'm surprised you didn't recognize me on the class roll in freshman English," Morgan said. "Cabell isn't a common last name."

"I was so plastered all the time, I gave up trying to learn the names of my students. I stopped even paying attention, except for the really smart ones and the really cute ones. So I definitely remember you and your boyfriend, the lacrosse star who became the famous AIDS researcher written up in the *Alumni Weekly*," Professor O'Koren said with a little laugh. "You didn't look like your father, though, so I never made the connection."

"Everyone always said I looked more like my mother," Morgan replied, not knowing whether to be shocked or flattered that someone took Ethan to be his boyfriend when they were freshmen. "I'm tall like my father and got his athletic build, but I didn't get his strong jaw and curly blond hair."

Professor O'Koren laughed again more softly. "Robert was so embarrassed about his hair, always combing it to make it lie straight. Then anything he did, rowing or bicycling or just standing in the breeze, the curls went tousling over his forehead again. It was the one completely comical thing about your father, now that I think about it, his constant battle with his curly hair."

"I would have loved his blond curls instead of my mousy beige hair. Funny, isn't it?"

"You have your father's eyes, though. I can't imagine why I didn't recognize those eyes, no matter how hung-over and fuzzy my brain was. The first time I met him in a pub in Cambridge, I got lost in those pale blue eyes. Robert was simply the most handsome man I had ever seen in my life. I searched all over the world, believe me, but I never found any man to equal him. I'm sure that's the biggest reason I stayed single, because no other man measured up. My therapist at rehab decided it was one major reason I drank and couldn't stay sober, on top of the leftover Catholic guilt."

"You were always someone special to him, too." Morgan wanted desperately to offer some sense of consolation. "Do you know that he kept the photographs you sent every Christmas? I found them after he and my mother died. He kept them together in a neat stack, tied with ribbon, in his secret drawer along with the letter from the Olympics Committee."

"Letter from the Olympics Committee?"

"Don't say that he never told you about the invitation to the time trials for Coxless Pairs."

Professor O'Koren's florid complexion turned a deeper shade of red as decades of pent-up rage came erupting to the surface. "That bastard!"

Morgan finally understood why his mother so often said *I'd prefer not to discuss that*, because some things are so thoroughly ugly, like his father's thoughtless treatment of his friend Brian. He exchanged business cards with Professor O'Koren and promised to stay in touch, resolving even before he left the chapel steps to mail him as a keepsake the battered copy of *A Room with a View* that his father had read at the beginning of every June, rowing season.

Morgan walked back to the hotel around midnight, knowing Ethan was still out boozing with his lacrosse teammates while Tony and Cameron were doing God-knows-what at their old eating club on Prospect Avenue. He felt tremendously sad that men like his father could not have wives and families *and* keep their male friends over a lifetime. Why did Big Bob need to make an absolute choice between his fiancée and his rowing partner?

Then Morgan suddenly realized had his father made the other choice and never married his mother, he himself would never have been born! The thought of never existing, with nobody realizing he was missing from the planet, sent a chill across his scalp. The ripple effect of his absence would have altered the lives of everyone he cared for. All their stories would have been different if Brian O'Koren, with his broad shoulders and Black Irish good looks, had triumphed over Leslie Carr in their quiet struggle for the heart of Robert Branch Cabell, the brilliant young economist and legendary oarsman of King's College, more than half a century before. But his mother understood more clearly than the two men, and with stronger revolve, the nature of Brian's threat and the most effective counterattack. Her silent disapproval and polite insistence upon correctness, nothing ugly and nothing unpleasant, had always proved the surest means for getting exactly what she wanted in life.

Morgan laughed out loud, knowing for sure what Eddy would have said if he had come along for the reunion weekend. "Jeez, you're just like Jimmy Stewart in *It's A Wonderful Life!*"

As he waited for the green light to cross Nassau Street, the smile lingered. Morgan felt a profound sense of gratitude that his life had turned out exactly as it did, with all the health challenges and romantic disappointments and hours of sadness, in order to experience every single day he shared with his crazy Cuban. There were tragic lives in the world, but he knew for a certainty that his life was not one of them. Sophocles was wrong. It *was* better to be born.

This sense came upon him more as a wave of serenity. He felt entirely satisfied, with no lack and no threat. Beginning so many summers ago in the old photographer's gallery in Santa Fe, the bitch goddess Success had diminished as the driving force in his life so completely that the obsession to prove himself had almost faded. Even when meeting his most successful classmates with their young trophy wives, their partnerships in prestigious Washington law firms, and their pictures on the covers of *Forbes* and *Fortune*—the things that should have sparked every deep-seated insecurity, every lingering sense of professional inadequacy and personal shortcoming—Morgan felt completely content. He had nothing to win and nothing to prove.

He had mouthed the words *What in this moment is missing?* for years and years, but on this still summer night as he left the campus behind, standing alone on the crooked curbstone, with all the parties that he chose not to attend still roaring in distant quadrangles, he felt an assurance in the core of his being. The longest journey that Father Mike described from the head to the heart had happened for him.

"Yes, sir," Morgan thought as he stepped into the crosswalk on his way to Palmer Square, deciding to sit quietly by himself on the park bench for awhile, watching the undergraduates stroll past in little groups of twos and threes without envy of their youth and future promise, until he would get up slowly and walk back alone to his hotel. "My life is enough."

This deep-down satisfaction had been a long time coming. Mostly the scattered experiences of a lifetime started falling into place on a grassy hill in Central Park, where two middle-aged men lay naked in the sunshine as if dozing, side by side on the grass, drying themselves after their swim in the lake and their shower beneath the angel fountain.

Without opening his eyes, Eddy edged closer and rested his head on Morgan's chest, listening to the strong steady beating of his heart. The touch had lost none of its special magic and Morgan started getting aroused.

The events of 9/11 marked the beginning of a new era when airliners were flown into skyscrapers and governments reacted with fear and fury, as they reacted in 1914, not realizing what consequences their high-tech attacks and troop occupations would set in motion when lashing out against a region and a religion. "Let's by all means grieve together," Susan Sontag was widely criticized for writing in *The New Yorker*, "but let's not be stupid together." Great civilizations clashed as they did when the Moors were driven from Grenada, and again when European powers took dominion over Islamic homelands in the aftermath of the First World

War, fostering the jihadist passions that spanned generations until coming back with such vengeance on September 11.

But men are resilient and can learn to tolerate almost anything. The globe was a large place. There were so many unlikely targets, most people felt secure enough to get on with their lives. Nietzsche was right, as Morgan long ago suspected when researching his senior thesis at Princeton. Whoever understands the *why* of his life can endure almost any *how*.

He and Eddy joined those who rebuilt, as their lives together rose like the phoenix from the white ashes which had almost consumed them. They continued to take yoga classes and attended Twelve Step meetings in church basements, and they were always trying the newest nutritional supplements. Morgan had season tickets at the Metropolitan Opera, and Eddy seemed to grow fonder of the performances and was actually excited when a new production of *Rosenkavalier* was announced.

Because they refused to live in fear, they took a vacation in Turkey during the summer of 2002. They stood upon Troy's ancient walls where Achilles avenged the death of Patroclus. Morgan bought more tribal carpets, like the first one received as a gift from his grandmother, and finally they visited Rumi's hometown. It was the fulfillment of Eddy's dream to sit in the poet's garden and read translations of his favorite verses.

> *Find a friend and hide,*
> *Laughing crazily and moaning*
> *In union of lover and beloved.*
> *This is the true religion. All others*
> *Are thrown-away bandages beside it.*
> *Whatever I was looking for was always you.*

As they had sought out the little mud-brick church in the northern valley of New Mexico, they came as pilgrim souls to Konya to find another resting place, in the quiet garden with its roses, beneath the glittering green dome of the mosque that served as the poet's mausoleum.

Morgan never became a Christian or regular churchgoer, preferring when in Santa Fe to read the Sunday *Times* at the coffee shop next to the local bookstore where five roads converged at odd angles, one of them the dirt road where Alan Sutton's gallery had been tucked away—now remodeled by some Texans as a vacation home, with a gigantic Hummer parked in the front yard where hollyhocks once bloomed—while Eddy attended Mass by himself at the yellow cathedral. But Morgan was drawn to places with long histories of worship, places made valid by generations of prayer, whether mosque or village church or ancient kiva, where he sat in reverent silence among the ghosts of the vanished builders. He liked sitting quietly in one of these hallowed places, or merely at a corner table in a coffee shop, just sitting, nothing more. He reckoned this was one of his true accomplishments in life. Once as he cradled a cappuccino in his hands, listening to the almost unhearable fizz of milk foam dissolving, he recalled a rare moment of tenderness from *Thus Spoke Zarathustra*: "Small things make the best happiness. Be still."

In Rumi's garden he sat cross-legged on the ground at Eddy's feet, in exactly the spot where the Sufi master sat with his beloved Shams, listening to his friend reciting poetry as tears brimmed in his eyes on a breezy afternoon. Morgan's heart had learned much from the day when he and Eddy nearly died in the collapse of the Twin Towers, and the sense of gratitude and high privilege for their years together seldom left him now. Gradually he learned to take his time, or maybe he learned to let time take him, as he made peace for the reality of growing older with an emphasis on *growing*. He was always excited about learning new things, even letting Eddy teach him how to read music and position his fingers on the keyboard of the piano. Eventually Morgan learned to play some of the easier preludes in the *Well-Tempered Klavier*, mostly the ones in minor keys, after long halting practice alone at night while his partner was working at his restaurant. One of the few Spanish phrases he ever learned *Aún aprendo!* came from the painter Goya at eighty—"I'm still learning!" He had come to appreciate time as a gift, not just a threat.

After working with charitable foundations for years, he accepted a fulltime faculty position at the NYU law school. He was already teaching part-time, one course per semester, and he loved the classroom so much that he wondered why he took so long to discover what he really wanted to do. The academic calendar meant that they had a four-week Christmas break and almost four months of summer vacation in New Mexico before returning to the city for the start of the fall semester. Finally Morgan had a title, too, along with Dr. Rees and Count Mallafré. He became Professor Cabell.

As they spent longer vacations in New Mexico, they added more rooms to their rambling compound including a library. Santa Fe's tourist economy did not come back quickly after the 9/11 attacks, and things got worse after the economic meltdown in 2008, so Morgan felt that any money spent locally was money spent supporting their adopted community. Now, too, Eddy had a place for the pianoforte Morgan bought him to celebrate their twenty five years together. The nineteenth-century Broadwood grand had somehow ended up in an antique shop in the Santa Fe railyard, in mint condition except for some warping in the lid from water damage. The period instrument was perfect for the Schubert sonatas that had become Eddy's latest passion after giving himself permission to fail with fiendishly difficult Liszt.

Now their house was complete. Time would blend the new parts into the earth from which the bricks had come until looking as if it belonged there forever, like the old tamarisk tree outside. From his favorite reading chair in the new library, Morgan could watch snow clouds gathering low about the Sangres. Those high places guarded the sacred trails where men for centuries built shrines and placed prayer feathers. When big white flakes began falling, those mountains would disappear, the pastures beyond the creek would disappear, and finally the poplars leading down to the guest casita would disappear. Birds stopped singing when it started snowing. The next morning when Morgan went outside for firewood, he would find the footprints of quail and cottontails in new-fallen snow. The early light would ripple blue over fresh drifts, and huge icicles would hang like stalactites from the canales

As the setting sun reflected off icy slopes and filled the room with rose-red light, Morgan savored the assurance that nothing evil could ever change the essence of this landscape. An arctic solitude brought the world to a standstill. Snow on the flat roof muffled every sound. Here he could live each day exactly as it presented itself, knowing that in the kitchen Eddy was scattering seeds on the window tray for bluebirds and towhees.

Morgan nicknamed their last new room the Merton College Library after Gatsby's library in the novel, inspired by Oxford's oldest college where Tolkien had been a professor. The heirloom carpet in front of the fireplace became a favorite place for him and Eddy to lie together on these winter nights, beneath landscapes by their artist friends Michael Bergt and Roger Montoya, as snow fell on stubble fields across the hushed valley. On these frigid evenings when the mercury dipped below zero, so cold that apple trunks cracked in their orchard, Morgan looked about this room at all the souvenirs assembled within its four walls, the sentimental loot of a lifetime, like his old swimming trophies and award plaques, and now also paintings by the early Indian artist Pina-yo-Pi and painted bowls by the young clay artist Diego Martínez. As he gazed, Morgan's mind followed the webwork of memory back over the long years, until he understood what his mother meant when she added near the end of her weekly letters to him, *I don't know where the time goes.*

Then Eddy would break the somber silence by saying something completely silly like "Remind me to tell you about the time I looked into the heart of an artichoke, some snowy night in front of the fire." He policed Morgan's sullen tendencies so strictly that he would not even allow him to buy the DVD of *Brokeback Mountain.*

For his fiftieth birthday, Morgan gave him a first edition of *A Room with a View* bought on eBay and signed by E. M. Forster himself. The novelist's spidery handwriting had inscribed "ONLY CONNECT!" on the title page where he dedicated the volume to someone named Bob Buckingham. Morgan finally got around to writing a love sonnet and had no trouble including his favorite Dante line—"Your eyes have shot their arrows into my heart"—because it was perfect iambic pentameter and an easy rhyme. He copied the poem neatly on stationery from the Loretto Hotel and folded it among the novel's pages, at a passage already marked in faded blue ink, impossible to know whether by Forster or his friend. This had become one of Morgan's favorite passages, too, where husky George Emerson said something about choosing a place where you won't do very much harm and standing there for all you are worth, facing the sunshine. Keeping this autographed volume on their bedroom dresser gave him a feeling of having Forster with them somehow, almost a spiritual presence hovering nearby in the still of the night, linked through their meeting one summer afternoon with the real-life Alec Scudder.

Neither man ever discussed retiring after the Wall Street meltdown shrank the value of their stock portfolios. Eddy simply sold his restaurant in Brooklyn and opened a new one in Tesuque, located in an old hacienda that had once been a well-known brothel. He named his new restaurant "Tía Sara" after his old friend who died peacefully in her sleep, at age eighty-six just a month before the grand opening, but not before he had wheeled her around the construction site and won her nod of approval. While his menu changed weekly, customers always looked forward to the chocolate cake based on the recipe by Helen Chalmers for her lunchroom at Otowi Bridge, and of course the restaurant's signature dish, turkey prepared in Sara Baca's special *mole* sauce. The recipe never appeared in any of the Eddy's cookbooks, not even in the glossy write-up in *Gourmet* magazine, remaining the one recipe with its secret ingredients of anise, plantain, toasted walnuts, mulato chiles, and the tiniest pinch of church-dirt from Chimayó he passed along only to Tony, who passed it along to Edward and Jonah.

Eddy made a custom of visiting Sara's grave twice yearly in the old Rosario Cemetery, beside her aunt Léona Baca, in the well-tended family plot bordered by iron cribbing. He always left a large bouquet of yellow roses, her favorites, on her birthday and the anniversary of her death. Those were the only two dates that he marked on his calendar at the beginning of each new year.

These years seemed to slide past more quickly now. Summer after summer, the two men sat on their sandstone cliff toward sunset and felt helpless as they marked the progress of the great bark beetle invasion that killed piñons by the thousands. The blighted trees looked ghastly, their fallen needles blackening the surrounding earth as if struck by lightning. Still wearing the same beat-up old cowboy hat that Eddy gave him for their second anniversary, Morgan could hardly bring himself to drive the Volvo SUV northward and hike the badlands where dead pines littered the sandy hills up the old ranch road beyond the red metal gate.

Eddy hired old José Mondragón, jack of all trades still hustling to make a few dollars, to clear the dead trees from their property and chop what he could salvage for firewood. Their handyman had been a wiry young buck with jet-black hair when they first arrived in the valley, now graying like themselves, his lean face wrinkled and scarred by the sun. He had a bad limp after an accident with a backhoe but still managed to get around, complaining and cussing with every other breath.

"Jesus Christ, why don't you sharpen your frickin' ax? Morgan'll kill hisself trying to split wood with this worthless sonabitch!"

His wife Lucille had died from cancer years before, and his four kids had graduated high school and moved south for jobs in Albuquerque, the youngest boy, Benny, with the Marines somewhere in the Middle East. Every year Eddy hired the scrappy worker to prune the orchards so their trees would fruit. In early summer he prepared the vegetable garden and planted seeds by the light of the full moon, always including some beans from his own family field. As a token of gratitude for steady work, Joe helped himself to the biggest pumpkin from their neighbor Demian's patch to decorate their portál between Halloween and Thanksgiving, no questions asked. Every three or four years he mudded their house, inside and out, and rubbed smooth the interior walls with sheepskins. Eddy the patrón always overpaid the locals, especially the ornery old half-pint Joe Mondragón.

Near summer's end when the wind brought indoors the scent of sagebrush, Eddy dried slices of apples and the whole house grew sweet with the aroma of his boiling jams and preserves. Before returning to New York, the two men always drove high into the mountains to gather pine knots, those legacies of long-forgotten trees, to store away for the pitchwood fire that they would light outdoors on Christmas Eve, just like their neighbors at the pueblo, to summon the playful spirits of the Towa-é who guarded their red valley.

They saw drought years when the sun blazed, dry winds blew, and the heavens turned hazy brown with dust. Beanfields withered under cloudless skies, and everywhere grass died and crackled under foot. Eddy's Lakota friend who ran the sweat lodge told him how the old medicine men journeyed to the four sacred mountains to perform a ceremony for rain. They believed that if their hearts were right, the rains would come. And sure enough, the western skies darkened and showers fell. Other years, they had steady monsoons when the vistas of the llano turned velvety green, alfalfa fields came alive with grasshoppers, and the hill country exploded in yellow wildflowers. In time, even the bark beetles retreated and tiny young piñons sprung up in the badlands.

They grieved the deaths of friends and coworkers, and they grew older with more acceptance of life's disappointments and forgiveness of other people, especially each other. Whenever Eddy spotted orange boxer shorts in a men's store, he bought them for Morgan.

One summer night as they climbed into the old Mexican four-poster, Morgan asked, "What do you imagine Forster would think about two men like us and the lives we've made for ourselves?"

The descendants of Alec and Maurice will embark upon a heroic landscape where there will be sex and sunshine. In other lands and other times, male lovers will cast off their clothes to brave the beauty of their naked limbs in the fullness of day. They will swim in sacred lakes and stretch out their bodies in the grass. Men will love differently then, openly in the light of day. Love will be born there in forest or desert, of what quality and into what worlds, only the future can decide. And some bright spark of Maurice and Alec will remain aglow like white heat somewhere deep inside those men's hearts and loins.

"You," replied Eddy as he opened the curtain, "think the weirdest stuff and you always will."

"Come here and I'll show you weird." Morgan lay back on sheets silvered by moonlight and opened his embrace. "Come here . . . Come here . . ."

ACKNOWLEDGEMENTS

This novel belongs to the twenty-first century—which means that it is haunted by novels of the twentieth century—continuing the story of E. M. Forster's *Maurice* (New York: W. W. Norton, 1971) as well as the brilliant screenplay by Kit Hesketh-Harvey and James Ivory for the film adaptation *Maurice* (1987). Material on the novelist comes from P. N. Furbank's authorized biography *E. M. Forster: A Life* (New York and London: Harcourt Brace Jovanovich, 1978); Christopher Isherwood, *Christopher and his Kind* (Minneapolis: University of Minnesota Press, 1976); Harry Daley, *This Small Cloud: A Personal Memoir*, intro. P. N. Furbank (London: Weidenfeld and Nicolson, 1986); J. H. Stape, ed., *E. M. Forster: Interviews and Recollections* (New York: St. Martin's Press, 1993); Michael Haag, *Alexandria: City of Memory* (New Haven: Yale University Press, 2004); John Sutherland, *Stephen Spender: The Authorized Biography* (New York: Viking, 2004); and Forster's own *Aspects of the Novel* (1927; rpt. New York and London: Harcourt Brace Jovanovich, 1955). I am grateful to Bill Burgwinkle and the Fellows of King's College, Cambridge, for hosting me to dinner—when one senior don, who remembered, allowed that "Forster never got pervy with the boys"—followed by a visit to the novelist's set of college rooms.

New Mexican episodes blend history and imagination from regional books: Willa Cather, *Death Comes for the Archbishop* (1927; New York: Vintage, 1990); Richard Bradford, *Red Sky at Dawn* (New York: Harper, 1999); Peggy Pond Church, *The House at Otowi Bridge* (Albuquerque: University of New Mexico Press, 1973); Frank Waters, *Of Time and Change: A Memoir* (Denver: MacMurray and Beck, 1998); and John Nichols, *The Milagro Beanfield War* (New York: Henry Holt, 2000). Similarly, the northern Italian episodes engage with Standhal, *The Charterhouse of Parma*, trans. Richard Howard (New York: Modern Library, 1999);

Ernest Hemingway, *Farewell to Arms* (New York: Charles Scribner's Sons, 1929); and Michael Ondaatje, *The English Patient* (New York: Random House, 1992). John Bierman, *The Secret Life of Laszlo Almasy: The Real English Patient* (New York: Viking, 2005), reveals the wartime love story was actually a homosexual romance with a German officer.

Reconstituting the collective memory of the 9/11 attacks on the World Trade Center relies principally upon *Inside 9/11: What Really Happened* by reporters of *Der Spiegel* magazine (New York: St. Martin's Press, 2001), and Jim Dwyer and Kevin Flynn, *102 Minutes: The Untold Story of the Fight to Survive Inside the Twin Towers* (New York: Henry Holt, 2004).

Quotations from Rumi are cobbled together from *The Essential Rumi*, trans. Coleman Barks with John Moyne (New York: HarperCollins, 1995), p. 10.

Excerpts from Chapters 2, 5 and 9 appeared previously as *Martin and Alan* in Miles Newbold Clark, ed., *Red Anthology* (Ithaca NY: No Record Press, 2009).

For their encouragement, I wish to thank early readers of the manuscript Demian Baum, Joel Castleberg, Ed Chisholm, Sterling Zinsmeyer, Lee Cagley, Steve Kruger, Del Kolve, Chuck Lichtenwalner, James Gasowski, Brad Thompson, Craig Dorward, Arjo Vanderjagt, and Andrew James Johnston.

CPSIA information can be obtained at www.ICGtesting.com
Printed in the USA
LVOW062310130812

294150LV00001B/8/P